# SEAL FOREVER

## KRIS MICHAELS

WWW.KRISMICHAELSAUTHOR.COM

# CHAPTER 1

*C*reed Lachlan pushed the throttle up on the four, 1,480-hp, diesel V-drive, inboards until the power under him lifted the nose of the one hundred-sixty-five-foot luxury yacht out of the glassy, late-afternoon, Atlantic. He held the controls at half power, listening to the throaty rumble with a skilled ear. He'd modified this baby's quad engines, and she was pushing enough horsepower to beat any tropical storm back to the safe harbor of Key West's Cow Key Channel. The gauges showed exactly what he needed to see. *Angelo's Princess* was once again purring, hitting all cylinders. The gauges held true as Creed inched the throttle forward. He flicked the throttle up a quarter inch. The plane of the bow surged further upright, and he braced against the pull as he balanced behind the wheel. He gripped the steering controls and tightened his muscles as he steadily increased the power to the motor. At the throttle's top end, he was almost flying the yacht over the water. The exhilaration from the deep growl of the motors and speed of the boat fed an addiction he'd been trying to forget. Like most of the men in his career field, he'd grown accustomed to jolts of adrenaline. *Check that... prior career field.*

When he'd been forced to retire, he'd commanded SEAL Team One. Six platoons. Ninety-six SEALs and a headquarters element—all before he fucked up his knee. Blew it out six ways from Sunday and needed a complete knee replacement. Oh, the Navy had offered him a job *'commensurate to his physical limitations.'* He'd take a pity job the day his rosy, red ass sprouted blossoms. Instead, he'd shown a middle finger to the paper pushers and had left on his own terms. At the advanced age of forty-three, he'd retired. *Fuck*.

Since then, he'd buried himself in the family business. His parents had built Lachlan Maritime Industries from the ground up and were still strong pillars within the Key West community, even though they'd handed the reins over to their three sons.

The coastline of his home reappeared as he brought the *Princess* out of her breakneck pace. Like a trained thoroughbred, she relaxed under his expert hand, and the deep vee of white froth behind her lessened to almost nothing. The heavy roar of the diesel engines died to a bass murmur. Creed took a moment to soak in one of the most beautiful sights in the world. Sunset in Key West. The setting sun glistened off the flat waters west of Cow Key Channel and painted the sky in epic orange and purple. Creed turned on the *Princess'* running lights and pulled back on the throttle to coast through the no-wake zone. He rounded the northeast side of the island and headed the yacht back to the massive commercial pier his father had built. As he approached, two figures trotted down the dock. They scrambled to tie off the *Princess* as Creed nudged the one-hundred-and-sixty-five-footer into its berth.

"I was getting worried about you, old man."

Creed glanced up but ignored his brother's smart-ass comment as it floated through the cabin's open window.

"What happened? Finally lose your hearing?"

Creed shifted his eyes again to glare at his brother. The little shit. He was about four inches shorter than Creed's six-feet, six-inches and easily eighty to ninety pounds lighter. Where he hit the gym regularly and had the bulked-up muscle to prove it, Thane had a swimmer's body. Hell, Thane's sun-bleached hair was more blond than brown. The only thing Thane had in common with either of his brothers was the color of his eyes. All three had deep blue irises, ringed in dark black circles and laced with flecks of gold. It seemed to be the only genetic gift from his mother's side of the family. Thankfully.

3

His mother, all four-foot-eleven inches of her, had a fire-laced temper with a hair trigger that brought all three of her boys to heel. Nobody messed with Caroline Lachlan. Nobody.

Creed didn't give his brother the courtesy of a response before his attention returned to the engine logbooks.

"Yo, dude, we're going to Sam's tonight. You in?" Thane braced himself on the doorjamb and leaned into the bridge of the yacht.

Creed kept writing but asked, "Cruise ships all gone?"

"Yeah, the last one pulled out about an hour ago." Thane glanced at his watch. "Missy should be there by now. She's going to hold a table for us."

Creed nodded. He could do with a cold beer. "I'm in."

"Seriously?"

He lifted his head at the sound of his brother's shocked voice. "Yeah, why?"

"Because you've never come with us before?" The 'duh' was implied.

"And still you ask every time." Creed returned to his work.

"Yeah, you know miracles do happen, and old, cranky shits like you are allowed to have fun."

"I'm only ten years older than you."

"And you *act* like you're ten thousand years old. Dude, you wake up, work out, come here and then go home. Wash, rinse, repeat. Day after day, week after week, month—

Creed snapped his book shut. "I get it."

"Do you? Do you really?" Thane crossed his arms and blinked like an owl before he shook his head. "I don't think you do. We live in a paradise, complete with sunshine, good food, great rum, teeny-tiny bikinis and hard, hot little bodies inside those almost nonexistent pieces of string. And still"—Thane paused for dramatic effect—"you live like a fucking monk."

Not quite. His brother made some big assumptions. "Partying until three in the morning has never been something I enjoyed." That was the God's honest truth. He'd never been interested in parties or the type of people who lived for the thrill of that atmosphere. His mom said he had an 'old soul.' These days his soul felt older than dirt.

Thane shifted on his feet. "What exactly do you enjoy, Creed? I mean it's been almost a year since you've been back. You don't date, at least not that I've seen. What exactly is it that gives you pleasure? Dude just tell me, and I'll find it for you. I know there has to be something out there for you." His voice softened, "Man, whatever it is that will bring back the man I used to know, I'll find it. I hate that you are so damn empty. I see it and it kills me."

Creed stood, automatically testing the cobalt-chrome device they'd replaced his knee with. His mind still believed the thing would fail. The doctors said that was normal. Normal. As if. He drew a deep breath and turned his entire focus on his brother and forced a smile. "You can't find what doesn't exist, but thanks for the thought."

Thane quipped, "You need a woman in your life."

"Not interested." Not any longer. He'd fucking searched for that elusive woman. Hell, he had the list. Truth be told, he wasn't asking for a supermodel crossed with a physicist. Looks faded; he knew that. He hadn't been looking for some image of perfection. He wanted a real woman, someone genuine who could hold his interest. As said woman's competition was his job, well, his former job, it had been a tall order. Over the last twenty years he'd dedicated too much time carrying on strained conversations with women whose names he promptly forgot to hold out any hope there was someone for a man like him. Obviously, he wanted a fucking unicorn, because the woman he'd been searching for didn't exist. There was never that 'click,' and no he wasn't channeling a romance novel or a *Lifetime* movie. He tucked his books under his arm, pocketed the keys to the million-dollar vessel and slapped his brother on the back as he exited the bridge.

Thane fell into step beside him. After a moment, he cleared his throat. "Danica is going to be there tonight. She's been asking about you. I'm supposed to hint that she's a good catch."

He stopped short, and his brother crashed into his back, bouncing off of him as he turned around. "Say what?"

"Well, Mom and Missy are worried, too."

He extended a finger and pointed it at Thane. His brother stiffened and backed up another step. "You're telling me that *your* wife and *our* mother are trying to set *me* up?" Incredulous didn't begin to cover the shock of that thought. He was forty-four-years old. If he wanted to get laid, he did. He just didn't make a spectacle of it. Fuck him for being discreet.

"Ah... yeah." Thane blushed and rubbed the back of his neck. "I promise I'll run interference tonight. Everyone will be there, and if you aren't interested in Danica... well then man, you're dead."

Creed chuffed. "Fuck you."

"She's *hawt*." Thane licked his finger and touched something imaginary making a sizzling sound.

He'd seen her hanging around with Missy. The girl *was* attractive. Okay, *hot*, but dammit, he was forty-four, and he had no desire to become a sugar daddy. He wanted the company of a woman that could actually hold a conversation and didn't post three hundred selfies to social media throughout the night. He kept walking and tried to picture what a date with Danica would be like. It was useless. He shook his head to clear his thoughts and muttered under his breath about the yacht he'd just run. He made a note on the invoice that they needed to send in the clean-up crew to wash and detail the ship before the owner took possession of her. Just for good measure he glanced over his shoulder at his brother and grumped, "She's barely legal."

Thane presented his fingers and made an act of counting before he piped, "Twenty-two."

Creed snorted. "That qualifies as barely legal, and she's literally half my age. I was in college at Annapolis when she was born. Think about that."

"She's the trifecta! Young, legal, nubile and H.A.W.T." Thane hustled along behind him.

"Idiot, that's four things, not three. Does Missy know you have hidden desires for this girl?"

"What's four then... a quadfecta? Who says they're hidden? Missy and I have had some awesome sex after talking about our fantasies." Thane made a growling sound behind him.

Creed stopped short, and his brother bounced off of him—again. He turned and held up a hand. "Never, and I mean never, tell me about your sex life. I don't want to know. Some things you can't unhear or"—he pointed toward his head—"mentally unsee."

A shit-eating grin crossed his brother's face. "But you did picture it, didn't you?"

"I'm having second thoughts about going to Sam's with you."

He could just as easily have a drink at his house. His cottage was small, but it was his, free and clear. The little home had been wiped out during the last hurricane. Having money saved, plus the insurance policy on the house and no real home in the military, he'd rebuilt his cottage with fourteen-inch-thick cinder block walls and even elevated it higher than the building code required. It was his forever home where he had planned to retire with a wife. He hadn't realized his retirement would come so soon.

"Right?" Thane's question made him realize his brother had been droning on.

He entered the massive storage warehouse where they dry-docked over four hundred boats. He glanced at his brother. "Right, what?"

Thane pulled up and scowled at him. "Dude, weren't you listening?"

He shrugged. "I rarely listen to you."

"Wow, I think I might be hurt." Thane put his hand over his heart.

He opened a spiral notebook for his notes that he carried along with the log books of the *Princess*. He ripped out a blank page and handed it to Thane.

The man's eyes bounced from the paper to Creed. "What's this for?"

"To file a hurt feelings report. You tell me all about those bruised emotions. Submit it, and in twenty or thirty days I'll send you a response guaranteeing I one hundred percent don't give a shit. You know, just to make it official." He spun on his heel and headed to his office on the far side of the warehouse.

9

"You know if you weren't my brother, I'd think you were a dick."

He turned and walked backward as he spoke, "You *are* my brother, and I still think you're a dick."

"Only because I am!" A smile split Thane's face as he threw the words across the building.

He shouted back, "Glad to know you have a skill!"

"We're leaving in a half hour!"

Creed lifted his hand in acknowledgment and chuckled. It had been a while since he'd been out with his brother. A drink or two while avoiding the trap Missy and his mother had set for him should be doable. He was a fucking SEAL after all. How hard could it be to avoid a tiny, five-foot-nothing blonde?

# CHAPTER 2

*E*vidently, pretty fucking hard. Creed shifted and moved the woman who'd taken up a perch on his lap. He'd give her credit; she was tenacious. With every polite refusal of her advances, she'd back off, regroup, and re-engage. Tenacious and too damn young. God, he felt old. Really fucking old.

"Seriously, like we should def go to the beach together tomorrow. All these muscles." Danica slid her hand up his chest. He grabbed her fingers and held them, keeping her from roaming further as he side-eyed Thane and Missy. His sister-in-law had the decency to look embarrassed, and Thane looked uncomfortable as fuck. Good.

He turned his attention back to his current problem. Danica had had about three too many Cuba Libres, and her words slurred enough to make that obvious. A drunken woman-child. Just what he didn't need or want.

She tugged at her hand and frowned before her face lit up like a fourth of July fireworks celebration. "Oh! We can go to yours, like now, and you can show me your muscles. In private." She reached down with her other hand and cupped Creed's cock, giving him a squeeze. "All of your muscles."

Fuck, when did groping in public become acceptable? Maybe he was over the fucking hill because it was that exact instant he decided he'd had enough babysitting. He stood, dropping her to the floor.

She giggled and jumped up and down on her toes. "Goody! Let's go!" She snagged his wrist and started toward the door.

He resisted her pull easily, and she lost her grip. She spun around and reached for him again. He managed to capture her free hand. Seriously, the woman must have been born an octopus. He swore she had eight arms. He waited until she actually looked up at him.

"Stop. We are not going anywhere together. I have zero desire to show you anything, including any of my muscles." He spun her and directed her, albeit gently, toward his brother and Missy. "Go find yourself someone closer to your age, because there is nothing happening here."

He didn't wait around to see if the woman did as he directed before he hightailed it outside the bar and onto Duval Street. He straddled his Harley and kicked the engine awake, noting his brother had followed him.

"Dude, leaving already?"

He glanced at Thane as he lowered the bike from its kickstand. "Yeah. Seriously not feeling it."

Thane stepped into the street. "Sorry, man. I've never seen Danica like that. What do you say you and I head over to the 'O'? I'll buy. We can leave the insanity here and just have a drink. It's been a long time since we've done that."

He threaded his hands through his hair. The close cut he still maintained was practical—or at least that's what he told himself. "That sounds solid, but not tonight. I'm heading home. I'll have a drink with you when you don't have the missus waiting for you."

Thane reached out a hand and Creed grabbed it, pulled his brother in, and gave him a hug, slapping his back before he let him go. "Get back to the party."

Thane smiled, winked and headed back into the bar. The sound of music and laughter floated onto the street, barely discernible above the throaty rumble of his hog's engine. Creed drew a deep breath as that old Danny Glover line popped into his head. Maybe *he* was getting too old for this shit.

The warm, humid wind caressed his skin as he turned south on Simmonton Street from Duval. Traffic was light as he cut left on Truman and then right on First Street. He leaned into the turn on

Flagler Avenue and headed home. His cottage came into view. He did a double take. A black SUV filled the driveway. Alert in ways he hadn't been in almost a year, he assessed the situation as he approached his home. A lone figure sat on the porch in one of his two Adirondack chairs.

Creed pulled the bike up and parked it at the foot of the stairs. He cut the motor and propped the Harley on its kickstand while his eyes scanned the vehicle, the outside of his home, and the man on his porch. Detecting no immediate threat, he walked up the stairs and leaned on a column of his front porch. The man waiting for him had Property of US Government practically tattooed on his forehead. In the ninety-five percent Key West humidity in the middle of fucking July, the black wool suit his visitor wore was ridiculous.

"Commander Lachlan." The man stood. His posture betrayed him almost immediately. The way he held his hands, cupped naturally at the seam of his pants, the ramrod straight back and the correct use of his military rank, yeah, the man was prior military. He may have sneered as Mr. Government gave him the once-over too. Good to know. He considered getting the measure of a person an occupational hazard from a lifetime's worth of training. Seemed Mr. Fed agreed.

"And you are?" He stood with his legs apart, ready

to move, still not comfortable with his unexpected visitor.

"Forgive the unannounced drop-in, Commander. My name is Silas Branson. I'm Assistant DHS Director, and I'm here because we have a problem."

Assistant Director for the Department of Homeland Security, now that was pretty fucking high up on the totem pole. "What can I do for you?"

"Ah, well in order to tell you that, I have some papers you'll need to read and sign." The man reached down to the small table between the chairs and produced a folder.

The bold red stamp was unmistakable, and his eyes flashed straight back to the man in front of him. A person didn't just carry around Top Secret folders. This wasn't a social call. It was his call-up. Bone Frog Command. Finally. "Care to take this inside? I have AC and single malt." He nodded toward the cottage door.

"Fuck me, I thought you'd never ask." Branson's shoulders dropped a bit, and a ghost of a smile spread across his face.

AFTER POURING two fingers worth of single malt for both of them and cranking the AC down low enough to freeze the tits off the Wicked Witch of the West, he sat down across the kitchen table from Branson.

"You know why I'm here?" Branson asked as he took the proffered glass.

"I am assuming Bone Frog has a mission for me."

He got a nod in return. "That would be correct." Branson swirled the liquor but didn't take a drink.

"Figured you'd lost my application."

The department Branson represented had recruited Creed as he processed through his retirement. At that point in his life, the offer of employment doing what he loved, even on an infrequent basis, was the ingredient he needed to keep his sanity.

Branson's brow furrowed. "Hardly, Commander. You were on hold until your knee rehabbed, and until now, there hasn't been a need to utilize your specific skill sets."

He knew when he signed on with this unit as a freelance contractor his knee would be an issue, especially if the organization needed him in the field. It was one of the many reasons he'd worked so damn hard to get back to one hundred percent, or as close as he could get with a replacement joint. His brother had pointed it out earlier today. His life was built around a schedule. Workout, work, go home. Wash, rinse, repeat. Thane had no idea why he was so damn committed to the routine. This, the opportunity sitting in front of him, was the reason he'd kept his nose to the grindstone.

He nodded at the folder. "Hit me with the paperwork."

Branson shook out two pieces of paper from the folder with his right hand as his left struggled to pull loose his wet tie. The man must have been sitting outside for one hell of a long time, or he had a perspiration problem because his shirt and under-shirt were visibly drenched. "How long were you waiting?"

"Well, our intel said you usually got home about five. I've been waiting since four thirty." Branson popped the collar button of his shirt and drew a deep breath.

Creed glanced at the clock. It was nearly ten. The man had waited outside for almost six hours. Branson had been pounded with the late afternoon sun for at least three hours before sunset. He got up and grabbed two bottles of water out of the fridge and handed them to his unexpected guest before he turned on his heel and rummaged around in the hall closet. It took a minute to gather what he wanted. When he returned to the small table, he plopped a towel, bar of soap and a change of clothes in front of the man. "No offense, but you stink. The guest shower is down the hall to the right. I'll read what I'm assuming is a reinstatement of my security clearance and a non-disclosure agreement while you shower. Take that fucking folder with you. I don't want to know what is in it until all the I's are dotted and the T's are crossed."

Branson narrowed his eyes at him and then nodded. "All right, but only because I do fucking stink."

They both laughed, and he watched the man grab the classified folder, place it on top of the pile of clothes Creed had just deposited in front of him, and head down the hall.

He crunched the now empty water bottles and placed them in the recycle bin. Once he heard the water start in the bathroom, he turned his attention to the documentation. It was the standard shit. Nothing he hadn't signed before. He initialed in all the appropriate spaces and scrawled his name across the heavy bond paper, twice, before he dated them and threw the pen on top of the papers. He nursed his two fingers of heaven and listened to the sounds of a complete stranger showering down the hall.

Since he was seventeen, he'd lived, eaten, slept and dreamt of nothing but serving in the United States Navy. He'd pursued his dream since the day he entered the hallowed grounds of Annapolis. Four years later, he exited that campus as a naval officer, but he had a higher goal, one he fought to achieve with every atom in his body.

He *knew* commitment. He understood service, and he'd made the sacrifices. The second he was eligible, he submitted his application to the Naval

Academy's SEAL Officer selection process. He'd been accepted. Fuck, a person had no clue what they were able to endure until they were put to the test. And the Navy fucking tested each and every candidate. The inner metal of a man who made it through BUD/S training was stronger than anything the average Joe on the street could imagine. The public now knew some of the training SEALs endured. Basic conditioning, diving, and land warfare, but then came training and certification with a parachute and from there on to advance training. Creed volunteered for every last one of the courses he qualified for and even put in for those he didn't. What was the worst they'd say? No? Fuck that. The air he breathed was laced with the blood, sweat, and tears of men who bled for this country. A SEAL was part of a team and he, and every one of the men that graduated from BUD/S, understood that. They all had sacrifice grafted into their DNA.

He worked like a madman for five years after he successfully completed initial training. Then he pushed a platoon before he'd been promoted to a position where he directed the operations and movements of larger forces at the headquarters element level. He'd risen to the pinnacle of SEAL command and then... He pushed the shit hand his fucking injury had dealt him back into the box he'd built to contain it. Now wasn't the time to dwell.

He also chased away the urge to speculate on

what his mission would be. Whatever was happening would play out as soon as a less-olfactory-offensive Assistant Director made his way back down the hall. He smiled. Branson was obviously a dedicated man. He could have taken his ass off that front porch and come back in the morning.

His eyes popped wide open at the sound of the bathroom door opening. He downed the last of his liquor and decided he'd pour one more. Something told him he'd need it.

Branson had rolled his suit into a tight, compact, cylinder. Yeah, the man had attended Packing 101 in the field. Branson glanced down and went through the papers he'd autographed to ensure both were signed and the appropriate language was initialed. Only then did Branson sit down, take a sip of his own drink, and open the classified folder. He kept his eyes on Branson as the man spoke.

"In the last eight months, the CIA, in conjunction with the FBI, Homeland, Guardian Security, and numerous foreign military entities around the globe, have prevented the detonations of four separate weapons of mass destruction."

Creed narrowed his eyes. WMD was a vast category, anything from poisonous gases to nuclear warfare. "Care to be more specific?"

Branson gave him a small nod before he flipped out two, eight-by-ten photos from a folder. He laid them in front of Creed. A quick scan showed a total of four devices. "Dirty bombs." Branson tapped the first one. "This was found in Tel Aviv. The Mossad is not forthcoming on the details of how they were tipped off, but it was discovered before the President of the United States and the President of Israel were to meet. It had been placed in the West Bank."

Creed sat back in his chair and glanced from the picture to Branson. "No press coverage of the attempt? Impressive."

Branson chuckled. "Not for the Mossad. They can close shit down hard." He pointed to the second device. "Note the same construction. This one was found in London, three days before the royal wedding."

"How was it found?" Creed examined the casing of the two devices. From what he could see from the photographs, all were exactly the same, down to the small metal clips fastened against the locking mechanism.

"MI6 received a tip from Scotland Yard. Seems one of their informants got wind of something huge happening along the procession route for the bride and groom. This device was attached to a cement barricade."

"Strange it was so out in the open. Something this big would be visible, wouldn't it?" Creed looked at the photo again. "What is this? About thirty inches squared?" From the photo, it would appear the second device was encased exactly like the other three.

"Twenty-four, by twenty-four, and no, it was located under a barricade made out of Styrofoam and painted to look just like the others. Due to the threat, Buckingham Palace changed the route, which meant the barriers needed to move."

Creed shook his head. "So it was found by dumb luck."

"100 percent, but because of that incident, the intelligence community has elevated the threat levels. The third one was found during Carnival in Rio, and that is what gave the international agencies and the CIA their first lead on the source. It was discovered in a diplomatic pouch. Russian. Of course, Russia claims no knowledge of the incident."

"There are four here. Tel Aviv, London, and Rio. Where was the fourth one found?" Creed tapped the last picture as he spoke.

"On a boat intercepted by the Coast Guard on a routine inspection. The origination point of that craft was Cuba."

"Fuck me." Creed scrubbed his face and absorbed the implications. "The Russians are making dirty bombs in Cuba?"

"One of the most likely theories put forth." Branson leaned forward and took a sip of his scotch. "Of course, the diplomatic channels are clogged with bullshit."

"You're not here because you need a diplomat."

"Obviously," Branson sighed.

"What's the government's position on the threat?"

Branson let out a snort of derision. "Depends on what fucking department you ask. What we have here is, at the worst, a potential for a nuclear threat on our doorstep. There are factions in D.C. that would rather shove their fingers up their asses than determine if this is an actual threat. God forbid we act instead of react. Fucking idiots." Branson drew a deep breath and studied the pictures, speaking to them rather than Creed. "The last operation went tits up, and I believe it was because there wasn't an operational focal point."

He understood the man's consternation. He'd had his hands tied by political maneuvering on occasion. When the chips were down, he broke the chains that bound him and his team. He did what he knew to be right, consequences be damned. People's lives mattered. On one such occasion, he'd stepped out and made the call to abort because of too little communication. Not enough reliable intelligence was being produced from the miasma called the Joint Operation Headquarters. One of his teams was cut off before they could abort and get to safety. They fought hard until Creed was able to deploy, but he did reach them, against orders.

Branson leaned back, his perfect posture not relaxed in the slightest. "Were you aware that the

Countering Weapons of Mass Destruction Office was recently formed under the umbrella of Homeland Security?"

"Can't say as I was." Seriously, who had time to keep up with the shifting sands in Washington? He shook his head. D.C. was a ball of snakes all intertwined. God only knew where one entity started, and another stopped.

"We took a chunk of one organization and mixed others into it, and presto, the Department of Homeland Security became the proud parent of the CWMD office." Branson raised the glass of liquor to his lips as he watched Creed.

He raised an eyebrow at the man across from him. "And this rearrangement somehow pertains to my portion of this mission?"

"Ah, well, in addition to several agencies appearing under the Homeland umbrella, one organization was formed to ensure critical missions don't get lost in a political quagmire or caught in an alphabet tug of war."

"Bone Frog Command." Creed threw out the name of the freelance contracting agency he'd signed on with when he'd retired.

"Indeed. Technically, we don't exist, but our activities are covered under the umbrella that my superiors have formed. I have been empowered by them to utilize certain contracted former members of the military and other organizations. Members with specific skills and management abilities. Leaders who could coordinate, direct, and if necessary, participate in the reconnaissance and execution of a mission that would unearth information, deter participants from going forward with actions detrimental to the security of the United States or eliminate any threat to the interests of the United States of America. You, Commander Lachlan, are one of those leaders and this is your formal notice."

Branson pulled out a small sheaf of papers. "You are hereby working for me, effective at 0900hrs, tomorrow morning. I suggest you get your affairs in order, sir. You have a mission to plan and execute."

He took the papers the man held out. A quick glance confirmed it was his banking information and a dollar amount. He set the papers aside. He wasn't doing this for the money. "What resources will I have available?"

"I think you'll find them more than adequate. I'll fill you in when we hit Hurlburt Field." Branson gathered his papers and tucked his suit under his arm. "I appreciate the loan of the clothes. I'll have them returned after they're laundered."

Creed waived Branson's offer off. "No need. Where do I meet you?"

"I'll pick you up, here. 0900. And Commander, I'm sure I don't need to remind you all this information is classified at the highest levels. Your departure shouldn't leave any ripples in any pond."

He crooked his head at the man and smiled. "Yet you did remind me. Interesting isn't it?"

"I'm just ensuring you know the scope of the mission."

Branson almost shrugged.

He wondered if the man was capable of such a relaxed movement. He doubted it. "I'll figure something out to tell my family. How long do you anticipate the mission lasting?"

Branson's lips tightened into a thin line as he thought. "Hopefully the recon will be completed within the next two weeks, but the potential for expansion based on what you find is high. I'd say at least three months. Worst case scenario, six." Branson nodded as if he were agreeing with his own assessment and headed toward the door.

He watched the man walk out of his home and drew a deep breath. He had a cover story, one that wouldn't be questioned by his brothers or parents. A fellow former SEAL needed help and had reached out to him. He was going to spend some time with an old buddy.

He stood and looked around his small home. His entire world was about to change. The stress of the unexpected meeting settled in his neck. He rolled his shoulders and a smile tugged at his lips when the reality of tonight's conversation hit him. If only for a little while, he was going back to the one thing that had meant everything to him.

# CHAPTER 3

"Why me for this particular assignment?" Creed moved, dropping into an uncomfortable chair in the small conference room inside a small, secure building on the tiny base situated on Key West. The air conditioner rattled and wheezed in a symphony of complaint. He'd refrained from asking any questions of Branson until they arrived at the secure location. Training curbed his tongue until he could be sure no one overheard the conversation.

"The obvious reasons, of course."

"Humor me, which of the obvious reasons?" He turned in his seat as he asked.

Branson moved away from the wall and put his hands in his pockets. "Leadership ability, to start. I need someone who is mature enough to handle the assignment, but young enough to be able to work it too. Based on the latest brief I received, you work out regularly, weightlifting, running and swimming. Your artificial knee still gives you concerns, but you are physically able to perform to the standard we require."

His brow furrowed at the backhanded compliment. *You're a gimp, but a capable gimp.* All right, then. "Thanks, I think?"

Branson's forehead pulled together in concentration. "Don't be offended, Commander. You'd be surprised how many who have had your type of injury let the injury win. You didn't. Another mark in your favor. In addition to your leadership and stamina, I am uniquely interested in your training. Specifically, the covert missions you've been instrumental in planning and leading. As a commander, you are respected by most of the agencies with whom you've worked. The Marines, not so much."

He threw back his head and laughed. Early in his career, he'd gone head-to-head with a Marine recon commander during a particularly dicey mission. He waved a dismissive hand as he continued to laugh at the memory. "Let's just say there was a difference in opinion about the exposure of our assets. The fallout wasn't pretty." But from that moment on, he'd grabbed and held that Marine officer's respect. Fifteen years later, that Marine was the Aide to the Chairman of the Joint Chiefs of Staff. They talked about once a month. Creed dashed Branson a cheeky smile. "The Marines love me."

Branson offered him a real smile in response. He shook his head as he spoke, "Apparently. Although that isn't necessarily a mark in your favor."

Creed laughed again. Branson did have a sense of humor buried under that suit. Who knew?

Branson continued, "You also speak Spanish. You've grown up on the water, and you can captain a large boat. Cuba is only an hour and a half boat ride from Key West."

Creed leaned back in the chair and crossed his hands over his stomach as he contemplated Branson's words. "Leadership ability and covert ops. How many am I taking in and where is the insertion point?"

Branson's eyebrows rose ever so slightly. Creed had never been accused of being a patient or a politically correct person. Oh, he could dance that dance if he had to do it. If it was necessary, he could perform the political cha-cha with the best of them. Four years in the Academy, and tutelage under one of the best fucking Captains in the US Navy had prepared him for a long career. He'd been on a very short list to make O-6 and wear the rank of Captain. Too bad his body hadn't respected that honor. Fucking knee.

Branson hoisted up the black briefcase that had been delivered to the small conference room as soon as they'd arrived. He pulled out a stack of at least fifteen folders. Creed instantly recognized the Naval personnel folders intermingled in the stack. He assumed the others were from other branches of the military, but by the array of colors in the pile, he'd bet there were several from other government organizations, too. Branson set them down and pulled out a chair opposite Creed. "The candidates for your team."

"All right, define the mission. "He didn't move from his comfortable position. It was about time to see exactly what he was getting into. Not that it mattered. He was doing what he loved, and he'd be the first one through the door, no matter if the mission was a walk in the park or a clusterfuck of epic proportions.

"First, although this mission is sanctioned by my office, if you or any of your men are captured, your official status is private citizen." Branson stared directly at him waiting for the weight of his words to sink in.

"Then we don't get captured."

"I'm sure that is also what the CIA team, missing somewhere in Cuba, told their handler."

He sat back and stared at Branson. "Is this a rescue or recon mission?"

"Officially, your mission is to determine if the dirty bombs are in fact being produced in Cuba, and if possible, to stop or disrupt those making the bombs–with prejudice."

"Officially."

"Except for the modifier I added at the end of the statement, correct."

Creed chuckled at that, but he needed to know the full extent of his mission. "And unofficially?"

"Commander, there are four Americans in Cuba who went in under orders to find the facility that was producing the dirty bombs and shut it down. Unofficially, I'm telling you to do whatever it takes to bring those men home."

"Without being captured."

"Of course."

"Then I need a team, a plan, and contacts in the country."

"Agreed. The team, you and I will pick. We'll develop and refine the mission based on the skill sets of your team. I have a contact in Cuba."

He leaned forward and steepled his fingers together. "I'd prefer to define the mission and then shop for the personnel, and I have final say on the talent." He'd done it both ways, defining the mission around the talent was an option, but getting the mission laser focused was essential and if they needed to adapt and overcome after that, so be it. A smile spread across Branson's face, and somehow Creed felt like he'd passed a test he had no idea he'd been taking. "Do you trust your contact in Cuba?"

"I do." Branson leaned back into his chair. "I've worked with him before. There is a risk, a grave risk, of being exposed when you get in Cuba. Rafael Diaz and his network are your best bet for getting through this mission alive."

"Network?"

Branson's eyebrow rose. "He is the organizer and head of Cuba's largest black-market operation and he is a ranking member of the G2, which is... hell it is the secret police. If anything is happening in that country, Rafa will know or can find out about it. Of course, to get that information, we will end up paying dearly."

"You trust a ranking member of the G2? Someone who could ruin us in a heartbeat?"

"I trust his greed. I've used him before. He wants money and if we are discovered and tied to him, he loses everything. He can't afford to cross us."

Creed held up his fingers and rubbed them together. "Of course, he is a businessman after all." Sarcasm dripped from his words. "Do we have the resources to pay?"

"We do," Branson confirmed. "Rafa isn't a man to be trifled with. He is extremely powerful, and because he is, the Communist party turns a blind eye to his activities. They need the products he brings in, and they need the money that Rafa puts into the country's economy."

"Why didn't the CIA use him as a way in?"

"Rafa isn't an easy man to contact or to persuade for that matter. It can take weeks to get a message to him if not longer. If the CIA tried to rush that process or pressure him…"

"Which I'm gathering from your tone is their norm?"

Branson shrugged. "I offered to smooth over any ruffled feathers. I was informed they had their own assets. The fucked-up thing about it is, the missing team disappeared less than twenty-four hours after setting foot on Cuban soil. From what we have pieced together, they wouldn't have had the time to meet the source who was supposed to be waiting for them, and the Cuban informant alleging knowledge of the dirty bombs hasn't been seen or heard from since."

"You think it was a setup?"

"Even odds between that, or the contact was caught when the agents were taken. Bottom line, there isn't anyone to help us find the source of the dirty bombs except Rafa."

"Have you communicated with this Rafa about the upcoming mission?"

"He knows we are coming, where to meet, and a timetable. No details on why we are there or what we want. That is for you to play as you see fit when you arrive. You will have complete operational control. Comms are suspect at best. We have CIA intel that says the Cuban government has invested heavily in monitoring systems. The government is trying to listen to calls inside the United States. With the frequencies the US military uses being sold off at an alarming rate and the amount of overall cell usage, it wouldn't take much to figure out what freqs our people operate on. But that's a topic for another mission. In this instance, I'll leave any communication once you are in-country to your discretion, but I think we should build the mission and all scenarios as if we have no comms." Branson tossed him a map and a pen. "Let me fill you in on what information the CIA was kind enough to share."

SEVEN HOURS, five cups of coffee, three bottles of water, and a halfway decent bag of sandwiches later, they had a plan and a tentative team.

Creed tapped two files. "I like these two. We can discuss them in a minute. The third member can be any one of those men." He pointed to a stack of four folders. He shook his head. "What I really need help with is our exit strategy. I'm looking for someone who can pass as a charter boat captain. I don't see anyone among this group I can use for that purpose."

Branson's eyes scanned the stacks of folders around them while he drummed his fingers on the table. After releasing a huge sigh, he reached back under the table and pulled out the black briefcase. Another thick stack of personnel files landed on the table. "These men are qualified, but for various reasons weren't my first choice. I saw two or three who had maritime experience."

They each took half the stack and started going through the folders. The files seemed to merge together as Creed tossed one after the other onto the 'no' pile. Until... *bingo*. He raised his eyes to Branson. "I've got one."

"Who?" Branson glanced at the jacket cover.

Creed tossed Branson the folder. "Dan Collins."

After a quick flick of the paper, Branson shook his head and placed the folder on the 'no' pile. "He's with a private contractor, Guardian Security, but his military service jacket shows disciplinary problems."

"Is the fact he is a Guardian an issue?"

"No, their personnel are top notch. I'm concerned about the disciplinary problems he had before he got out. According to Jacob King, my counterpart at Guardian, Collins is a solid asset. I'm not so sure. I don't like what his military jacket shows."

Creed reached for the folder, placed it in the center of the table and flipped to the man's disciplinary record. "Other than the one episode, he has an excellent service record. This looks to be an isolated incident."

Branson's forehead scrunched in concentration as he scanned the paper again. "He hit a superior officer. You don't need a question mark like him on this operation."

"That is where you're wrong. That is exactly who

I need on this operation. I need men who will think on their feet and stand their ground. Collins' record was exemplary, minus that one instance." He flipped to the single sheet of paper sent by Guardian. "He is highly recommended. Water-based operations are his expertise." He couldn't see why this conversation was happening. This was the man he needed.

"He received disciplinary action under Article Fifteen of the UCMJ." Branson shook his head and put the folder back into the no pile.

Creed reached over and put the file firmly back on the 'yes' pile. He opened it and flipped the page. "According to this, he was busted two pay grades and still finished his hitch without any further disciplinary occurrences. He speaks some Spanish, and he has his captain's license. I want him."

"Fine, he stays," Branson conceded with sigh. "So, we have Collins, and you want those two?" Branson motioned to the folders that Creed had pulled earlier.

He reached for them and flipped open the cover of the Naval personnel folder. "This individual could be a liability, but we need his expertise."

Branson glanced at the orange folder sitting beside Creed. It was the only one of that color and for a good reason. "Ahh…Whitehead. Yes, I agree. He is needed."

Creed set aside the Naval folder for a moment and picked up the orange folder, flipping it open to confirm his assessment. Whitehead was a nuclear physicist who had worked in the U.S. government's nuclear program and consulted for the Nuclear Regulatory Commission. On his down time, he ran marathons and had no radical affiliations. He was currently taking a sabbatical from the university where he worked when he wasn't consulting, to train for the Iron Man Marathon. Branson told him the consulting gig was for the CIA, so the man had clearance and experience. No immediate family, only a few close friends. Christopher Whitehead would be the one to determine if there were indeed nuclear components being made into dirty bombs in Cuba.

"McGowen is the other choice?" Branson slid the folder Creed had set down before he picked up Whitehead's orange jacket and scanned the contents.

"Tigger McGowen." He'd had to double check the man's name when he'd opened the folder. "What parent is so cruel as to name their child Tigger?" He shrugged. "That could explain why McGowen is one badass motherfucker."

Branson chuckled and glanced through the jacket.

McGowen's military training and certifications impressed, but it was McGowen's off-duty certifications Creed was most interested in utilizing. The man held a black belt in Muay Thai, and an eighth-degree red belt in Jiu Jitsu. He'd had to leave the room, get his phone out of the locker, and go outside to Google that shit. He'd found out a red belt is reserved for those at the pinnacle of the discipline, surpassing black belt status. If the team got into trouble on the ground, he needed someone who could work silently. This wasn't a shootout type of mission. Stealth, observation, and operation discipline were the only way they'd survive in country long enough to find the contact, locate and scout the sites, and confirm or disprove the CIA's information about dirty bombs being constructed on Cuban soil. Oh, and bring out four CIA agents who may or may not be held by the Cuban government.

"Both McGowen and Whitehead are athletes. Both have discipline, granted one is an academic, but if he's training and running world-class marathons, he's tough up here." Creed tapped his temple. "McGowen was honorably separated. His jacket is nothing but commendations. Do you know why he left before he was eligible to retire?"

"His parents died. They went over the edge of a cliff during a blizzard. It took two months for the car to be spotted. His little brother was still at home, underage and alone. McGowen's normal schedule had him deployed over two hundred days a year. He told his CO that his brother deserved better. Separated on a hardship discharge and opened a gym in his hometown." Branson tossed the story out as he was going through the other folders.

"Where does that leave us? Is the brother still at home?" Creed glanced at the folders Branson was rifling through.

"No, he is now enrolled at Oxford. It seems McGowen did well with the kid. After he was discharged, he invested the parents' life insurance so the kid would have an educational fund. He sold his old man's eighteen-wheeler to get the kid counseling and made sure he had everything he needed to succeed. McGowen has friends, is well-liked and accepted in the community. No relationship at the current time. If we provided him a cover story, he'd be able to leave. His management is capable, and from what our surveillance has reported, trustworthy." Branson tossed a folder toward him.

He caught it before it slid off the table and held the folder in his hands. "The cover story for McGowen can be the same one I used. A friend from the military is having a hard time and needs his help. He owes the man his life, and he's taking the time to repay that debt. No one will question it."

Branson nodded and scribbled into his notebook. "All right."

Creed lifted the folder in his hand. "Who is this?"

"Sage Browning. He lives in Tampa. He's worked several jobs in the past. Never fit in anywhere except the military." Branson shrugged. "He'll do what he's told when he's told. A solid man who will have your back."

"Why did he get out?"

"Traumatic Brain Injury. He stutters. Bad. No

other physical or mental issues. He was discharged for the TBI."

He looked up at Branson. *There was something...* "You know him."

A single dip of the chin confirmed his suspicion. "He served with me." Branson leaned back and leveled a stare at Creed.

He paged through the file. He saw nothing that would make Browning a liability, and if he had Branson's endorsement, he was onboard without further question. Creed threw the file in the 'yes' pile. "Done."

"So, Browning, McGowen, Whitehead and Collins." Branson stacked all but those four folders and pushed the big pile to the side of the table. Branson stretched as he spoke, "That leaves our contact in Cuba."

"What background do you have on him?"

"Rafael Diaz." Branson reached into his pocket and produced a small black notepad. He flipped through it until he found the page he needed. "His parents were caught up in the revolution when Batista was ousted and Castro took over."

Creed stopped the man for clarification. "Caught up?"

Branson frowned and read his book for a moment. "Reports are they were executed as Batista supporters."

Creed leaned back in his chair. "Were they?"

Branson shook his head. "Unknown. At that time,

it didn't seem to matter who you were sympathetic toward. Bloody mess."

"You said you've worked with Diaz before?" Creed wanted as much information on the man as he could get.

"Yes. He's debunked false information and provided access to certain items that had managed to find their way to Cuba through back channels. Items that if made public would damage reputations of certain high-level government officials."

"So, you trust him?" Creed pushed the question.

Branson shrugged. "Trust is a vague term."

Creed blinked several times before he stared at the man in front of him. "No, it really isn't."

"You'd think that, but believe me, one thing I've learned, trust isn't a solid process." The darkness in Branson's expression seemed to grow. "We have the money to pay him. I trust he wants that money. I trust he either knows, or will find out, if the CIA agents are alive and where they are being held, and I trust if dirty bombs are being made in his country, he will assist us in finding out where. His cooperation, as always, is available to the highest bidder. We arrive and feed him information as he needs it. If there are no other clients, and plenty of money, he will do what it takes to get what he wants. Therefore, my trust is a relative term."

"Not for a SEAL." His statement was emphatic. Trusting his team was instinctive.

"Granted, but you won't be dealing with people you've gone through hell with this time, Commander. Your team needs time to grow that level of trust, and time is a luxury we don't have. Suspicion, gut feelings, and instinct will be the tools you'll need to use to keep your team alive." Branson stood and rolled his neck, cracking it. "Your talent for knowing when to pull back or charge forward and your ability in handling the unforeseen shit that explodes in your face during missions tagged you for this assignment, Commander Lachlan. Your country is asking you to get in, find that location, shut down the manufacturing process if possible, and bring home those agents."

Creed stood and extended his hand. "Then let's get to it."

# CHAPTER 4

The sun had no mercy, and if it were possible, he'd have melted hours ago. Creed tipped his baseball hat back and wiped a forearm across his brow, catching the sweat that continued to drip into his eyes. He caught the sleeve of his t-shirt and mopped up the remaining beads as they trickled down his face. The forty-five-foot luxury fishing boat with all the bells and whistles they were using was a gift from heaven, also known as Guardian Security. The vessel was registered under the Grand Cayman flag and made getting into Cuba that much easier. Fortunately, Guardian had a docking permit for another operation, but according to Branson, this op had jumped in priority and Guardian slid Homeland the permit. Golden fucking ticket.

He powered down the engine and glanced over

the ladder to the deck below. Four unfamiliar men, men whom he and Branson had vetted and selected, scrambled to pick up fishing poles and cast a line in the water. The out-rigging of fishing gear was for plausible deniability. They were still out far enough they were not required to start hailing the Cuban Port Officials. He trolled the boat at a slow speed and waited for the rest of his team to join him on the raised pilot deck.

Dan Collins climbed the ladder first and dropped into the seat next to him. "I'll hold her while you do the briefing."

Creed did another double take. Fuck, the man could be a double for that actor who starred in all the dinosaur and superhero movies. He'd talked with the man extensively over the last twenty-four hours. Initially, he wasn't sure about Collin's captain rating, but when he watched the man maneuver the craft into its slip when they both arrived, he was impressed. Collins had given him a tour of the boat. He acknowledged both Collins' knowledge and experience. The Guardian was a solid asset.

Sage Browning popped up the ladder followed by Whitehead, with McGowen bringing up the rear. They all stood around the small, detachable table Creed had pushed into place. A map of Cuba landed in the middle and he began. "We are fifteen nautical miles from Cuba." He pointed to starboard side of the boat in case there was any question as to which

44

direction the country lay. "We will stay at this distance until sunset, then Collins will take the vessel into Hemingway Marina. Cuban laws require we start hailing the port when we breach thirteen nautical miles. The port officials use handheld radios. We won't have contact until we're four miles out. That is when Whitehead, McGowen and I will cut loose on the skiff. We will skirt to the south under darkness and put in here." Creed slipped his finger to the south and east of Hemingway Marina.

McGowen leaned in closer to see the cove he indicated. "That's Havana, isn't it? It's a populated area."

Creed shook his head and swiped at the sweat trailing down his temples. "No, the reconnaissance we were able to obtain from Branson's sources shows the apartment complexes are condemned. No one lives in this area, and the location is closed off with razor wire so the locals can't pilfer from the buildings." He pulled out several satellite photographs and indicated the fencing. "There are zero heat signatures."

McGowen nodded and stood to his full, intimidating height. "Exit strategy?"

He held up a finger. "I'll get to it. First, Collins and Browning will probably be told to drop anchor outside the port until the authorities come back to work in the morning. We have all the documentation." He opened a drawer and handed a packet each to Collins and Browning. "These contain your passports and all the information the customs and immigration personnel will require when you enter the port. Getting in and cleared could take three to four hours."

"W-Why s-so l-long?" Browning's jaw clenched tight, and his eyes drilled holes in the packet.

Creed leaned back. "They can bring anywhere from two to twelve men onboard to search the vessel as well as drug-sniffing dogs, health officials, agriculture department officials, and even the Guarda Frontera." He glanced at Browning, whose eyes popped up to his in question. He clarified, "Their version of the Coast Guard."

"We'll need a cruising permit." Collins rubbed his chin and pointed to the map. "We can cruise from port to port. What is your timeline on meeting your contact?"

Creed leaned back and braced his hands on his thighs. "Tomorrow before dawn. I'll go alone to make contact. On the off chance that this goes south, we need a way to signal you we are ready for extraction. UHF and VHF radios are out as the state monitors all transmissions."

"WiFi?" Whitehead crossed his arms, his legs braced as the craft rolled with the swells of the ocean and the trolling motor slowly pushed them forward.

"Also monitored by the state. No cell service as all calls are monitored, and no satellite phones. I think the only time we will use our burner phones is if hell has frozen over and the devil is wearing ice skates." He chuckled and rubbed the back of his neck, wiping his drenched hand on his board shorts. "We are going to do this old school. Collins, you figure out a cruising schedule. Something that won't cause any raised eyebrows. We have no way of knowing how long the recon and recovery will take. You're here as our emergency exit."

"Skipper, I know you need us out here, but I wish like hell there was something more we could do." Collins flipped his eyes toward Browning who nodded in agreement.

"I get it. Sitting on your ass and waiting is hard, but when we need to get out, you're the ones who are going to make that happen. Build the schedule. Two months. If it takes longer, start the cruise schedule over."

"That should work. We have a year on the fishing permit, once it's granted." Collins stood with his hands on his hips. "Still, if you need us, we can dock and make a restocking trip to one of the grocery stores they let tourists go to. Wouldn't take too much to get lost on the way."

"Noted. We can work on that after we get this nailed down. Make sure each of us has a copy before we separate. Make this look legit. I want you and Browning to fish. Fill these coolers to over-flowing if necessary. If you're boarded or inspected while you are cruising, I want a foolproof cover story."

Collins nodded before his eyes flicked to Browning. "You ever done any deep-sea fishing?" Browning shook his head in response. A broad smile crossed Collins' face. "Get ready for a treat."

"Where do we make contact with our person on the inside of this mess?" Whitehead glanced from Creed to McGowen.

Tigger shrugged and pointed a thumb towards Creed. "His rodeo."

"All three of us are going into Havana. There are enough Americans from the cruise ships that we will blend in. Be tourists, but be here"—he pointed to the map of Havana he'd pulled out—"at seven a.m." He dropped his index finger on the National Cathedral. "Wait no more than five minutes. If I'm not there or fail to show, follow the port docking list that Collins is developing. Each of these marinas is surrounded with fencing. Tie two plastic bags along the fence line on the easternmost post." He glanced at Browning and Collins.

"Why two?" Whitehead's brow furrowed.

"One bag could just be trash blowing around. Two? It is a signal," McGowen answered for Creed.

He nodded and pointed at McGowen and Whitehead. "Grab a couple bags each from the galley and shove them in your shoes under the soles. They will conform to your arch, and you'll always have them.

Collins and Browning will check for a signal before they depart each marina. If your signal is there, they will fish, crisscrossing in the waters just to the east of that port. Then from midnight to three a.m., Collins will drop anchor no more than two miles out and wait for you. At dark, you and McGowen swim to the boat. Then you get yourselves back to Miami."

"And the guy who is supposed to be helping us?" McGowen braced his big arms against the frame of the overhang as he spoke.

"I'll meet with him. If things look legit, I'll rendezvous with you at the Cathedral, and we will head out."

"How long to canvas the entire island?" Whitehead scratched the dark scruff on his face. The man held himself in a way that impressed Creed. Although he appeared thin, to be an Ironman triathlete the guy had to have stamina.

"Depends on the intel our contact gives us." He glanced at Collins and Browning. "The spare fuel tank is full. You have enough money and an unlimited credit card to fill up at any of the seven marinas that have fuel available. Don't run too low. A high-speed run to Miami or Key West will drain both tanks."

"I got it. Not my first rodeo, Skipper." Collins' smile softened the cautious jibe.

"I have no doubt, but if our information is right

about what is going on inland, we have more than just our lives hanging in the balance."

"Roger." The smile on Collins' face disappeared as the devastation the detonation of a dirty bomb would create weighed on all of them.

Creed reached into the drawer again and passed a money belt to McGowen and Whitehead. "American dollars."

Whitehead held the belt like it was a snake about to strike him. "Why do we need money? I thought the plan was we stayed under the radar, as in no one will know we are on the island."

Creed threw back his head and laughed. Browning, Collins, and McGowen joined him.

Whitehead swiveled his head from person to person. "What the fuck is so funny?"

Creed banked his laughter so he could speak. "All plans are perfect..."

"Until the first contact with the enemy." McGowen and Collins finished the statement, and Browning snapped his fingers and gave a thumbs up in agreement.

Whitehead dropped his hand. The belt snaked along the floor. "What does that mean?"

McGowen reached out and squeezed Whitehead's shoulder. "That means we plan for the worst-case scenario; hope this mess doesn't go to hell in a hand-basket, and you glue yourself to me. If shit goes south, I'll get you out of Cuba."

Creed couldn't have scripted a better answer. McGowen was a damn good asset. He'd accepted he was paired with Whitehead, and he knew why. Creed would take the high-risk asset in Cuba as his partner. If shit went downhill, he had no doubt McGowen would get himself and Whitehead out safely or die trying.

"But wait, if we get caught in Cuba, won't they like execute us as spies?" Whitehead's head whipped from Creed to McGowen.

"See, that right there? That's why we don't get caught." McGowen gave the smaller man a wink and glanced over at Creed. "We done here?"

"Until sunset. Relax until then." He folded up the map of Havana and put it into the waterproof pouch he would affix to his money belt.

He glanced at Collins, hovering over the map of Cuba. The man turned to Browning. "The stuttering, is it permanent?" Browning nodded. Once. "Ever think about learning American Sign Language?" Browning frowned, and he gave a sharp jerk of his head. "Hey man, don't get upset. I have a friend, he's a doctor. He had problems talking because of a traumatic brain injury. He communicated faster in ASL than he could trying to get his mouth to form the words his brain wanted to say. As a Guardian, I've learned it, and I use it. We're going to be on this boat for one hell of a long time, and I'm going to get bored if you don't talk, so we need to figure something out."

Browning narrowed his eyes at Collins. "W-why?"

"Why what? Why do I want to help you learn?" Browning nodded his head again. "Easy. You're a brother. Don't matter we aren't serving anymore or that we didn't serve in the same branch." Browning lifted a very expressive eyebrow, and Collins laughed, holding up a hand. "Oh, don't think I'm not going to rag you, sailor boy, because I am. That's another reason for you to learn ASL. I can't wait to hear your squid-ink tainted comebacks! Come on, let's get into the air conditioning or I'll drip all over this damn map. Then we'll be up a shit-creek without a paddle."

Browning glanced quickly at Creed, gave him a brief nod and headed down the ladder. Creed reached out and stayed Collins. He nodded toward the ladder. "Thank you." With the direction of the wind, there was no way Browning would hear his low statement.

"He's got a fucked-up sentence, yeah? Probably stuck with that disability for life. Has to be frustrating to have your mind go faster than you can talk. I can teach him if he's willing to learn. Might be helpful."

Collins made a move to leave, but Creed tightened his hold on the man. "What happened to get you busted when you were in?"

Collins turned and faced him. "Why? Does it matter?"

He nodded. "To me it does. To me, you appear

squared away. What happened to cause you to hit a superior officer and then punch your ticket and get out of the service?"

Collins drew a deep breath and cast his eyes toward the horizon. "Let's just say superior officers shouldn't be allowed to cast homophobic slurs around and then make moves on guys that are too terrified of the man's position to report him." He turned his attention back to Creed and leveled his stare, making solid eye contact. "Is that going to be a problem?"

He shook his head. "Not for me, but I would've loved to have seen that fucker's face when you put him on the ground."

Collins winked at him and headed to the ladder. "Wasn't near as good as the face he made when I threatened to tell his wife." The man smiled wickedly before he disappeared.

He dropped into the Captain's seat and smiled to himself. He had a fucking phenomenal team. For the first time in over a week, he took a liberating breath of humid air. The chances of this operation being successful got better with every minute that passed.

# CHAPTER 5

"Why me?" Mariella stood in her uncle's office, her arms crossed over her chest. She was pissed and not afraid to show it. Tonight, she was supposed to meet the inbound shipment. She always went. It was a privilege Rafa had given her just over a year ago. She and her crew ensured the contents of the shipment made it to the distribution points and from there to the people it was intended to reach, not the party officials who would consume it or sell it for ten times the amount Rafa charged. It was a delicate dance, one she was good at. Damn good. Although her crew was armed to the teeth, they'd never had to use their weapons. The distinction was an honor she'd earned through quick wits and brazen attitude, an attitude she skillfully wielded. "Send someone else."

Her uncle glanced at the closed office door. He

crooked a finger and beckoned her closer to his desk. When she stopped in front of it, he motioned for her to come around to his side of the desk. He motioned with his chin toward a live video feed on the computer screen. A man lay bruised, bandaged, and curled on his side. He'd seen better days. Wait…she recognized that room. It was the safe room under the house.

Still gazing at the man on the monitor, Mariella dropped to her knees beside her uncle. "Who is he?"

"I don't know his name. Paco's people found him injured and unconscious and brought him to me."

Mariella snorted and shook her head. She knew better than to believe her uncle. "Yet he is here. That means you know something."

Rafa shrugged. "There are rumors very powerful people in our government have recently acquired three Americans who did not process through customs, and they look for a fourth."

Mariella slowly pulled her eyes from the screen and gazed steadily at her uncle. "You think this man is that American?"

"I do. They actively seek an injured man. They know he is hurt. If he is hurt, someone must be hiding him, or they would have found him already. Of course, they want information. Where do you think they will come first?"

"To you." Her uncle was skilled at balancing the Communist party's more aggressive loyalists on a razor's edge. As a senior member of the G2 he was feared. He applied just enough pressure to keep the regime away from his illegal "import" business, but they expected things in return. Information was a regular form of payment.

He nodded. "Which means I should remain here in case they seek answers from me."

Mariella shrugged her shoulders and straightened her back to release the building tension. "Just give them the man."

"No, he is too valuable." Rafa gave her a wink.

"Valuable? To whom? Give him up. Make your money and make him go away. He doesn't need to complicate things here."

"The Americans you will meet will pay more than the people making inquiries. If I'm right, the Americans are here looking for the ones the regime is holding."

"How do you know this man is an American?

"He's American. Just look at the clothes. He tried to blend in, but…" Rafa shrugged a shoulder and a sly smile spread across his face. "The Americans will *pay*." He released a small evil chuckle and picked up a European cigarette from the leather-covered box on his desk. "They will pay enough I could retire to Greece or Italy and live happily for the rest of my life."

Mariella studied her uncle's face. She loved the man, and after a fashion, he loved her, too. Uncle

Rafa's true love would always be money. "So, we ask the Americans for money tonight?"

His brow furrowed. "No. The dance is more... delicate. The Americans will ask us to locate the people the regime has in their possession. We agree to look for them. Learn what you can from the Americans, and then mention we have heard rumors." Rafa motioned toward the screen again before he flicked a silver lighter and flamed the tip of his cigarette. "These men, they are our goose that lays the golden egg."

Mariella sat back on her heels. The essentials Rafa's network supplied sustained lives even though they made a profit from the misery of others. She tried not to dwell on that aspect. They provided a service. Period. "What happens when we get the golden egg? Would you really leave? You are needed here."

Rafa waved a hand in the air. "Not for much longer. Things are changing. Besides, when there is a void, it is filled."

"Yes, but by whom?"

Rafa stroked his chin for a moment before he drew on the cigarette in his hand, igniting the tip with a flick of his lighter. He blew out the smoke and speculated, "There are a few. Adalberto probably."

Mariella shivered and rubbed her arms against her revulsion at that name. Adalberto DeJesus was Rafa's second in command and below Rafa in rank at the G2, which made him lethal and dangerous. His lecherous glances and inappropriate comments directed toward her made her feel…vulnerable. She avoided that sensation at all costs. She'd built emotional armor. She acted hard and tough because any weakness would be a way for Adalberto and people like him to gain power over her, something she would not allow. So, she'd put on a front and learned to fight from some of the best men Rafa had in his employ. Still, the warm breeze from the open windows did little to alleviate the chill that invaded her at the thought of Adalberto in a position of power without Rafa to control him.

"I didn't think you'd leave our people to suffer under him." Mariella's disgust dripped from her plea.

"Adalberto is a good businessman and looking to advance his position within the G2. You could do worse."

Her eyebrows crept up at his horrifying suggestion. When would Rafa understand? "There is no one I consider worse than that man. It's only because he fears you that he leaves me alone." Of that Mariella had no doubt. The lecherous man barely restrained himself.

Her uncle sighed and reached forward to tap his ashes into an ashtray the size of a dinner plate. "You need someone to look after you, someone to provide a good life for you."

"I don't need anyone! Besides, Adalberto wouldn't

give me a respectable life. You and I both know that. I don't want to be kept by a man the likes of Adalberto. I do fine on my own. You raised me to provide for myself." Mariella glanced at the screen. The man's arm moved while he was unconscious... or perhaps asleep. Her gaze followed the motion.

"I won't be around forever, my hissing kitten. We must make plans for that eventuality." He drew long and hard on his cigarette, closing one eye against the smoke tendril that rose heavenward as he looked at her. "You should be married with babies. You're an old maid."

Mariella scoffed and then laughed at the familiar argument. "I am turning thirty-five, not seventy, Rafa. If I want a man, I go out and find one." She hadn't exactly lacked for sexual partners, but they weren't something she actively sought out, either.

She'd had a total of one serious relationship, but that ended when she discovered the man wanted her for her connection to Rafa. Since then, she'd made sure her partners were anonymous, but, sex with no emotional attachment had lost its appeal. A physical release for the sake of release wasn't all it was cracked up to be, so celibacy had happened. Not necessarily by choice but more forced by her job, commitments to her people, and circumstances. Due to her position at the top of her uncle's organization, she couldn't afford to become distracted by the things most women her age already had...a family and someone who wanted more than a sweaty tumble in a strange bed.

Rafa stabbed out his cigarette while throwing her a fierce scowl. "I don't want to hear about your sex life. It isn't proper."

She pointed to herself. "Thirty-five, not sixteen, not seventy. I don't need a man to provide for me." She didn't need it. Want it, maybe…at times.

"Other than me, you mean?"

She snorted. It was an inelegant and sharp noise to let her uncle know he was treading in dangerous territory. "I work for you. What you give me is fair for what I do for you. Don't pretend it isn't."

Mariella was third in command and should be second, at least in her opinion. If she were a man, there was no doubt she'd run Rafa's organization. But she had power. Her word was law unless countered by Adalberto or Rafa. Being the only close relative of a powerful G2 member bestowed that privilege. "I am better with the people than Adalberto, and I make better decisions in the field."

Rafa grumped, "You shouldn't be in the field."

"Yet you want to send me to Havana to make contact with the Americans." She stood and patted her uncle's shoulder. "You contradict yourself, old man."

"There is a reason I'm sending you." He batted away her hand. Rafa didn't like to be touched and had rarely touched Mariella when she was growing up.

The hugs he did give her she could count on one hand.

"I don't trust anyone else to do this." He nodded toward the monitor. "For some reason, the Americans have risked sending four men here and now more arrive. Politics between our countries are strained on a good day. Ask yourself why the Americans would risk this obvious intrusion. Twice. According to my contact, the matter is urgent."

"Do you know why?" She leaned against his desk, half sitting on the hardwood surface.

"Not yet. There was an attempt at contact from the American side before we found this man. It was suspicious, so I ignored it. My contact, one I trust, reached out almost immediately afterward. Things are tense on the American side of this event." He shook his head and glanced up at her. "What I do know is the money they will provide us will make any action we are asked to take lucrative. My instinct tells me there is a dangerous reason they come here, come to me. An important reason. That is the information we need. Go to Havana. Meet the American and bring him back here. Find out what you can." He looked up after he fished another cigarette out of the little box. "Information is power."

"With power comes responsibility." She arched an eyebrow at him. "Responsibility to the people who work for us to ensure they are not gathered up by the regime."

"No. Power is wielded much like an umbrella. I control who it covers. Your responsibility is to me and only to me, Mariella. Protection for all of you is provided by my power. My reputation"—his shoulder lifted in a slight shrug—"and to a degree, yours." He lit another cigarette as he looked up at her.

"Did that hurt?" she snipped. Her uncle snarled a response she didn't exactly hear, but it didn't matter. Rafa giving her a compliment was a rare thing. Mariella shook her head in disbelief and reminded her uncle, "And yet you want to push me toward Adalberto who would demand my loyalty to him. He's almost fifty, and he is cruel. Sometimes I wonder what is rattling around in your brain, Rafa." She leaned down and kissed his balding head.

He ducked out of her reach and watched her from his chair. He drew in another lungful of smoke. "In another country, you would be my successor. Not here. If I were to leave, the men would look to Adalberto, not you."

She growled and snapped, "It is time for people to change."

Rafa moved his shoulders. The action more acceptance than anything else. "You can't change an entire culture overnight."

"Then there is no future for me here." Mariella's words landed flat and heavy in the room.

"At last we agree on something. We get the golden egg, and we leave." Her uncle glanced up at her. The statement was the first time he'd ever mentioned *her* leaving Cuba. She blinked at him and nodded, shocked at his words.

"It is decided then. Adalberto will keep the business running while we deal with the Americans. He cannot know what we are doing, or he will want to profit from it. I will only use those I know are loyal to us."

"And he isn't?"

"Adalberto is loyal to Adalberto. I control his access to power, so he obeys my orders, but he is also ambitious. Ambitious people are dangerous."

Mariella cocked her head. "You fear Adalberto?"

He gave a devious smile. "Fear fuels weakness. No, I don't trust ambitious people." Rafa drew the last of his cigarette and regarded the tip. "This, we will do." He motioned between them.

Mariella smiled, the same evil little smile Rafa had given her a few moments ago. A chance for her to leave Cuba, to live where necessities weren't rationed, withheld, or forbidden. The kernel of hope had been planted not more than two minutes ago by Rafa, and it was already taking root. Yes, the Americans would be the way out. She sat down on the desk and faced her uncle. "Tell me where and when to meet the Americans."

# CHAPTER 6

*T*he locals in Havana called the seawall at the ocean's edge the world's largest open-air bar. Known as El Malecon, the structure ran from Boca de la Chorrera to the Canal de Entrada, but people tended to congregate on the stretch between Calle 12 and Av De Los Presidentes. Mariella found a vacant space across from the Jazz Cafe. It was a nightclub the visitors from the cruise ships frequented. The club was a mirage, the image the Cuban government wanted to project. Wealthy tourists did not want to see the empty grocery stores or the desperate need prevalent in her country. Mariella gave a mental sneer. If they only opened their eyes, the poverty of her countrymen would smack them in their overprivileged faces.

She studied the area on the part of the wall she'd claimed. A typical night at El Malecon. locals sat or leaned against the rock and mortar wall, entrenched in conversation or obsessed with their phones. The government had a WiFi system they allowed people to log into. It was monitored, and access was granted to only certain controlled sites, but the thrill of the internet called to the people who lined the sea wall. Mariella kicked her feet in a natural swinging motion as she sat on top of the low wall. She received several looks, and double takes, as she sat alone. Some were from men who were cruising for a partner for the night. Her ice-cold stare sent those men on their way. Other glances were more surprised. Widened eyes and hurried footsteps passing by spoke of their knowledge of who she was.

Mariella glanced down at her shoes. What a ridiculous signal. One orange and one lime green shoelace. Her uncle's idea so the American would be able to identify his contact. She'd dressed differently for this meeting. Shit kickers, camo pants, and a tank top were her normal daily attire. Tonight, her hot pink canvas high tops matched her tank-top. Or at least they were both pink. The shoes had once been red, but the sun had faded the canvas. Her little toes peeked out of holes years of use had worn through the fabric. The short denim skirt was once a pair of jeans that had been altered when the threadbare knees had finally given out. She liked the short skirt. It showed off her long legs as she swung them back and forth slowly, advertising the ugly neon colored strings of braided cloth.

She played mindlessly with the bottle of rum she'd bought from one of the men who tried to sell tourists knock off liquor and cigars outside the authorized government shops. Her uncle did not dabble in cigars or liquor. The trade they conducted was primarily for essentials—food, sanitary supplies, car parts, and clothing. The local officials knew the people who sold the knock-off cigars and liquor were there, but the government bureaucrats received most of the sales revenue as kick-backs so they looked the other way. It was the way of things. Those who were in power fed off those who were not.

Mariella glanced at her watch. Boredom kept her eyes roving. Muted portions of conversation flitted across her attention although she focused on the sidewalk, well actually the shoes that passed by, not necessarily the people walking past her. Keeping her gaze down helped avoid interaction, and she didn't want to invite any conversation. Instead, she kept her eyes focused on the walkway and the small bottle of rum in her hand. Her mannerisms screamed 'do not approach.'

"Want someone to share that with you?"

Mariella looked up. Ah, well there were always those who were ignorant or arrogant. Three men stood in front of her. She purposefully glared at each one of them in turn, memorizing their features and looking for weaknesses. She recognized them for what they were, locals that skimmed just under the national police's attention. The wife-beater t-shirts displayed shoddy tattoo work. Muscled? Yes. Brains? That was yet to be determined. They were minor league, the type of people her uncle wouldn't touch. No loyalty could be found in these types of men.

"I don't think so. You need to leave. Now." She scanned the area. The two trusted men her uncle had handpicked to shadow her while she was in Havana edged toward her. When they moved to close in, she caught their attention and gave a small shake of her head, stalling them. They had no idea what she was doing in Havana. They were told only to be available if she needed them.

The men confronting her missed the exchange. The one in the middle chuckled and playfully nudged the bigger man on his left. The big man sneered and moved away from the asshole in the middle. Apparently, he didn't like being touched. Mariella noted that there would be no help for the middleman from that corner, at least not immediately. Moron middleman stepped forward. Doing so he simultaneously declared himself spokesman and made him her first target. "I don't think so. I know we can give you a good time."

*Game. Fucking. On.* She'd warned him off. The damn fool. "You want to give me a good time?" Mariella hopped off the wall and carefully set the rum bottle down before she approached the mouthy man in the middle. He was several inches taller than her. Not very bulky, but he was muscled. Mariella glanced to the man on Mouthy's right. He practically vibrated with nervous energy. This would be the one to come to the fucker's aid. She smiled and cozied up to the middleman, rubbing her breasts against his chest.

"Fuck yes, bitch. All three of us are going to show you a good time." He laughed, and his arms went around her, tugging her into him. He ground his hardening cock against her. The fucker slapped her ass and grabbed it with a painful grip. He meant it to hurt. She could see the evil in the bastard's eyes.

Mariella elevated her hands, running them up the man's arms. She leaned forward and whispered. "Let me show you *my* idea of a good time." Her knee slammed into his groin at the same time her hands cupped the back of his head. She dropped her knee as she pushed the fucker's head down and jacked it up again, driving the man's face into her thigh as it hurled upward. The sound of cartilage breaking punctuated the man's high-pitched wheeze.

Nose and balls busted in less than five seconds. Rafa and his men had taught her well. The man's body crumpled. She planted her tennis shoe against his chest and pushed. Her shove sent him back onto the concrete. Curled in on himself, he didn't hit his head. Dammit.

Mariella dropped into a slight crouch and wiggled her fingers at the two other punks, focusing on the one on the right. He started to move toward her, but the other slapped his shoulder and nodded toward her uncle's men who'd pressed through the gathering crowd. She let out a low evil laugh that mimicked Rafa's. She used it as a weapon to intimidate men who thought she was inferior simply because she was a woman. "Oh, don't worry about them. I don't let others fight my battles."

The one on the right snarled at her, but he stepped back and helped his smarter friend pick up the bastard curled on the ground. Mariella noted the blood on the concrete and the crimson stain down the front of the asshole's shirt. His nose was swollen and twisted. She smiled at him. "That is what I call a good time, asshole."

She spun and hopped up onto the wall again. A crowd had gathered and gawked at her. "What?" she spat while staring down those who were bold enough to still stare at her. People found other things to focus on–quickly. Her uncle's men surveyed the area, shadowing the three assholes before they melted back into the thinning crowd.

Mariella stayed on the damn wall. For hours she'd dangled her feet, advertising her stupid neon colored laces. The night wore on, and with each passing hour, her anger grew. Her uncle should have pinned down a meeting time with the American. The vagueness of the location was concerning, but coupled with the uncertainty of *when* the meet would take place– Mariella felt like a worm on a hook. *Sometime before dawn* gave her far too much time to sit and brood. For the second time in twenty minutes, a pair of old Converse sneakers ambled by. She noticed the shoes the first time because the laces were new and white with the plastic tips still intact. That was something that was rare in the people who frequented El Malecon this late at night, or should she say this early in the morning. Sunrise was only an hour away. The brightly colored laces she wore were pieces of cloth braided together. Things like shoelaces were a luxury. Shoelaces, toothpaste, bar soap, manufactured shampoo and lotions, all were luxuries. She had access to them through her uncle, but the majority of the Cuban people did not.

The new laces appeared before her again, hesitated and then approached her. Mariella lifted her eyes. The jeans connected to the sneakers were old and worn thin, and they clung to bulky, muscled thighs. As her gaze rose higher, one of her eyebrows rose. The jeans were tight enough to advertise what the man was packing before a light blue t-shirt's V-neck exposed well-developed pecs, ropey neck muscles and magnificent shoulders and arms. Mariella clicked her tongue and did one more up and down appraisal of his smoking hot body before she steadied her gaze on the man's face. He had dark hair, and his tan could help him pass as a native of the island, but something told her he wasn't. Something besides the damn shoelaces. She hopped off the wall and then leaned back against it, feet crossed, her stupid laces displayed prominently.

The man came forward and leaned on his forearms next to her, looking out toward the ocean. She turned and mimicked his stance. Their arms brushed together as they watched the water in silence. A tingle of excitement ignited and sent gooseflesh over her arms. She spun the small bottle of rum in her hand, waiting for the man to initiate the conversation. Not her typical demeanor, but her uncle had cautioned her to keep her mouth shut and her ears open. Again, not her typical behavior. The stranger casually reached over and grasped the bottle she spun. *Oh, sweet Mother in Heaven! His hands were huge, and his biceps were larger than her thigh.* Okay, that might have been an exaggeration, but not by much. Mariella gave him a sideways glance. She smirked when she met his intense blue-eyed stare.

"You don't look like a Rafael." The words were no more than a whisper, for which Mariella was thankful. If anyone heard them speaking in English, they'd be reported within minutes. Paranoia ran deep within the inhabitants of the country, and for a good reason.

She sent a split-second smile his way. "Actually,

I'm told I do resemble him. I'm his niece." Her whisper was just as quiet as his.

The man turned his attention to the water. "Where is he?"

"Busy." She took the rum back from him, opened the bottle and took a sip.

"Are we compromised?"

She shot him a withering glance and let loose with her patented inelegant snort. She pushed the rum back toward him. "As if I'd be here if you were compromised."

He accepted the bottle but didn't take a drink. Whatever. She'd take it back home with her because she wasn't going to let the rum go to waste. It wasn't a big bottle, and for a knock-off, it wasn't horrible.

Sunrise was the earliest they could safely leave, less than an hour away by the lighter shades of blue that punctuated the eastern sky. Waiting until there were more cars on the roadways would give them the anonymity she desired. It wasn't as if the military or police needed incentive to pull people over, but there was no need to draw attention to the fact that she'd been in Havana. Getting in and out of Havana without being seen was relatively easy, as long as the Americans cooperated.

She tipped her head and stared at him with narrowed eyes. Scrunched like this he looked like that movie star in the ancient Roman warrior films. Not Brad Pitt, the other one, Gerard Butler. She prized her small shelf full of old VHS tapes and DVDs. She'd watched them so many times she could speak the lines with the actors.

His intense blue eyes widened momentarily as if her squinting and staring at him was a surprise. She'd bet a lot of women studied this man. It was a rather enjoyable pastime. One could make it a hobby without too much effort.

"I need to speak to your uncle immediately." The man shifted closer to her when he whispered his demand. She was now practically enveloped by his large frame. His arm came down over her shoulder. From the sidewalk, they would appear as lovers. For reasons she didn't want to consider, she shivered against his embrace. Oh, who in the hell was she fooling? She'd consider this man's...*reasons*...all day, every day. He was tall, built and had a handsome square jaw. He was intense, in a coiled-way-too-tight-and-ready-to-pounce type of way. She would definitely do him. Three or four times at least, muchas gracias y si, por favor. The fact that she hadn't been this intimately close to a man for over a year probably had something to do with the desire that coiled low in her belly. Messing around sexually with the American had advantages and disadvantages. He'd be gone, and she wouldn't need to worry about his ulterior motives. Sex with him could complicate her uncle's golden egg scenario. So... regretfully... no, not happening.

Mariella shrugged, moving the weight of his arm when she shifted her shoulders. She reached over and took the bottle out of his hand and saluted him with it before she took another pull from the small container. His eyes lowered and watched her. The devil on her shoulder laughed with delight. The American *was* interested. The things she could do with that knowledge filtered through her brain in a stream of evil, delicious photos.

She lowered the bottle and licked her lips. Slowly. The man's eyes followed her tongue. Oh, if only this American wasn't her uncle's magical goose. But he was, and that thought once again doused the flame that had sparked inside her. She was here with this man to work. More importantly, the completion of this mission meant escape for her, although leaving her people to the likes of Adalberto left a rancid taste in her mouth. She'd spent her life trying to provide things for those who had no way of obtaining them. The tourism trade was expanding. It was only a matter of time before the black-market would be irrelevant. Years, perhaps, but changes were happening, some for the better.

"Where are your men?" She spoke in Spanish because others had filled in the space near them.

The American turned around, leaned against the seawall, and maneuvered her in between his legs. She ended up with her hands on his chest. His decidedly hard, wide, muscled chest. Those big hands of his rested lightly on her hips and his scent surrounded her. The aroma of his soap, deodorant, and after-shave married with the smell of the man himself. It was a mixture she could bottle and sell by the gallon.

He leaned in and nuzzled her neck. "Close by. Yours?"

Fluent Spanish caressed her ear when he spoke. Gooseflesh rose over her arms in response to his whispered words. She leaned away from him just enough to see those blue eyes and smiled sweetly. "I don't have any of my men with me."

His eyes narrowed as he scanned the sidewalk behind her. Ahhh... the big American didn't trust her. That ticked her opinion of him up a notch. He was careful, and that type of person didn't make stupid mistakes. She could work with careful people, and something told her that Rafa's goose needed something more from them than just the location of the missing Americans.

She leaned up on her tiptoes, bracing her hands against his shoulders as she leaned in. "We need to leave when the tourists are active. This, what we are doing, will work to keep others from being suspicious." She purred the last portion of that comment. She pulled back to examine his expression expecting to see desire, and secretly hoping for lust-filled, heavy-lidded, eyes.

Except, she saw nothing. The complete and total lack of expression from the man was a red flag waving in front of her as clearly as any matador would wave his cape at a raging bull. He didn't consider her sexually attractive. *She would accept that challenge.* Unfortunately, the schemes she was building in her imagination needed to wait for an appropriate time, which sucked because she wasn't a patient person, but she'd wait until her actions wouldn't complicate her uncle's plans.

She stepped back and extended her hand to him. He glanced up and down the seawall one more time before he took it and moved away from the bricks. His arm dropped over her shoulder when they started walking. He tucked her close to his big, hard body. "Where is your uncle?"

Mariella's head snapped up at the sound of a siren in the distance. The warbling shriek faded instead of strengthened. Sirens were rare where the tourists could hear them. Something serious had happened. She glanced around making eye contact with her men. They followed at a discreet distance.

The American had asked her something... what was it? "Oh, Rafa is at home."

"Is home here in Havana?" He followed her lead as they crossed the street, moving toward the Jazz Club. She could hear drunken laughter and both Spanish and English floating from the inside of the bar.

"No." With a nudge, she maneuvered them toward a roadway heading to where she'd parked her uncle's car. "He has a house near Punta Macurijes."

"How far?" The American's eyes traveled the length of the road they were walking. Sharp and observant. Those were traits to be admired. At least in her mind.

"This is an island. Most everything is within a day's travel." The roads were not congested, but the ones away from Havana were riddled with potholes and wide cracks. Not that it mattered. Traffic was limited to the essential. The price of gas was too steep for joy rides.

"My men will meet us at seven."

"Where?"

He nodded down the street. "We're going in the general direction."

"You don't trust easily, do you?"

"I don't trust people I don't know. It has kept me alive."

Mariella laughed at the comment but took the time to examine the man in greater detail. He had a trace of grey in his dark brown hair. Deeper lines at the corner of his eyes showed a longer life than his exquisite physique would suggest.

"Trust is built, this I understand. When I stop going in the right direction, let me know?"

Her feet left the ground when the American jerked her into a side alley, and none too gently flattened her against a brick wall. He pulled an automatic from a concealed holster at the back waistband of his jeans. Mariella lifted an eyebrow. Dammit. She hadn't noticed the concealed weapon. "Two men are following us. If they're yours, speak now."

"Not mine. They are my uncle's men." She reached for his t-shirt hem and pulled it up. He slapped her hand away. Mariella reached for his shirt again. "Seriously? I didn't see your gun and I looked. I want to see what holster you use." She pulled at his shirt. The deep "V" cut of his obliques sidetracked her attention for a moment. She twisted and caught a glimpse of the dark plastic clipped to the inside of his jeans before he twisted and pulled down his shirt.

His hand went around her throat and pinned her to the brick. He didn't tighten his grip, but he got her attention. Mariella raised her eyes to meet his heated glare. The man was all business. Devious thoughts raced through her mind. She was going to have so much fun ruffling this one's feathers. He might be on a mission, but she was too, and her mission was to get as much information from him as she could. How to do that was yet to be seen. She relaxed her muscles and sighed. Those ocean-blue eyes dropped to her mouth for a fraction of a second. Obviously, she had the ability to get beneath the man's stone-cold exterior, but would he let himself relax? No, she doubted it.

Even lost in her own musings, she heard the distinct sound of his weapon as the hammer was pulled back and locked. "You said you were alone."

"Not true. I said I don't have *my* men with me.

Those two belong to my uncle. My men are working a shipment tonight." She shrugged, or attempted to. His big hand still circled her throat. "I would advise you not kill me. My uncle is a vindictive son of a bitch. You'd never find the Americans you're looking for—or see the shores of your country again, for that matter."

The man's body tightened at her words and his eyes narrowed. Suspicion and surprise flared across his expression, discernible only because they were mere inches away and staring at each other. She could see the micro-movements of his features.

"Who said we are looking for Americans?" The man's fingers flexed just enough to remind her he was in charge.

A shiver ran through her at the thought of this man's dominant position. He could snap her neck in a second. Against every survival instinct she'd developed working for her uncle, she smiled at the deadly force currently holding her life in his hand. "Are you going to tell me you're not looking for four men?"

The man's hand that held the weapon lifted and pointed toward the opening of the alleyway. His focus stayed on her. Confused, she shot her eyes toward the opening. It was then she heard footsteps. "They will be my uncle's men. Kill them, and he won't be happy."

"Get rid of them." He didn't lower his weapon.

They were far enough in the shadows that the man's gun wouldn't be seen.

"Mateo." Her voice elevated so the approaching men could hear her.

"Mariella, are you all right?" They'd stopped short of the opening of the alley. Smart men.

"I'm fine. I'll meet you back at Rafa's." She waited, still staring at the American. His intense blue eyes never left hers although in the darkened alley the color had deepened, like the sky before a tropical storm, tumultuous and filled with energy.

There was an unintelligible exchange of words before Mateo called back, "Rafa will have our asses if we leave you."

Mariella jerked her head to the side and glared down the alleyway. "Are you questioning my orders?"

Anyone who worked for her uncle had seen evidence of the quiet rage that boiled just under her skin. The question was a warning hiss and the rattle of her tail, all rolled into one. Again, the men exchanged words, too soft for her to hear. "Answer me!" Her shout silenced the men immediately.

"No." Mateo's sullen answer did little to soothe her or the American.

"Leave me now, or you're going to have to deal with me, not Rafa."

"Neither Rafa or Adalberto would want us—"

"I will end you before you have to worry about Rafa or Adalberto. Question my authority again, and it will be the last time, Mateo." She'd had enough of this shit. Her hands flew up to push the American away and caught him by surprise. His arm and hand tensed. For all her effort she ended up with a gun lodged against her forehead. She growled. In English, she spat, "If you were going to kill me, you would have by now." She clenched her fists and shouted, "Mateo throw the keys to my car into the alley. You and Iker take the bus home."

"The bus?" Mateo's voice grew petulant.

"Yes, take the fucking bus unless you want to walk back. Idiot!" she snapped. A few seconds later, the sound of a ring of keys landing in the alley reached her. She could hear her uncle's men arguing as they walked away.

She leaned back against the wall and glared at the American. "You're welcome."

"For what?" The sounds of Mateo and Iker grumbling as they left was enough incentive for the man to lower the hammer on the automatic and release his grip on her. The man didn't relax one muscle.

"For what? Saving you the ammunition, and the inevitable run we'd have to make if you shot that damn cannon. You do realize that gunfire isn't necessarily an everyday occurrence around here, right?" Mariella walked up the alley. She bent over searching in the inky darkness for the small silver ring of keys.

"I have plenty of ammunition."

"Good. When you get the hell out of my country,

81

you can leave it for me. Surprisingly weapons and ammo aren't that difficult to get, but I'll take any freebie available." A shadowed pile to her right caught her attention. She stopped and kicked the ground. Nope, that was a piece of garbage. She pulled her hair to the side and held it, keeping it out of her eyes.

"I need to speak to Rafa."

Mariella stood and turned around in frustration. She couldn't see him clearly, but she didn't need to see him to tell him off. "You are a broken record. I told you that I would take you to him. So it doesn't make us targets, we will leave when the tourists are awake and swarming." She turned back around and kept working the dark alleyway looking for the keys to Rafa's car.

"I don't think you understand the urgency of the situation."

Mariella could hear the frustration in his voice. She continued looking for her keys. Men, especially Cuban men, were always telling her she had no place in the hierarchy of Rafa's business. She'd been told she should stay home and make babies. It seemed the fucking American was cut from the same cloth. The venom of her answer was built from a lifetime of anger at being dismissed as simply a woman. "I understand the urgency of *not* being caught by the police," she sneered. "No, you're right. I probably don't. You know us, *stupid* women. We never understand the dire consequences of a man's world."

A hand grabbed her arm and pulled her away from her search. Mariella caught the full force of the man's angry stare.

She jerked her arm away with a vicious yank. "Help me find the damn keys."

CREED STARED down at a woman of either incomprehensible bravery or one with a death wish. Regardless, he'd be damned if he was going to lose control of this meeting, again. "Mariella."

The woman blinked up at him as if her name had cut through the rage that gripped her. She straightened and asked, "What's your name?"

Nope. Not going there. Names made things personal. That's why he'd used her name. It was an advantage. He caught her name from the assholes that followed them but giving her his wasn't going to happen. He could see the sky turning a lighter hue. He glanced at the watch he wore. They had little time before the city woke and he could meet his men. "That isn't important. What *is* important is that we reach Rafa as soon as possible."

"Then help me find the damn car keys."

She pulled at her arm, and Creed loosened his grip to allow her to move. He stood still and started scanning the alley for the keys. He started his visual assessment at the mouth of the alley doing a quick grid search of the area. A glint of metal caught his eyes about five feet in front of where she was currently looking. He strode forward and picked up the keys, jingling them as he straightened. Her head popped up. Creed tossed the keys to her, and she caught them.

"Thanks. We'll go to my car. It is three blocks from the cruise ship terminal. The Americans will start leaving the ships early. Once the tours start, we drive out of the city."

Creed fell into step beside her. He grabbed her arm, stopping her before they exited the alley. She sighed and rolled her eyes. "They're gone."

"Forgive me if I don't trust someone who has already been proven untrustworthy." Creed felt her tense as he peeked around the corner of the lime-stone building. The street appeared empty.

"I am not untrustworthy."

Creed glanced down at her quickly before he glanced around the corner again. "Right. You were so forthcoming about the men trailing us." There was no movement. He tugged her along with him.

"I'm tired of you yanking on me." She tried to rip her arm from his grip.

Creed stopped and made a point to glare at the woman. He'd memorized those huge, chocolate colored, doe-eyes, long-as-fuck lashes, and thick, pouty lips. Despite what Thane thought, he wasn't a eunuch. No, this time he glared down for effect. He extended his arm, pushed her away from him and straightened his fingers to drop her arm with the same arrogance as a millennial dropping a fucking mic.

Spinning on his heel, he headed in the general direction of the National Cathedral, lengthening his stride. It was time to move this meeting to his wheel-house. Her uncle's reputation as a greedy bastard gave him the leverage he needed. If Rafa was as smart as everyone seemed to think he was, the woman would come scurrying after him. He heard a low growl of frustration and a string of muttered words right before a series of hurried steps.

"You're an asshole, you know that, right?"

"I suppose you wouldn't be pissed if you were met by someone you weren't expecting, followed into an alley and lied to by a contact you were told was trust-worthy?" Creed kept his stride long and regular as he spoke.

"No, I'd have been pissed, but I am trustworthy, and I wouldn't have been an asshole to you." She hustled to keep up with him, but he stopped short. She went on several steps before she realized it and spun around to face him. She snarled, "What now?"

Creed took in the woman in front of him. Too damn bad she was irritating as fuck, because, in his opinion, the woman was arresting, feisty and sexy as hell. She snapped her fingers in front of his face. "Did you go on some sort of mental trip there, mi amigo? Why are you stopping? It's almost time for the cruise ships to start letting the people off."

He snapped, "Give me one reason to trust you. Just one. Otherwise, I'm out of here, and your uncle is out one hell of a payment." He'd call this mission in a heartbeat, and he was a nanosecond away from doing just that. Branson would have to find some other way to get them some intelligence. Hell, with the team he had now, they could regroup and think of something.

The woman stood there gaping at him like he was insane. Creed shook his head and started walking, this time in the opposite direction of the cathedral. He was calling it. When he didn't show, his men would rally at the meeting point. After securing two bags to the fence line at Hemingway Marina, they'd be picked up tonight and in contact with Branson by midnight.

"Wait."

Creed kept walking.

"Hey, I said wait." The woman ran up beside him. "An asshole *and* deaf." She got in front of him and braced her hands against his biceps. "We know where one of the Americans is located."

"I know where several thousand are located." He glanced over his shoulder at two cruise ships towering over the buildings behind them. Creed sidestepped her and kept walking. "I don't have time for games."

"It isn't a game. I've seen him. He was injured," Mariella snapped back.

"Nice try." Creed couldn't take her words at face value, that much he'd ascertained.

"I know where he is located right now."

That stopped him.

"Where? And don't give me any vague shit, I want an exact location." His gut said the woman was telling the truth, or at least a version of it.

"He is with Rafa. In our safe room. He's in a bad way, and he isn't conscious, or he wasn't when I saw him."

"Then you need to take me to Rafa." Creed spun on his heel and headed back towards the National Cathedral. This little tit for tat had cost time. He glanced at his watch and lengthened his stride.

"That's what I was trying to do!" Her voice lowered, and she complained to herself, "Are all Americans crazy? Why couldn't he be Canadian? Those people are nice. They have manners." She caught up to him and hustled to stay with him as he walked. "My car is parked one block that way with the rest of the vehicles staged for the tourists. When we get your men, we will all go to the car and drive out like the others that have been hired for the day."

The cobblestone under his feet was damp from the morning dew or a recent shower. The street blocked the morning sun, preventing it from burning the wet overlay off the ancient cobblestone. He glanced at his watch. They were back on schedule.

An impressive cathedral rose on his left. He slowed, taking in the architecture. He ran his finger along the building wall. The white bricks looked to be sandstone or limestone, but from glancing at the fossils in the brick, Creed assumed the blocks were made of coral. The doors facing Calle Empedrado, the street they were walking on, were sealed shut. He veered to the left and walked on the small sidewalk. The building to the right had a distinct tangerine color going on. Typical for the tropics, but Creed liked the ancient feel of the stone and mortar cathedral formed into a Baroque bastion of history. They entered the plaza that already had tourists walking along the cobblestone court. The main doors to the cathedral were set back from the stone framed opening. An ornate wrought iron fence enclosed the small elevated portico and a matching gate stood sentry before the massive opening to the church. With a final glance at his watch and another quick three-sixty to ensure no one was following them, Creed nodded toward the entrance of the cathedral.

The four stone steps leading to that opening were slick with morning dew. He grabbed Mariella when her foot slipped. Her arm jerked out of his hand. "You are meeting your men here? At the Havana Cathedral?" She looked up at the bell tower on the left and then swung her gaze to the one on the right.

"Yes. I thought it was called the National Cathedral?" At least it had been in most of the documentation he'd studied.

She shook her head. "The party calls it the National Cathedral. We call it the Havana Cathedral." She waved him forward. "I'll wait here for you."

"I don't think so. You're coming with me." Creed moved to the side so a party of tourists could enter the church.

"Yeah, about that. You're standing awful close." She gulped and stepped away. "If I go in there, a lightning bolt will strike me, and you'd be collateral damage."

"What?"

"My aunt, she taught me about God. Religion here isn't condoned, but my aunt she knows. She told me all about God and his rules, his Son. He is all-powerful. Vengeance is mine." She all but whispered the last words.

He stifled the laugh that bubbled up at that image. "I have never heard of God striking someone down for entering a church." He gently placed his hand on her waist and extended his hand not wanting her to think he was manhandling her again.

"Yeah, well, that's because I've never set foot in one of them. Remember, I gave you fair warning."

She ducked her head when she entered the cool

interior. He followed her in, standing to the side to allow his eyes to adjust from the morning sun to the shaded hues inside the cathedral. Crystal chandeliers dropped down from massively arched ceilings at least forty-feet high. Dark mahogany pews stood in straight lines over white and black marble floors. Along the central nave were side isles. Statues lined those walls and roped access points drove everyone to a table where rosaries were being sold.

Creed drew an easy breath when he saw McGowen and Whitehead. McGowen acknowledged his presence with a discreet flash of three fingers. Creed crossed his arms over his chest and left one finger extended giving the countersign. McGowen tapped Whitehead, drawing his attention from the papal statue he studied.

Mariella shifted from foot to foot beside him. Her eyes flitted from the front to the back of the sanctuary. The anxiousness that rolled off her was palpable.

Creed moved closer. "What is it?"

Wild brown eyes turned to him. She hissed, "I told you! Nothing good can come from me being here. I've never been inside a church." She glanced around and shrunk into herself even more.

It took a few seconds for him to realize she wasn't joking. "And yet you believe in a God so powerful he can smite you from the face of the earth."

She nodded, her eyes still casting around the interior of the church. "With all my heart." Her voice cracked with emotion, which was... unusual.

While he waited for his men to make their way to the door, he tried to decipher the woman next to him. Reading people and their motivations was part of his job, and he was damn good at all aspects. Hell, during some missions, his gut was his best asset. Right now, he didn't have a good grasp on the woman sent to be their contact. Was she setting them up? No, he didn't think so, but he wasn't going to trust her farther than he could see her. Figuring out Mariella shouldn't be difficult, but he couldn't read her... yet. Was she sent to seduce him or help him? It wouldn't be the first time the Samson and Delilah ploy had been played against him or one of his men. Creed gave a mental shrug. The woman could very well be playing with him. He glanced down. She'd inched behind him, cowering.

One thing he did understand, she was deeply spiritual, but not religious. At least, she hadn't been brought up in the Church. All in all, she was a puzzle, but if he had to make a call, he'd bet she was playing games with the sexual innuendo she flipped on and off like a flashlight. Yeah, he'd wager his entire bankroll the woman had been fucking with him. Especially when you added in the way she'd silenced Rafa's men and her comments about being "just" a woman? She'd seen his physical reaction to her and was using it. Smart, sexy and bossy. Just what he fucking needed. Not.

Creed glanced at his men. Whitehead's eyes trailed over the walls and exhibits of artwork. McGowen's scanned the interior of the church, too, but for an entirely different reason. Couples sat in the pews in quiet reflection. The whispered words of others strolling through the old church provided a white noise that mixed with the outside sounds filtering through the massive doorway. McGowen directed Whitehead out the door when the man would have come over to Creed. Should anyone be watching, they needed to keep a casual distance from each other. Creed waited another thirty seconds before he shifted to leave. Mariella was on his six in a heartbeat. The woman did not like being in the church and took zero prompting to exit the structure quickly.

She ran her hands over the exposed flesh of her arms and glanced back at the stone façade of the cathedral. Creed glanced at his men and then lowered his head and whispered, "No lightning strikes."

The woman wrinkled her nose at the building before she glanced up. "We aren't very far away. I wouldn't bring a curse upon yourself if I were you." She nodded toward the plaza in front of the church now crowded with American tourists. "Your men?"

"Will follow us." Just in case his gut was wrong,

Creed wasn't going to out them. He had been out of the game for a year, and he might be rusty. He'd hedge his bets for a while yet.

"You realize I'm here to help you, right? Me getting caught assisting you would mean the police would have justification for taking me. I'm not going to risk that." She started down Calle Empedrado, going back the way they'd come.

Creed fell into step with her, knowing his men would follow at a discreet distance. "Your uncle wouldn't allow that."

"Ha. A lot you know." Mariella shook her head. "Leverage is a tool you wield carefully in Cuba. It is a balancing act on a high wire. Push too much one way, and you fall. Don't push enough and you can't maintain your position, and you fall. I know not to expose myself. I would never ask my uncle to upset the balance to rescue me. It is not the way things work here."

Creed held his tongue. She was right, he didn't know the way things worked in Cuba, although he couldn't imagine a scenario where her uncle wouldn't at least try to arrange his niece's release should she be detained. That was him inflicting his belief system on this culture, one of the many things he'd learned not to do during the years he'd led missions all over the globe.

They stopped at the street corner. A 1957 Chevy passed them. It was hot pink and had a fake raccoon tail waving from the antenna. From what he could see, the car was in pristine condition. They waited for the roadway to clear before they darted across the street. The crowd of tourists from the cruise ship grew as they moved. The throng of people kept them weaving. Knowing McGowen would keep up, he resisted the urge to look back for McGowen and Whitehead.

They crossed the street, and that's when the teenage gearhead inside of Creed smiled and rubbed his hands together. Classic cars lined a huge parking area. Mariella waved her arm in the direction of the vehicles. "Not a car newer than 1959. That is when the revolution happened. When Castro took over, he allowed citizens to keep what they owned. Cars and houses or apartments are part of the family, only treated better. The cars, they don't have doctors. If we have accidents in Cuba, which is extremely rare, we ask how the car is before we ask about the passengers or the person who was driving. A car is part of the family here. It is passed down from generation to generation. We make parts if they fail or wear out."

She stepped off the sidewalk and headed down the long row of vehicles. Every conceivable configuration of classic car was front and center. Convertibles, hard tops, muscle cars, roadsters and even a couple of European beauties. Mariella stopped in front of a purple and white 1957 Chevy Bel Air

SEAL FOREVER

Custom convertible. She opened the trunk using the key he'd retrieved from the alley. He watched as she inserted a funnel into the gas tank.

"Do you need help?" He stopped admiring the vehicles and moved to the trunk.

"You can pour." She handed him a glass gallon jug.

Creed arched an eyebrow at her in question.

"Fuel is very hard to acquire. When it is available, we use containers to get what we can and store it. Pour that into the funnel. Slowly, so you don't spill." She motioned to the piece of plastic stuck into the gas tank of the car.

Creed twisted off the top and set it on the ground, not willing to damage the old, well cared for paint job on the car with the residue of gasoline that might be on the lid. A slight tip to the jar started the trickle of gasoline. Through his peripheral vision, he saw McGowen. He glanced up at the man and nodded to the car. He and Whitehead placed their packs and a third that belong to Creed onto the back seat. He drained the container he was pouring and carefully replaced the lid. Mariella handed him another one, and he repeated the process. He split his attention between pouring the gas, Mariella, and his men.

She waited for him to hand her the container, set it in a grid compartment made specifically for the jars, and shut the trunk. She pushed past Creed and headed for the driver's side door and slid into the driver's seat of the old car. "What are you waiting for?" She motioned to the passenger side door.

Whitehead's eyebrows reached towards the heavens, but McGowen chuckled and opened the passenger door, flipped the lever to lean the front seat forward and gestured for Whitehead to get in. The man gave Creed a glance but moved into the vehicle, taking the seat behind Mariella. McGowen settled in the back behind the passenger seat after he piled all three backpacks in the center of the wide bench seat.

Creed got into the car and turned to Mariella. "Take me to your leader."

McGowen's laughter split the air behind him. She rolled her big brown eyes so damn hard he swore he could hear the groan the action might have caused in her brain. The hot Cuban sun beat down on them, even at the early morning hour. Mariella put the car into gear and eased off the clutch, rolling out into the tourist-lined parking area.

# CHAPTER 7

"You did what?"

Mariella cringed at the sharp edge of her uncle's low, angry words. She'd driven to her uncle's complex in record time and had shown the men to their assigned quarters. The American leader was pissed when she claimed her uncle was unavailable until dinner and suggested they rest until then. God knew she wanted to sleep for a couple hours. The American in charge hadn't believed her, but there was nothing he could do but wait. Rafa's compound was vast and well-guarded, and the Americans were under constant observation, a point the men noticed as soon as they entered the fortified walls. The Americans were outnumbered and outgunned. Keeping them secluded while she talked to her uncle was her only goal at the moment.

"I had to tell him the man was here. He was leaving, and it was the only way I could get him to stay. Do you want this payout or don't you?" She stood her ground. She had one card to play, and she'd thrown it on the table. Rafa loved his money.

"What have you learned from him?" Her uncle plopped down in his chair and reached for his ever-present cigarettes.

"He plays his cards close to his chest. He's smart, and he doesn't trust me. This one is ...more? It is hard to describe." He was scary as fuck and yet so enticing at the same time. Did her fascination with the man stem from that shiver of apprehension and trepidation she felt whenever they were together, or was it his base, physical attraction? Likely a healthy portion of each if she was honest with herself.

Her uncle drilled her with a cold, hard stare, then he cocked his head and smirked. "More?"

She nodded and shrugged. "He reminds me of the man who came here once. The one in charge of the camps." That man had unnerved her the same way the American had. They both had harnessed power, but while the man who visited her uncle radiated evil, the American? She didn't feel evil, just... resolute... or maybe intent?

"What does your instinct tell you about them?" Her uncle brought a cigarette to his lips and lit it while staring at her.

"Whatever they are after is bigger than the man downstairs. He is important, but... When I told him we had one of the men, there was no indication of relief. In that aspect, he is impossible to read."

Rafa took a long draw off his cigarette and inhaled, holding his breath as he looked at her. He blew out a lungful of smoke and pointed at her. "Then tell me in what aspect is he easy to read?"

Mariella narrowed her eyes and glared at her uncle. The man was extraordinary at drilling down to the point of the matter. A small smile tugged at the corner of her mouth. Just enough to let her uncle know she was confident in her next statement. "He wants me. I don't think he will act on it. He is very disciplined."

Her uncle kicked his boots up on his desk and motioned to the chair beside his desk. "Describe him and his team."

Mariella gratefully plopped down onto the soft cushion and leaned back into the warm leather. "Smart, careful and very observant. He knew Mateo was following us and was ready to kill if he wasn't one of ours. He speaks Spanish very well, no pauses or misspoken words, although he sounds highly educated... polished. His way of speaking will raise eyebrows in any city outside of Havana. His men... one is just like the leader. Their eyes never stop scanning. Their minds are looking for danger, assessing all the time. The third, I don't know what to think of him. He watches, but not like they do. He seems... in awe of what he sees, maybe? I would guess he does not have the same background as the other two, which makes me question why he is with them. I do not think he is a soldier."

Her uncle stared at her for several moments before he slowly nodded his head. "Then the missing people aren't what they are here for. It is something else." He stubbed out the smoldering butt of his cigarette and picked up another one. "We will use the man we have as a bridge. Offer him up and see what the American says. Flies to honey."

Her uncle had often tempted government officials with items they could not get in order to obtain information or access to things he needed. Using the tactic on the American was a wise decision. "Has the man regained consciousness?"

Her uncle nodded. "Amelia said he is awake, but he says nothing. I don't know if he can talk or if he is damaged in the head. Our doctor will be here tomorrow. He couldn't leave before then without raising suspicions."

"What do you think the American wants?" Mariella leaned her head back and closed her grit-filled eyes. She needed a nap before she had to deal with the Americans again.

"I don't know. When did you tell them I would see them?"

"For dinner."

"Go, rest until then. We will have our answers tonight."

"What about Adalberto?"

"I've sent him to deal with an issue."

Mariella opened her eyes and found her uncle. "What kind of issue?"

"We had someone from within our organization stealing from us."

"Who brought them into the organization?"

"He did."

Mariella had seen the obscene way Adalberto had dealt with people who'd crossed Rafa. Having this form of disrespect from someone he'd brought into the organization was a huge disgrace. She immediately said a prayer for their soul. Rafa paid well to keep his people loyal. Stealing from him meant stealing from everyone who depended on Rafa. That list of people was extensive. She sighed, "He will make an example of the man."

"The woman." Her uncle's eyes met hers.

She knew her uncle could not condone the theft, but Adalberto... "Rafa?"

"I sent two of my men with him." Rafa lit the cigarette in his hand and drew a deep pull from the tobacco. "Go to bed."

Mariella held his stare. She knew better than to question him in these matters, but this wasn't an everyday occurrence. The people who worked for Rafa were loyal to a fault. "Are you sure? Is there proof?"

"Adalberto said there was proof."

"Have you seen it?"

Her uncle uncrossed his legs and dropped them to the floor. "I have not, which is why I sent two of my men. Go. To. Bed, Mariella." He pointed to the door and dropped his ash into the huge ashtray. "I want you back here with the Americans at seven. I'll have the man downstairs ready."

"All three of the Americans?" She stood and rolled her shoulders; the long hours were settling into her muscles.

"Yes. I want to see if my assessment and yours match." Her uncle turned toward his computer dismissing her.

An inward groan protested the constant tests her uncle put before her. "I'm right."

"We shall see. Now go." Her uncle again dismissed her.

"We will revisit the woman. I need to know what happens."

Her uncle turned and regarded her with narrowed eyes. "You need to know only what I tell you."

Maybe it was because she was so damn tired, but she challenged her uncle again, "So I'm no more than one of your paid employees?"

He spun his chair toward her. "You are my niece, and I love you. What I don't tell you protects you."

"What you don't tell me? How much don't you tell me, Rafa?"

"Far more than you could imagine, my dear." He spun and started hen pecking on the old keyboard in front of his computer, ignoring her presence and terminating the conversation. Mariella knew she wouldn't get any more from her uncle, at least not now. She turned and headed to her private quarters at the far side of the compound.

$\mathcal{C}$reed inspected every inch of his room. There were no listening devices or cameras that he could see. He continued his inspection of the common room that connected his men's rooms with his. McGowen stepped out of his room and shook his head, indicating he hadn't found any monitoring devices either. Creed nodded towards Whitehead's room. McGowen nodded and lightly rapped on the exterior door before he stepped in.

A systematic search of the room found nothing. McGowen exited Whitehead's room and shook his head. Creed motioned to the far back corner of the room.

"Nothing."

"Did you check the outlets?" McGowen pointed toward the one plug in the room.

Creed nodded. One screw held the faceplate in

place. He'd popped the sucker off in record time. There was nothing that he could see, and he was up to speed on the latest monitoring devices.

"Why are we being delayed?" McGowen leaned against the wall, his whisper only a shade above the sound of an exhale.

Creed shook his head. He was antsy as hell. They needed to get to Rafa and start the man's network in motion. Mariella meeting them and bringing them here to meet with Rafa tonight had delayed his mission by over twelve hours. How much of a dirty bomb could be constructed in twelve hours?

He motioned towards Whitehead's room. "He's asleep?"

"Crashed immediately."

"You go. I'll wake you in three hours." Creed watched as McGowen nodded and headed back to his room. They still had their weapons, nobody had asked for them and he sure as fuck wasn't going to offer them up. The entire meeting and trip here were total deviations from the norm, but he was used to adapting and overcoming the obstacles placed in his path. Right now, his team needed rest. McGowen first.

Creed slid a rattan chair into the corner that allowed him to watch McGowen and Whitehead's bedrooms plus the door to the small apartment. He would use the next three hours to organize a plan for tonight's meet with Rafa.

First, he'd learned that Rafa had one of the CIA team members here in the compound. He needed to talk with the man and gather any intelligence he could on the op that failed so miserably for that team. The CIA hadn't used Rafa, so the man could reasonably be eliminated from suspicion of leaking the information that the team was in country. Could he imagine circumstances where Rafa could have manipulated something? Sure, but he had no reason, at this point, to give that scenario any weight.

Foregoing any information from the agent, the path ahead was straight, if and when they actually received an audience with the great and all seeing Rafa. Creed snorted at the image of a little fat man behind an emerald curtain. No, Rafa's organization was run by a hard as steel man. Hell, he had to be strong to deal with that niece of his. The woman was a hot mess. Strong, volatile, resilient, and fuck him standing if the woman wasn't sexy as fuck.

Creed rubbed his chin, absently scratching the five o'clock shadow that was about twelve hours old. He kicked his foot out, extending his rebuilt knee and relaxing his leg. That woman invaded every sense he used. Her physical beauty had smacked him with the force of a left hook when he'd first passed by her perched on the seawall early this morning. All he saw that time around was her long-ass legs, the fullness of her breast in the neckline of the tank top and that mass of dark brown hair that fell over her shoulder. He detected a hint of high cheekbones before he forced himself to concentrate on the shoelaces of others he passed. Not one other damn pair had orange and green laces, except hers. Creed walked the seawall again just to make damn sure. When he approached her, it was her eyes that captivated him. They were huge, dark chocolate brown, and displayed every emotion that raced through her mind.

He'd been enthralled... until she opened her mouth. He still hadn't decided if the woman was ADHD, full of senseless bravado, or just naturally prone to saying shit to see what response she could draw from others. Perhaps it was a combination of all three? Who the fuck knew? Certainly not him. Thankfully, she had completed her mission, and he'd meet Rafa soon. He glanced at his watch, noting how much time had passed. McGowen still had an hour or so to sleep.

The door to Whitehead's room opened, and the man stumbled out. His hair stood straight up on one side, and the crease of where he'd slept against the pillow marred his face. He rubbed his eyes as he glanced at Creed. "Sorry. I was exhausted."

Creed motioned to the chair next to him, and Whitehead plopped down. His jaw jacked open in a yawn.

"You still have four hours before we need to leave. You can sleep longer." Creed kept his voice low.

Whitehead nodded and dropped his head back on the couch. "I'll go back in a minute. Just wanted to make sure I was pulling my weight."

"You'll do the heavy lifting when we start searching."

The man rubbed his face with both hands and yawned again. "Yeah, readies are not nice toys to be playing around with. Someone should tell them that." He nodded towards the exterior door to their small apartment.

"Readies?"

"Radioactive Dispersal Devices. Someone tagged them as readies, ready to go." The man shrugged, yawned again and hung his head. "It fit at the time, and it stuck. Whoever is doing this isn't thinking the event through. The thing about a dirty bomb is there isn't really a nuclear impact. Yes, there is radioactive fallout over a very small area, and yes it can render the area uninhabitable until responders manage to decontaminate it, but as far as deaths associated with the radioactive material? Not so much. There is a saying in my career field that dirty bombs aren't so much weapons of mass destruction as they are epic dislocation devices."

Creed leaned forward and locked onto every word coming out of Whitehead's mouth. "So, you're saying the intent of a dirty bomb is to dislocate people?"

Whitehead shook his head. "No, I'm pretty damn

sure the intent is to terrorize the world, but if you look at all the aspects of a conventional explosion being used to disperse the radioactive material, the primary impact of the radiological element besides terror would be dislocation. City blocks being evacuated to prohibit the spread of the contaminants."

"How much clean up would it take?" Creed had never given much thought to the after-effects of the bomb. His focus had been on preventing the making and explosion of the damn thing.

"Well, that would depend on the quantity and type of radioactive material and whether it was a fine powder or a different medium encased in the bomb. Deaths would result initially from shrapnel, concussion of the explosive, and perhaps the panic and confusion caused by the detonation. The long-term effects of any radioactive poisoning event would need to be scrutinized, but speaking from a strictly scholastic standpoint, the use of the radioactive additive in a conventional bomb causes a mass dislocation of people from the area for years, if not decades, depending on the country's ability to provide resources. Think Chernobyl, but on a much smaller scale." Whitehead stared at him and cocked his head. "Why?"

"It just occurred to me that we were chasing the tail of the dog and not necessarily looking at why the animal is wagging it."

"Huh?" Whitehead shook his head quickly and blinked. "I didn't understand that."

"Why are all of these bombs cropping up now, and should the positioning of the bombs be more relevant than where they are being manufactured?" Fuck... he wished like hell he could get on the phone to Branson, but the phones they'd brought would be used for extreme emergencies only. Until then, he'd gather as much information as he could.

"Putting them out of business is the only way of stopping the placement, right?" Whitehead stood and walked over to the small kitchenette in the corner of the room. There was a hot plate and dishes, but only a few bottles of water on the shelf that Creed assumed was the pantry. Whitehead grabbed two bottles and tossed one to him.

Creed caught it and inspected the bottle before he opened it and downed half. "Correct, but what if the placement of the bombs is about more than a terrorist attack? What if someone is trying to dislocate people away from a specific target?"

"Like what?"

Creed had at least twenty scenarios assault him at once. "A financial district, a political target, a transportation hub, a national landmark or even a bank..."

Whitehead sat down and stared at the bottle in his hand for a moment. "Not all of the placements of the dirty bombs so far have been in those areas, right? So that can't be the reason."

"Unless the placements so far have been to conceal the real purpose?" Creed's gut told him he was onto something. There was no rhyme or reason for the placements so far, and the fact that the bombs had been found *before* they were detonated was too fucking neat. No, there was something other than your garden variety terrorism happening here, he just couldn't put his finger on the pulse point. He needed to talk to Branson, but Whitehead was right. Stopping the manufacture of the bombs would, at a minimum, slow down an attempt to actually activate the devices.

He'd table those thoughts until he could talk to Branson and that conversation could be weeks from now, so he needed to focus on the task at hand. "Speaking strictly from your expertise, what is the danger to the team during the hunting phase of this project?"

"Hunting? Well, I guess we are hunting for a site, aren't we?" Whitehead asked.

"Exactly. When I speak to Rafa tonight, I need to know exactly what we are looking for so he can dispatch his people."

"Smart money would be on a remote location, but one with easy access for vehicles and maybe to a sea or airport. They don't want witnesses, so vacant buildings."

"That's a needle in a very large haystack. You've seen the number of vacant buildings in Havana." Fear that they'd never locate the site ghosted along his consciousness.

"But that's just it. They wouldn't want this in a populated area. If there were an accident and people started to get sick, the government of Cuba and maybe other nations would investigate. So, a remote, vacant building with decent access that has power. There is no way they'd risk building this type of contained system without an adequate power supply. The radioactive material in the bombs already found had been vacuum sealed, and the soldering was elaborate. To do that, they need power." Whitehead shrugged and scrubbed at his face. "A generator would work, so if his people see something like that, it would be of interest to us, but yeah, it could be a huge undertaking and hell, who knows, we could miss them altogether. We don't know how many of these devices they are making or how much radiological material they have access to. So many damn unknowns."

"Let me worry about that." Creed needed to talk to the CIA agent that Rafa had stashed somewhere in this compound. The man could fill in a shit-ton of blank spaces. Hopefully. "Back to the dangers to the team while hunting these assholes. What is our primary concern?"

Whitehead rolled his head toward Creed and arched an eyebrow. "You mean besides bullets and spontaneous death via pissed off terrorists?"

Creed laughed. Whitehead had a wicked sense of humor. "McGowen and I will do our best to ensure spontaneous death by terrorists is eradicated from your concerns."

"Yeah, well minus those threats, our primary concern would be accidental exposure. I have a bag full of small clip-on badges we can wear should the situation dictate it. Branson had them produced for me. They look like Cuban flags. If the white stripes turn black, we've been exposed. I have a field kit that I can use to mitigate any contaminants that touch our skin. What we need to be is extremely cautious not to ingest or breathe in any of the material. That type of exposure will kill."

Creed spun his half-empty bottle in his hand. "You will be in charge of the approach should we locate any sites."

"Deal, as long as you two make sure there are no bad guys who are going to snipe my ass."

Creed laughed again. "Deal."

McGowen's door opened, and he lifted a hand in greeting before he wandered over to the supply of water and grabbed a bottle. He drank the entire thing in one go. When he finished, he moved his chin indicating Creed. "You need some shut-eye, skipper."

"Roger that." Creed stood and stretched. All the concerns wrapped around the mission would have to wait. He'd be worthless unless he could think straight and that required sleep.

The bedroom held a full-size bed with well-worn linens. The small six-foot by ten-foot room had been scrubbed recently. No dust or spiderwebs in the corners. Just like the rest of the apartment they'd been given, it was sparse but clean. There was one small pillow encased in a patched blue linen case. He'd slept on far worse. With a flick of his wrist, he unclipped the concealed holster at his back and removed the hard plastic from his belt. He removed the weapon from the holster, held it in his hand until he positioned himself diagonally across the bed so his feet didn't hang too far off the corner. He tucked the small pillow under his head, laid his hand with his automatic on his stomach, placed his trigger finger on the upper receiver of the weapon, so he didn't shoot himself while sleeping, and closed his eyes. His mind drifted over an image of Mariella. Those big brown eyes and smiling lips chased him into imme-diate slumber.

# CHAPTER 9

*C*reed and his men followed the guard sent to escort them to the main house to meet with Rafa. His stomach growled at the aroma of food as they entered the modest building. It was comfortable, not elegant. The furniture was old but well maintained. There wasn't an ostentatious item to be found in the comfortable living area. Everything had a function. Not quite utilitarian, but it was the home of someone who didn't need to present airs. Rafa scored a point in his books there. The man lived the way his people lived, at least as far as Creed could determine. Of course, this portion of the house could be a façade, something the man presented to those who visited.

"Rafa will be here shortly." The man who escorted them backed out of the room and shut the French doors. He turned his back and stood in front of the doors, in full view of the men he'd deposited into his employer's home. He cradled his rifle across his chest and pointed his attention outward. Creed glanced at McGowen who raised his eyebrows. He'd noticed it too. Who was the guard keeping out of the meeting?

"Gentlemen." Creed's head snapped toward her voice. Mariella stepped into the room from a hallway. She was dressed in camo pants, shitkickers, and a white tank-top. He immediately noticed a large knife protruding from a sheath at the top of her boots and a holstered automatic weapon strapped to her thigh in a quick-release rig. The natural way in which she wore the weaponry implied it wasn't for show. This woman was used to carrying the armament, and that meant she was used to danger. She moved toward a small cart in the corner of the room. She took five glasses from the bottom shelf and poured a couple fingers of amber liquid into one. "Rafa will be here in a moment."

She picked up the glass and downed the contents, immediately pouring another. She nodded to the cart. "If you want it."

Whitehead glanced at Creed as if asking permission. He gave the man a subtle shake of his head. They needed to stay sharp. Mariella groaned and tossed back the second drink. "It's good quality, and one drink won't hurt."

"I agree with my niece. I never conduct business

without sharing a drink, or at least offering one." Creed swung his attention to the man who entered the room from a door at the far corner. Strong. That was the overwhelming vibe coming from the man in front of him. A power player and those sharp brown eyes missed nothing as he took inventory of Creed and his men. He zeroed in on Creed and moved forward extending his hand. "My name is Raphael Diaz."

"Creed." The handshake was brief and powerful.

"Just Creed?" The man strode to the liquor cart and poured himself a drink, turning and lifting the glass in question.

"Yes, just Creed and thank you, we're good." He spoke for his men who'd taken up position behind him. He could feel McGowen working the room, looking, waiting and watching. Whitehead was to his left. The man was watching the interactions as if he'd stumbled upon something interesting but didn't know quite what to do with the situation.

"Your loss." The man moved to one of the couches and motioned for Creed to take a seat. "You have a business arrangement for me?"

Creed glanced at McGowen who nodded a fraction of an inch and casually found his way to the corner where he could observe the entire room and all entrances. Creed motioned Whitehead to a chair close to McGowen. The man wasted no time in planting his ass in the creaky rattan chair.

Creed settled in and watched as Mariella moved behind her uncle. Well, the chessboard was set, and it was time to move his first piece. "We need information, and transportation."

"Of course you do. What information, specifically?" Rafa took a sip of his drink, but his eyes never left Creed.

"May we speak openly here?" Creed cast his eyes around the room, landing back on Rafa.

"I have men posted outside. They cannot hear, and there will be no interruptions. The room itself was swept for listening devices just before you entered. Anything you say in this room stays in this room. I do not include blackmail in my business endeavors."

"We are looking for a location. A remote building that is vacant but has recently had activity, and the building would have power, either from the island's infrastructure or a generator." In his peripheral vision, Creed saw Whitehead nodding in agreement.

Rafa set down his drink and leaned forward, propping his elbows on his thighs. "This is information I can obtain, but my question is *why* am I looking for this building?"

"To stop the construction of dirty bombs." The man's eyes had narrowed ever so slightly when he dropped that explosive bit of information.

"How do you know that these *things* are being built in my country?" Rafa's eyes flicked to his niece.

Creed glanced her direction. The shock in her expression spoke volumes. She didn't know, and if his gut was right, neither did Rafa. The man was pissed, that was obvious by the tone of his voice.

"A joint task force has tracked the latest in a string of dirty bombs being placed around the globe to Cuba."

Rafa reached for a small box on the table and removed the lid. He pulled a cigarette out of the box and brought it to his lips before he replaced the lid. "You want to find where they are being made?"

"Yes." Creed acknowledged.

"You said transportation. What do you have planned?" The man leaned back in the cushions and dug a silver lighter out of his pocket. He flicked the cap open and torched the cigarette all while staring directly at Creed.

"Once we've located the facility used to build the bombs, my men will secure the radioactive materials, and then we will leave."

"I'm assuming by securing the material you also will be..." Rafa leaned forward. He pinched his lips together, and his jaw muscle clenched. "You will also be killing some of my countrymen?"

Creed wasn't one to blow smoke up someone's ass. "We will get that material, and we will stop the production. It is not our intent to kill anyone, but our intent is out the window should we need to act to secure the devices."

Rafa blew out a lungful of smoke and stared at Creed before he shook his head. "We must talk to the man Mariella told you I found. He is an American, but he doesn't speak to us. Perhaps, he will talk to you. If he has knowledge of this, it will expedite the places where we must look."

Creed nodded. That made sense. "I'd like to speak with him—alone."

"But of course. He is not a hostage, and neither are you." The man stood and waved at Mariella. "Take him downstairs and let him talk to his countryman. His men and I will stay here and stare at each other. I'll drink. They can watch me. We'll all be happy." Rafa chuckled as he rose from the couch and headed to the liquor bottles.

Creed followed Mariella to a small door and had to turn sideways to follow her through a narrow passage. It opened wider after about six feet. The stairs down were cement and wide. The exposed bulb overhead cast shadows along the unadorned grey concrete. Creed saw an older woman sitting outside a solitary door.

"How is he tonight, Amelia?"

"He is stubborn. Will not eat, will not drink. He will kill himself this way." The old woman glared at Creed as she spoke.

Mariella snorted and pulled open the door, waving him through. Creed noted there was no locking mechanism on the door. "I'll wait for you out here."

Creed stepped inside the room as the door closed quietly behind him. The man on the bed didn't move. The room was as simple as the rest of the compound. It held the bed, a clean chamber pot, and a chair. There was a cup and a clear pitcher containing water sitting on a solitary shelf. A small bundle of what he suspected to be food was wrapped in a wax-type paper sitting beside the pitcher. The room was clean, and so was the man lying on the bed. Creed reached out and shook the man's leg gently. With a moan, he rolled onto his back. The black, purple and red bruise that covered the right side of the guy's head had to have come from the butt end of a rifle. The shape of imprint was undeniable.

"Hey man, can you wake up for me?" Creed grabbed the small chair, spun it around and straddled it, wanting to give the man the allusion of a barrier between them. He wanted the guy to relax and towering over him while he asked the man questions wasn't the way to accomplish it.

Small slits of eyes showed through the swollen mess of the man's face. "American?"

"Yeah, dude. We are here tracking the same shit you were. Our source in country is the man who brought you here and has been taking care of you." Creed glanced up at the water pitcher. "The water and food are safe. Our source wants money and poisoning you will not get him any bonuses." Creed nodded up at the pitcher. "You want a drink?"

"I don't know you." Creed could see suspicion warred with the man's thirst.

Creed poured a cup of water and downed the entire thing. He poured half a cup and sat down on the chair, holding the water. "My name is Creed Lachlan. You're CIA and came in with three others. We lost contact with you within twenty-four hours of you hitting land."

"Martin Street. They were waiting for us." The man moved his hand beckoning Creed closer. "Professionals. One was an American woman. I waited until they left and crawled to find help. I heard a truck. Rolled into a ditch. Cuban army vehicle drove right past me. They took my team. They were waiting for us."

Creed nodded. "You think someone inside tipped them off?" The man nodded and tried to wet his dry lips. Creed supported the man's head and fed him small sips of water until the water in the cup was gone. He lowered the man to his back again and waited as he drew several ragged breaths. He'd had the shit beaten out of him. "Mission classified. Need to know only." He grabbed Creed's arm. "Don't trust anyone."

Creed put his hand over the man's and gave it a gentle squeeze. "Did you have a location?"

The man closed his eyes and shook his head. "General idea. Camaguey and Las Tunas border area."

"All right. We've got this. You rest up. Eat and drink." He started to lift up, but Martin caught his arm again.

"Who is your contact?"

"Rafa."

The man let out a shuddering breath. "Team leader told them to wait and negotiate with Rafa. Suits wouldn't agree to it." A weak hand patted Creed's arm. "Don't get killed."

"That's the ultimate goal, man." Creed stood and moved the little chair back to the position it was before he took it. "I'm sending in Amelia. Let her take care of you."

The man nodded, but he wasn't going to be conscious for long. His injuries, self-imposed lack of food and water, plus the conversation, had exhausted the man. He was asleep before Creed opened the door.

"He will eat and drink when he wakes." Creed stopped and squatted down in front of the old woman. "Thank you for taking care of him."

Wise, old eyes stared back at him. "He has dreams, very bad. You find who did this to him, and make sure they don't do it again."

"I'll do my best." Creed gave the old woman one of his best smiles before he straightened and motioned down the corridor to Mariella. "Why is he down here?"

"Because this is our safe room. The passage we came down is the only way in or out, and when the back wall is in place, it is nothing but a closet. No one will find him here if the compound is raided or searched." She stopped at the base of the stairs and put a hand on his arm, stalling his forward momentum. "The people who bring these materials to our country must be stopped."

Creed squared on her. The urgency in her eyes pleaded with him. "That is our intent." Maybe the woman wasn't as disinterested as she let on?

She nodded. "Good, then we are on the same page." She pivoted and headed up the stairs. He followed her as his mind raced with the implications of Martin Street's information. The CIA's covert team was compromised. The mission was need-to-know only. That limited who could compromise the team even further. Shit was getting darker and darker in this scenario. His primary mission hadn't been rescuing the CIA team, but that priority had just been upped. Creed was finding those bombs and freeing the CIA team. Somebody way up the food chain had fed that team to the sharks and was probably hoping the Cuban government would execute them.

He turned sideways and exited the small entrance. Mariella stood out of his way, so he could exit, and then slid the back panel into place. The doorway was completely obstructed. She pushed the rain jackets on the hangers to the center of the rail, further disguising the entryway, before she pulled the string turning off the closet light.

"Did you get any information from him?" Rafa asked from his position on the couch.

"We need to concentrate our efforts in the Camaguey and Las Tunas border area." Creed did a silent check in with McGowen who gave him an almost imperceptible nod.

"Excellent. I will start the search. In the meantime, there is food, and you must be hungry." Rafa led the way through the house to a large dining room table.

Creed accepted a plate full of food. Pork, beans, rice, and plantains. He stared at his food, Martin's words sat front and center like blinking neon signs in his mind. He turned his gaze to Rafa who was staring back at him.

"What is it that has you worried?"

"Just a gut feeling." The CIA hadn't wanted to use Rafa for a reason. They'd hurried the covert team in without a known contact.

"I've lived this long by trusting my gut. I would encourage you to do the same." Rafa used a tortilla to capture a piece of pork.

Creed leaned back in his chair. "Don't trust anyone, Rafa. Something is off." It stunk so badly that the rancid smell turned his gut in a way not many things could. "We can't expose ourselves. Either your people or mine."

Rafa finished chewing his food and leaned back in his chair. "This is my life. I trust very few. It keeps me alive. Your man, he warned you?"

"He did."

"He would know." Rafa sighed and nodded. "I think I may have a way. It will require sacrifice on both of our parts, but it may be the only way. Let me work the details. We will eat, then I will work. Tomorrow, you will go north to the Camaguey and Las Tunas border area."

Mariella straightened from her position on Rafa's right. "Without being reported by the Comité de Defensa? The CDR will report this."

"CDR?" Creed asked for clarification.

"They are eyes at the neighborhood level. Eyes for the government," Mariella explained before she turned on Rafa. "They expect us to work shipments, but you know they will be paranoid if we start poking around."

Rafa shrugged. "It is my concern. I can use my influence in the G2. You just do as you're told. I need several hours." He nodded to the food and then at Creed. "Eat and rest. I have a feeling you're going to need it, my friend."

Creed considered the interaction and eyeballed the man who'd just shut down his very intelligent niece. Pieces of the Mariella puzzle started to move together. Rafa and his chauvinistic attitude probably accounted for a healthy chunk of the reason she'd gone off on him in the alleyway. His eyes slid to her. Head down, shoulders slumped. Defeated. Nothing like the woman he met earlier this morning. What a shame.

# CHAPTER 10

*M*ariella raised her boot to her kitchen table and tied the laces. She'd slept for shit last night. Her dreams of the American, Creed, and his team being slaughtered had disrupted any chance of sleep. The specters that wiped out the Americans were faceless and unrelenting. Mariella's skin crawled at the memories the dream had left with her. She'd tried to reach them, but every effort to save them was useless. She watched as a faceless entity sliced Creed's throat. It was her own scream that shook her from her sleep. The vivid dream still sent shivers down her spine even though she knew it was the result of an overactive imagination and the ominous warning the wounded American had issued. She'd heard everything the man had said to Creed, and after the Americans retired for the night, she'd repeated the entire conversation to her uncle. Rafa had accepted the information and dismissed her so he could work.

She'd spent the evening in a fruitless, one-sided conversation with herself. The evil of the world had invaded her life. Granted, working with her uncle, she dealt with devious, corrupt people all the time. The militant faction of their government was capable of horrible atrocities, and most who lived on the island knew of or had seen the acts firsthand. Was change happening on the island? Yes. Were things getting better? Mariella gave a mental shrug. It appeared with American tourism, and the recent events at the top of the party, change *could* happen. The people of Cuba needed that hope. The young ones like her had never known a life outside of communism, and older people who spoke of such things did so at a risk to their own freedom. The whispered conversations sparked dreams inside her. Dreams she couldn't afford to feed or foster. Doing so would only lead to disappointment. She would never be allowed to leave the country. No matter what her uncle said, she doubted either of them would live a day outside the borders of Cuba. The people who ruled could not allow it. Rafa was a powerful man in the G2; he knew too much.

The combination of the nightmare and the continuous loop of hopeless and useless wishes and wants dredged up and floating in front of her had her awake, showered and dressed far too early. Out the door with the first rays of morning light, she made her way to the main house. She nodded at several of the guards who watched the complex during the hours of darkness. The heavenly scent of coffee met her at the kitchen door.

Amelia turned as she entered. "You are early." The old woman's gruff exterior was a ruse. If there was a heart bigger than Amelia's in Cuba, Mariella hadn't found it.

"I couldn't sleep. How is our guest this morning?" Mariella poured herself a cup of coffee and accepted a thick piece of homemade bread with a smear of jelly that Amelia pushed in her direction. She jumped up on the counter with her breakfast and coffee and bit off a huge chunk of the bread.

"He drinks and eats now. He will be all right." Amelia sliced another hunk of bread and smeared the wild berry jam on top. She looked up at Mariella. "There is a table. You act like the men around here."

A bubble of laughter escaped before she jumped off the counter and joined Amelia at the table. "I don't need table manners for what I do here."

"You need a future." Amelia tore off a small piece of bread and ate it. "You need to leave this"—the old woman waved her hand around in the air—"times are changing, and that is always dangerous. People who face change are afraid, and scared people do stupid things. Your uncle worries about what to do with you."

"What to do with me? He doesn't need to *do* anything with me." Mariella shoved the rest of her bread into her mouth.

Amelia put her coffee cup on the table and leaned forward. "Cuba is changing. The old way of doing things is dying. There is hope for the first time since I was a little girl. It may take years, but what your uncle does will one day become a thing of the past. When he no longer holds power, he is vulnerable. Where will that leave you?" The old woman held up a finger when Mariella opened her mouth to respond. "Don't. Not everything is a joke to be laughed off. Think about this. Think what your life is, and what it isn't." Amelia slowly rose from the chair. She shuffled over to a small pail that had a cloth over it which was undoubtedly food for the American. Mariella watched her shuffle to the small closet entrance. The old woman turned and pinned her with an old, knowing stare. "What is it you truly desire? Answer that question, Mariella, and be honest with yourself, for once."

She lowered her gaze to the coffee in her mug. Small dots of oil pushed to the surface as the coffee cooled. She studied them as she thought about what Amelia asked. What did she truly desire? The easy answer was security. She was tired of being afraid... no... not afraid, on guard. Constantly wondering if a conversation will be recorded, worried if the shipment will be raided, what could happen if the government tipped the delicate balance that her uncle had worked so damn hard to maintain. She assumed her uncle had money, but it probably wasn't as much as everyone believed. She'd seen her uncle use his resources to help out his countrymen. Did he make money from them? Yes. Did he give back? Yes, but most never saw it. It came in the form of paying off the government to remove spying eyes from people and towns. The payment for information from citizens, most of which was useless, the care for those who had nothing, all of it was anonymous and all of it was from her uncle.

What did she truly desire? Security and someone to share it with. Oh, she slapped down all her uncle's insinuations that she should be married, but the picture wasn't unappealing, except she'd rather chew off her right arm than be tied to Adalberto. Mariella shivered and lifted the coffee to her lips. Speaking of the man, he should be back today. Hopefully, after the Americans left. She rolled her eyes and leaned back in the chair, relaxing with her coffee. If she knew her uncle, his men would ensure Adalberto's trip back ended after Rafa's business with the Americans was done.

At the sound of footsteps, she focused her attention on the kitchen door. Her uncle strode into the kitchen and poured a cup of coffee before he said a word. He wasn't a morning person. He brought the cup to his lips and turned to lean against the counter. "I will need you to assist me with the Americans."

She sat up and turned toward him. She had no problem with that. She could drive to whatever meeting point her uncle set up. Or perhaps he wanted her to shadow them. "What do you need?"

"I need you to marry the American."

She snorted at his joke. "Right. I'll just go get Padre." She chuckled to herself and took another sip of her coffee.

"I have Padre coming here in an hour." Rafa narrowed his eyes at her, and she realized he was not teasing.

She bolted up from the chair. "Wait, you're serious? You *can't* be serious!"

"Stop the hysterics and sit down." Her uncle's sharp reprimand snapped her gaping mouth shut.

Her knees may have given out because her ass hit the wooden chair a lot harder than she'd intended. "Please explain yourself." Okay, that was a calm, clear question. She gave herself points for control and restraint that she didn't normally possess.

"We need to get the Americans into areas where they will stand out. There can be no questions as to why they are there. None. For that reason, we need a purpose for them to be in the area. One that will not raise suspicions. Who you are will keep most out of our business, but not all." Her uncle smiled at her, obviously seeing a connection she wasn't.

Her mind raced trying to put the dots into some semblance of order, but she was damned if she could figure out the rationale behind his words. "How does my marrying the American make this happen?"

"Who do you know in Santa Lucia?"

"Cousins, Tia Josefina, and a half dozen of our contacts," her response was immediate.

"And in Guaimaro?"

"More distant cousins and contacts?"

"So, what would be a legitimate reason you, my niece, would travel to Santa Lucia and Guaimaro?"

Mariella dropped her head into her hands and shook her head as she spoke. "To introduce my extended family to my new husband." She shifted uncomfortably. "How do we explain his sudden appearance?"

"An arranged marriage. Arranged by me through distant relatives in Spain. I have the Americans' passports being made and the customs forms for their arrival two days ago have been filed using the passport numbers Geraldo has in his possession. We just need photographs to complete the work."

"So, it is a pretend marriage." Mariella nodded her head. "Okay, I can deal with that."

"Unfortunately, no. The only thing I can't control in this entire scenario is the documented marriage reports to the government. You are my niece, everyone will look. The license is real and will be filed along with the clergy's documentation, which the party cares nothing for." Her uncle elevated his cup and took a sip while staring at her.

Dread dropped low in her gut. "I don't understand how that is a factor."

"People watch us, closely. If there was no wedding on record, the American's cover would be blown."

She spun to face him. "I could introduce him as my fiancé."

Her uncle frowned. "When was the last time one of our relatives traveled to introduce an intended?"

Mariella shook her head. "Never, but that doesn't mean I couldn't. I'm not exactly traditional, am I?" She waived at her camo pants and holster.

"You are not, but why raise eyebrows? Our intent here is to give these men a legitimate reason to be in the area. Visiting my family and introducing your husband is legitimate."

Icy tendrils of realization laced their way around her, sending her into a panic. "Rafa, this is ridiculous!" She stood up again. "There has to be another way."

"I'm willing to listen. What would you suggest?" He reached into his pocket and grabbed a pack of cigarettes, shaking one up from the package, lipping it while he put the pack away.

"Ah... they could be new to the organization?"

"Because we send new people into areas where they are not known to work," her uncle retorted.

No, they never moved people out of the area where they had influence and experience. That would never work. "What if we introduce them as potential partners?"

Rafa rubbed his neck. "We would take them to Santa Lucia and Guaimaro to do what? There is no reason to take partners to the area. Partners would be interested in the books and import points, not small towns in the middle of the country that receive and pay for only a tiny percentage of the supplies we import."

Mariella groaned, "There has to be another way, Rafa."

"I have spent the entire night trying to come up with a different solution. This is the only way we can get the Americans where they need to go. Word has traveled to me that there are two, perhaps three places that are remote, deserted, with access and suddenly have a power source. Two are close to Santa Lucia. My cousin Victor is waiting for your arrival today. He has been told you are marrying this morning and to have a wedding celebration ready for you tonight. Of course, I will be sending money, food, and tokens of my gratitude to them before you get there to thank them for hosting the event."

Mariella clenched her fists. "How in the hell does that get the Americans closer to the sites?"

"His men will be free to wander the area while you and your husband... retire for your wedding night." Rafa pushed off the counter and walked toward her. "There may be people making bombs with radioactive material in the center of our country. From what you heard, the Americans face a difficult task even if we get them to the right place. The payout for this one mission will be enough that both of us will be rich. What is your real objection here?"

Mariella crossed her arms over her chest and spun away from her uncle. Her real problem? She was terrified of marrying someone in the eyes of God and then making a mockery of that relationship. There was no divorce in the eyes of God, at least that is what Amelia told her. Amelia had taught her marriage was a sacrament and not to be violated. Granted, her education about the politics of the Church was lacking, but that didn't mean falsely entering into a relationship would bode well for her. Could she ever tell her uncle her reasons? No. Her beliefs weren't his.

"The American won't agree to this... besides, he's probably married."

"I doubt all three are married." Her uncle lit his cigarette and took a deep draw filling his lungs with smoke.

*What?* No. He wasn't serious. Mariella blinked at her uncle. He didn't care which American she married? Was her life really so... disposable?

Rafa blew out a cloud of smoke and spun to fill his coffee cup again. He spoke as he worked, "I will talk with Creed. You need to go change. The priest will be here soon, the paperwork has already been completed. Pack for the road and be back here before Padre arrives so you and your future husband can provide a united front when he arrives."

"What if they don't agree?"

"Then they go back to America, and they try something else." He put the coffee pot back down and raised his mug. "This is the only realistic, feasible option to reach his goal. He will agree."

She watched as he strode out of the kitchen. Married. To a stranger. Today. She closed her eyes and drew a deep breath. She had no rational explanation for her deep-seated belief that the Catholic God of her Aunt Amelia sat in judgment of her every action. The communist regime had rigorously attempted to stamp out the influence of the Roman Catholic Church in Cuba without success. While the government-monitored attendance at mass was poor, almost every elderly Cuban held an ingrained belief in an all-seeing God and a benevolent Jesus that bordered on superstition. *He* would be aware she was marrying in front of one of *His* priests and *He* would hold her to her vows regardless of the circumstances. She set aside her anxiety. The American would never agree to this. She'd go to her rooms, change, and pack, but it would all be for nothing. The American wasn't someone to be backed into a corner. He was strong, decisive and nobody's fool. A smile spread across her face. It had been a long time since she'd wished to see her uncle's plans stymied, but right now her money was on the American, and she had no doubt her uncle would have to regroup if he didn't want to lose his golden goose.

# CHAPTER 11

*C*reed listened to Rafa's plan carefully disassociating his distaste for the ruse from the feasibility of the actual structure of the mission.

McGowen leaned forward. "The logical groom is you. Whitehead needs to be able to roam, and if we are calling it like it is, I'm able to make sure nobody follows us. Quietly."

Creed nodded, acknowledging McGowen's words.

"Wait, you mean you are actually going to marry this guy's niece?" Whitehead's head swiveled from Creed to McGowen to Rafa. "Am I the only one here who thinks this is bullshit?"

Creed was frustrated, too, but the plan Rafa had drafted would get McGowen and Whitehead into the area quickly and without suspicion. McGowen's

Spanish would cover for any limitation Whitehead might have with the language.

Creed addressed Whitehead, "Do you have any alternative that will give us a reason for being in the area and moving around without question?"

Whitehead sighed, "Well... no, but Skipper, this is just wrong."

Creed smiled at the title Whitehead had automatically copied from McGowen. "It is the best plan we have, and I've explained the necessity for keeping us under the radar." The fact the CIA could harbor a traitor didn't sit well with any of them. They'd discussed scenarios most of the night, but Rafa's plan was damn near perfect. The only objection he had with the scenario was *actually* marrying the woman. He'd always thought when he said those two little words that he'd say them meaning 'until death do us part,' not, 'until this mission is over.'

His glance shifted to Rafa. "What do you need from us?"

"First, passport photos. Then you and I will speak of financial concerns." Rafa led them to a white wall and used a Polaroid to take their photos. The camera spit out the sheet and Rafa handed each man his photo until he finished. He took all three photos and dropped them into a folder, sealed it and marched it out to a man who was waiting on the patio. Creed had seen the man on his way in. He watched through the window as the guy dashed across the complex with the folder as Rafa came back into the living room.

"Now, gentlemen, there is coffee and food in the kitchen." Rafa dismissed his crew. Both McGowen and Whitehead snapped their eyes to Creed. He nodded once. Whitehead left first. McGowen swept the room again and pegged Rafa with a deadly look before he followed his charge. "That man, he would die for you." Rafa pointed toward McGowen as he headed into the kitchen.

"As I would for him." Creed acknowledged. "But that is not what we are here to discuss."

"True." Rafa agreed. "I will need much to pay for the favors I am calling in."

Creed had been authorized to negotiate the price. "And what would be fair compensation?" He couldn't wait to hear the exorbitant amount Rafa would spout. Branson was sure the man was going to cash in, and Creed had been told to agree to any terms. The agency had access to deep and unmonitored coffers.

"Ah, there are several things I will need. First, I need one million Euros." Rafa watched him carefully as he spoke.

Creed drew a breath and shook his head. "That is a lot of money." Branson had batted the word a million around like he expected Rafa to want at least seven figures.

Rafa laughed. "Not for you. I have worked with

this organization before. But I am not done with my list of demands."

Creed leaned forward and placed his elbows on his knees. He leveled his stare at the man across from him. "Demands?"

"Oh, yes, these are demands. Make no mistake. You will honor them." The man's face split in an evil smile.

Creed didn't like to play games. "What do we get for a cold hard million?"

"First, I have found the other three in Mr. Street's group. They are heavily protected. We will watch and wait and get the information to you as to what is happening to them. In the prisons, I cannot help you. In transit, you will not be alone when you take them back."

"How will we get them in transit?"

Rafa cocked his head at him. "I have my ways."

Creed leaned back. Taking back the four CIA agents was his intent from the start of this mission. "What else?"

"So far, I have been told of three locations that meet the criteria you stipulated last night. All close enough to areas you will be visiting to allow your men access to the sites without suspicion. You will have to be very careful. In the interior of the island, there is a rampant fear of the government. This comes from a lifetime of suffering, and if anyone believes your presence will bring more pain to their way of life, you will be reported. However, as we are framing this endeavor, you will become my family and will be welcomed by our relatives."

"And if these sites turn up nothing?" Creed wouldn't put all his eggs in one basket.

"I am still waiting for word from more remote locations. We will find this manufacture point should it actually exist." Rafa leaned forward and opened the small box on the coffee table and withdrew a cigarette.

"What other demands do you have?"

"I want safe passage for Amelia and me to Greece." Rafa lit his cigarette and drew in a lungful as he stared at Creed.

Amelia, the old woman who was watching Street? Wait, what about... "You mean Mariella?" Was the bastard planning on leaving her in fucking Cuba to deal with the mess his disappearing would cause? That sent a spike of pissed-the-fuck-off through him. It was an asshole move on every level.

"No, I mean Amelia. Mariella goes to America with her husband." Rafa blew out a cloud of smoke and smiled. "You stay married to her until your agency makes her an American citizen." He brought the cigarette to his lips again. "Those are my terms. They are non-negotiable." Drawing on his cigarette, he sucked the smoke into his lungs before he smiled and spoke again, "Four CIA agents, the location of the dirty bomb manufacturing point and the people making the bombs, should you be skilled enough to capture them without killing them. All for the bargain price of one million Euros, transport for two old people, and a marriage to a beautiful woman. What is your answer, Creed Lachlan?" Rafa blew out the smoke and stared through the hue at him.

The fucker had him over a barrel. Obviously, Mariella had told her uncle what she'd overheard last night from his conversation with Street. Creed's name included. The son of a bitch had his retirement fund and exit strategy planned down to the last detail.

Creed had no doubt Branson could pull strings and get his soon-to-be *wife* citizenship. Getting Rafa and the old woman out of the country would be simple if they could get to Gitmo. There was no way that old woman would be able to make the swim to the yacht for extraction. Rafa would be iffy with the number of cigarettes the man inhaled.

Gitmo would be where he needed to get the CIA personnel, Amelia and Rafa. The base had unobstructed passage off the island. The million Euros was a matter of an electronic funds transfer to complete. "The money will be transferred when we have the people and the site. Not before."

"Understood. I have people I can leverage, once and only once, to get the prisoners transferred. When you are ready, we will arrange it."

"Then we will take you off the island with our people."

"We have an agreement then, Mr. Lachlan?"

"As long as you keep your end of the bargain."

Plans were great until first contact with the enemy, and in this mission, the enemy wasn't clearly defined. His only allies now were the head of Cuba's largest black-market entity and his niece, a woman he was being forced to marry and take back to the States. He trusted McGowen and Whitehead, but everyone else was suspect. Mariella had told Rafa everything she'd heard from his conversation with Street. Her allegiance wasn't in question. It was to Rafa and Rafa alone. Which was appropriate, but dammit for some reason he'd hoped she was enough of her own person to function independent of her uncle. The whole marriage scenario bothered him, though. Rafa's plan was too convenient, too thought out and complete to be something the man mashed together last night.

"Of course. You will marry my niece shortly." Rafa's head snapped to the window as the same man ran across the open area in front of the house. "Ah... your passports." Rafa lifted off the couch and snubbed out his cigarette in a large ashtray next to the sofa. He strode to the door and took the envelope. Rafa examined the back of the large packet. He tossed it to Creed. The flap had been sealed with wax. Creed broke it and reached in to retrieve three red leather passports. Gold embossed wording of *Union Europea España Pasaporte* labeled each. He cracked one open. Whitehead's picture was attached to the name Santiago Garcia. He flipped to the next. McGowen was now Alejandro Garcia, and Creed was Esteban Garcia. The holographic overlay covering the photo and typeset was in place and from what Creed could see, perfect. He flipped his to the back and noticed several entrance stamps. The latest of which landed him in Cuba as of two days ago. He glanced up at Rafa. "Your people do good work."

"My people do excellent work. It is what you are paying for. A botched passport could mean the difference between success and failure in this country. We've learned to make sure there are no mistakes." Rafa stretched and yawned. "Forgive me. I was up all night working." He glanced at the clock. "Come, Mariella will be here shortly. We need to make sure all four of you tell the same story when the priest shows up." Rafa's hand landed on Creed's shoulder. "Welcome to the family."

Creed rolled his shoulder and dislodged the hand. "Can't say as I'm thrilled to be marrying into your family, Rafa."

The man threw back his head and laughed. "Don't worry about the entirety of my family, my friend. Mariella will be more than enough for you to worry about."

Creed reached down and grabbed his coffee mug

before he headed into the kitchen where he could hear McGowen and Whitehead talking. Creed had no doubt about that statement. Mariella was a concern and a distraction. One he shouldn't have to worry about, but it seemed as if her life ass-planted in the middle of his op. He stacked all three of the passports Rafa had given him and slapped them against his hand. They had a mission to do. Surprise marital vows aside, Branson and the rest of the world needed to know if the dirty bombs were being made in Cuba.

He followed Rafa into the kitchen and grabbed the mug that McGowen handed him. There was a tray of meat and cheese along with bread. McGowen passed him a sandwich and Creed straddled a chair and devoured it. Lessons he learned early in the military were basic and simple. Eat when you can, every time you can. Never stand when you can sit. Never sit when you can lie down and never stay awake when you can get some shut-eye. He had no idea what the rest of the day had in store... other than getting married, so he reverted to the basics.

He watched Rafa talk with his men and made another sandwich. He drained his coffee and Whitehead refilled it.

Mariella opened the kitchen door, and all conversation stopped. Creed swallowed the last of his sandwich with a large gulp. The woman wore a cream-colored dress, knee length, and form-fitting. Her hair was swept up and pushed to the side. Her long lashes had been enhanced with mascara, and she wore a bright red lipstick that accentuated her pouty lips. Her nervousness was clearly visible. She frowned at Creed. "What? He told me to change. Wait? Did you say no?" Her face lit up in a brilliant smile.

"I said yes." Creed stood and took the backpack out of her hand.

The smile she wore faltered before she dropped her eyes. "Oh."

Fuck him. She didn't want this any more than he did. Her hands fell to her sides before she elevated her head and straightened her back. "Then we have some information to go over, yes?" Her voice trembled slightly. She'd obviously hoped he wouldn't go through with the plan, but it was the only way to move forward.

"My name is Esteban Garcia. This is Santiago"—he motioned to Whitehead and then to McGowen —"and Alejandro Garcia."

Mariella wrinkled her nose and arched an eyebrow. "You do not look like an Esteban."

Rafa put down his coffee cup and pointed at Creed. "The story is that your father arranged this marriage with me after you fell into some trouble in Spain. Santiago and Alejandro were sent with you to make sure you didn't fuck up again." Rafa shrugged. "It is a common thing, to make sure a miscreant of a son is chaperoned. You will be relocating to Cuba. Your father's decision. Not yours."

"I take it I'm not happy about that?" Creed crossed his arms and stood with his feet shoulder-width apart.

"Your story to tell, I don't care. The marriage is one of convenience. Your father is one of my main suppliers from Europe, and it is well known that I want my niece married."

"You make me sound like something to be passed off," Mariella huffed.

"I'm using my concern for your wellbeing to sell the cover for these men. My people know I think you need a strong hand."

"Now I sound like a dog or a horse." She glared at her uncle.

*There was the woman he dealt with in Havana.* "Is there anything else we need to know?" Creed tried to put a stop to the bickering.

"I'm sure there are a vast amount of details, but we won't be able to cover everything. Keep the story basic. Don't elaborate and you'll be fine." Rafa shrugged. "The priest will be here soon. I have some clothes in storage. Come see if you can find anything better to wear." He turned on his heel and walked away, expecting them to comply.

"Go with him. See what you can find. I want a moment." He addressed McGowen who nodded and ushered Whitehead out of the kitchen.

"I'm sorry." Her whispered words barely made it to his ears.

*For what?* "Was this your idea?" Creed asked.

Her head snapped up. "What? No!"

"Then you have nothing to be sorry for. As this farce is an arranged marriage, I don't expect anyone would believe us being happy with the situation. I'll keep my distance." He'd offer her that politesse at least.

Mariella stared blankly at him for a moment before she chuckled and then laughed. "Oh, you are in for a surprise." She shook her head, still chuckling, and went to one of the three cupboards and pushed aside the curtain. She grabbed a glass and a bottle of clear liquid. She held up the bottle. "Courage." She cocked her head at him. "Want some?"

He shook his head. She shrugged and pulled the cork out of the top of the bottle with her teeth. "Too bad." The words formed around the cork sounded like "ooh aad."

She poured a couple fingers worth of liquid courage and recorked the bottle.

Damn, dressed like a lady and chugging liquor like one of his men. Why in the hell did that impress him? He shrugged off the thought and brought his mind back to the conversation at hand. "Care to tell me what you mean by that?"

"Courage?" She glanced over the top of the glass at him.

"No, that I'm in for a surprise." He watched her toss back the entire glass.

She blew out a breath and sucked another in. "Damn, that is strong." She wiggled the cork out again and poured another glass before she looked up at him. "My uncle's family is preparing a wedding celebration for us tonight. We will be forced into close company. Yes, this is an arranged marriage, but it is still a marriage that will be toasted, celebrated, and there will be certain assumptions made." Mariella closed her eyes, shook her head as if she was trying to clear her mind of images she did not want to see, and then shot the liquor. She grimaced again and pulled another deep breath. "Whoa."

"Assumptions are not my concern. Look, neither of us is happy about this event, but I need to get up there so we can recon the area. I'll play my part." Creed dropped his crossed arms and rubbed the back of his neck. "I'll make sure you get your citizenship."

Mariella's eyes snapped up to him. "Excuse me?"

"It was part of the deal. You go to the States with me when we leave, and I stay married to you until you receive your American citizenship."

Mariella slammed the glass down on the counter and screamed, "Rafa!" She spun on her heel and headed into the house. "Rafa, dammit! Where the fuck are you!" Creed hurried after her. Obviously, the woman had no idea of the conditions Rafa had put on their marriage. "Rafa, you bastard!"

The man in question opened the door that led into the living room. Standing beside him was a small, slight man wearing a black suit and white collar. "Ahh, Father Augustus, may I introduce my lovely niece, Mariella."

"Yes, I heard her before I saw her."

The priest's eyes traveled over his future bride. The judgment in his gaze was enough to make him cringe, and he wasn't Catholic. Creed blinked at that thought. Didn't he need to convert or something to make this legal? And why would he worry about something like that? This marriage was a sham.

He moved to stand beside a stunned-silent Mariella and extended his hand. "Father Augustus, may I introduce myself. I am Esteban Garcia, recently of Spain."

The smaller man took his hand in a limp shake. "A pleasure to meet you." He glanced at Rafa. "You have the paperwork? The government requires it to be completed prior to my conducting the ceremony."

"Yes, of course it is complete, and the gratuity for your travels to our home." Rafa pulled an envelope out of the jacket he was wearing. "Esteban, your cousins were able to press your suit for you. You'll find them down the hall."

Creed excused himself and exited to get ready for his Cuban wedding to the niece of a black market kingpin. What layer of reality had to warp to for him to think that thought?

# CHAPTER 12

*T*hank God she'd downed two strong shots of tequila. It was all she could do to control herself as her uncle paraded the priest around like he was his own personal body armor. The man never left the priest's side. Seething, she stared daggers at her uncle. The man had the audacity to wink at her over the head of the priest.

Creed and his men entered the room and distracted her anger momentarily. They wore slacks and button-down shirts. Creed wore a black jacket that accented the blue of his eyes. She met his stare for a second before she returned her furious gaze to her uncle. Creed walked in front of her. She shot him a fraction of the deadly glare she'd been slaying her uncle with and moved so she could continue her visual assassination of said uncle.

Creed leaned forward and whispered in her ear.

"Once we get through with the ceremony, we can discuss this, but do not cost me a chance at this mission because you can't control your emotions."

She leaned back and shifted every ounce of her anger to the man in front of her. She spat out a whisper, "*Your* precious mission! You do understand that I'm marrying you, right? That I'm sacrificing my one chance at a family to help you find the people you're searching for? What about *my* dreams and *my* hopes for a future? Oh, that's right, they don't matter, because you and Rafa struck a deal." She spun and headed out of the room.

"Where are you going?" Rafa shouted after her.

"To powder my nose!" She yelled and nearly ran down the hall. She slammed the door behind her, resting her head against the doorjamb. Tears streamed down her cheeks, and that pissed her off even more. Crying when she was angry was a fault she'd tried so damn hard to fix, but she never could… because she was a fucking woman. Anger skidded across her like a car on wet coral pavement, careening and out of control. She sat down on the toilet and wadded a piece of toilet paper in her hand. *Damn Rafa.* She hated him for expecting her to accept his decision that she go to the United States with the American. She thought back to her uncle's words two days ago. Yes, they would both leave. He'd made sure she'd be gone, but what would she do in America? Was there a need for a woman who knew the black market? No, she couldn't imagine there was.

A light rap on the door startled her. She wiped her cheeks as she answered, "What?"

"Open the door. Please." Creed's voice sounded from the hall.

"No." She blew her nose and tossed the paper into the small trash can.

"Mariella, open the door for just a moment." She glanced up at her reflection in the mirror. Streaks of black ran down her cheeks. She swiped at the running mascara again before she unlocked the door.

"What?"

He leaned against the doorjamb. "Thank you."

"For what? Opening the door?" She flicked her wrist dismissing him. The American may be physically attractive, but he was a self-centered asshole who would use anyone or anything to complete his damn mission. It was probably why he was here. His country knew he'd succeed at any cost.

"No." A tiny smile ticked one corner of his mouth up. "I had no idea you'd been forced into this arrangement. If it helps, you'll be marrying a person who doesn't exist, and I'm not Catholic. The Roman Catholic Church will not recognize this ceremony as legitimate. When we get to the States, and your citizenship is confirmed, we can have the marriage annulled and you'll be rid of me."

He smiled at her as if that was the answer to all

her problems. *Ha.* Her problems *started* there. What would she do alone in America? She didn't know a soul in that country. How would she live? She had a small amount of money, but nothing that could sustain her for any length of time. Especially living in America.

Mariella grabbed a washcloth and wet it. She used cleaning the smeared black streaks off her face as a way to delay conversation and keep all the worries and questions from spilling out of her mouth. She was being plunged into a situation and a future where she had no control. She glanced at her image in the mirror. She'd struggled so damn hard to make a life for herself here. To be respected and in her small way, contribute to the country she loved.

"I get that your arm was twisted. I'm sorry about that, and if I had any plan that would hold a snowball's chance in hell of working, I'd use it. I don't like that you're being used without your consent."

She sniffed and dabbed at her nose. She had no option but to follow her uncle's orders. Without him, she was nothing. Her eyes flitted up the mirror. With him, she was nothing.

"Look, I understand you don't want…" Creed's words trailed off as loud, angry, and mostly unintelligible words reached them before Adalberto's clearly heard protests echoed down the hall.

"What in the hell do you mean she's getting married? You know I've been waiting for your permission. You've put me off for years. If she marries anyone, she marries me!"

Whitehead appeared at the door, his eyes wide as he lowered his voice and spoke in English. "Skipper, you need to get out there."

Creed nodded. He stopped long enough to speak over his shoulder. "Stay here."

Mariella blinked at him and then turned and looked at her reflection in the mirror. *As if*. She could hear Rafa's voice. Oh, her uncle was pissed. He reserved those coldly calculated words spoken in that sharp, low, tone for only the most dangerous of people. Adalberto fell into that category. She drew a deep breath and made the decision to take part in her destiny instead of letting the men who surrounded her dictate her future.

She walked down the hall letting the heels she wore tap out a staccato announcement of her arrival. She entered the room, and every head turned her way. Her uncle barely acknowledged her presence before he returned his focus to Adalberto. Creed's eyes narrowed, probably pissed she didn't stay cowering in the bathroom like he'd instructed.

She glanced at the priest who trembled in the corner like a small mouse. Walking toward the liquor cart, she spoke into the sudden silence. "I'd never marry you, Adalberto. I've told you this." She poured a small amount of her uncle's prized port wine into a glass and walked over to the priest, handing it to him.

The man's hand shook horribly as he took the offered glass. "Drink it, Padre." The man did what he was told and downed it all.

"You were promised to me. I will have you, making me next in line for all of this." Adalberto waved his arm indicating something larger than the room they were in.

Rafa's words were precise and enunciated, "I promised you nothing, Adalberto."

Mariella took the distraction her uncle offered to assess the situation. She counted three guns on Adalberto. One strapped to his leg, one he carried in a shoulder holster and one in his boot. She knew her uncle had guns stashed throughout the house, but she hadn't seen any on his person since the priest had been in the house, and she'd seen proof that the Americans carried concealed cannons. If one person pulled a weapon, everyone in the room could die. Keeping this tense situation from becoming a bloodbath was imperative. She had to distract Adalberto, his temper and evil streak were notorious, and he was damn good with a gun.

Adalberto squared off on Rafa. The rage that ran through the man made the vein in his forehead pulse. "You complain about your old maid niece, how she needs a strong man." Adalberto thumped his chest. "I told you I was willing to make her behave like a woman." He swung a finger toward Creed who watched, poised and ready to launch. It didn't escape her that the big man with Creed had moved silently to remove her and Father Augustus from any cross-fire. "He isn't part of this organization."

Her eyes scanned the scene. What could she do to distract Adalberto enough that the Americans could act? Other than... Mariella threw Creed a pleading look before she filled her lungs and threw back her head laughing. Adalberto and Rafa's attention shifted to her. Not enough, so she put her hand on her hip and sneered at Adalberto. "Really? That is your objection to my marriage to Esteban? Adalberto, you are a fool. *You'll* make me behave like a woman? You'd never be man enough. And as for all this being yours someday? Since when? Was there an announcement I missed? Rafa, have you drawn up papers leaving everything to Adalberto? No, I didn't think so. *I* will inherit everything, and there is no way I would marry you and give you a legal claim. You disgust me."

Adalberto surged across the room. Mariella knew what was coming and she braced, expecting the backhand that whipped her head around and sent her crashing into the wall. Pain exploded across her face and shoulder. Black and red spots blasted in front of her eyes and grew until they pushed most of her vision into blackness. She felt herself sliding down the wall but could do nothing to stop her fall. She gasped and cowered when she saw a quick movement at the far reaches of her vision. Shouted words filled her mind like the roar of a crashing wave seconds before darkness consumed her.

RAGE CONSUMED him in less than the time it took to blink. Creed launched across the room at the exact same time as McGowen and Rafa. He was closer and reached the bastard first. The heel of his right hand snapped out, connecting with the bastard's nose. His left connected with the fucker in an uppercut that released every ounce of fury that raged through him. His right caught the motherfucker on the way down, his slack jaw shattered under Creed's assault. He followed the man to the floor and rolled him on his back. The fuckwad made his last mistake. He tried to swing at Creed. Creed laid into the bastard fully intending to kill him, stopping only when McGowen pulled him off the son of a bitch and restrained him. Creed snapped at Whitehead in Spanish, "Get his fucking weapons!" His man scrambled pulling two automatics, one revolver, and a knife from the crumpled body.

Rafa appeared in front of him. The man's cold stare assessed Creed for several seconds. Creed pulled at his arms and McGowen released him. Whitehead shoved the weapons toward McGowen and hurried to where the priest hovered over Mariella. Blood from her split lip trickled down her chin, but she was conscious and pushing herself up, despite both Whitehead and the priest encouraging her to stay down. Creed ground his teeth and kicked the man at his feet as he glared at Rafa.

Rafa lifted an eyebrow and waited for Mariella to stand with assistance before he spoke. "Mariella, with everything that has happened today, you have a choice to make. Do you want to marry Esteban and commit to the arrangement we have?"

The woman trailed her fingers through the blood that lingered on her chin. Her eyes moved from her uncle to Adalberto and then to him. He saw her take in his bruised hands and the blood that had transferred onto his borrowed clothes.

Creed pointed to the man at his feet. "Regardless of your decision, I promise you this man will never touch you again."

Her eyes snapped back up to his. She didn't believe him. The sadness buried in her eyes as they traveled from him to Adalberto to her uncle told him she knew what her future held, and it fucking killed him that she didn't believe him. He got it. He would be leaving, and if she walked away, Adalberto would still be part of her future. She was damned to a life that involved that fucker if she stayed and if she left with Creed? What would her life be like? It wasn't as if he'd be able to take care of her once Branson worked his political magic.

She glanced at the priest. "I am sorry for the

before-wedding theatrics, Father. If you give me a moment to clean up, we can start."

The small man shook his head. "I don't think that would be wise. Perhaps when cooler heads prevail, my child."

Rafa stepped forward and took the priest by his elbow. "Surely, you've witnessed other family squabbles prior to a wedding, Padre?"

The little man shook his head. "This man needs a doctor."

Rafa glanced down at Adalberto. "I guarantee you he will be well taken care of. Now, perhaps I can increase my contribution to the Church as a way of saying thank you for your discretion and cooperation." He escorted the priest to the door of his office before looking back. "Mariella, five minutes? And please have Paco take care of the mess." Her uncle's deadly stare left no doubt as to the intent of his instructions.

MARIELLA NODDED and flinched at the pain the motion caused. Slowly she shifted and made her way through the kitchen to the back door. She opened it and gave directions to the guard posted outside. He glanced back at her and did a double take, shock at her appearance showing instantaneously. "Go," Mariella said lifting her chin toward the apartments

Paco and the guards used. The guard nodded, shot a look past her into the house and then trotted across the compound.

She wet a kitchen towel and dabbed at her lip and chin. Her head throbbed. The rush of adrenaline that had been sustaining her waned, leaving her knees shaking. She leaned against the sink and closed her eyes.

The sound of several feet running across the porch could be heard before the back door slammed open. "Mariella? Where is Rafa?" Paco spun her and winced at the bruising that no doubt had already started to show.

"Rafa is fine, Paco. You need to take Adalberto away. He attacked me. Rafa will give you directions, but keep him secure until he tells you what he wants done." Mariella pulled away from his gentle hold and headed for the bottle of tequila she'd taken a couple hits off earlier. She glanced at the clock on the wall... was it really less than an hour ago? She blinked at the hands of the clock and tried to clear her vision. Less than a half hour. The liquid sloshed from the bottle into the same glass she'd used earlier. She hoisted the glass and sipped it awkwardly, trying to avoid the cut her teeth had slashed into the inside of her lip. Several of her teeth were loose. She must have hit the wall pretty damn hard, or Adalberto had hit her with his fist. Probably the later.

"Here." Creed appeared in front of her and took

the glass away. He stood directly in front of her. So damn close his scent enveloped her. He dabbed the wet cloth across her chin and down her neck. "You made him go after you." He moved her chin, so she was forced to look at him.

She shrugged. "If I didn't, guns would have come into play. You have a mission to complete, and you can't do that if you're dead." Tired, she leaned forward the few inches that separated them and rested her forehead against his shoulder. Not an intimate gesture, but rather one of exhaustion. "Adalberto?"

"Taken care of by your uncle's man."

She felt the man's arms circle her and dammit if she didn't let herself lean into his warmth. *Just for a moment.* Then she would put her armor back on and move forward with the sham marriage. She'd deal with the spiritual repercussions of lying to a priest and God. It didn't matter if the marriage wasn't "legal". She was taking vows to be a wife to this man with no intention of honoring them. Vows made in front of God and witnesses. It had to be wrong.

"Skipper, they're ready."

She didn't move at the words spoken by the big man who reported to Creed. McGowen, the soft-spoken giant who hovered, acting as Creed's extra layer of protection, not that the man needed it. She'd seen the aftermath of his altercation with Adalberto. Adalberto was damn good with his hands. She'd seen

165

him destroy people in 'friendly' sparring matches. Creed Lachlan had bested him. That defeat would sting more than her callous words. Adalberto was evil and consistent. He couldn't stomach being second best, and Rafa was right when he'd said that Adalberto was ambitious. She just didn't realize a marriage to her was a real part of that ambition.

"Are you ready?"

Wrapped in his embrace, she felt the rumble of Creed's voice. This man wasn't here to protect her. He was here to do a job, and she was a means to that end. She drew a deep breath and forced herself to stand up and step back. Carefully, she mentally drew her armor around her. She'd do her job and trust… she glanced around the kitchen. No, she wasn't ready to trust anyone. One thing the last thirty minutes had taught her was she couldn't count on anyone but herself. Rafa and this American had made an agreement, and she was just a pawn. One Rafa was willing to sacrifice to win the game and get his golden egg.

# CHAPTER 13

"So, you're married then?" Whitehead helped Creed load their gear into the trunk of the '57 Chevy they'd driven into the compound not more than twenty-four hours ago.

"Nah, man, 'Esteban Garcia' is married to her not Creed Lachlan. The fake name and the fact I'm not Catholic qualify this union for a real fast annulment if it's even legal—which I doubt." Creed moved one of the gallon jugs and noticed someone had filled them. He checked the tops to make sure they were sealed.

"Personally, I wouldn't be in such a rush to drop her. She's pretty fucking amazing. She baited that bastard this morning, didn't she?" Whitehead opened his bag and pulled out a baggie of small Cuban flag pins.

"She did. He had weapons, and she knew we

needed to get a jump on him or shit would have gotten deadly, fast." Creed flexed his fists. They were swollen and sore, but he was beyond happy he'd been the first one to that motherfucker. Seeing him hit Mariella with a closed fist had set him off like a brick of C4. Nobody deserved to be treated that way, man *or* woman.

As Creed worked to pack the car, her comments in the alleyway came back with a vengeance. How long has she been told that she was... less? That her opinion wasn't equal to that of a man's? He hated that shit. People mattered, dammit. Gender didn't play a role in capability, nor should it ever play a part in the way a person was treated. Creed believed that with his entire being. Mariella was intelligent and quick-witted, and she was willing to sacrifice herself for others. There was a lot about her that he, well fuck... he guessed he admired. The woman needed to know what she thought and felt mattered to him.

He glanced at where she stood talking with Rafa. Rather, Rafa talked, and she stood with her eyes glued to the ground and listened. She'd gone through with the sham wedding and was preparing to leave her home, her family, everything familiar, potentially for the last time in her life, and she had zero say in that scenario?

*Son of a bitch*. He knew exactly what she was going through. The look of resignation on her face was one he'd worn when he'd been told by the doctors that his life was being stripped away from him. He *understood* her pain. Hell, he'd been in her shoes. Circumstances had rearranged his life, and he'd had absolutely no say in it. The feeling of helplessness sucked on a basic level. His heart hurt for her. Fuck, it was a loss he still felt, so yeah, he empathized with her, and if he could walk away from this mission to save her that pain, he'd do it. He wished like fuck he could, but his direction was set in stone and he couldn't change it. Not even to spare her.

"What did he say about Street?" McGowen asked as he stacked in the last two backpacks.

"He'd bring Street with him when it was time to extract the others." Creed shut the trunk and leaned against the car carefully. "The CIA's team was compromised. We have to believe it was an inside job, so any contact we have with Branson could also be monitored."

"Thought we weren't going to have contact with him until we made it back to the boat?"

Whitehead's gaze was on Mariella and Rafa, too. Hell, they were all staring. Rafa had stopped talking, and Mariella shrugged. God dammit. The woman looked lost. She stepped off the porch and headed their way.

"It looks like the extraction point for the agents may end up being Gitmo, depending on what happens." Creed turned his back, giving himself and McGowen a few sheltered words. "If something happens and we get split up, remember nothing important gets said to him unless you can guarantee no one is listening. Got it?"

McGowen nodded, and his eyes flitted to Mariella. The crunch of gravel indicated their private conversation was over.

Creed spun and opened the passenger door for her, pushing the seat up. "McGowen will drive. You could use a rest."

She halted. Suspicion shone just as brightly as the bruise that was forming on her cheek and under her eye. She extended her keys toward McGowen. "Do not get in an accident." She dropped the keys into his hand and slid into the backseat.

"You heard the lady." Creed slid into the backseat with her and Whitehead took his place in the front passenger seat. McGowen slid in and cranked the old lady up. Creed turned his head and stared at Rafa as they left. The man stood motionless on the porch, his stoic expression never changed.

They'd put the old rag-top up on the car, but the air blew through the windows, keeping the interior cool. Creed saw Mariella's head bounce to the side several times. Convinced she'd end up with a wicked case of whiplash, he tapped her arm. She blinked up at him, confused. He extended his arm. "Use my shoulder."

McGowen eyes met his in the rearview mirror and returned to the road almost immediately.

Mariella shook her head and tucked herself into the corner of the back seat. "Wake me when we get to the outskirts of Santa Lucia." She folded her arms across her chest and rested her forehead against the car. It looked uncomfortable as fuck. Creed shook his head. He *wasn't* the bad guy in this scenario. Although right now, with Mariella's rebuff grating against him, he felt like it was his fault. Wasn't that some seriously fucked up shit? He was just a man doing a job under damn near impossible conditions while infiltrating a foreign country.

The trip took just over three hours. Creed placed his hand on Mariella, bringing her out of a light slumber. She rolled her neck and leaned forward, hanging over the front seat. The bruising on her face looked horrible. Her lip was swollen, and the ragged rip was caked with blood that had dried. If a relative of his had arrived looking like her new husband had beaten the fuck out of her, he'd kill the motherfucker. Creed could only guess at the reception he and his team would receive.

"The next street up, no not this one, the one by the blue house, turn there." Mariella pointed out of the windshield.

She gave McGowen directions, and he navigated the rut and pothole-filled roads, ensuring the car avoided the majority of the roadway hazards. They pulled up outside a salmon-colored house. The hue wasn't quite a pink, but not brown either, some mish-mashed color in between. At their arrival, a flood of people exited the house.

"Get ready to play the happy groom." Mariella waved and shooed Whitehead and Creed out of the car. She got out and jumped into an older man's arms.

He hugged her and then held her at arm's length. "Mariella! What happened to your face?"

"Uncle Jose, I tried to wear heels. I tripped and fell into the corner of the wall! It was so embarrassing!" Mariella reached back to Creed and smiled. "May I introduce my husband, Esteban Garcia."

Creed came forward and gripped her hand, extending his other to the older man in front of him. "Sir, it is a pleasure to meet you."

The man stared at him and then at Mariella. "From Spain, yes?"

"That is correct, sir." Creed immediately replied.

"Very proper, isn't he?" The old man smiled at Mariella.

"Maybe you'll pick up some manners." An older woman pushed her way through the crowd. She held Mariella in a stern gaze before both of them started laughing.

He was suddenly wrapped up in a three-way hug, which was just plain awkward.

"Esteban, this is my Aunt Josefina."

"He's hitting you already?" The woman glared at him like he was the devil incarnate.

"No! Esteban did not do this!" His bride of fewer than four hours jumped to his defense. "He is a good man. This was an accident. Besides, you know I'd never let a man hit me." She scolded her aunt while protecting his honor.

The woman stared hard at Mariella before she nodded. "This is true. You would never allow it."

Creed let out the breath he'd been holding. The mission required them to be here and to be free from undue scrutiny. The bruises on Mariella's face could have caused problems, but the woman handled it all while holding his hand and pretending she hadn't been decked by a fucking thug hours earlier. She continued to impress him. Strong, stoic and dedicated. Why was she so dedicated to her uncle, especially after the arrangement he'd forced on her today? He'd yet to understand it, and it was a concern he'd get an answer to when they were alone. He didn't like not knowing what motivated her.

With ease, Mariella introduced him to her extended family and effortlessly pulled Whitehead and McGowen into the mix.

Tia Josefina smiled, or at least she attempted a smile. It looked more like a sneer. The woman didn't buy the accident line, and he couldn't say that he blamed her, but she invited them in any way.

"Come, in the backyard we have food and drinks to celebrate."

Mariella pulled his hand, and he glanced around at McGowen who was surrounded by three or four women. Whitehead had two more family members pulling him into the house.

Creed glanced down at his 'bride.'

She shrugged and whispered. "Food, embarrassing stories, and rum. A price you must pay to be here."

She moved away from his side and spoke to a group of women who eyed him with curiosity and a healthy dose of suspicion. He glanced at his men and then followed Mariella into the fray. He'd fought Satan's minions through the sin-stoked valleys of hell, how hard could it be to meet her family and convince them he wasn't an abusive dick?

Obviously, pretty fucking hard. The sideways looks continued all night. Mostly from Josefina, but the cool reception from others added to the weight of trying to pass the marriage off as legitimate. The only good thing about the awkwardness was the fact that everyone knew the marriage was arranged as a way to further Rafa's business. Creed was positive that tidbit of information was another black mark against him…or rather Esteban.

When the festivities finally dwindled, they were shown to their room. Josefina waved them into a tiny space with a twin sized bed. She glanced at him and sniffed, "You can sleep on the floor," before she kissed Mariella and left. The last glare she gave Creed should be taught to investigators around the world. The acid it contained could peel paint off the wall.

Creed turned around to see Mariella sitting on the bed, her hand supporting her forehead. She had to be exhausted and in pain. He grabbed his pack and dug through it until he came up with a packet of pain relievers. He opened it and poured her a glass of water from the stand beside the bed. "Here." She jumped as if she'd forgotten he was in the room with her. "For your headache and the pain." He had several resealable plastic bags of medical and personal supplies. He'd learned to pack for virtually any situation.

She extended her hand and examined the pills he'd dropped into her palm. "Thank you." The words were the first real conversation they'd had since they'd left the vehicle.

"How bad is it?" He sat down beside her and took the glass from her after she'd swallowed the medicine.

"I've had better days." She closed her eyes and sighed.

"You take the bed. I'll sleep on the floor." He rose and grabbed his pack to shove it in the corner.

"Why? We have to be ready to go in a couple hours, and we both need sleep. Just lie down with me. I'm not going to jump you, and you don't need to worry about my reputation." She sat up straight and pulled her arms inside the t-shirt she'd worn to travel in. Creed averted his eyes but didn't miss the bra that dropped to the floor before her arms reappeared. She toed off her espadrilles and stood before she unbuttoned her jeans and allowed them to drop to the floor. Mariella turned and pulled the sheets and thin blanket down to the foot of the bed.

Choking was a serious possibility. His eyes slid down her back, over her perfectly shaped ass encased in tight white panties, to her long, shapely legs. She slid into the bed and turned to face the wall, leaving him over half the available mattress space.

Creed hadn't told her they weren't going out tonight. McGowen and Whitehead were doing recon on the facility four miles away if they could slip away without being noticed. According to their estimation, it was the least likely to be used because of its proximity to the town. Tomorrow they would scout out the other site, the second of the three sites that Rafa's informants believed might be utilized. If it showed signs of use, they would slip out after midnight and make the six-mile run to investigate it further. He, McGowen and Whitehead would have no problem running twelve miles. Mariella on the other hand? Well, she could stay in the house and rest. He didn't know her physical capabilities and wasn't willing to risk the lives of his team on an unknown.

Creed dropped his head back between his shoulders and studied the plaster of the ceiling. The swirls did nothing to stop his physical reaction to the woman in the bed. Hell, thinking about the mission hadn't even stopped it. He was so fucked.

"Stop overthinking it and get some sleep." Her mumbled words broke through the verbal chastisement he was giving his suddenly overactive libido.

He reached for the small battery-operated light that Josefina had given them and switched it off. His boots and jeans landed in the corner near hers. He positioned himself, careful to keep his body curled over the corner of the thin mattress not touching the vast expanse of beautiful skin that lay behind him.

*You've slept in more awkward positions.* He closed his eyes. True. As a SEAL he'd slept standing up or more commonly sitting in the back of a deuce and a half as it trundled down pothole-strewn backroads while soaked in freezing mud or baked in the desert heat. This was a walk in the park. He could do this. Falling asleep was a trained skill. He started his routine, relaxing his muscles one by one, thinking of lying in a hammock in a dark room repeating 'don't think,' 'don't think' until the quiet overtook him. His eyes shot open the second Mariella moved. Her back now reclined against his and her hair fell in a silky cloud against the back of his neck. A cough down the hall registered along with snores coming from the room next to them. Mariella's body heat warmed his back in the darkness. He scooted away, clinging to the fraction of the mattress he'd allotted himself. Yeah, sleep...he closed his eyes again. He could do this. Maybe.

# CHAPTER 14

Mariella woke up and grimaced. Somehow during the night, she'd become tangled in the sheets. She couldn't move her legs, and she was hot. She lifted her head and looked down to the foot of the bed, but the darkness was complete, and she couldn't see anything. An arm around her waist pulled her from her foggy sleep in an instant. She blinked into the darkness. Creed, she was sleeping with him, and she was in Santa Lucia. She dropped her head and drew a breath. The pain medicine he'd given her had wiped away the dull headache that had been building since Adalberto had hit her. She'd tried to stay happy and animated today, but she knew her great aunt had seen underneath the pretense. Of course, Josefina assumed that Creed had caused the bruises and no matter what she said, the old woman had continued to think so.

Creed's breath moved the hair at her temple. He was a good man. Of this, she had no doubt. He had a staunch sense of duty to his country, and he had always been kind to her, even when he thought she'd set him up. In that Havana alley, he could have hurt her, but he didn't. He could have left her to her own demons yesterday afternoon when she found out about Rafa shoving her on him, but he didn't. He could have let Rafa deal with Adalberto, yet he was the one who took Adalberto down.

When she first met the man, she was willing to play a game with him. This, the marriage, wasn't a game to her. He was a good looking man. Very good looking, and he was compassionate. It was that tenderness that she fought to stay away from because it scared her worse than Adalberto's anger. That tenderness and compassion made Creed dangerous. Why that was she didn't know, but deep inside she realized that getting close to the man would lead to disaster.

She carefully laid her hand on his forearm. He twitched in his sleep. His breath stuttered for a moment before his breathing resumed a steady pattern. A protector. Creed was a protector. Whatever woman won this man's heart would be lucky. Unless he already had a woman. When she looked this morning, there was no tan-line or indention on his ring finger, not that that meant much. Wedding rings weren't always worn.

She traced her fingers over the hair on his fore-arm, barely caressing him. She couldn't deny her attraction. She didn't doubt he would be good in bed. He was athletic and kind. She could almost feel his gentle touch as he made love to her. She smiled into the dark. Perhaps he was a possessive and aggressive lover. She could picture the tension in his muscles and the intensity of his focus. Without a lover for over a year, her body reacted to her imagination. She squeezed her legs together and moved her hips slightly, trying to alleviate the need for friction. Creed tensed, pulled her back into his chest and then relaxed. Mariella held still although with every fiber of her being she wanted to slip her fingers down to her clit and provide her swollen sex with relief.

She squirmed a bit. With her hips pushed back into the man behind her, the pressure she could give herself was almost enough. Her sex throbbed with need. Her mind's sex tape featuring the man wrapped around her now looped on repeat. Her nipples peaked against her t-shirt. Mariella bit her lip and slowly ground one leg against the other, trying to trap her desire and grind against it. It had been so long, and she needed release so badly. She squeezed her legs tighter, and then rocked her hips. Creed's hips pushed back against her ass. She released a silent gasp. He moved his leg, draping it over hers. The added pressure demanded she move again. She clenched and rocked her hips, no longer able to disguise what she was doing. His body reacted, and she felt his cock thickening against her backside. She stifled a moan and ground back into him again. Fuck it, she was an adult and so was he, right? They could have sex. Creed's hand slid down to her hip, and he pushed her back against his cock. She bit her lip and gasped when his fingers brushed her sex.

His body rocked into her for several seconds and then he woke. He stiffened and pushed away. She heard the thud as he landed on the floor on his ass. Mariella rolled over and reached out for him. In the darkness, her hand connected with his cock.

He hissed and scrambled away from her, banging into the bags they'd cast into the corner. "Fuck!"

She fumbled for the battery-operated light. She flicked the button and blinked at the sudden brightness.

"Are you all right?" She crawled off the bed and over to him.

He pushed up and away, practically crab walking over the bags. "Fine. I'm fine." He scrubbed his face with his hands and blew out a long breath. He waved toward the bed. "If I did anything, fuck, I'm sorry." He looked everywhere but at her.

Mariella sat back on her heels. She could play it off, or she could admit her need. Her need won. "You didn't do anything I didn't want."

"What?" His head snapped around to fix his eyes on her.

"I liked it. I want more." She pulled her legs up in front of her and wrapped her arms around them.

"More?" He blinked at her as if she'd spoken in a foreign language.

Maybe she had? She nodded, and in English, she whispered, "I want sex. With you." There, she'd said it as clearly as she knew how.

He gulped, his Adam's apple moved along the strong column of his neck. "No. That can't happen. It isn't a good idea."

"Why?" She couldn't see a downside to it. "Don't you want me?" She glanced down at the very visible bulge in his briefs.

He snorted. "It's rather obvious I do."

"Then what is the problem?" She ran one of her fingers up his exposed leg, noting the texture of the hair there. It sprang back, tickling the palm of her hand. She reached the bottom of his briefs and her eyes tracked up his body to his face.

"We're working."

She cocked her head at him. Honorable, kind and by the quickly growing length under the snug cotton, just as needy as she was. She shrugged. "We aren't working now."

He shook his head and shifted his legs, removing his visible desire from her view. "Mixing business and sex is a recipe for disaster."

"What kind of a disaster do you think would happen?" She moved again, sitting up on her legs.

The move aligned her next to him, her thighs touching his hip.

"I don't know, and I don't want to find out. I'm here for a reason. I can't lose my focus." He moved next to the wall, as far as he could get from her.

"Yes, the mission. It is very important. I agree. You need to complete your mission, but…" She leaned forward, now on her hands and knees, and crowded him against the wall. "I'm your mission now, too. True?"

His head snapped toward her. "No. You're not."

"But I am." She leaned forward and placed a kiss on his shoulder. "You find the location." She spoke as she slid her lips along his collarbone. "You catch the men building the bombs." Her breath ghosted against his pulse at the base of his throat. "We rescue the ones the regime has." She licked up his neck to his jaw and nibbled on it. "Then you take me to America and divorce me. Until then, I am a part of your mission." She pulled away enough to see the desire in his eyes. "It is our wedding night, husband."

"We are not legally married, and sex was never part of the arrangement." He pushed off the bags as his arms wrapped around her. They stood on their knees, bodies pushed flush against each other. She could feel his strength and heat and trembled with her own need. "I would never presume…"

She laughed. No, this man was as opposite Adalberto as it was possible to be. He had honor. He would never act against a woman's desires. She understood why he'd backed as far away from her as he could.

She motioned between the two of them with her forefinger. "This, what happens between us, this is for *me*. This is what *I* need, what *I* want. I can't control much in my life, but this? I can and will control who I sleep with." Mariella slid her hands up his arms following the mounds of muscles to his shoulders and wrapped her arms around his neck. "Please, give me what I want." It wasn't a request.

"Are you sure?" His grip tightened on her as he asked.

Her hand slid between them and grabbed his substantial cock. "I'm sure."

She stroked him, and he bucked into her hand. He dropped his lips to hers, and she gasped at the explosion of desire the gentle kiss ignited. The chemistry between them had been strong, but the feel of his lips on hers, his tongue as it invaded her mouth and discovered every secret she held... it was almost magical. Desire pulsed through her like an explosive electric current. With one kiss he possessed her will. She felt him move her and clung to his neck as he lifted her onto the bed. His big body covered hers, and she opened her legs, letting him slip into place.

He kissed her bruises, tender and caring. She knew he would be. He grabbed her shirt, pulling it over her head. His eyes traveled over her body followed closely by his fingers, his lips, and tongue. She groaned when his mouth found her breast, and he feasted on her nipple. He lavished attention on one and switched to give attention to the other. He had no idea how much she needed to be loved. To be made to feel like she was beautiful and important. His worshipful touch and reverence acted as a soothing balm to her exposed and raw emotions. Was it wrong of her to use him to satisfy her needs? Maybe, but she deserved this. His fingers stayed at her nipples, tweaking and rolling them as he kissed lower down her abdomen. She opened her legs to make room for his broad shoulders after he'd removed her panties.

She gasped at the first flick of his tongue across her engorged clit. Her hands grasped his shoulders, and she bucked her hips up into his touch. "Please!" She was so close. She needed release.

"I've got you." He murmured the words against the inside of her thigh. The muscle there shook as he kissed her. The scrape of his whiskers against the sensitive skin amped up the indescribable urgency of her aching need. He wrapped his arms around her legs and used his fingers to spread her sex.

Mariella arched off the bed, her hands threaded through his short hair. Air heaved out of her lungs. Sweet mother of everything holy, her body clenched at the feel of his lips, teeth and oh, God, that suction.

She gasped and pleaded. Needed, oh god, she needed...

Her orgasm shattered through her, dropping her off a cliff she didn't remember climbing. She panted for air as he crawled up her body. His lips and tongue still working her oversensitive skin. He stopped at her breasts and worshiped them again. The heat that had detonated minutes ago banked and smoldered against the new fuel he provided. She wanted to feel him inside her. Wanted to have that connection with this man.

He shifted out of his briefs and t-shirt. His cock was hard and full. He moved and reached over her for his backpack. She watched as he sat up and ripped open a silver packet he'd pulled from the pack. He took out the condom while staring at her. His chest was flushed dark red.

"Now would be the time you tell me to stop." He rolled the condom over his impressive erection.

She ran a finger up his thigh and watched his cock dance in reaction to her touch. She shook her head, "No, now would be the time I tell you I want another orgasm just like the last one."

He smiled at her words and dropped to his elbows above her. "Bossy, aren't you?" He positioned her leg over his hip and made space for himself between her legs.

"Yes, I am. I like sex. Sex with you? I think I like it a lot."

"You think?" A smile played at his lips.

She shrugged. "I think I need another orgasm to know for sure."

"I can do that." He stared down at her as his body entered hers. His eyes closed, and the muscles of his neck strained. "God, so fucking good." The words came out of him on an exhaled breath after he'd seated himself deep within her. "So fucking perfect."

Mariella closed her eyes and pulled him down to her. She didn't want him to open his eyes and see the emotion or the tears in hers. No one had ever been so attentive to her needs before, and none of the men she'd been with had ever told her she was perfect. His nose bumped her cheek, and she turned her head to capture his lips. Their kiss lasted until they had to breathe.

His body moved, his hips thrust and rotated, lighting up her insides, sending trickles of wonderful sensations outward. Her arms tingled, and she trembled with a vibrating need she'd never felt before. There was nothing outside this sensation, this moment. No reason to exist except to let Creed push her through the hurricane of desire that raged inside her. The sensual assault demanded she submit to the lashing storm bands of ecstasy, and that is exactly what she did. His mouth covered hers and his lips captured her cry of euphoria. She gasped for air when he surged upward. He pulled her body onto his cock as he thrust forward.

His body tensed, hard and unyielding over her as he climaxed. Sweat trailed down his temple. His dark hair had become nearly black from the dampness it had collected. He swayed above her, catching his weight on his elbows. "Holy fuck."

He kissed her shoulder, and she shivered at the touch, and her nipples ached as the hair on his chest teased their tight peaks. She was exhausted, but her body was on board for more from this man.

"Was that a good holy fuck, or a bad holy fuck?" She ran her hand up his bicep to his shoulder.

He collapsed on top of her and laughed. "That was..." He rolled and pulled her toward him. "The best in one hell of a long time." He kissed her forehead.

That thought made her happy. She wasn't sure if she'd ever been anyone's best and rather liked the idea that she would be memorable for this American. Her eyes closed of their own accord. She felt him move and take care of the condom and heard the little battery-operated light's switch click off. She didn't have the energy to move and make any of his tasks easier for him.

He pulled her back, adjusting them so they were spooning and comfortable on the bed. "Please don't regret this in the morning."

His whisper floated to her ears, but again exhaustion prevented her from responding. Regret this? No, there would be no regrets in the morning.

# CHAPTER 15

"We should probably talk."

Creed lifted his eyes to her as he took a drink of his coffee. He'd been given a cup by one of the cousins and had found a quiet place under a palm tree. The rest of the house milled quietly about as it woke up after the celebratory party. McGowen and Whitehead were back and sleeping in the small screened in porch where they'd been given cots. He glanced around. There was no one around to listen, but... "Here?"

Mariella shrugged. "Nobody is up and out here yet." She sat down next to him and leaned back against the cement brick wall that fenced in the small yard. She glanced at him and opened her mouth as if she was going to speak but closed it again and shook her head.

"What?" He turned so he could see her a little

better. Her bruises had bloomed. The purples and reds bled across her smooth skin, but the swelling had started to recede.

She stared at a dent in the metal cup she held, her finger tracing the divot. Finally, she held him with a steady gaze. "I need you to not make this weird."

Creed stopped mid-sip and blinked at her. *Him* make it weird? *Seriously?* "Excuse me?"

He watched as she tipped her head back and settled it against the brick wall. She closed her eyes and spoke. "Yeah, I mean, it was just sex. I'm not asking you to marry me."

Surprised, he laughed so hard he almost spilled his coffee. Mariella's mischievousness let him know she'd meant to lighten the mood. "What? I'm not good enough for you?" He transferred his cup to his other hand and flicked away the coffee that had sloshed out.

She chuckled and took a sip of her drink. They sat for several minutes in a comfortable silence before she nudged him with her elbow. "Seriously, last night was good, but let's not complicate what is happening here with any idea what happened meant more than it did."

"First, last night was better than good." Creed raised his cup in a salute and was rewarded with a blush. "Second, I agree. The mission is paramount."

She let out an exaggerated breath and sighed,

"Thank God. I don't know what I'd do if you'd gotten all clingy and needy."

Creed threw back his head and laughed again. The woman was priceless. "I'll try to curb those tendencies."

She smiled and winked at him before she rose. "See that you do, Romeo. I'm going to clean up and then help with breakfast before I take you for a tour of Santa Lucia."

He watched her walk away and chuckled again as a wave of relief washed over him. This morning could have been awkward as fuck, by all rights should have been. The fact that she wanted to move on, keep the focus on the mission, and not make a big deal of what had transpired between them last night was fucking perfect. He frowned into his coffee...wasn't it?

"What's with the corrugated tin?" Whitehead asked as Mariella led them down the street toward the town center. She glanced over at the house he was talking about and then surveyed the neighborhood. "When the revolution happened, each Cuban citizen was allowed to keep the home and vehicle they owned. As families grow, there must be new rooms. Those are additions. The materials you see are scavenged or bought on the black market."

"You mean the entire family lives in one house? Like everyone?" He swung toward her.

She nodded. "Some younger people move into government provided apartments. If they have a family and outgrow the place the government assigns? It becomes difficult. We can't buy new homes. If a family wanted to move, they would have to find someone willing to swap houses with them. Selling the house makes it the property of the government. We swap our properties when we can find someone who is willing, although money almost always changes hands. The exchange of money isn't reported. There was new legislation proposed recently to allow the sale of homes, but no one knows how that will affect us. So, we wait and watch."

"The compound Rafa lives in? I saw new construction." McGowen spoke for the first time since they started their walking tour over an hour ago. Creed swept the roadway again looking for any potential threat. Mariella seemed comfortable and relaxed, but he didn't like being exposed.

"The government turns a blind eye to us because Rafa buys them off and because of his rank within the G2. He provides for all who work for him and their families in the compound. He gave me my rooms." She swung her gaze around the neighborhood. "He does what he can." She motioned to several men who lingered at the front step of one of the larger homes on the block. "I need to go talk with my cousins. Just a minute. I'll be right back."

Creed watched as she jogged across the street. He was pretty damn positive the men weren't her cousins, but he waited, primed and ready to react if he needed to move.

MARIELLA DIDN'T SAY a word before Rafa's man spoke, "Adalberto escaped. Rafa was injured, but he is all right." Her gut dropped at the news. Adalberto was free. Granted, he'd been hurt, and he'd need to heal, but once he was able, the man would be a formidable enemy. As she turned to leave, her contact stopped her. "Rafa and Paco will find him, but Rafa told me to warn you and your husband, and to tell you to stick to the plan."

Mariella nodded her understanding and dashed back across the street. She was ending the walking tour. Thank God Rafa's men had waited to show themselves until they'd returned to her aunt and uncle's neighborhood.

She jogged back across the street. "Come, it is time for a drive." She didn't look to see if the men were following her but moved forward quickly. Creed fell into step beside her, and the others followed.

"What happened?" Creed dropped an arm over

her shoulder and pulled her into his side as if he was her lover. She wanted to fold into his strength, but she wouldn't give in to that desire. Not again. Dealing with the morning after had been awkward enough. She played the night off, easy and light. Creed seemed relieved, and that reaction told her exactly what she needed to know. She could very easily let the attraction she felt for Creed turn into affection—or more. Okay, the affection had already started. She'd admit to that much, but his reactions and attitude this morning assured her he did not share her inclination.

He stopped, his arm bringing her around in front of him. "Are you okay? What did your cousin say that upset you?"

Mariella blinked and shook her head to clear her thoughts before she spoke quickly, telling him what Rafa's contact had told her.

He frowned at McGowen before he asked, "Does Adalberto have people in this territory? Would he know we've come here?" Creed walked with her to the car and waited for McGowen and Whitehead to get into the back seat.

He caught the keys as Mariella tossed them to him. She pointed down the street they were parked on. "That way. Make a right at the end of the street."

They got into the car, and she waited until they'd turned on the street she'd indicated before she answered his question. "I don't know if he will know where to look for us, but it is a small island. He'll need to lie low and lick his wounds. How many men will remain loyal to him and risk Rafa's wrath? I don't know." The constant backstabbing and conniving for position and promotion in the G2 made Rafa's current situation tenuous.

Adalberto had a small core of very dedicated people. How many would stand with him against Rafa? That was yet to be seen. Rafa was good to his people, but Adalberto was brutal and vindictive. Fear had a way of influencing people. How far Adalberto's influence traveled was something Rafa needed to determine.

"Has Rafa been challenged before?" McGowen's voice drifted from the back seat.

"Yes, many times, but never by someone inside the organization." She closed her eyes and captured her hair, stopping it from whipping her in the face. She gave directions until she saw the turn off she was looking for. "Here." Creed pulled the car into the small flat spot off the roadway. "Follow it back." There was a small meadow hidden by trees. She'd used this exact spot to transfer goods from one truck to another many times. "Pull back farther." She glanced back to ensure they couldn't be seen from the road. "The warehouse should be this direction." She pointed to the northeast.

The men unloaded from the car, and each shouldered a backpack. Creed locked the trunk and handed her the keys to her uncle's car before he let her lead the way toward the building they wanted to inspect. The heat was oppressive as no wind penetrated the sawgrass and palm strewn underbrush. Sweat trickled between her breasts, soaking her bra and shirt. She pulled her hair into a sloppy bun trying to alleviate the stifling heat. The quiet was punctuated by the sounds of boots scraping on outcroppings of rocks or the rasp of sawgrass catching on fabric. As she neared the building, Creed took the lead, sandwiching her between him and Whitehead. He set a grueling pace which they all followed.

The roof of a large, dilapidated building suddenly loomed over some stunted palms. She took a knee when Creed did and watched the men gear up. The backpacks were stashed behind a low hedge of sawgrass. Weapons were checked, and Whitehead took out several small kits, clipping them to his belt before he nodded to Creed indicating he was ready. Mariella started to stand, but Creed grabbed her arm. "Wait." His voice stilled everyone.

The low, distant sound of a motor flattened everyone to the ground. She watched as Creed crawled along the ground, maneuvering behind a trunk of a fallen palm. She could hear the vehicle but couldn't see it. Creed shifted slightly. He watched from his vantage point. The motor stopped. Voices could be heard as the occupants opened and then closed the vehicle doors. She heard something scrape... a door perhaps? Mariella glanced at McGowen. Both he and Creed were poised and ready to strike. She heard more sounds, conversation, and a laugh, before the motor started again, and the vehicle drove away.

Creed lowered and belly-crawled his way back to where they lay. "Four men armed with Russian made weapons carried in two large boxes. It took all four to lift each box and get it into the building. After the offload, only two guards exited while I was watching. I can't tell if there is power to the building or not. It is isolated. Something is going on here. I saw two other guards posted on that side of the building." He nodded toward the path they'd traveled. "Let's get out of here, regroup and make a plan of attack."

Mariella fell into position and followed Creed, moving low and slow until they were out of visual range of the building. They jogged out of the over-grown underbrush and headed for her uncle's car. The backpacks stowed, they hightailed it out of the area. Mariella guided Creed to a back road, and they found a place to park. McGowen passed out bottles of water, and they all chugged them, dehydrated from the heat-laced jog through the dense foliage.

"Okay, so what happens now?" Whitehead crunched the plastic bottle he had and capped it, handing it back to McGowen.

Creed turned in his seat, so he faced her. He

tapped his empty water bottle against the white leather bench seat. "How hard would it be to get word to your uncle and set up a rendezvous with him?"

"We could send a runner back to the compound or drive down. It is only a few hours away. Why?" Mariella wanted to know what was going on behind those blue eyes.

"This is my thought process. McGowen, chime in if you see a flaw in my plan. We need to sit on this place and monitor it. According to what Street told us, the location is right. It has vehicle access as we witnessed just now, and we know it is being used. Power is the only question and according to Whitehead, whoever is making the bombs definitely needs a power source."

Mariella glanced into the backseat and McGowen gave her a quick smile.

Creed tapped the plastic bottle again and nodded his head. "We will be able to figure that out tonight when it's dark. You and Whitehead will sit on that warehouse tonight. Mariella and I can monitor it during the day."

"What about her relatives? Won't they think that's wonky?" Whitehead's eyes flitted from Creed to McGowen.

"Not if we pack up and leave today under the pretense of going on to meet more relatives," Creed suggested.

"No. Not tonight. It would be suspicious for us to leave this late. The CDR would report the sudden departure as suspicious. If we tell them tonight we are leaving in the morning, it won't raise any questions, but leaving before eating a dinner they cook in our honor? That would be... rude." Mariella knew some of her relatives wouldn't understand. "There is no need to spark questions or rumors."

"Agreed." Creed thumped the bottle and stared over her shoulder, lost in thought.

Nobody spoke.

Mariella watched as the American stared off into space, his mind working hard as they all waited. He blinked and glanced back towards McGowen. "We need to run scenarios. If this is the place, we'll need backup and a timetable. Most likely you and Whitehead will be here while Mariella and I travel to wherever the prisoner transport is happening. Events will need to fall precisely as we plan. Otherwise, we jeopardize the potential for us to get out alive."

Whitehead closed his eyes and dropped his head back on the car seat. "I did not need to hear that."

"You need to hear the truth. Dealing in ignorance enhances room for error." Mariella whipped one of her uncle's canned responses out. Rafa had never sugarcoated any truth for her. Creed turned his gaze to her. "What? Am I wrong?"

Creed gave her a small smile. "No. You're absolutely correct." His praise warmed her from the inside. The happiness that bloomed because of Creed's acknowledgment was to be expected... wasn't it?

"Okay, then deal me the truth here, would ya? I need to hear these scenarios so I stop freaking the fuck out." Whitehead stared directly at Creed.

"Alright, let's start." Creed's knees pushed against hers, and he sent a quick glance her way. Mariella felt a blush rush to her cheeks and fought to concentrate on the plan Creed was laying out. She pushed her tingly emotions to the side when McGowen started asking questions. The complexity of the scenarios was intimidating, but McGowen and Creed spoke with authority and assurance. Three hours later, they'd laid out three viable strategies that each hinged on Rafa and his plans for getting the CIA agents transferred.

"Any questions or concerns?" Creed rolled his shoulders as he spoke.

"I think it would be best if we traveled back to Rafa to coordinate the transfer and figure out the timeline. If we know firsthand, we can narrow it down to one option and work that plan."

"Won't work. We need some major league support to monitor the building during the day." Whitehead spoke before anyone else.

"No, not necessarily."

Her head snapped in Creed's direction when he corrected Whitehead.

He continued, "If we can get a couple of Mariella's or Rafa's men up here, McGowen can watch nights. You'll monitor the building during the day. He'll be here so you can wake him if you have questions. Right now, we are gathering intel, but we'll have to breach that building, eventually." He glanced at McGowen. "McGowen will show you what to look for. If you see something that isn't right or you think they are packing up, you wake him up."

McGowen nodded. "It could work. I could sleep close to where they are watching, and it would enable you to firm up our plan. I'd like to have only one scenario to concentrate on." He leaned back and stretched his arm along the back of the seat. "Whitehead and I can handle the surveillance from this end. You take Mariella to help you spring the CIA agents. We both get support from her team or Rafa's. I don't see a downside."

"The downside is you won't have support until we make it to Rafa's compound, hammer out the details and get Rafa's men back up here."

"It isn't my first mission, Skipper. I can go a night without sleep." McGowen smiled and pointed at Whitehead. "He can watch the building while I doze if there is a delay. He won't admit it, but he's digging this double-oh-seven shit."

Mariella swung her head just in time to see Whitehead flip off McGowen as he looked at Creed.

"No spontaneous death by terrorists or bullets, that was our deal, remember?"

Creed laughed and turned to start the car. McGowen held out his knuckles toward Whitehead. "We got you covered, my man."

Mariella watched as Whitehead bumped McGowen's outstretched hand. They both reached forward extending their fists to her. She laughed and bumped fists with them. The friendship and comradery between the men was something new to her. Oh, she'd seen it between the men on her team, but for them to include her? It would never happen. She was a woman and Rafa's niece. The Americans didn't seem to care about either.

She leaned back in the car and stuck her arm out the window realizing that for the first time in years, she was happy. As that thought resonated, she lost her smile. Happiness had always been an elusive goal for her. She thought she'd obtain it when she led her own crew. And she was happy with herself–for a while. Rising to be Rafa's number three took determination and hard work. She should be happy and content with her position, yet she wasn't because she knew it was only because she was Rafa's niece she was afforded much of the respect she'd been given.

Granted, she viewed the fact Rafa trusted her enough to send her to meet the Americans as an accomplishment, but she wasn't necessarily happy to be doing his bidding. Yet here she was, traveling with three American agents, hunting people who were making horrible bombs, talking about exit strategies and associated risks and *this* was where she found happiness.

She examined Creed covertly. The man excited her, physically and mentally. His vision for the operations, quick wit and intelligence titillated a part of her no man had ever excited. Oh, she could talk to Rafa, and sometimes he gave her glimpses into what he was doing or planning, but these men included her as if she was an equal.

She found herself glancing at Creed again and again. The afternoon sun accentuated the light touch of grey at his temples. Physically, he was a magnificent man. The sex they had last night had set a new standard for her. Never had a lover taken the time to pleasure her before he found his own release. Of course, she'd never been into foreplay and kissing. It was too personal, but with Creed? The way he made her body sing was... well it was wonderful and exciting and... dangerous. Yes, danger was written all over her feelings for Creed Lachlan. They were written in large bold print, and still she walked past the warnings her mind flashed at her, all caution signs systematically ignored.

She wanted more of the man. More of his touches, more of his kind words, and more of his approval. Closing her eyes, she leaned back and let her head drop to the headrest. Deep inside, she knew the desire for more would end in heartache. The man had been forced to marry her, and even though he didn't believe the marriage was real, she couldn't help but believe that in God's eyes it was. Stupid? Maybe. The legalese of Church politics was beyond her. She chuckled to herself. *So, the man was forced to marry me, and then I demanded he make love to me last night.* Yeah, she could just imagine his report to his superiors. Or would he even mention it to them? Who knew? What she did know was he was doing everything in his power to complete his mission and comply with Rafa's demands.

That took character. A rare trait, yet all three of these men seemed to possess it. Even Whitehead. Mariella could tell he was out of his element, but he still pushed forward. Creed didn't get upset at the questions he or Mariella asked when they needed clarification. Both Creed and McGowen had this gentle giant thing going on. Creed was a wound tight and almost ready to explode version, but she could see this man as the protector he was. Dominant and a natural leader, yes, and... dangerous. To her at least. She rolled her head and looked at Creed. The wind whipped through the window of the vehicle blowing his short hair and making the t-shirt he wore wave against his hard muscles. He was beautiful. She'd guard her feelings, or she'd become enamored. In the back of her mind another sign blinked, "too late." She ignored that as she'd done all the others.

# CHAPTER 16

*C*reed shut the small bedroom door behind him. Mariella's family had turned out in force again tonight. The food and conversation lasted until well after dark as the news of their imminent departure seemed to energize the evening's festivities.

He glanced at the small bed and then at Mariella who stood in the middle of the room. He chuckled and rubbed a hand at the back of his neck. "I'm in uncharted territory here." He had no idea what the protocol should be or what she expected.

Mariella glanced at the bed and shrugged. "So am I." She sat down on the bed and started to unlace her shitkickers. "What do you want to do?"

Creed sat down next to her and untied his own boots. "What do I want to do, or what do I think we should do? Because they are two very different things."

Mariella toed off her boots and stuffed her socks into the top of each. She leaned forward with her elbows on her knees, her hands folded together. Her hair fell forward concealing her face as she spoke, "What do you think we *should* do?"

"Turn off the light, lie down and go to sleep. I'll sleep on the floor. You take the bed." It was the absolute correct answer. They needed to keep the focus on the mission.

She nodded, her hair brushing his arms with the movement. She turned her head to look at him and fuck him if he didn't see desire in her eyes. "What do you *want* to do?"

Creed reached out and pushed her hair over her shoulder and then cupped her cheek, his thumb carefully trailing over her bruises. "What I want to do is to push you back onto this bed and spend the night lost inside you." There was a hunger deep in his gut. It gnawed at him with sharp teeth. It was a feeling he couldn't ignore.

That was the truth. He wanted more of her. The taste he'd been given last night whetted his appetite, and the craving lingered just under his skin, alive and consuming him little by little.

He watched her tongue dart out to wet her lips. This time he could tell the act was born from nerves, not from seduction, the way she'd tempted him at the seawall a few nights ago. She dropped her focus to her hands again. "And which will you choose?"

Creed trailed his finger down her arm. She shivered under his touch. "What we do isn't my choice. You are the one with the power here." He'd be damned if he would make this decision for them. Did he want her? Fuck yes, he'd admitted as much, but he would never pressure or presume. It wasn't the way he was raised or the type of man he wanted to be.

She nodded and continued to stare at her hands. "I want more of you." The simple words sent a jolt through him, but they weren't enough. She flicked a quick glance his way. "I need boundaries, so this doesn't become... an issue. This is temporary. When this mission is over, so is this thing between us. Right?"

Creed's gut clenched, and he had no idea why. Those *boundaries* protected both of them. Boundaries front loaded the expectations and limits instead of forcing Mariella or him to deal with any awkward expectations later.

"Agreed." Her head dropped just a little. Maybe in relief? Did she think he wouldn't agree? Hell, it was a perfect scenario. Absolutely fucking perfect... wasn't it? So where did that niggle of dissatisfaction come from? He watched her intently. She gave him a sideways glance and a half-hearted smile before she stood to take off her shirt.

The soft, perfect skin over her stomach and ribs

caught his attention. He dropped to his knees in front of her and placed a kiss on that expanse of exposed flesh. Her muscles jumped under his touch. Her hands landed on his shoulders and traveled down his back. He slid his hands up her back to the clasp of her bra. The second he flicked it open, her hands left him, and the damn thing disappeared. For that, he was eternally grateful because he wanted all of her body available to his taste and touch. He licked the underside of her breast, and she moaned. Fucking moaned. God, when had a woman ever been so responsive to his touch?

He slid his hands to the button of her jeans and moved the fastener out of its anchor as his tongue laved the underside of her breasts. She stepped out of her jeans when he pushed them down her legs. Her hands pulled at his t-shirt, and he leaned back far enough to drag it up and off and fling it into the corner.

"Your jeans," she said before she stepped back from him. He stood, stripped and had her back in his arms in seconds. Their lips met as he ran his hands down her long spine and cupped her round ass. Her soft, warm skin against him fueled the smoldering fire that had been burning for her all fucking day. He delved into her mouth as their tongues dueled in a sexy dance of give and take.

She slid her hands up his arms and pushed away. He chased her lips, bringing a laugh from her. "Wait, there is something I want to do." She pushed him and laughed when he didn't move. "Sit." She pointed to the bed.

He wasn't very interested in sitting. Actually, he had vertical images in his mind and pretty definite ways of getting there already planned out.

"Sit down." She extended her index finger and shoved him with it.

Her eyes flashed at him, and dammit if he didn't plop his ass on the bed.

She lowered to her knees in front of him. "You're too tall to do this with you standing." She reached for his cock, and his eyeballs spun in his head like a fucking slot machine. Her small hand barely circled his girth, but the feel of her stroking his shaft broke a sweat out on his forehead. He dropped back to his elbows and watched as she moved her hand.

A drop of pre-cum glistened at his slit.

She glanced from his cock to him and smiled. "My turn."

Slowly she lowered toward the head of his cock. She didn't drop her gaze, and his eyes bounced from her to his cock. Another drop of clear liquid pushed out, sending the first on a slow trail down the side of his shaft. Mariella smiled and stuck out her tongue. The warmth of her breath hit him seconds before the soft velvet of her tongue swiped the drop's path. She swirled her tongue around the head of his cock, and his hips kicked forward. Coherent thought quickly vacated the premises, leaving only the blissful sensations of her touch.

She smiled and lifted her eyes to his as she opened her mouth and went down on him. He closed his eyes and let his head drop back between his shoulders. Her hand worked the lower part of his shaft as she took his cock further into her mouth. She gagged slightly and pulled off, only to drop down again. This time the head of his cock hit the back of her throat. *Fucking hell!* She nudged forward, and his cockhead entered her throat. He leaned onto one elbow and reached out to grasp her hair. Not to direct her, because holy fuck, she needed absolutely no direction, but to ground him to her... to this moment. His eyes popped open when she took him in her throat and swallowed.

His hand curled in her hair when she rose, preventing her from going down again. She opened her eyes and gazed at him. "You are fucking amazing, but if we continue like this, the night will be over far too soon."

She rose and crawled over the top of him. "Well, here's to a long, long night."

Creed maneuvered them so he was lying on the bed with her straddled on top, which was a fuck-ton harder done than said, especially since neither one of them wanted to break the kiss they shared.

He reached out and found his backpack. His left hand

dug vigorously in the front pouch. She growled against his mouth and broke away, pouncing on his backpack and dragging it toward them. She pulled open the pouch, grabbed a condom and ripped the pack open with her teeth. Without a word she straightened and scooted back. A mischievous smile split her face. She winked at him, put the condom in her mouth and...

*ohmyfuckinggodwhatinthehellisshedoing?*

Her hot mouth encased him. She worked down his cock before she lifted away and smiled.

"With your mouth?" Yeah, so what if his voice sounded like he hadn't hit puberty yet. How in the hell had she put the condom on with just her mouth? Her hand pushed the condom down further. His mind was completely fucking blown with that maneuver. "Where the hell did you learn to do that?"

She laughed and arched her body low to skim over his stomach and chest as she moved up him. "Do you really want to know?" She kissed him, and he could taste the latex that lingered on her tongue.

She moved away, the playfulness in her expression told him he probably wouldn't get a straight answer anyway.

He shook his head and murmured, "No, not at all." He grabbed a handful of hair and brought her lips down to his again.

She shifted and reached between her legs, grabbing his cock. He kept their lips together as she pressed down over the head of his cock. Her tight heat surrounded him, and they both gasped. They shared a breath as she slowly sank down on him.

"So fucking good." His words were a mere whisper, and he wasn't sure he'd actually said them.

"So fucking good." She agreed before she braced both hands on his pecs and sat up. The motion sank him deep inside her. She ground down on his cock sending a shit-ton of sensations racing through his body. She elevated and looked down at him when she lowered onto him. Her hips moved as she did and *oh, my fucking hell*, that little twist of movement slammed into him. He wasn't going to last. The woman was a treasure trove of sexual torture. He grabbed her hips and hefted up into her.

That got her attention. He moved his hands from her hips to her breasts, cupping both. "Lean over." His hands supported her as her weight came toward him. He trapped her nipples in between his thumbs and index finger and rolled them as he thrust his hips and slammed into her.

Mariella gasped. Her hands grabbed his forearms, and she dropped her head, sending her hair in a fall around both of them. The moment held in the air as they stared at each other. Her beautiful chocolate brown eyes mesmerized him. They moved together, working toward their climax. He lowered his arms, and she relaxed into his support until they could kiss.

His fingers still rolled the hard pebbles of her nipples, and his hips moved in a slow, purposeful rhythm.

"Please."

He'd been waiting for Mariella's plea. He flipped them and grabbed her leg, bringing it up over his hip. He thrust into her, grinding when he bottomed out, bringing friction against her swollen clit. She clutched at his back, her fingernails making indentions in his skin. It felt fucking fantastic. All of it. The heat in the room rivaled any tropical sun and the tension as they fought to find a climax, together, was a physical thing. It stretched tight between them, pulling them closer to each other, closer to being... whole. Creed closed his eyes, unwilling to admit the sexual tension between them was morphing into something else. At least for him.

Mariella's body tensed, tightened as her back arched off the bed, melding into him. He captured her mouth as a silent scream pushed from her. He felt her climax. The fluttering pulse around him broke his reserve. He couldn't help himself. He pounded into her, chasing his release. Five hard thrusts later, he split in half, shattering as lightning raced upward from the base of his spine. He dropped to his side and pulled her with him so he didn't slip out of her. *Not yet. No, not yet.*

Their breathing was totally erratic and quite loud. "Damn."

At her low roll of laughter, his eyes snapped open.

"I thought last night was a fluke." She glanced at him and winked. "It wasn't."

Creed chuckled and wiped a trickle of sweat from the side of his face. "We are quite combustible." He dealt with the condom quickly and resumed his position.

"Combustible... that's a good word," Mariella said and smiled as she closed her eyes. "I like combustible."

Creed did too. He watched her as her body relaxed, and she fell into a slumber. They were combustible, but beyond that, they were... compatible, complementary. No, it was more than that. They were damn near perfect together. He stared at the darkness and shook his head. Not that anything happening now mattered. *Dammit.*

## CHAPTER 17

Mariella checked her sidearm before Creed pulled into the drive that led to the compound. She had no idea what to expect since Adalberto was so embedded in her uncle's organization. Creed slowed the car near the checkpoint. Her gun was leveled and ready to shoot as was Creed's. She recognized the men but didn't lower her weapon. A man stepped forward, his rifle hanging off his back and his holster clipped shut. Creed's attention was on the other side of the road.

She knew the man who stepped out in front of them. He did a double take and smiled. "Mariella. Does Rafa know you are coming? He didn't alert us."

"No, I didn't tell him we were coming back."

The man glanced over his shoulder and lowered his voice. "You heard about Adalberto?"

She nodded and sent a surreptitious glance past the man in front of her. "Adalberto's man?"

"Was. Just be cautious." The man glanced at Creed. His eyebrows raised at the cannon the Creed carried. She'd little doubt Adalberto's man would be dead before he could lift his weapon in her direction.

"When have I ever been anything but cautious?" She smiled and winked at the guard.

He chuckled and backed away from the car. "You are your uncle's niece."

He lifted a hand, and the other guard moved out of the car's path. "Watch him." Creed cautioned as he drove past. Mariella turned to keep her attention on Adalberto's man as they entered the compound. He didn't move, just watched as they proceeded.

"You're worried about him?" She asked when they turned the corner in the long drive blocking the vehicle from the guard's view.

"I'm worried about you," Creed replied as they pulled into the compound. Normally that type of comment would piss her off. Nobody needed to worry about her. She was able to watch out for herself, but the possessive tone in Creed's voice injected a sense of warmth and familiarity, which made her insides flutter just a bit. She'd admit Creed worrying about her made her feel safe and wanted.

She had about six seconds to internalize that feeling before her uncle was beside the car. "What happened?" His hand was on his pistol.

"Nothing we need to discuss out here." Creed opened the door and dropped his cannon back into its holster.

Mariella blanched at the cut across Rafa's left cheek. It was deep and held together by butterfly bandages. "Are you all right?"

Rafa backed away from her hand as she reached out to touch him. "A scratch. It is nothing." He motioned for them to move into the house. "Why are you here?"

"We believe we may have found the location, but we need assistance." Mariella dropped into a chair in the front room as Rafa sat on the sofa. He reached for a cigarette as Creed took up a position standing behind her.

Rafa glanced up at Creed. "What do you need?"

"Support and coordination." He put a hand on Mariella's shoulder. "How long will it take to arrange the transfer of the CIA agents?"

Rafa leaned forward and lit his cigarette. The entire time, his eyes never left Creed's hand. He drew a deep lungful of smoke and shrugged. "It won't be easy or fast. The timing would be difficult to know."

Creed removed his hand and crossed his arms over his chest. He rocked from the balls of his feet to his heels as he thought. "Where would you get them transferred to?"

"Why?" Rafa asked.

Creed arched an eyebrow. "I'm forming an exit strategy. If we take out the manufacturing location before the transferred prisoners are enroute to us, or even before they get to our location, it could alert the government. If this is actually the facility we are looking for, our intent, for now, is to monitor the warehouse unless we can determine a bomb is ready to be sent out."

Mariella listened to his rapid-fire layout of almost everything the team had discussed yesterday.

Rafa grunted in response before his eyes met Creed's. "You don't think it is?"

"The box I saw them take into the warehouse was a sealed unit. Heavy. It took four men to carry it, and they barely managed. It could have been lined with lead."

"Which would shield them against the radioactive material." Rafa acknowledged.

Creed nodded. "But we can't be certain. I need my men to monitor the facility while Mariella and I continue to search the rest of the locations your people have identified. To that end, my men need support to monitor the facility 24/7. Two or three trusted people who won't ask questions."

"That can be arranged." Rafa carefully scratched alongside the healing wound on his face. "I have identified five more locations within the interior and one along the coast to the north. I'd start with that one. While it is near the coast, the warehouse is sectioned off with razor wire. There is power, and only recently there are guards."

"You have the locations so we can take a look at the map?" Mariella spoke for the first time.

Rafa nodded his head distractedly. "How will you let me know when to coordinate the move?"

"Coordinate the transfer now." Creed glanced at Mariella who was intently watching her uncle. "When we have the details of the transfer, we can agree on the rally point. What I would suggest is that you, Amelia, and Street meet in a location near the transfer point."

"No. Adalberto is too much of a threat. He wants me dead, and I know he has eyes inside this compound. I will keep his attention on me. When I know the exact time of the transfer, after I get the information to you, I will make my move. If I don't make it, you will take Amelia to America with you." His words were addressed to Mariella.

She bounced out of her chair in an instant. "What? No, you were supposed to retire to Europe."

"And I will, but I will not leave until I have taken care of this business with Adalberto." Rafa drew another long pull off his cigarette as he watched her.

"He will go to the government if he catches wind you are working with the Americans. They won't let you step foot off this island."

"They will try to stop me, but, with the right distraction, I can slip away." Rafa shrugged and blew out the smoke. He watched the plume dissipate. He turned his attention to Creed, dismissing the worry that ran through her veins and pounded at her heart. "Should I dispatch Adalberto before the transfer, how will you get us off the island?"

"Guantanamo," Creed responded immediately.

"Then we will tell my contacts the Americans need to be moved to the interrogation center near La Maya. It is the closest facility to the American naval base." Rafa flicked his ashes into his ever-present ashtray and pointed to Creed. "They will let us on base?"

"Yes, but I'm going to need a few more burner cell phones. I know your government has invested heavily in monitoring devices, but if we move around and use burners far away from where we believe our business will happen, it could work to our benefit. Even if your government intercepts the call, stopping the transfer or mobilizing any response force should come too late." Creed rolled his shoulders and sighed, "Unless whoever compromised the agents is involved with the transfer."

Rafa stared at the end of his cigarette. "We would be wise to account for this possibility. I will stay in the local area. There is a villa in Playa Cazonal owned by a high-ranking government official. He owes me many, many favors. I am going to ask him to allow my niece and her new husband to honeymoon there. I'll make the request after we have narrowed down the dates and the transport details are firmed up. That should give you time to examine the other sites, coordinate with your men and get everything ready for the final run."

"How far is the villa from the detention facility and from the site in Santa Lucia?"

Mariella could almost see Creed's mind turning and building scenarios.

Rafa blew out a puff of cigarette smoke and gazed at Mariella. "Maybe a half-hour's drive from the villa. Santa Lucia is hours away."

"How far is the detention facility from Guantanamo?" Creed finally uncrossed his arms as he waited for Rafa's answer.

"Depends. With an armed escort, not long. If you are trying to fly under the radar? Much longer." Rafa smashed out his cigarette and picked up a new one, leaning forward to grab his lighter. "I suggest an armed escort."

"Straight to the base. Run over anyone in our way?" Mariella chuckled. "You've wanted to do that for years."

Rafa let out a bark of laughter. "Exactly."

Creed moved over and sat in the chair beside Mariella. "Do you have maps?"

Rafa lit his cigarette and nodded as he inhaled. "Hand drawn. The maps the government produces are, shall we say... optimistic."

Mariella laughed at that and agreed, "Yes, we have

a wonderful road system... on paper. The conditions of some of the roads make areas unpassable. It is our business to know the dirt roads and ways around obstacles that are not documented on maps."

"We need to check those roads when we travel to Playa Cazonal." Creed glanced at Mariella when he spoke.

"Not a problem." It wasn't like they had many options or much time for making sure they had a perfect layout of the land. The maps were kept up to date out of necessity. "What if your men need to move before the transport happens?"

Creed leaned forward on his knees and drew a deep breath. His brow furrowed as he thought for a moment. "McGowen knows finding that manufacturing site is the priority. He'll take it down as quietly as possible and get out." He glanced at Mariella. "He knows his exit strategy if that occurs, and it isn't the same as ours."

"What is his exit strategy?" Rafa's attention snapped toward Mariella.

She blinked at her uncle's question and then glanced at Creed before she swung her gaze back to her uncle. She shook her head and extended her hands. "Why are you asking me? I don't know." Although she did. She knew everything there was to know about how McGowen and Whitehead were going to get off the island and the precautions they were going to take with the radioactive material if they recovered any and how they would get any possible informants out to a boat. The plan was intricate and dangerous, for the informants, but the men had a solid way out.

Rafa narrowed his gaze before he flicked his eyes to Creed. "Are my men going to be in danger?"

Creed's lips pressed into a thin line before he spoke. "There are an unknown number of guards with Russian made weapons. Yes, it is dangerous. No, my men will not intentionally put your men into harm's way, but there is always a risk."

Rafa tapped his ash into his hand. He considered the grey material in his hand before he spoke. "Then single men only. I'll let Paco know. The married men will stay with me, here in the compound. They have a vested interest to keep Adalberto and his people away. Their families live here." He reached over and dropped the ashes into the ashtray. "Street, your man is... not right. The blow to the head did something. He is always dizzy and nauseous. He is off balance. I have put a man with him as he is too big for Amelia to hold up. Amelia will continue to keep him comfortable."

"Concussion?" One of her men had suffered a fall from the back of a truck. His head bounced off the gravel road. He was never the same.

"Probably. Our doctor could not say without tests. For now, he is to be kept quiet and move as little as possible. The trip to Playa Cazonal will be hard on him, but..." Rafa raised his shoulders to signify it was unavoidable.

"All right. We need to look over this map." Creed stared at Rafa as he spoke.

"I agree. Mariella, we need lunch and drinks." Rafa dismissed her.

"No." Creed held out a hand, stilling her from rising... as if she was going to. Rafa's dismissal wasn't anything new, but this time it seemed... intentional. "She needs to be part of this. If something happens to me, she'll be in charge."

Had it been for any other reason, the surprised look on her uncle's face would have been comical. But it wasn't funny, especially when his brow furrowed, and he asked, "Her?"

"Yes, her. Why the hell wouldn't she be the one? She is smart and intuitive. Street is down and won't be able to run the operation. My men have their orders, they know what to do. If you aren't there until the last minute, which is what I am assuming your plan is, you won't be up to date on the issues that we've discovered and worked through, so yes, Mariella is the logical choice should I be taken out of the scenario."

Rafa leaned back into the cushions of the couch and stared at Creed. To say she was honored by Creed's words would be an understatement. Never had anyone shown such confidence in her. Rafa had tried. She would acknowledge that fact, but Creed accepted her as competent and capable. Her uncle measured her by a different standard.

"It is your operation." Rafa conceded with a shrug.

"One that you both have a vested interest in seeing successfully completed." Creed nodded toward the kitchen. "Why don't we go get something to eat and talk through our next steps?"

Mariella stifled a laugh when her uncle's eyes popped open. Other than getting himself a cup of coffee in the morning, her uncle didn't go into the kitchen. Creed stood and waited. Her uncle threw a frown at her and she laughed.

"Rafa isn't good in the kitchen. I'll make us some lunch while we all discuss what to do next. If I make it, it will be edible." She stood and made her way into the kitchen.

Creed followed her and helped her gather the items she'd need for sandwiches. She worked and listened as he spoke with Rafa. Her inclusion in the planning process was normally her uncle telling her how things would happen. In the field, she had proven she was smart and could adapt to anything thrown her way. It was the reason she'd become Rafa's third. But she realized she'd never be considered an equal, by him or anyone in the organization. She glanced at Creed, who was following her movements as she worked. He spoke to Rafa without stopping his perusal, and she felt the heat of a blush bloom on her cheeks. She smiled at him and dropped her eyes back to the task at hand. She couldn't help wondering what it would be like to be this man's woman. To be respected and valued for more than cleaning house and cooking food. She dropped a sandwich onto a plate and chastised herself for fairy tale thoughts. What she was to Creed was a requirement of the mission. They'd defined the relationship. It was temporary. Done when the mission was over. She sliced the sandwich with a bit too much enthusiasm and handed it to her uncle. He raised his eyebrows before a knowing smirk spread across his lips. *Damn Creed for making her want more.*

# CHAPTER 18

Creed pulled out of the compound with his automatic in his grip. He didn't trust that bastard, Adalberto. Taking a snipe at Mariella seemed well within the man's wheelhouse.

"Why did you tell your uncle you didn't know our exit strategies?" The question had been at the tip of his tongue since she lied to her uncle.

She turned in her seat and regarded him for a while before she spoke, "Because that information does not belong to him. You trusted me, asked for my input, and used the information I gave you to make your decisions. Rafa is an information broker. It is how he manipulates people and gains access. There is no need to manipulate you or your people. The end game is the same for all of us. Find the manufacturing point, get any information and materials out, safely and quietly, and rescue the team that has been apprehended."

He turned onto the main road and slid his weapon's selector lever to safe before he holstered it. "You failed to mention getting you, Rafa and Amelia off the island."

"That doesn't come into play unless we find the location of the dirty bombs and recover the missing Americans. Rafa told me the agreement."

"Did he tell you about the million Euros he would be getting, too?" Creed assumed he hadn't by the momentary shock in her eyes. Fuck that. He wasn't going to let her uncle take all the money and run. He had no idea how to make the man... well *man up* and take care of his family. Hell, who was he kidding? Rafa could be making plans to set Mariella up in the States, but his gut told him Rafa was dumping her on the government and walking away. "Your uncle is a piece of work."

"My uncle took me in after my parents died. He didn't have to do it. He raised me the best way he knew how. He is a good man in his own way." She turned and looked out the window.

He'd agree to disagree. Rafa was infamous, and even after Mariella had proven herself to him, he still didn't recognize the raw talent and intellect Creed had clearly witnessed. Was she infuriating? Yes. Did she push his buttons? Oh, hell yes. But if he could build a team, she'd be on it and not because she warmed his bed at night. She was an asset, plain and simple. Would she encounter a steep learning curve? Fuck yes, but he didn't doubt for a second she'd be able to conform and adapt.

"The tarps and blankets you wanted me to put in the trunk? They are because you don't want to sleep at the casas particulares?" Mariella's comments snapped him back to the car and out of his own head.

Casas particulares were rooms that private citizens rented out to travelers. Creed didn't want to take the route Rafa offered because the fewer eyes on them the better. "No, even though the rooms offered in the small towns would suffice, we don't need to run into anyone who might question us. It is a precaution."

"It is smart. What is a precaution is the insect repellent I put in with the tarps and blankets."

Creed laughed when she gave a full body shudder. "I also have repellent in my pack, so we are well protected."

"Why did you want to leave now instead of later?" She leaned back in the seat and turned to face him as she spoke.

"Why would you think that I would?" He threw the question back at her. She narrowed her eyes at him, so he added, "I'm curious to know if you'd figured out my rationale."

She tapped her hand on her jeans for a moment before she propped her arm over the open window ledge of the passenger's side door. Her hair whipped wildly around her face as she looked at him. "You've got something planned that you didn't tell Rafa."

"That's right." Creed agreed.

"Because you have an extra burner phone now."

Creed shook his head. "I have three extra burner phones now." Not counting the two in his pack that he'd brought with him from the States.

Mariella's eyebrows shot up, and she gave him a wide smile. "You stole two phones from Rafa?"

"He had five of them." Creed wasn't going to apologize.

Even with the best networks in the States, tracing a call took time. Here? If he kept the call under two minutes and then dislodged the battery and sim card while chucking that motherfucker as far as he could? The government wouldn't be able to trace a fucking thing. Could they record the call? Sure, but there was nothing he was going to say that they would be able to understand. If he'd known the infrastructure in the interior of Cuba was as old and antiquated as it was, he'd have brought more burners of his own. Hell, he was going to give Branson some shit about that. The man's organization could tell him the location of a birthmark on any of his men, but they couldn't decipher the interior of a country ninety minutes away. His team could not be the first team to enter Cuba. Branson had a shit-ton of work to do in the coordination part of his division because that information would have been good to have.

"He'll be pissed."

Creed rolled his eyes. "Like I give a shit? Besides, he'll be well compensated."

She grabbed her hair and held most of it to keep it from flying into her face. "People don't piss off Rafa. They tend to... go away if they do."

"Like Adalberto?"

She pursed her lips and nodded. "He almost ruined the plan Rafa was working. For that, he'll be hunted down."

"What?" The word was out of his mouth before he could stop it.

"What, what?" Her brow scrunched up, and she regarded him like he was a crazy man.

"Adalberto needs to have his ass handed to him for hitting you, not for fucking up Rafa's op."

She laughed and shook her head. "You already did that. Rafa didn't punish him for hitting me. He wanted Adalberto to learn his place, and his place wasn't to question anything Rafa directed. He told me before we left for Santa Lucia that I was stupid for provoking Adalberto's wrath, and he was right. I deserved what I got."

"You're fucking kidding me, right?" Creed jerked the steering wheel to the right, pulled over to the side of the road, and twisted in his seat.

"Why are you stopping?" Mariella glanced up and down the roadway.

"Because right now my mind is trying to wrap itself around the idea you think you deserved to get hit." There was no reality where hitting her was condonable.

"I got hit because I poked a rabid dog. I knew what I was doing. The asshole is predictable."

"Hey, look at me." She glanced his way, her eyes defiant and filled with challenge. One he wouldn't take. "You know I'm not okay with that, right?"

She spun in the seat and almost snarled at him. "You're not okay with me defusing the situation before guns came into play? Good to know. You and Rafa make one hell of a team." She crossed her arms over her chest and snapped her head around to look out the window. "We need to fucking leave before someone stops to see what the problem is."

He threw his arms up and looked around. "Who, Mariella? Who is going to stop? There isn't a car on this fucking road except us. And if they stop, fine, let them stop. For your information, I wasn't talking about you defusing the situation. I am perfectly fine with that and thank you. What *I'm not* okay with is you getting hit by that bastard or any bastard—ever." Okay, that might have come out a little more heated than he'd planned, but the idea she thought she deserved to be hit or lumped him in with the likes of Rafa and Adalberto just fucking lit his fuse.

Creed stepped on the clutch, put the car into gear and attempted to calm the fuck down. "Do me a favor? Stop jumping to conclusions. I *am not* like your uncle or Adalberto!" Yeah...that didn't come out so calm. *Way to state your case, Lachlan.* He checked to make sure the roadway was clear before he let off the clutch and eased back onto the road, even though he wanted to jam his foot against the accelerator and launch the old car. The silence as they traveled was deafening. He knew where he was going and didn't need any directions, and obviously, Mariella wasn't in the mood to talk. Creed drove to the top of the small range of hills he'd seen on the way back to the compound. He maneuvered the car to a narrow pasture adjacent to the road, parked, and got out.

Palming one of the two phones he had on him, he powered it up and waited for it to acquire a signal. The second it did, he dialed the number he'd memorized. Mariella sat quietly beside him, looking out the window. Was he wrong for correcting her and standing up for himself? Nope, not even a little. Was he going to apologize for it? Not likely. He wasn't like those assholes, and yes, he put Rafa fully into the asshole category.

"Go." Branson's voice was crystal clear.

"We have a tentative location on the primary mission. Secondary assets have also been located." The words were chosen carefully to let Branson know they'd *believed* they could have found the location where the dirty bombs are being made, and they'd located the CIA agents.

"Duration?"

Branson wanted to know a timetable. That was tough, but Creed could give them a ballpark. "Working the timetable for assets. Location is more fluid."

"Departure as discussed?"

"Yes, as of now for the primary. Secondary assets to southern exit." McGowen and Whitehead would get to the yacht where Browning and Collins were waiting for them. "Total count for southern departure point?"

"Total of eight."

"Repeat count?" Branson came back immediately.

"Eight. Non-negotiable, part of the terms."

"Affirmative."

Creed added, "I'll contact you when information is firmer."

"I copy and understand and will alert secondary." Branson was going to call Gitmo.

Shit, Creed couldn't let him do that without knowing what Street had told him. "Be advised, secondary assets were compromised from inside."

There was an audible pause from the rapid-fire conversation. Finally, Branson responded, "Acknowledged. We are in the dark. Be careful."

"That's my middle name. Out."

Creed ended the call, cracked the case and pulled

out the battery and SIM card. Damn, the old flip phone should be in a museum, not scattered over the island, but... Creed pitched the battery one direction and put the SIM card under his heel, crushing it against the coral underfoot. He turned and chucked the phone as far as he could in the other direction. Was it necessary? Who knew? But taking chances during an op wasn't going to happen, so better safe than sorry.

He got into the car and started the engine. Mariella still seemed to be in no mood for conversation. Whatever. He pulled back onto the roadway and headed to Santa Lucia. He needed to brief McGowen and Whitehead on the plan forward and give McGowen an extra phone. Any updates would be given to Creed via Rafa's people. For those that were for his ears only, they had the burner phones.

The mission could go to hell in a second. Tigger needed to know he had operational control and the authority to make any decisions he needed to make to get himself and Whitehead to safety. McGowen was solid and the man would finish his portion of the assignment and get the fuck off the island with Whitehead and what information and materials they could take with them.

He glanced back at the road behind him through the old rearview mirror. Damn, he wished he could see the path forward as clearly as the empty-as-fuck road behind him.

"WHAT'S with the tension between the two of you?" McGowen tipped his head toward Mariella, who was engrossed in a conversation with Whitehead and one of her uncle's men who'd pulled in minutes behind Creed.

"Fuck if I know, man. I tried to clear up some shit I didn't agree with. She lumped me in with Rafa. Told me I was just like him." Creed hated to think she actually believed that shit.

McGowen leaned back against the car. They'd passed the baton, or in this case, burner phone, and McGowen was ready and capable of handling any situation. Splitting the team still grated on Creed, but they'd always known that was a possibility. The man crossed his arms and cocked his head as he regarded Creed. "And you did what to prove her wrong?"

"Whoa there, big guy. Why do you assume I'm the one in the wrong here?" Creed barked a laugh that drew everyone's attention. He lowered his voice and turned his back to the others. "That woman went off like a firecracker." Creed lifted his hands and popped his fingers out like an explosion.

"Ah huh... and you did nothing in response, right, Skipper?" McGowen tried damn hard to hide a smile, but he was failing miserably.

Creed narrowed his eyes at his man. "I may have

voiced my displeasure in being put in the same category as her uncle and that fuckwad that hit her."

"Yeah, and just how did you do that?"

McGowen wasn't even trying to hide his laughter now, and that was... irritating as fuck. "I told her."

"Told her or yelled at her?" McGowen's laughter moved his shoulders now.

The fucker.

Creed crossed his arms and spread his legs as he glared at McGowen. "Fuck you very much."

McGowen bent over laughing.

The fucker's glee was contagious, and Creed broke a smile, too. "Shut the fuck up, man. I get it... I'll make it right." Creed glanced over at Mariella who quickly shifted her gaze past him. "Maybe I overreacted."

"You think?" McGowen straightened and cuffed Creed on the shoulder. "You got time with her. Apologize, and if this shit happens again, apologize again. That woman is a stone-cold keeper, Skipper, and she deserves to know it."

"Yeah, yeah... where the hell did you learn to decipher women?" Creed leaned on the car beside his man.

"A long time ago I was involved with a fantastic lady. She taught me." McGowen's features softened when he spoke.

"What happened?" Creed knew the man wasn't

married or involved. Branson's intel had been damn thorough.

"She needed someone who was home all the time. She deserved better than me. I wasn't going to leave the service, so I walked away from her." McGowen shrugged. "It was for the best."

"When you got out did you look her up?" Creed had never had that type of connection, but he didn't think he'd walk away without a fight.

"Nah, it hurt enough leaving her the first time. I didn't want to see her with another guy. That would have torn my guts out." McGowen put his hands in his pockets. "So, I spent my time and resources making sure my brother got everything he needed to succeed. The kid is smart, and he's going places in this world."

"I read that he is in Oxford?" Creed wasn't going to push McGowen, if the man wanted a topic change, he'd follow.

"Yup. He is a Rhodes Scholar. He came home all excited and talking a mile a minute. I had no fucking clue what a Rhodes Scholar was, and I had to GTS."

"Google That Shit. Seems I live by that term most days. I had to GTS your belt. That's really fucking impressive."

McGowen rolled his eyes. "Yeah, I can fight. Spent a fuckton of time training after I got out of the service and moved up a bit."

"A bit?" The fucking biggest understatement of the year.

"A lot. It kept me sane." McGowen nodded toward Whitehead. "He's a newb, but he'll do. You picked the right person bringing him on board for this op. He's been briefing me, telling me what to expect if or when we actually breach a facility."

"Monitor the location for patterns. You know humans." Creed scuffed the ground with the sole of his boot.

"Creatures of habit." McGowen nodded. "Can we readdress the exit strategy for you if I have to go first?"

"Nope. I'm heading to the secondary point." He'd get a military airlift back to the states. Having the boat in Cuban waters for any longer than necessary wasn't going to happen.

McGowen frowned. "If I have to bug out first, I'll have Collins position just outside the waters controlled by Gitmo, that way we can head back and debrief together."

Creed shook his head. "You'll need to get the material and people to Branson."

"Which I can do with a simple radio call from the boat. We will make the exchange and then get our asses to Gitmo. Collins, Browning, Whitehead and I can meet up with you. Tell me you won't need the assistance once you take on that prisoner transport. I will not leave anyone behind, Skipper. Can't do it."

Creed nodded but focused his stare somewhere in the distance. This was what he missed. The unity. Fuck.

"What do you think the political ramifications will be if we do prove there are dirty bombs being made here?" McGowen nodded with his chin toward the small hamlet of Santa Lucia. "They are good people."

Creed watched as Mariella and Whitehead walked toward the truck Rafa's men had arrived in. "I talked with Branson about that. Our government can never acknowledge the CIA op or this one, but pressure can be levied, and you know those political black door talks happen all the time." He looked down and kicked a small rock that he'd dislodged. "I'm fucking glad I'm military and not a politician. That shit takes a certain type of person."

"Yeah." McGowen agreed. "Won't lie to you, I don't like many of them, those politicians."

"Yeah." Creed agreed, but they'd both sworn an oath. One they both still held as sacred.

"Thinking about Collins. He's with Guardian. Full time. He said they are restructuring and looking for good people."

"You'd give up your gym?"

"I have people who can manage it." McGowen glanced at him. "Tell me you wouldn't give up what you have going on to come back to this."

"I couldn't. I'd be lying." Creed would admit that freely.

"You should consider working for Guardian. You know they have the best toys and the best pay."

"I never even considered private security."

"They are international." McGowen shrugged. "I'm going to talk to Collins about it. No matter how fucked up things out here get... I feel alive."

Creed nodded. He got that. Fuck, this assignment had shown him just how much he'd been treading water back home. He glanced back when movement in his peripheral drew his attention. Whitehead and Mariella had started back toward where he and McGowen stood. "You do what you need to do, Tigger. Don't hesitate. Use your instinct. If you need to pull out, do it. Move. Don't hesitate. Take care of him and take care of yourself."

"You got it, Skipper." McGowen sent him a sideways look. "And remember what I told you. Apologize."

"Yeah, yeah." Creed pushed McGowen, and the man laughed as he fake stumbled away. Creed shook Whitehead's hand when the man approached. "Be smart, don't risk any exposure and listen to McGowen."

"Will do. You take care of her." Whitehead nodded toward Mariella who rolled her eyes.

"She does a damn good job of taking care of herself, but I hear you." Creed slapped the man on the shoulder and waved one last time at McGowen. He might not see either man again. He fucking hated it, but that was the way the dirty bomb crumbled. God, he hoped not. He slid into the driver's seat and waited for Mariella to get in before he put the car into gear. He needed to shift gears, literally and mentally. For now, he was a newlywed getting to know his wife all while trudging around a hostile environment looking for explosive radioactive materials. Good times.

Creed chuckled to himself. What a seriously screwed-up turn of events. If someone had him told three weeks ago he'd be married and on his "honeymoon" in Cuba, he'd have told them they were fucking insane. Life was fucked up for sure because, seriously, nobody could make this shit up.

# CHAPTER 19

*M*ariella needed to apologize. She really didn't want to and that pissed her off more than the fact that she'd screwed up. Because she *had* screwed up. From the moment she'd met him, Creed had been honest with her. He'd treated her with respect, well minus the minutes in the alleyway in Havana and that had *technically* been her fault. Who knew he'd be so adept at recognizing he was being followed. She had omitted the truth, and he'd called her on it. No, she couldn't hold those actions against the man.

She drew a breath and gathered her nerves.

"I'm sorry–"

"I apologize–"

They spoke at the same time. She blinked at him, and he smiled at her. "Let me." There was laughter in his voice, which was good. She'd let him talk, but she wasn't sure what *he* had to apologize for.

He glanced at the rearview mirror before he spoke again. "I didn't need to yell at you when we were discussing the situation with Adalberto. For that, I apologize. I have no defense other than to say it really bothered me that you thought I was like your uncle and that fucktard."

"Fucktard?" That was a new word.

Creed shrugged. "Trust me, it suits Adalberto."

"Ah, well I accept your apology, but I should also apologize. I was defensive. It is my default setting." She grabbed her hair and held it at the side of her neck.

"Your apology is also accepted." He threw her a quick smile. It looked relaxed and not strained. Thank goodness.

"I don't think you are like Rafa, and definitely not like Adalberto." She shook her head. "Rafa isn't a bad person. He was raised in a different time. He rarely goes into Havana, or any town for that matter, and the influences of the rest of the world are slow to trickle back to him. Even though he deals in information and is connected to the pulse of this island, his cultural base is antiquated. He tries."

Creed nodded, but she didn't think he really believed her. At least he wasn't arguing the point, and she had to defend her uncle because she loved him and would always be indebted to him. The sun-warmed leather of the seat felt good against her skin. She leaned back against the car seat and relaxed for the first time since they'd exchanged heated words earlier in the day.

"Was the man you were talking to on the phone upset at the number of people you were going to try to get off the island?"

"He was expecting five. Almost double was probably a shock." Creed smiled at her. "He's working it. There isn't going to be a problem. What do you want to do when you get to America?"

"What? You mean besides be an American? I have no idea." She gave her best carefree laugh but refused to look at him. Temporary. That was the word she was holding on to like a life preserver. She had perfected the mask she wore while dealing with men like Rafa and Adalberto. It wasn't hard to slip back into. "What would you suggest someone with illegal black market experience do in America?"

She rolled her head to look at him. His jaw was taut and the relaxed man she'd been talking to moments ago was gone. But why? Perhaps he wasn't happy about her asking for any type of assistance in America? Okay, she could avoid that topic. Two weeks, three at the outside. She'd play the Juliet to his Romeo, but she wasn't going to drink any poison. This thing between them was a fling for him. Nothing more.

"What exactly do you do for Rafa?" Creed asked after an awkward amount of time had passed.

"I manage inbound shipments, take care of most of his inventory although we don't have warehouses. Most of what we get into the country is gone within days of arriving on the island. A few items are saved to bribe the officials to look the other way, and I manage the distribution of what we get in. There are... markets, I guess you'd call them, for lack of a better word. The people who need what we have know how to find us."

"Is the business changing now that Americans are coming in droves?"

"Ahh... well, probably for the people working in Havana. Restrictions have been lifted on how much money can be sent into the country. The Cuban money attached to the dollar is the CUC. One CUC equals twenty-four or twenty-five CUP, or our Cuban Pesos. Remember, we are a communist country. The money tourism brings isn't retained by the person who earns it. All revenue goes to the government who then "divides" it amongst the people of the nation. I'm told the workers can't keep the tips that they report and all CUC tips must be reported. Unreported tips in American dollars or other currency are what help the people of Havana."

"Is life in Cuba getting better?"

"Better? That I don't know. The way of life here is changing. Slowly. There is still so much poverty. It's how we live. Each concession from the government is a major shift in our life. Things Americans take for granted are valued here. My generation has never known life outside communism. The previous regime, Batista? From what the old ones tell me, he was a dictator. Oppression by our government is something everyone knows, but..."

Describing the oppression was difficult. How did one tell someone about going to school hungry because there was nothing to eat? Do you tell those things? Do you complain because you watch someone who is in favor with the government receive what you can't have? Was it necessary to describe the joy she'd seen on parents' faces knowing they could feed their children with the food she was able to smuggle into the interior of the island? Or the glee she'd seen on the faces of tobacco farmers when a tourist bought ten cigars for a dollar each. That money would augment the food the farmer had grown so his family would not be hungry. The markets where people shopped in Cuba were not the same as she'd heard of in America. No, the markets in Cuba had random items from different countries–if items were available at all. Government sanctioned markets boasted shelves that were mostly vacant, and her people bought food off of pushcarts that traveled the streets of the small towns. Plantains and local fruits and vegetables were the staples that fed most

Cubans. It was a hard life, but they were proud people, and they would survive. They always had.

"What did Adalberto do for Rafa?"

Creed's question pulled her from her thoughts. "Ah, well Adalberto was the enforcer. He was the muscle that made everyone fear messing with our system. Rafa had him under an iron fist. Adalberto is a ruthless man who has no compassion. If he were to take over the operation, people would suffer. Don't misunderstand, Rafa makes a profit, but under Adalberto's control, most goods would be priced out of reach for the common people, those we serve who most need it. Adalberto has said many times because there is now foreign money coming into the country, Rafa should raise his prices. Rafa won't do it."

"So basically, he's a giant dick." Creed glanced over at her.

She laughed. "Yes, Adalberto the giant dick."

She motioned to the right. "About ten kilometers up, there will be an offshoot of this road to the right. Take it. The first location is about an hour and a half from here."

"We aren't going there." Creed smiled at her. "Pick a number."

"What?"

"Look, I know you trust Rafa, and I do too... to a point. But I don't trust anyone in that compound right now. So, the map Rafa gave us has our route all plotted out. Who else besides Rafa saw it or had access to it?"

Mariella shook her head. "No one."

"That we know of. Even if Rafa took precautions, for us not to do the same would be foolish, don't you think?"

"Okay, so we are going to go out of order?"

"We are."

"Which one are we going to go to first?" She pulled the map out of the glove box where she'd stowed it.

"Pick a number, any number, but not the one he suggested we visit first."

"Okay." Mariella studied the map. "He wanted us to go to the coast first." She pushed the map against the dashboard so Creed could see. "So instead we go here. Rio Cuarto."

"Perfect. You're the navigator. Plot us a course."

CREED USED a bottle of water to bathe the sweat off himself. They'd found the warehouse that Rafa's men said met the criteria. There was power and activity, although it appeared to be local officials using the small warehouse as a storage place for antique furniture and various odds and ends. They managed to get inside, and Creed was certain the building wasn't the facility they were looking for.

The power was minimal and fluctuated, browning out in waves.

"We move on tonight?" Mariella wrung out the small piece of cloth she'd used to wipe down. She glanced up at the clouds that were building and blocking out the abundance of stars that populated the night sky.

Creed took a look at the clouds and nodded. "We can, or we can stay here. Sleep in the car tonight."

Mariella glanced at the old car and shrugged. "It won't be the first time I've slept in this car. The front seats lay back, almost flat. It isn't particularly comfortable, but it beats being rained on."

"We'll make it work." Creed grabbed one of his packs and motioned toward the car. Mariella jumped into the passenger seat. Creed opened his pack and pulled out two MREs. "They aren't the best tasting things in the world, but they fill you up." He handed her one and tore into his.

She watched him for a few moments before she tore her plastic pouch open. "This is food?"

"Yep. Meals Ready to Eat. They are the rations we had in the field when we deployed. Like I said, they aren't the best tasting things, but they fill you up."

Mariella held up two packets. "Peanut butter and crackers." She smiled at him. "I love peanut butter. I want this for dinner."

"No, that's snack bread. Kinda similar. Here." He dug into his pouch and pulled out his crackers and peanut butter and handed them to her. "There is a shit-ton more food in that pouch." He pointed to her plastic bag. "You've got beef stew in there, probably some kind of drink additive and if memory serves you have the brownie in that meal, plus condiments."

She glanced down and nodded. "Okay, I'll eat the rest tomorrow." She placed the bag on the floor and ripped open the crackers he'd given her. She carefully peeled the plastic away from the crackers only breaking the top sheet. Creed opened his heating system, dropped the tablets into the bag and poured water in the pouch before he dropped his entree of chicken and noodles into the pouch.

Mariella watched him as he worked and reached out to touch the bag when the water started steaming.

"Careful, that water is boiling hot."

"How?"

"Chemical reaction to the tablets."

"And this is safe? You put your food in this chemical reaction?"

"Yeah, the food is inside the plastic, we don't drink the water, and so far, I've heard of no deaths from MREs." He'd heard horror stories about gastric issues caused by eating MREs, but that was a subject he hoped to avoid.

She shook her head and tore a tiny hole in the packaging for the peanut butter. "Do you have enough water?" She glanced out the car windows.

"Rain is coming. If you want some more, you should probably get it now."

Creed looked up and saw a wall of water working its way towards them. He shoved the rest of his MRE onto the seat and darted out to grab a couple bottles of water from the trunk along with some things from his other pack. He just made it back into the car before the first big drops started to fall. They rolled up the windows and popped the corner windows, which prevented rain from falling directly into the vehicle but gave them air movement. The sounds of the rain on the old ragtop were almost deafening.

"It doesn't look like this is a small sprinkle." Creed glanced around him. Their windows had started to fog over, but from what he could see, the drenching rain wasn't moving on quickly.

"Nope."

She carefully divided the peanut butter between all her crackers and the snack bread. She took a bite out of the first one and moaned. The sound went straight to his cock. He pulled open his heater and fished out his meal. The chicken and noodles weren't his favorite, but he'd learned to eat what he could when he could. He ripped the top of the plastic pouch and shoved his spork through the semi-congealed mess.

"That smells... nasty." Mariella's cute nose crinkled and turned up.

He shrugged. "It tastes about the same as it smells, but it's food."

"Mmmm... I'll take your word for it." She popped another cracker into her mouth.

"So where do we go tomorrow?" Creed shoveled the noodles into his mouth. The slimy texture made "shovel and gulp" the best method to get the food down.

She made a small sound, and he glanced her way then paused. Her eyebrows had risen to her hairline.

"Do you always eat that way?"

"Ah, no, but for this MRE it's best if you don't leave the food in your mouth long enough to actually taste it. Your beef stew is pretty good." He swallowed the rest of the food in his mouth and washed the taste away with a drink of water. "Where to tomorrow?"

"Ah... not the coast, because if someone knew the schedule, they could assume we are just held up."

"Excellent, so where should we go?"

"Depends. Do you have cash for gasoline?"

"I do."

"Then I say the location near Vazquez." She opened the glove box and fished the map out, pointing to the small town with her pinky finger, careful not to get peanut butter on the paper. "I have cousins here. We can stay with them, or we can sleep on the ground. I would recommend the house. Adal-berto does not have a strong presence in this area, and if word has traveled that he and Rafa are at war, the people here will side with Rafa."

"They would be expecting you to arrive with your husband in tow?"

"No, but they will keep their mouths shut. They are loyal." She shrugged. "Besides, word has already spread that I'm married."

Creed crammed the rest of his noodles in his mouth and chomped down on them, trying not to breathe. He waited to speak until he swallowed. "How do you know that?"

"What? That word has spread?"

"Yes."

"There isn't a lot that is fast in this country. Gossip is the one thing that the government cannot censor or stop. Believe me, if something noteworthy happens, it travels quickly through the bus lines and is told in hushed conversations. It is amazing how accurate the information that travels this way remains."

"Really? I would assume any information traveling by word of mouth would be inaccurate, or at least exaggerated."

"If lives didn't depend on the information, I'd agree with you. People out here don't have cable television or cell phones that feed us information. We have the radio, and the stations we receive are broadcast by the Cuban government. At night we can pick up stations from Miami. The people have learned that the most accurate information we get is by word of mouth."

"So they know you're married."

"They should," she acknowledged.

After their meal they cleaned up. Mariella collected all the empty packets and wedged them into the glove box, shutting the door.

Creed fiddled with the lever to lay his seat back and chuckled when it fell with a thud.

"Ah, that one only has two positions. Flat or straight up." Mariella laughed with him.

"Thanks, good to have that information." He moved his weapon, so it wasn't digging him in the side and chuckled as he raised his head and slid his arm under it. She adjusted her seat slowly and lay on her side facing him.

"You'll enjoy the States." He reached over and pushed a lock of hair away from her eyes.

"I don't think I will."

"Why not?" Creed turned and propped on his elbow looking down at her.

"I told you. What will I do in America?" She closed her eyes and shook her head, rolling onto her back. Her hand lay on her stomach as she seemed lost in observation of the fabric of the ragtop. "I have no place there. I have an education, a degree in accounting, but I've never used it."

"Not even for Rafa?"

She shrugged and sighed. "Not to any extent. Like

I said earlier, I took care of the limited inventory we had, and made sure the shipments weren't missing items." Her eyes rolled toward him. "Why?"

Creed lay down on his side, so they faced each other. The worn, cracked, white leather was soft under his weight. "I don't think you'll have a problem finding a place in America. You work hard, and you'll be a citizen. There won't be any doors you won't be able to open."

She chuckled sadly. "With no money? Living alone in a foreign country whose customs I don't understand? Speaking a language that is not my own? I wish I had your confidence." She closed her eyes. "Never mind me. There are bigger worries."

Creed sighed and rolled onto his back, careful to avoid hitting the pedals by his feet. He didn't agree with her. A woman like Mariella would always find a place to belong, but she was right. At the moment they had bigger worries. "Yeah, I need to check for voice messages from McGowen." He pulled the cell and battery from his pocket. He slid the battery into place and powered up the phone. He waited for a connection and gave it an additional minute before he shut it down. No voicemails or text messages waiting. That meant McGowen and Whitehead were still waiting for an opportunity to get into the warehouse. Tigger had indicated there was activity, and more armed guards had arrived when they had traveled back from Rafa's compound. Getting into the facility was going to be harder than anticipated, but people were creatures of habit and McGowen could get Whitehead in and out if he was given a chance. Night, when McGowen was watching, would be the best possibility, but McGowen would wait and observe before he made a move.

"Nothing?" Mariella asked. The rain muted her words. Not so torrential, it now fell against the car with a quiet patter.

"No, but I didn't expect anything today. McGowen and Whitehead need to watch and ascertain the best way and time to get into the facility."

"Do you think it is a waste of time to check the other sites?"

"I don't know. All of us sitting on that location while waiting for an opportunity to get inside and inspect it is a waste of manpower. We are better off eliminating other potential sites. When McGowen confirms or eliminates that site, we will respond appropriately."

"It would seem it is the location, based on Street's information and the guards." Mariella's voice softened. Her eyes fluttered shut before they opened a fraction of an inch.

"It would. You should rest now. Sleep." Her eyes closed and her features relaxed. He rolled onto his back and stared at the ragtop, putting thoughts of Mariella back into the "to be considered later" compartment.

He watched as water seeped into the car from a small hole near the corner of the convertible top. The day had been long, hot and busy. Rafa had his hands full tracking down Adalberto and coordinating the transfer of the CIA agents. He couldn't assume the person who'd offered the agents on a platter wouldn't know of their pending transfer, which made the attempt to free the agents riskier, if that was possible.

His gut told him the site McGowen currently monitored was where shit was going to go down, but he couldn't disregard the other possibilities. Fuck. He'd love to have ten more men and a fuckton more firepower, but that wasn't within the scope of the mission he and Branson had established. He tapped his stomach with his fingertips. He needed to talk at length with Branson, and it needed to be sooner rather than later. There was only one way to do that.

# CHAPTER 20

"*I* thought we weren't going to the site on the coast?" Mariella glanced at the map and then at him.

"We aren't going to the site." Creed acknowledged. He was going to make a phone call tonight that was longer than one hundred and twenty seconds. So, a detour this morning was in order. "I need to make a quick stop, then we'll travel to the location near Vazquez."

"A stop? Where?"

"There is a port up the coast. I just need a few moments to leave a signal."

"A signal? For who?"

"The rest of my team. We are going to meet with them tonight." Creed's head snapped in her direction, "You can swim, can't you?"

She gave a very inelegant snort. "I live on an

island. Of course, I can swim."

"Maybe I should rephrase that. How far can you swim?" He glanced at her and raised his eyebrow.

"Oh, that sounds like a challenge." She laughed and spread out her arms. "I'm a good swimmer. If I pace myself, I can swim far, but if you want me to swim to Miami, I may need some of those, what do you call them?" She made a motion around her arms. "Balloons that the tourists put on their babies."

"Water wings?" Creed sputtered. The thought of her wearing inflatable arm flotation devices just did not compute.

"Yes, water wings. "

"No, I promise it will be a shorter distance than Miami." Hopefully. He had no problem with a long haul. He'd need to make sure he maintained a slow, steady pace so she could make the swim, too.

He navigated the winding roadways and avoided some treacherous areas where the pavement had heaved, leaving massive cracks and potholes. They stopped in Morón, and Mariella was able to buy gas for the car with his American dollars. He watched as she argued with the owner of the filling station over the price. She was a vivacious live wire. When she'd settled on a price, she went down the street to see about getting them something to eat. "Other than the toxic sludge MREs." Her words, not his.

The man who worked or owned the gas station ambled out of the shaded concrete building and nodded at him. Creed nodded back and noticed the age in the man's face as he neared. Deep lines framed his eyes, and there were etched indentations around his mouth. When he smiled, Creed could see why they were there. "Your woman is not very respectful." The old man chuckled at Creed's snort of laughter.

"She is many things. Respectful is not one of them," Creed agreed readily enough. He didn't want to examine the warmth he felt hearing Mariella referred to as "his woman."

The man cocked his head. "Where are you from?"

"Spain." He left it vague. It was easier that way.

The man studied Mariella as she stood at a window. Creed assumed it was a paladares, a family-run type of eating establishment. Not necessarily a restaurant, but a place where they would cook what food they had and sell it to those who had money to buy. They were prevalent in the interior of Cuba. From what he understood the paladares were run by the ruling faction and Cuban citizens couldn't eat there. Rafa's G-2 connections no doubt. He'd seen some of the offerings and thought he'd more likely eat an MRE than anything Mariella brought back.

The man was staring at him when he looked back. Creed raised an eyebrow and waited. It was obvious he had something to say.

"She needs a firm hand." The old man nodded down the street.

"She is a handful." He agreed and laughed when

the old man let out a cackle. More and more, though, Mariella seemed like a handful he'd like to have as a permanent fixture in his life.

"I can tell by the way you watch her. She is the reason you have grey hair." The old man pointed at Creed. "Women like her are not women you can leave alone. They need a man's attention. I have a woman such as this one. She has kept me on my toes my entire life."

"You look pretty spry." Creed acknowledged.

"It is true. Fifty-three years I've been married to my Lucia. She has been my life. Take care of this one. Women full of such life are a gift." The old man lowered his head and laughed as he shuffled off. "Love, it makes a man strong, my friend."

Creed swung his gaze back to where Mariella stood, visiting with an unseen person at the window. She was exceptionally beautiful, in a natural, honest way. Much of her beauty came from within, not from artificial enhancement like so many of the women that he met in Key West. Hell, even before that. She was genuine and honest. Now that he knew her, he could see that she wore her heart on her sleeve. She tried to bury her kindnesses, but his vision was 20/20 now, at least as far as she was concerned. She was a woman any man would be lucky to know and they'd be blessed if she gave them her heart.

He glanced down at the toe of his boot. If he'd met her in Key West, he would have asked her out. Or

KRIS MICHAELS

he'd like to think he would have. Really, he didn't know. Before Branson had reached out to him, he'd been focused on one thing. Getting back to this. To work that mattered. Yes, he knew this mission was a one-off, and the likelihood that he'd be called up again was slim to none. That bothered him.

He had nothing waiting for him back in Key West. He drew a breath and gave himself a mental shake. That wasn't true. He had his family. His brothers and his parents, but even though they were there, his life was empty.

McGowen's words echoed in his mind, and he mulled over the thought of working for a private company. He'd heard some amazing shit about Guardian. He didn't have a clue if any of the things he'd heard were true, but if even half were credible, the company might be worth looking at. After this mission was done. After Mariella was provided a new life. He examined the fluffy clouds as they moved across the sky. He should be good with that. Good with getting in, getting done and letting her go. Should be, but he wasn't, and that was …disturbing.

Mariella threw back her head and laughed before turning to look back down the block toward him. When she noticed he was watching her, she smiled and waved for him to come to her. He lifted his hand to the old man who'd taken up his seat in the shade again and wandered down the street.

"Come, we are eating here." She nodded to a small

bench of cinder block and scrap wood. Through the years many asses had polished the wood to a soft sheen. He accepted a piece of brown paper which held three corn tortillas, a pile of some sort of meat and some cooked veggies, by the look of them, cucumbers and squash. He sat down with her and watched as she used the tortillas to scoop up small portions of the meat and vegetables and put it in her mouth. He followed suit. It wasn't bad. The garlic and onions provided a familiar taste.

They ate silently, and after Mariella had thrown away the paper, they ambled back to the car. He started it and pulled back out onto the horrible high-way. The ragtop was down, and the drive to the marina took only about an hour and a half. Navigating to the marina, he parked and while still seated in the car, took off his boots.

Mariella watched silently as he pulled two white trash bags out of the bottom of his boots. He tugged his boots on, laced up and got out. He shut his door and rounded the car, opening her door and extending a hand to her. He'd tucked the plastic bags into his pocket. She glanced at the back seat one more time to check it was empty. Before getting to the marina, they'd locked their gear in the trunk along with the newly acquired jars of gasoline. Casually, they strolled along the edge of the pavement and moved toward the water.

"What are the bags for?"

"What do you think they are for?"

"Two bags." She glanced at him and shook her head. "Are we going shopping in one of the markets the government has for tourists?"

"Nope." Creed could only imagine Mariella's expression if she entered a Whole Foods Market or even a Super Walmart. The selection alone would probably overwhelm her. "These are for the signal I told you about earlier."

They walked hand in hand along the roadway just outside the marina. He watched as her eyes scanned the boats currently docked in the berths. "To one of these nice boats?"

Creed smiled and winked at her before he double checked his directions and tugged her hand. They moved forward and up into the overgrown brush toward the end of the fence.

He pulled one bag out and looped it through the chain fence and then followed suit with the second. His eyes scanned the boats and instantly found the one he was looking for. Guardian's luxury fishing boat was moored out in the harbor. He saw movement on the deck, and although he couldn't be sure, it looked like both men were outside. He grabbed her hand and headed back to the car. Tonight, they'd take a swim and then he'd have that one-on-one talk with Branson.

$\mathcal{M}$ariella fought off a sense of unease. After leaving the bags tied to the fence, they'd traveled to the nearest site on Rafa's list and checked out the building. The warehouse was unlocked. There was no electricity, and it had been stripped of everything of value. The wall studs stood exposed where someone had cut out huge portions of drywall. She'd seen it countless times. Desperation led people to do things they normally would never consider. Stripping and stealing building materials and anything of value from abandoned buildings was a way of life on the island. A source of concern was why it had been included on the list Rafa had given them. It met none of their qualifications as a potential lab for dirty bombs.

They'd returned to the marina several hours later, and with dusk settling in, Mariella got out of the car and stretched her back by easing her arms over her head. She'd expected the cool breeze from the ocean to kiss her as soon as she stepped out of the car. That wasn't going to happen tonight. The air was muggy and heavy around them. The clouds in the east were low and threatening. Creed had parked to the east of the marina, shielding the car from the road behind a low hill that had a large outcropping of seagrass growing out of control.

Creed locked the car doors before he dropped the keys into a plastic bag and stowed them in a pocket of his cargo shorts. He'd insisted they change when they were in the empty building and had some privacy. Mariella appreciated the man's muscled calves and enjoyed the way his light tan shorts hugged his ass, but shorts were impractical for almost everything, and she'd told him that in no uncertain terms.

"The mosquitos will eat us for dinner." Mariella slapped at one offending bloodsucker.

Creed laughed and held out a hand to her. "Not for long."

She reached out and put her hand in his. This was one thing she'd miss. Nobody ever touched her. Not really. Rafa, well, he wasn't a hands-on type of person. The men she'd been with had wanted one thing, and there was never any cuddling or caressing before or after. Her choice and she didn't regret it. Not really.

They walked in silence for a while, pushing through a clump of thick sawgrass. Creed carefully pushed the razor-sharp leaves out of their way and helped her through the dense foliage. They didn't speak until another mosquito buzzed her ear. "Okay, where are we going?"

"Just over here a little bit." He motioned toward the rocky beach ahead of them.

She slapped at the whiny bug and groaned. "Obviously, you have the type blood that mosquitoes don't bother to drink. These monsters think my blood is a special treat and the little bastards fly from all over the island to take part in a Mariella Diaz buffet." She swatted at another mosquito and motioned back to where they'd left the car. "Please get the bug spray. I'd rather die of toxic poisoning than itch myself into an early grave."

"Come on, if we get a move on, we won't be a banquet." He pulled her toward the small clearing directly ahead of them. It was so dark she could only see the occasional glimpse of the ocean as they worked their way through the vegetation.

"There isn't a strong enough breeze tonight. Walking on the beach isn't going to get rid of all of them." She disliked the whine in her voice, but dammit, she hated mosquitoes. For the most part, the prevailing winds would keep them from the beach area, but it was almost breathless tonight. She glanced up at the sky. The clouds hung low and were moving in rather quickly, snuffing out the full moon and the glow it provided. It was dark. She stumbled over something and glanced back at it trying to figure out what she'd tripped over.

"Are you okay?" Creed stopped, the hand that wasn't holding hers made its way to her waist as he steadied her.

"If you'd give me an idea why we are making this trek in the dark, I'd be better." They were steps from the beach. Gentle swells rolled onto the rock and sand. She glanced to the west. Tiny lights that she assumed were the boats in the marina danced in between the leaves of the foliage that hung over and obscured a direct view of the area.

"Time to go for that swim." Creed pulled off his shirt, slipped off his shoes and put the small plastic bag with her car keys into his shoe. He wrapped his shoes in his shirt and shoved the entire thing into the middle of a clump of sawgrass. Well, she'd have to concede, nobody in their right mind would think to look for anything there.

Mariella crossed her arms and glanced from the exquisite man in front of her to the dark ocean waters. "This swim is important?"

"It is. I need to make a phone call, one that lasts more than a few minutes." Creed motioned to her shoes. "If you want to come, lose the shoes."

Mariella swung her eyes to the water and scanned the waves for something... ahhh... a large boat was out there. It wasn't running its lights, but it was there. She judged the distance. It would be a challenge, but...

Shoes toed off, she picked them up and tossed them on top of his clothes. "You're going in there to get them when we get back."

"Never assumed anything else." He pulled her to him and dropped a soft kiss on her lips. "Tell me if you need me to slow down or if you need to tread water to rest."

Mariella pulled back to look up at him. "I won't take any chances." She wasn't a fool. Obviously, this was going to be an easy swim for him.

He nodded, dropped a quick hard kiss on her lips and led her into the surf. She waded out until the rolling waves took her feet out from her and started to stroke. She kept Creed on her right. His strokes were smooth and seemingly effortless. She matched his pace and lost herself in the repetition of the exercise, trusting him to keep them true to their target. She concentrated on the rhythm. Breath-stroke stroke, stroke, stroke, breath-stroke. The salt water burned her eyes. The roll of the tide made her feel like she was swimming in place occasionally, but Creed was beside her the entire time. Finally, his hand touched her, bringing her out of her focus. She pulled her stroke and tread water. Twenty-five feet to her left was a boat. And what a fucking boat it was.

"Follow me." Creed huffed.

Thank God, he was winded too. Mariella had

been considering asking him to stop for the last five minutes or so, but pride had prevented her. She did a breaststroke behind Creed, and followed him to the aft of the ship where a metal ladder glinted against the muted light of the cloud-laden night sky.

She grabbed the ladder and followed Creed up.

"Skipper? What the fuck happened?" She heard the concern in the man's voice immediately.

"I need to use the SAT phone to contact Branson. Do you think your agency can scramble the Cuban government's listening tech for ten or fifteen minutes?"

Creed reached back. She grabbed his hand, stepping up and onto the ladder.

"Whoa... hello and who are you?"

Mariella flopped her soaked braid behind her and squeegeed the salt water out of her eyes.

"This is Mariella Diaz, our contact in Cuba."

"All right." The man extended his hand and offered her a large fluffy towel. She grabbed it and pulled the luxurious material up to her face.

"You will want a shower." He glanced at Creed. "Give me fifteen minutes. Our tech people are the best in the world." He turned to leave but stopped, spinning on his heel. "Oh, Browning is in the galley. He'll have food waiting for you. Figured the swim would leave you hungry. Ma'am." The man nodded at her and sprinted toward the cockpit.

"Come on. Let's get the salt off us and get some

food." Creed took her hand and led her to the middle of the boat.

She could smell the aroma of onions and garlic coming from the galley. Her stomach growled in appreciation. Creed opened a door and light spilled out onto the deck. Mariella almost gasped at the luxury she saw. The wood was expensive and well maintained. She followed Creed's tug on her hand as she tried to capture every detail of the luxurious furniture. It was low and dark blue. There was a large chrome and glass table and one, two, three... eight chairs! She swung her head around. A bar with crystal decanters and glasses in the corner was situated so people could talk or watch... oh my God! She'd never seen a television that big!

"Are you rich?" The words fell unbidden from her lips.

Creed glanced over his shoulder and glanced at the room they were tracking water through. He shook his head in a dismissive manner and pulled her further into a hallway. "No, this isn't my boat. Guardian Security owns it. Collins, that's the man we just met, he works for Guardian, and he and the boat are on loan for this operation."

"Oh." *Eloquent as always, Mariella.* The hallway was painted white, and the same brass that adorned the fixtures in the luxurious sitting room was in the hallway. Creed opened a door and pulled her into a bedroom. The blue and white theme continued. That had to be a king-sized bed. She'd seen them in the movies that she'd watched, but they weren't really a thing in Cuba. Those that had them did not mingle with people like her.

"Here." Creed walked through the room and turned on a light in the adjoining room. She followed him, and if possible, her eyes got wider.

"Shower is here. Turn it on like this. This way for hotter water; this way to make it cooler. There are towels here. Soap, shampoo and conditioner are..." He opened a cupboard and nodded. "Here. Also, a toothbrush and toothpaste." He held up the new toothbrush still in a plastic package. "I'll pop over into the other bathroom and take a shower after I put some clothes on the bed for you. Sorry, but you'll have to wear my extras until we can get your shorts washed and dried."

Her response was distracted. She couldn't stop looking at the unimaginable luxury. "Why do that? We are swimming back tonight, right?"

"That's the plan." He reached behind her and wrapped the nape of her neck guiding her into him. "Take your time. I'll meet you in the galley when you're done. Follow your nose." He dropped down to kiss her. His lips lingered on hers.

Mariella shivered, and it wasn't because the air conditioner was on frigid. No, it was because the way the man possessed her with a single brush of his lips against hers. *Yes, it was.*

He dropped his forehead against hers. "You make me want things I shouldn't."

*God, you do, too.* "Wanting isn't a bad thing." She whispered the words and meant every one of them. She wanted this man so badly her heart ached.

"Perhaps, but when I should be concentrating on my mission, wanting is dangerous." His lips brushed lightly against her cheek as he spoke.

"I won't compromise your mission, Creed." She closed her eyes and swallowed back a heart-rendering sob that threatened to escape. "I won't compromise you. We know what this is and what it isn't." His head jerked up, and he stared down at her. She shook her head and reached up to trail her fingers down his jaw. She put her fingers over his mouth when he started to speak. "Don't."

She couldn't bear to hear him say it was temporary because the feelings she nurtured for this man were not the temporary kind. These feelings were seedlings that put down deep roots. Unfortunately, these seedlings wouldn't have the time to blossom and bear fruit. Temporary did not have blossoms and lasting beauty. Temporary had right nows and carefully squirreled away memories secreted into portions of her mind where she could protect them and re-visit them when life became hard and ugly.

"Skipper?" A knock on the door broke them apart.

Mariella turned toward the shower. Creed's hand trailed across the small of her back before she heard him step away and shut the bathroom door. She closed her eyes and leaned back against the cool, tiled wall. The majesty and opulence of the boat faded in comparison to Creed Lachlan. She glanced at the small room and the luxury it contained. None of it mattered. When the mission was over, she'd be in the United States where she might possibly have the luxurious things in the cupboards. None of it would mean a damn thing if she didn't have Creed.

CREED STALKED across the bedroom and jerked open the door.

"Sorry to bother you, but I was lucky enough to get through to Jewell King. I gave her our SAT phone information, and she was thrilled. She said, and I quote, "Tell your Skipper that he can talk for an hour and those bastards will never know he's there."

Creed narrowed his eyes at Collins. "Is she really that good?"

"No, sir. She's better." Collins lifted his eyebrows and smiled a goofy ass smile. "Some say she's the best in the world. If she's not, I won't split the difference between her and the one at the top of the tech heap. It would be too close to call."

"Okay, give me five minutes, and I'll meet you in the cockpit." He headed to the cabin he'd taken when they'd boarded the luxury fishing vessel and pulled out a dark blue graphic t-shirt that was almost too tight on him and a pair of athletic shorts with a drawstring. He threw a pair of thick socks on top of the pile and popped back to the room where he'd left Mariella. He listened to the soft sounds of the shower for a few seconds before he headed back to his room. He grabbed a change of clothes and made a dash to the other bathroom on board. He dropped his soaked clothes and rolled them in a towel before he turned on the tap and waited for the hot water to run. Knowing that Mariella was also in the shower, he did a three-minute wash and rinse, not wanting to take much of the hot water from her. With a clean, dry, set of clothes on, he headed to the galley. Browning looked up as he came in and nodded at the table mounded with enough food to feed a small army or one hungry SEAL.

"This looks great. When Mariella gets here, make sure she eats, okay?" He got a blink in response before the man nodded. Creed grabbed a biscuit and took a bite as he walked through the galley heading to the cockpit. He stopped in his tracks and groaned. "Fuck me standing, Browning, this is the best biscuit I've ever eaten." He did an about face and walked back, grabbing two more. "For the road." He got a smile and a silent chuckle from the man for that one. Creed stuffed the rest of the first into his mouth. He had his third half-finished by the time he reached the cockpit.

"Those are fucking magic, aren't they?" Collins nodded to the biscuit in Creed's hand. He nodded, swallowed and then shoved the last half into his mouth. "Fucking awesome." The words came out muffled, but Collins knew what the fuck he meant.

The SAT phone rang, and Collins answered it. "Roger that. Thank you."

He hung up the phone and handed it to Creed. "The line is secure. Nobody is going to listen to you. She assured me that you are blanketed. You can talk as long as you want."

"You trust her?"

"With my life, which it very well could be if the Cubans trace your call and come after Browning and me." Collins nodded to the door. "I'll go keep your lady friend company and translate for Browning. Could be awkward if she asks him a question and he can't answer."

"Thanks. She speaks damn good English, but it can't hurt, and Collins... about her…"

"Skipper, I don't assume a damn thing. Keeps my life a lot easier that way. Unless you want me to bring her here, I'm happy to visit with the beautiful woman until you are done." The man winked and gave a low laugh as he left.

A phantom of jealousy slithered across his skin even though he knew Collins was gay. He straightened and put his hands on his hips. His assumptions didn't mean shit if Collins was bisexual. And fuck him standing if he didn't just assume Collins was gay. The man never said he was, just that he stood up for the men in the unit. Fuck it all. Creed scrubbed his face with his hands and dropped into the captain's seat. Every time he tried to bring up the possibility of something between them after the mission was over, Mariella shut him down. Maybe it was easy for her to silence him because he wasn't sure what he wanted. No... that wasn't true. He did know what *he* wanted. What he wasn't sure about was what *she* wanted. Would she entertain the possibility of more than just here and now? That fucked with his thoughts more than he cared to admit.

He reached for the phone and drew a steadying breath before he punched in Branson's number. It was fucking late on the East Coast, but it wasn't like Branson didn't know he had a mission going on.

"Branson."

"We are on a secure line. I need to talk to you."

"Lachlan? How is this a secure line?"

"Collins reached out to Guardian. The Sat phone is blanketed."

Branson lowered his voice. "What the fuck? Is everything okay?"

"Right now, it is. I'm aboard the Guardian vessel. Listen, I've had plenty of time to think. What if the dirty bomb placements to this point have been... practice?"

"Say what now?" Creed could hear Branson

moving, and the sounds of a television in the background quieted.

"I was talking with Whitehead while we were waiting to meet with Rafa. He said that dirty bombs are more a weapon of mass movement rather than a weapon of mass destruction. What if the bombs we've intercepted to this point are just decoys, practice runs?" Creed leaned back and closed his eyes. "Just think big picture for a moment. What building or business would someone want to close down so badly they'd play hide and seek with dirty bombs? Factor in none have exploded, and there are always anonymous tips that lead to finding every single one of them before they've detonated." Creed leaned forward and put his elbow on his knee. "Then add in that someone really fucking high up in the CIA has sold out four of his or her own people to keep them away from the dirty bombs being built in this country. Hell, you and I know there are people who enter Cuba every day from countries other than the United States who don't get a second look. What if the people who are building these devices are planning something?"

Creed stopped talking and waited... and waited... He looked at the phone. It was still connected. "Have I lost you?"

Branson cleared his throat. "No. As a matter of fact, based on intel we've been working with other agencies, it makes an alarming amount of sense. What about the sites you've inspected so far?"

"That's just it. I have McGowen and Whitehead sitting on the site we believe is the workshop. It is heavily guarded, and McGowen is waiting for a pattern or a break to get Whitehead in so we can determine if that is the hot location. In the meantime, Rafa gave us another list."

"And?" It was as if Branson knew Creed had stopped before he let his instinct speak again.

"We've only visited a couple, but it feels like he is getting us out of the area. Moving us away from the main site."

"Us?"

"His niece Mariella is with me. She's been invaluable in this operation." Creed wasn't going to sell her short.

"What do you have on the transfer of the agents?" Branson asked.

"Not a damn thing. Rafa said he'd let us know when it was arranged."

"Okay, barring that call, what can you learn from the asset you have on hand?" Branson's comment suggested a course of action he didn't like looking at but fuck him, he agreed it was time.

"I don't know what she knows. My gut tells me she is in the dark, too."

"She might know his contacts, and she could make some discrete inquiries."

"Man, the network down here doesn't work that way. It is all about absolute power, but I'll see what I can learn. Do you think Rafa is negotiating with someone else?"

"I haven't heard anything, but the man is known for his money-lust. I've never heard of him crossing wires once a deal has been struck, but there is always a first time for everything." Branson sighed. "What do you need from me?"

"What did the CO at Gitmo say?"

"He's not happy. If you get to them, they'll take you in and give you a way off the island, but don't look to maintain a presence there. I'm having my bosses reach out and try to get more cooperation."

"Got it. Okay, when we are getting ready to move on the suspect site, I'll reach out to you. You give Collins the word, and he'll get his ass to the waters just off of Gitmo. Ask the base commander to have a water transport ready. We'll get to this boat and fly to the nearest US port. We'll need a Coast Guard escort as soon as we reach US waters."

"Can do. Tell Collins to be on that horn as soon as you're onboard with which port he's heading toward."

"Affirmative. I'll try to get Mariella to work in the background and figure out what is happening with the transfer." She was probably as much in the dark about the prisoner transport as he was, but he also knew she'd help as long as it didn't cross her well defined lines of loyalty. "In the meantime, I'm disregarding the rest of the sites that Rafa has given us. My gut says what we're after is in the warehouse McGowen is sitting on, and I'm not playing around any longer. We are doing this. I'm taking the second skiff and going back before dawn. Mariella and I are going to head to that warehouse, and she can babysit Whitehead while McGowen and I get in and find out what we've got inside."

"Do you have the supplies you need?" He could hear Branson flipping paper in the background.

"Between McGowen and I, we have two bricks of C-4, blasting caps, det cord, and timers if we need them. We have our personal weapons, and I'll be taking enough M4s for all of us."

"You trust your asset enough to give her a loaded M4 and turn your back while she has it?" There was a bit of laughter in Branson's voice, but the question was serious and to the point.

"Yeah, I do. She could have told Rafa our plans for extracting the radioactive materials and if possible, to grab the people building them, but she didn't. She has a very defined sense of duty. We've shown we can be trusted, and she's proven the same thing to us." Creed hesitated for a moment before he asked, "Speaking of trust. Who the fuck sold out the agents?"

"Still working on that. Clearly, I can't storm into

Langley and demand an accounting. We have coordinated a covert look into the people involved."

"When these guys show back up on American soil, shit is going to roll downhill." Creed wouldn't want to be involved in the fallout.

"Yeah, don't I know it. There are several people who want to keep them under wraps while we debrief them and try to find out what actually happened."

"I think that would be the smart thing to do, but if I was one of those agents, you could bet money I'd be demanding answers."

"That is why I'm thankful you're not one of those agents. Do you need anything else from me?" His handler was a no-shit type of guy, and that was all right with Creed.

"Nah. The primary purpose of my call was to drop the suspicion about bogus bombs. Speaking of which, did your sources tell you if the bombs that were found were actually operational?"

Branson gave an evil chuckle. "We definitely think alike. I'm working on getting one of our specialists to examine the devices that are in the CIA's possession. Of course, I'm doing that without raising flags. For some reason, I no longer trust the intel from the CIA."

"Roger that. I have burner phones now. I'll call when I have more." Creed snapped his fingers. "Before you go, you realize that the intel you got about the capabilities of the Cuban government was bogus, right?"

"I've put that together, and I'm learning my connections with the CIA need to be examined."

"The CIA seems to be the common thread in this operation."

"Indeed. Take care, Creed."

"Roger that. Out." He hung up the cell which rang almost immediately afterward. Creed answered the phone but didn't say a word.

"Commander Lachlan? Will you need any further assistance tonight?" a low, husky, female voice asked.

He scrambled mentally. This had to be the Guardian tech Collins spoke with. "Ah, no. We're good."

"Roger that. I'll drop the cloak and keep the few Cuban tracers that reached out pinging across the globe for another thirty minutes or so. If you need our help again, have Collins contact Alpha. He was just lucky I happened to be at the workstation where his call was routed. Have a good night, Commander." The phone disconnected.

Creed turned off the device and set it down before he stood and stretched. His muscles were tight from the swim, but he felt good. The reason he felt good had more to do with the fact that he had a plan and was going to execute it. No more treading water.

# CHAPTER 22

*M*ariella sat at the table in the small galley. The food in front of her was a bounty of excess, and she was guilty of enjoying it. She'd have eaten more but the swim back to the shore, even assisted with the tide, would not be easy, especially on an over-full stomach. She eyed the selection of food and marveled that the men on this boat weren't fat and slow.

"Aren't you hungry?" The man who'd identified himself as Collins asked.

"We are swimming back to shore tonight, and I don't want to overeat, but I've enjoyed the meal. Thank you." Mariella smiled politely. She pulled at the shoulder of the huge t-shirt Creed had given her to wear. The shorts were impossibly large—she could put all of her in one leg—and since the t-shirt reached her knees, she wore only the dark blue shirt

286

and the socks, which she'd rolled down to her ankles. She felt exposed and vulnerable, especially since Creed wasn't in the galley when she'd wandered down the hall, following her nose as he'd directed.

"Browning over there can cook. He was raised on a ranch in Texas. I tell you I got the best part of this mission. Fishing all day and eating like a fucking king." The man's eyes bugged out. "Sorry, ma'am. My language is rough. I'm not around ladies much."

Mariella laughed. "Me either. Please don't censor your language for my benefit. I'm not offended." She liked the man. It would be impossible not to. His face had a permanent smile on it, and if he wasn't actually smiling, his eyes were sparkling with mischief and mirth. He was... what was the term? Ah... charismatic. And he looked so familiar. There was something about him that tugged at her memory.

Mariella tucked into the corner of the bench seat pulling her soda back with her. She had no idea what kind it was, but it was offered, and she wasn't self-disciplined enough to refuse the treat. "Is this your boat?"

"Nah, this boat belongs to the company I work for." Collins laughed and pointed at the quiet man who was now washing dishes at the counter. "Soon to be his company, too."

Mariella glanced from one to the other. "Yet you help Creed who works for the government?"

"You bet." Collins spun his coffee cup on the top of the table. "We work as a team."

Mariella took a drink of her soda, relishing the icy coldness. "This company, what does it do?"

"Oh, hell, you name it. There are overseas teams that do work like this. Domestic agents that work basic law enforcement and hybrid teams that do both. We are the world's largest private security company, and we are getting bigger every day."

Mariella nodded. Teams that did this... what she was doing now... maybe...

"Tell me you saved me some food." Creed's voice preceded him into the cozy galley.

"Plenty. Your lady friend didn't eat enough to keep a bird alive." Collins stood up so Creed could slide onto the bench next to her.

"Why?" His head snapped to her, and he rattled off in Spanish, "Do you feel okay?"

She answered him in Spanish, "I'm fine. We are swimming back to the shore soon. I didn't want to sink like a lead weight."

"We aren't swimming back. I'm taking the skiff back to shore. We can pull it up and hide it in the sawgrass."

"I can make the swim back." She wasn't going to let him risk exposure because he didn't think she could swim back.

"Not about you. We have some equipment that

needs to go to shore with us." Creed grabbed a plate and put it in front of her.

He switched back to English. "Browning, can I get another plate?"

The man nodded. A plate appeared seconds later along with a platter full of fish. A separate plate of vegetables and a third containing a rice dish reappeared. Mariella had already sampled all the dishes, but Creed brushed aside her objections and filled her plate with food.

She sighed when he set the plate in front of her. "You are going to make me fat."

All three men laughed at her. "Ma'am, no offense, but a strong wind would blow you off the deck."

"That's not true. I'm very strong." She looked at Creed. "Aren't I?"

"She is. The woman has grit." Creed spoke between bites of food.

Mariella wasn't sure what grit was, but the way the men all nodded she assumed it was good.

"So, what's the scoop, Skipper?" Collins stood again and poured himself another cup of coffee. The quiet man made several hand gestures, and Collins nodded. "We're getting tired of being lazy." The silent man nodded and leaned against the counter, crossing his arms over his chest.

"Lazy time is about over. Where are the charts of the island?" Creed asked as he paused between forkfuls of food.

"Hang on." Collins spun on his heel and darted out of the galley while Creed pushed several dishes out of the way.

"Here." The man returned and laid out the charts, and Creed pulled them to him. He examined the map as she glanced over his shoulder. The map was the first of its kind that she'd ever seen.

"Here." He pointed to the southeastern corner of the island.

Collins looked up at him. "When?"

"That's the unknown, but we won't have a warm welcome at Gitmo. They want us off the installation as soon as we arrive."

"Drive-th-through?"

Mariella jumped at the deep voice beside her. The silent one could talk.

"Exactly. We'll have the four agents, Mariella, her uncle and his...?" He looked up at Mariella. "What is Amelia to Rafa?"

"His aunt." Amelia was her great aunt.

"So, a full house?"

"Yes, and then a full-out run to American waters. If we are lucky, we will also have the radioactive material and someone for Branson et al., to interrogate."

"Shit." Collins' eyes scanned the boat. "From Gitmo to where, and why the fuck is the commander being a dick?"

"I don't know why we are getting the cold shoulder. Branson's working that issue, but we are planning for the worst and hoping for the best. The location we sail to will be for you to tell us. I need you to work the routes. Once we reach American waters, the Coast Guard will give us an escort."

"Whitehead can tell you for sure if this shit is contained, right? He has the equipment?"

"Yeah, he does." Creed acknowledged. "What we don't know is timing."

He shifted his eyes to hers, and she saw something in them.

"What?"

"Do you think you can contact your people and find out when the transport will happen?"

Mariella blinked and pulled away from Creed, putting space between them. "You want me to go behind Rafa's back?"

Creed sighed and relaxed against the bank of cushions. "I'm asking you to get the information and validate it. Yes."

"Why?"

"Let me answer that question with a question. Why are we checking buildings that don't even have power to them? What are we doing up here on the north side of the island except chasing our tails?"

Mariella stared at those brilliant blue eyes. They were tired and resolute. He knew the answers to the questions he posed. She searched for an answer, only she didn't have one. "Maybe he got bad information?"

"Or maybe he wants us out of the way. The question is why?" Creed leaned forward, closing the space between them. "Why would he do that?"

"I don't know." Mariella shook her head.

Creed pinned and held her with a stare. "Has he ever, to your knowledge, made an agreement with one entity and then taken a higher offer?"

"No. His word is final. He has never done anything like that." She shook her head adamantly. "No."

"Then what would cause him to keep us away from the middle and southern portion of the island?" Creed picked up his coffee cup and took a drink.

Mariella's gut dropped. "Adalberto."

Creed's head snapped around. "What?"

"He could be trying to keep us out of an area where Adalberto has people." She shrugged. It was the only reason she could think of that would force Rafa to put them on a wild goose chase.

Creed closed his eyes; his powerful arms were crossed over his chest. She glanced from him to his men. Collin's eyes were glued to the floor. The other man, Browning, was looking at her. He didn't need to speak to ask the question.

"Adalberto is my uncle's second in command. He and my uncle split ways after we got mar…" Mariella snapped her mouth shut. Dammit, she bit her tongue.

"Got what?" Collin' eyes were now fixed on her too.

"Married." Creed finished the sentence.

"Say what now?" Collins' question shot out as both he and Browning stood away from the counter where they'd been leaning.

"It was orchestrated to give us a reason for being in the interior of the island and give us a cover while we looked for the possible location." Creed flipped out the explanation.

"Hey, here's an idea. Couldn't you have said you were Canadian or German or some other country that is friendly with Cuba and tell them you were a tourist and lost?"

Mariella blinked up at the man. "That wouldn't have worked. Yes, there are many tourists in our country, but they don't go looking through random buildings. They hike or bike along the beaches and stay in the small towns that have rooms for rent. Where we were looking, this doesn't exist. If he, McGowen and Whitehead were to show up and start asking questions, the locals would have feared them and contacted the government. Never underestimate the hold the Cuban government has over the people of this nation." Ignorance of what her people lived through made assumptions like his easy. The truth, however, wasn't a pretty picture.

Collins stared at her for a moment. "My apologies."

"Accepted." She acknowledged him.

Collins tossed a look toward Creed. "You found the site?"

"We believe so. McGowen has had a couple days to gather intel. We are heading back down when we reach shore. As soon as we ascertain what is in the building, I'll pressure Rafa to get the transport online." Creed gave her a steady look. "I'm still going to ask you to make inquiries. We can't know for sure Rafa isn't playing us. I'm sorry, but I won't risk my people or you. "

Her stomach clenched. What Creed said was true. Rafa worked many different angles, pulled strings, and made arrangements. Keeping them out of the way may, in fact, benefit another deal he was work-ing. Creed stared at her for a moment, driving his point home before returning to his conversation with Collins and Browning. She listened as he recapped what had happened since they'd arrived on the island and why he felt the inland site was their target. She grabbed her soda and pushed back into the corner of the bench seat again. *Rafa what are you doing?*

Creed leaned back in his seat and pushed away his empty plate. His thigh rested against her foot. She burrowed her sock covered toes under his thigh. He glanced over as he spoke and smiled at her. His hand landed on her feet, the warmth of his contact sent a sense of safety through her. Her eyes closed and she leaned back against the seat cushion. The rock of the boat, a full stomach, and physical exhaustion joined forces against her attempt to stay focused on the conversation the men were having. Creed's deep voice covered her like a warm blanket. If this was what heaven was like, she'd be happy.

BROWNING REACHED over the small counter that separated him from the table and carefully took Mariella's soda glass out of her hand.

"She's out." Collins chuckled.

Her head lolled to the side, and her steady breathing was readily noticeable in the quiet galley.

"Are y-you m-m-married?" Browning asked quietly from the other side of the galley.

"No. I had a fake name and a fake ID," Creed responded immediately.

"Wait, she used her real name?" Collins pointed at Mariella.

"Yeah, why?"

"Umm... I don't know. That would make it a legit marriage. You're lawfully wed unless you prove that your fake name covers another crime. Even then you'd need to petition to get the marriage nullified." He glanced from Creed to Browning. Browning shrugged and signed something.

"Yeah, there was that case in Texas. Not sure about Cuba, Skipper, but..." Collins scrubbed his face.

"I think she's married to you. Just because you misrepresented who you are doesn't give you a get out of jail free card. I'm almost positive..."

"Excuse me?" Creed blinked from one man to the other. "Stop bullshitting me."

Collins glanced hesitantly at him. "I'm not bull-shitting you, boss. I think you're actually married."

"Fuck me..."

"Did you tell Branson?"

"No."

Browning sat down next to Collins and looked at Mariella. "Are y-you going t-t-to t-t-tell her?" He pointed at the sleeping woman.

"Tell her that we may be married? Hell, I think I need to find out the correct legal answer first." He glanced at Collins. "Do some research while you're out here fishing all day, would you?"

"You got it, Skipper."

Creed glanced up at the clock above the door. "We need to get some sleep. Can you get the skiff ready? I need M-4s, ammo, and personal protective equipment. Throw in the NVGs when you load the PPE."

"How are you getting all that shit to the site?" Collins translated Browning's hand signals.

Browning glared at Collins, and the man laughed quietly. "Excuse me, my colleague asked how you would transport the equipment. He gets pissy if I paraphrase."

Browning sent a flurry of signals again, and Collins nodded. "Yes, you did learn the alphabet for a reason."

"Ass," Browning said and flipped Collins off as he headed out of the galley.

They sat in silence for several minutes. Creed was lost down a rabbit hole. Could he actually be married to Mariella? What would she think about that? Hell, what did *he* think about it? He waited for the emotional sucker punch. The visceral dread he assumed he'd feel if their marriage was legitimate instead of staged just wasn't there. What this meant for the two of them in the future, he had no way of knowing. Fuck, another thing he did not have the time or resources to fix at the moment. He needed to focus on the mission. Blotting out the nonsense Collins had thrown onto the table was necessary.

"Browning is a solid man. He's worked hard at learning sign language. He gets frustrated because spelling out everything takes forever. But he's learning the signs for words. He'll be better than me before long." Collins turned to Creed and raised a brow. "Do you need one of us to go with you? The Cuban government hasn't even looked our way since we paid for our permit in Havana. There are boats out there that don't have permits. Shit is not what we were told to expect."

"We've learned that. I could use Browning. When you catch up with him have him load his full pack and his gear on the skiff, too." Creed swirled the last of his coffee in his cup. "What exactly do you do for Guardian?"

"Me? Ah... I guess you'd say I'm an underwater demolitions specialist, and I can pilot any kind of vessel you can put in the water." Collins chuckled to himself.

Creed nodded and narrowed his eyes at the man. "Has anyone ever told you that you look like—"

Collins held up a hand and gave a sharp, loud, laugh, interrupting him, "Not again. Yeah, I get that a lot." He stood and nodded at Mariella, who stirred at Collins vehement denial. "Get some sleep, Skipper. I'll go help Browning and wake you at three. That will give you time to eat, grab some coffee and get to shore before the sun starts to rise."

Creed nodded and watched the man go down the hallway after Browning. "He does look like him." Mariella's words were sleepily muttered. "I told him that, too."

Creed extended his hand. "Come on. A soft bed for a couple hours." He slid out of the bench seat and got an eyeful of thigh as she scooted out behind him.

"Where are the shorts I gave you?"

"They were too big." Mariella scratched her arms and shuffled toward the stateroom where she'd taken a shower.

Creed slowed down and looked at the woman as she walked away from him. So, she wasn't wearing anything under that t-shirt? He rubbed the back of his neck as he followed her down the hall. He stopped at his cabin door and waited for her to reach hers. When she realized he wasn't following her, she gave him a tired, confused look.

"This is my cabin." He nodded at the door.

"Then what am I doing in this one?" She pointed to the cabin door where she stood.

"I didn't want to presume you wanted me or wanted my men to know."

Her gaze slid from the door where she stood to him. "Are your men going to come into this room?"

"No."

"Are they going to come looking for you?"

"They could."

She scratched her arm and stared at him. "I'm willing to risk it."

Creed lifted an eyebrow in question.

"Unless you're not interested." She shrugged her shoulders and walked into the cabin, shutting the door behind her. Creed dropped his head against the doorjamb letting the blow hurt just a little bit more than he wanted it to because he was a fool. A fool to be thinking of the woman when all he should be thinking of was sleep and then the mission. A fool for being weak. A fool for wanting to be with her and the world's biggest fool to hope they *were* married and there could be something past the stolen time they had together. Fuck him. He was a freaking court

KRIS MICHAELS

jester. Put a three-pointed hat with bells on his head and ask him to perform. He slapped the doorjamb and pushed away.

The cabin was dark when he opened the door. He slid inside and stood by the wall letting his eyes adjust.

"What took you so long?" Her soft purr reached his ears.

"I was arguing with a fool." His t-shirt was off before he took a step toward the bed. His shoes and socks were off before his shins hit the bed frame and his sweats and boxers dropped to the floor a second before he knelt onto the bed, blindly finding her naked body. The interior cabin was draped in darkness with the exception of a small sliver of light from the hallway that crept under the cabin door.

Creed felt her hands run up his arms and twine behind his neck. Her skin was silky and warm under him as he lowered his body against hers. She ran her foot down the back of his leg.

"Who was the fool you were arguing with?"

Her fingertips drew swirls against his back setting a match to the explosive need for her that lived just under his skin.

"I'm the fool." He lowered and took her mouth.

Her taste was captivating, beguiling and habit-forming. He loved the way her tongue dueled with him, feeding her own need. She was a woman who knew what she wanted, and she took it. Fuck, that was liberating. He didn't know how many more moments like this they had, but he'd remember them because when he was with her, he was as close to complete as he'd ever been.

His lips trailed across her skin, and he studied her body's responses. Their past encounters had been fevered and urgent. Not tonight. Tonight they were safe, and they had privacy. He found the areas that made her shiver when he kissed or licked them. When he kissed the small space directly behind her ear, her whole body trembled. Ditto for the insides of her knees and each side of the delicate V of her legs. Creed drove her to the edge and then relented, starting the attack from a new angle, assessing, testing, learning. Her hands curled in his hair, and her body shook under him.

She muttered in Spanish, begged in English, and threatened him in a language he didn't recognize. He rose from her to reach for the nightstand, and she clung to him. "I'm not leaving." God, he fucking hoped there was a condom in the nightstand. There was a supply in his cabin when he boarded the ship, hopefully... yes... he pulled several out and tossed all but one on top of the nightstand.

Suiting up took only a few seconds and thank goodness for small miracles because while he'd been teasing her, he'd denied himself.

He lowered over her and rested on one elbow. His finger trailing down her jaw to the column of her neck. "You are amazing." He believed those words. "You are everything I didn't know I was looking for."

"I'm not." Her dark eyes caught a bit of the light from under the door and shone in a way that made him stop breathing. Fuck, why had he found her, now, here and under these circumstances? It was some sort of cosmic sucker punch. It had to be.

"I don't want this to end."

She chuckled and moved her legs to accommodate his size, "I don't think you've started yet."

He centered over her, rolling to both elbows and stared down at her. "Don't. Don't turn this into a joke."

She lifted her hand and ran her finger along his bottom lip. She opened her mouth to say something, something Creed was sure he didn't want to hear. He lowered and took her lips in a kiss, stifling whatever it was she was going to say. He moved his hips and breached her, feeling the delicious smooth heat of her envelop him. Her fingernails scored his shoulders as he hilted inside her.

"So good." She moaned and pushed her hips up. "So good."

It was better than good. They fit, in bed and out of it. He shifted and grabbed her leg, hefting it over his hip so he could drive them both insane. He thrust, and they both groaned at the wonderful sensation. Coherent thoughts all but disappeared. He let his base instincts lead while he consumed her with a multitude of kisses, breaking away only when they had to breathe, and even then, they shared air with their lips hovering mere millimeters from each other.

Mariella cupped his face with both her hands and whispered, "This isn't a joke to me."

He crushed her lips under his and pushed them both towards orgasm. His hips snapped forward, driving and relentless. He pulled away, sucked in a lungful of air and growled to keep his release back. He slid his hand between them and found her sensitive nub, rubbing it in time with his thrusts. Her body tightened, suspended bow-tight as he pushed into her.

Her orgasm shattered her, and within two thrusts he'd followed her into a chaos of bliss. He dropped his head to her shoulder and kissed her damp skin. She shivered under him. Fuck, he'd had good sex before, but this... this wasn't just sex. At least not for him.

He rolled off her and took care of the condom. He found the sheet at the foot of the bed and pulled it up over both of them.

"Your men?"

"Will keep their mouths shut." He pulled her into him.

"Creed?"

He nestled against her. "Yes?"

"I wish we didn't have to go back." She threaded her fingers through his and sighed.

"Me, too." But what they were doing was bigger than what they'd found together, and they both knew it. He closed his eyes and kissed her hair. "Someday this will all be over."

"And then what?"

"Then perhaps we can go on a date."

Her laughter was low and tired. "I'd like that."

"Go to sleep."

She hummed and snuggled back. Happy, at least for now, he closed his eyes and let sleep overtake him.

# CHAPTER 23

Mariella hopped out of the skiff at the same time as the men. She helped to pull the thing up onto the beach. Browning and Creed grabbed the bags and dropped them by the sawgrass before they found a small pathway in the foliage and shoved the boat deep enough into the shrubs that it was invisible from the beach and from the road.

"I knew I'd end up getting that stuff out of there." She muttered to herself.

"What?" Creed called back to her.

"Nothing." She turned and rolled her eyes before she braved the sharp leaves to retrieve their shoes, Creed's shirt and the keys to the car. She didn't manage to make it through the needlelike fronds without several nasty scrapes. *Damn shorts.* She couldn't wait to get back into her camos and shit-kickers.

The men were waiting at the car when she approached.

Browning pointed to her leg. She glanced down at the red scratches with small rivulets of blood trailing down her thigh and sighed, "Yeah, the sawgrass is unforgiving." She tossed the keys to Creed. "I need my boots and pants."

Creed popped open the trunk and pulled out her backpack, handing it to her. "We need to reorganize the trunk. You've got a couple minutes to change."

She nodded and headed to the front of the car. With both men behind the open trunk, she slipped out of her shorts and into her camo pants. By the time Creed closed the trunk she'd put on her boots and stowed away her flip-flops and shorts. She opened the passenger door and slipped into the back seat.

Browning made a motion catching her attention and pointed to the back seat. She shook her head. "No, you sit up front." The man shrugged and got in. Creed slid into the driver's seat, started the car and backed out of the small clearing where he'd parked it. "What do you need in order to check on the prisoner transport?"

Mariella considered her response. She'd thought of little else all morning. "I could go behind his back, but I honestly don't think he's double-crossing you. I want to call him, assure him you are not with me, and I want him to tell me what is happening."

"Wouldn't that let him know that we think something is going on?"

"No, it would let him know *I* do and that I'm pissed, which is what I would normally do. If I make even one call to his contacts, he will find out. If I ask anyone who has knowledge of the prisoner transport questions that have already been asked by Rafa, we threaten the entire mission. People are paranoid and terrified of the regime. Loved ones still disappear. This is not America."

Creed's eyes met hers in the rearview mirror. "When do you want to make the call?"

She glanced at the sun. It was just coming up. It was still early. Rafa would be going over the daily runs and shipments until about nine. "Let's get to McGowen and Whitehead. I'll make the call when you and Browning are getting a debrief."

Creed chuckled. "Learning the lingo, aren't you?"

"Damn straight." She quipped, and Browning laughed. She smiled up at Creed and winked.

Mariella leaned back and closed her eyes. She needed the distance from Creed to sort through his words last night. They scared her and made her insides all jumpy in a good way. Creed Lachlan had invaded her life and infused her existence with hope. She hadn't realized how resigned she'd become to the confines of her future. Having experienced the way

Creed and his men treated her, versus the way Rafa and the people who worked with her treated her, had been a revelation. One she couldn't un-experience. The Americans—Creed—had changed her.

She opened her eyes and stared without seeing out the car window. She wasn't sure she could describe her transformation. The sensation was almost like waking slowly from a dream, or maybe this was how a caterpillar felt when they emerged from a cocoon? She was the same Mariella, but she wasn't. Her eyes flitted to the front seat and the profile of the man that had been the impetus to that change. When had she ever trusted so easily or followed instead of pulling on the constraints of her life? She couldn't remember a time. She was a rebel. Her uncle called her a handful and thought she needed someone to take care of her. She didn't. A keeper wasn't what she needed or wanted. If she'd been asked a month ago what she wanted she'd say to be second in command and to be away from Adalberto's lecherous attentions. She wanted respect and power, and she wanted to be important. Yes, that was what her life boiled down to prior to going into Havana and meeting Creed Lachlan.

Her eyes tracked back to the countryside as it passed. All the things she'd worked so damn hard to obtain from Rafa and his men were freely given to her by Creed and his men. She had their respect. Her input to their plans was important. She was impor-

SEAL FOREVER

tant to the success of their mission, and she held a power she'd never thought she'd have. She had the power to make herself happy.

She sighed and closed her eyes again, letting the cool morning wind and the motion of the vehicle relax her. She was happy and wasn't that stupid? Why would traipsing around in the interior of the island with a band of Americans bring her happiness? She gave a mental laugh. It all pointed back to the people, rather person, she was accompanying. She was happy because she was with Creed Lachlan.

The car slowed down, and Mariella startled, blinking against the sun when she opened her eyes. They were slowing to turn into the small area where they'd left McGowen. She'd been lost in her thoughts longer than she realized.

Whitehead and one of Rafa's men stepped out of the foliage after they stopped the car and got out. She smiled at Whitehead, and he waved at her. Creed and Browning went to the back of the car and unloaded the packs they'd brought from the boat. Creed handed her a phone and then took his watch off and handed it to her. "No more than two minutes. I'm not sure what your government's capabilities actually are, but we aren't taking any chances, especially when we are this close to the end game."

She nodded and slipped the heavy black metal watch onto her arm. She waited until Creed had diverted Whitehead and Rafa's man, giving each a pack to carry back to the campsite. She powered up the cell phone and waited for it to acquire a signal. She dialed a number and it connected.

"Rafa."

"What the hell are you doing, Uncle? Do you think I'm stupid?" She groaned. "Don't answer that, of course, you think I'm stupid. What the hell, Rafa? There isn't even electricity to the sites you are sending us! How long before Creed becomes suspicious? What the fuck is going on?"

There was silence on the other end of the phone. Mariella pulled the phone away from her face and glanced at the damn thing to make sure they were still connected.

"I did it to keep you out of the area. Adalberto isn't someone to mess with."

"I can take care of myself, and you know the others I'm with won't hesitate to take him out if he tries anything."

"No need to worry. I found him last night." Rafa gave a pained grunt.

"How badly are you hurt?"

"I'll live. Is the American close?"

"No."

"Tell him the transport will happen three days from today. They leave Havana at nine in the morning. I don't have the route, and I don't think I can get it, but they are taking the prisoners to the interrogation center near La Maya. That limits the approach.

We can determine the best way to stop them before they get to the facility."

"Where will we meet you?"

"Call the day of the transfer. I'll let you know."

Mirella glanced at her watch. "You better be there, old man." Her tone was tender. She could tell he was hurt worse than he was letting on.

He gave a tired laugh. "I'll be there. Go, tell the American what I said." The line disconnected and Mariella turned off the phone and pulled the battery as she'd seen Creed do.

"McGOWEN IS SLEEPING. He was up all night." Whitehead pointed at a patch of smaller sago palms that had several cut boughs woven through them. He could see McGowen's form in the shade.

"We'll let him sleep until Mariella comes back." Creed acknowledged. Whitehead dispatched Rafa's man to watch the back of the building. His Spanish had improved. The man seemed happy to oblige.

Whitehead waited until they were alone before he asked, "What's up? Why is Browning here? Is there trouble?"

Creed shook his head. "No, nothing like that. We need to get into that facility and find out what is happening. Mariella is reaching out to her uncle and hopefully getting answers to questions that will allow us to make plans. I brought Browning to help McGowen and me infiltrate the facility." Creed spoke while watching Mariella make her way through the trees and underbrush toward them. He glanced back at Whitehead when he realized he was staring. "The three of us have the same training, and although we haven't worked any operations together, we're SEALs. That training lasts forever, man." He reached out, and Browning bumped his fist.

"Dude, I don't want anything to do with going in there. There are a ton of guards." Whitehead rubbed the back of his neck as he spoke.

"A ton, is that a euphemism or are there literally two thousand guards?" Creed didn't try to hide his laughter, and neither did Browning.

Whitehead flipped him off but laughed as well. "Screw you. McGowen's got that information. We were able to put one of the Cuban flag pins against the door. I can see it through those high-tech binoculars he has. There hasn't been a change in the stripes, so there are no outward signs of radioactive material, which is a fucking godsend because if the inside of the facility is like the outside, I'm not looking forward to dealing with the conditions that exist around that radioactive material."

Mariella had held on the edges of the camp. Creed motioned to her, and she approached.

"Sorry, didn't want to interrupt." She shoved her hands in the front pockets of her camos.

"What did you find out?" They needed information before they woke McGowen and made plans.

"Rafa was sending me out of the area because of Adalberto and using you as the vehicle to do that. He caught Adalberto last night. Rafa was injured. I don't know how badly, but he didn't sound good."

"I'm sorry to hear that," Creed acknowledged.

"Yeah, well other than that, the transport of the CIA agents will happen three days from today. Rafa said the transport will leave Havana at nine in the morning. He didn't know the route, and he said he didn't think he'd be able to obtain that information."

"What good does that do us?" Whitehead gave Creed a frustrated look.

Mariella held up a hand. "We do know the agents are being taken to the interrogation center near Le Maya. That limits the roads they can use. I know my uncle. He will post people on all the access routes, and we will know which way they are coming in time to set up."

"That's what I needed to know. Whitehead, go wake up McGowen and get him back here." He watched as the man damn near sprinted across the clearing.

"T-Timing is k-k-key." Browning spoke for the first time since they exited the car.

"You're right." Creed motioned toward the small cooler and a couple of dead falls that had been pulled up as a makeshift seating area. They moved over, taking the equipment with them.

McGowen and Whitehead headed back across the clearing. Creed could hear Whitehead talking a mile a minute, no doubt trying to bring McGowen up to speed.

"Skipper, Browning." McGowen acknowledged them before he glanced at Mariella. "You still hanging out with this loser?"

Mariella blinked in surprise before the joke registered. She smiled and shrugged. "I've finally got him trained."

That earned a low ripple of laughter. Creed smiled and winked at her before he tugged the map out of the pocket of his pack.

He opened it and motioned, bringing everyone closer. "Okay, we have a date for the prisoner transport. Three days from this morning. The point of extraction is near Le Maya." He pointed to the location on the map and then tapped lower, indicating the base at Gitmo. "We need to get from there, to here before the Cuban government knows we have retrieved the agents."

McGowen rubbed his face and yawned. "You ready for a report on this facility?"

"Go."

He pulled out a hand-drawn map and placed it over the map Creed had laid down earlier. He pointed to the main structure indicating the two doorways. "Access to the building here and here. There are twelve full-time guards. They are split in half, doing twelve-hour shifts. They are outside the facility unless they are carrying supplies. A small structure five or six hundred feet from the facility on the west side functions as their living quarters." McGowen indicated the map and snaked his finger along a line he'd drawn. "They are armed with Russian AK's and have no hand-held radios I've been able to detect. Each rifle has one magazine. I've seen no indication of additional ammo, either on their belts or in the guards' bed down area. There is one radio. It is a hand crank system. I saw an old piece of equipment like that in Afghanistan. It is ancient, but it's worked every time they've checked in."

"When do they check in?"

"Fuck, Skip, they have no schedule. No rhyme or reason that I can identify. So far it has only been used when they need supplies or when the civilians are leaving."

"Last supply transport?"

"Two days ago, so they should get a truck this afternoon," Whitehead answered.

"Civilians?" Creed glanced between McGowen and Whitehead.

"Yeah, probably the people building the bombs." Whitehead nodded his head agreeing with McGowen.

"Are they in the facility right now?"

McGowen shook his head. "No, they left last night."

Creed flicked his eyes between his men. "Do they do that often?"

"No. Last time they came back the next day with more equipment. There definitely isn't a sense of urgency."

"Where are the civilians bunking?"

"In the warehouse." McGowen acknowledged.

"Then we go in tonight." Creed glanced from Browning to McGowen.

Whitehead raised his hand like he was in a fucking classroom. Creed smirked at him and raised an eyebrow. The man dropped his hand and in exasperation asked, "What if the civilians come back?"

"Then we hope they are sound sleepers." Creed hoped like hell they didn't show back up, but they'd deal.

"What is the plan?" McGowen prompted.

"First we get in and determine if this is the site we're looking for."

"Validating the obvious at this point, Skipper." McGowen rolled his shoulders.

"Roger that, we may be, but there is no room for assumptions or chance."

"Who and w-w-when?"

Creed pinned Whitehead with a stare. "Square deal here. Do you have to go in for us to validate they are making the bombs?"

Whitehead shook his head. "No, but I need to go in to ensure you aren't accidentally exposed to toxic levels of radiation."

"Can you teach me to use that damn meter?" Creed didn't like the idea of taking a civilian through armed guards.

"Yes and no. There are different settings, and each one supplies information I won't be able to explain to you in the time we have before night falls. Look, I know I'm not a SEAL. I get that, but I can keep up. You brought me here for a reason. Let me do my job." Whitehead held Creed's stare.

"Okay, this is the plan. Mariella, you'll provide the perimeter for us. You and Rafa's men will keep shit quiet unless we are in jeopardy of being found. Then you make a distraction and pull the guards away from us."

Mariella stared at the map and nodded. "Got it."

Creed motioned to the map McGowen had drawn. "Where are the telephone and power lines?"

McGowen drew his finger from the building back ghosting alongside the road he'd drawn in. "Power lines are here. I haven't seen any indication of a phone."

"Browning, you will be close in defense and over-watch. You'll deploy first." Creed glanced at Whitehead and McGowen. "Which door do the civilians use to enter and exit the facility?"

"Here." They both pointed at the far corner of the map at the same time.

Creed examined the map again. "Okay, that's where we will go in."

Whitehead's head shot up. "That's where the lights are."

"Until I cut the power." Mariella sniggered.

Creed nodded. "Smart girl. You'll need to go back a distance. I don't want them to know it has been cut. Just a random power outage."

"That happens on the island all the time," Mariella said almost to herself.

"Good. Send one of your men out as soon as we break and have him trace the feeder line back as far as he can. He'll need to disrupt power at exactly eleven thirty." Creed pointed to McGowen. "I'm assuming the day shift will be fed and hunkered down by that time?"

"Most are out by ten, eleven every last swinging dick is snoring." He glanced at Mariella. "Sorry."

She chuckled and waved him off. "No problem."

Creed nodded and pointed to Mariella. "Eleven thirty on the dot."

"It will be done." She confirmed.

He pointed at Browning. "Close in defense then overwatch. Make sure you grab a set of NVGs and find a way to give us cover without exposing your-self. Take a look at the perimeter during the daylight. Find your position. We'll deploy from the same location." Creed pointed to the map where they would hold up and wait for the power to go out. "Once you go in, I'll give you exactly three minutes to reach your position and set up before we follow you."

Browning lifted his eyes and gave him a single nod. Creed liked the focus he saw in the man's gaze.

Creed motioned to McGowen. "You and I are taking Whitehead inside. NVGs for each of us. I brought what we had on the boat. We can't do something stupid like kick over a fucking chair and bring the guards in after us."

"Roger that. I get the initial confusion over the power outage will be our way in. What is our exit strategy?"

"Cover is one hundred feet away. Browning will move from close in defense to the overwatch position fifteen minutes after we get inside the building. That will give us enough time to call the mission if we need to do so. Otherwise, fifteen minutes and he'll shift to here." He drew his finger down to the corner of the dense foliage. "If we need to get out sooner, he'll provide cover fire. My plan is to walk out when the guards change."

"Will that work?" Whitehead's head swiveled between McGowen, Browning, and Creed.

McGowen put a hand on Whitehead's shoulder. "Got a better plan?"

"No."

"Then we make it work, yeah?" McGowen

dropped his hand and rolled his shoulders. "Skip, I'm going to need an hour or two. I'm wrecked."

"Get back to it." Creed pointed to Browning. The man made a circle in the air and Creed nodded his understanding. Browning was going to take a look at the facility.

"What do you need me to do?" Whitehead asked.

"Get your equipment ready. Make sure anything that makes a noise is taped down, strapped shut or otherwise silenced."

"I can do that." The man nodded and headed off toward his pack.

Creed glanced at Mariella. "How is Rafa?"

"I don't know. He didn't sound good."

"What happened between him and Adalberto?"

"He didn't say, but if Rafa is alive, Adalberto isn't." She shrugged and looked down at her fingertips.

"Hey, he's a tough old coot. He'll meet us."

She drew a deep breath and released it slowly before she nodded. "If this is the place, how are we going to get all of this to the boat or to Santiago De Cuba?"

"I have a plan." He winked at her and before she could ask, he finished, "First we confirm what's inside."

CHAPTER 24

*C*reed tugged the black electrical tape around the metal portion of the sling of his M-4. The padding of the electrical tape would ensure there wasn't a metal-on-plastic noise when they moved because his rifle wasn't going to be slung across his back. No, that fucker was going to be locked, loaded and the firing selector on 'semi.' He was prepping for the worst and hoping for the best. Standard operating procedures, especially when working with a team he hadn't trained with or seen in action.

Whitehead sat on the opposite fallen tree trunk and studied him intently. The man then mimicked his actions, making his own equipment as soundless as possible. He waited until Creed looked up and raised his hand. "I have a question."

"Dude, put your hand down. This isn't a classroom. What's your question?" Creed shook his head and released a small chuckle. The guy was really a nerd in an athlete's body.

"What happens if we go in there and the bombs are done and ready to deploy?" Whitehead shrugged.

The hair on the back of Creed's neck prickled. "What makes you think that is a possibility? Have you seen or heard something?"

"Nothing really. Well, it could be nothing, or it could be something, maybe."

"Fuck, just spit it out," Creed ground out.

"Right. Well, they came back the last time with what looked like a new soldering gun. I think that's what it was. I'm not one hundred percent sure, but I saw it when they carried it in. If these guys know their shit, the soldering would happen after the radioactive materials are vacuum sealed. You're talking maybe a day to finish the electronics, triggering, timer, etcetera."

"So, you think these guys are done, and they aren't coming back?" Creed's mind flew through the possible scenarios.

"I don't think so. I mean they didn't take anything with them, and they are staying here, you know? I'm pretty sure they'll be back. Besides, the device or devices still need to be transported out of here, right?"

Creed narrowed his eyes at Whitehead. "Did you tell McGowen what you're telling me?"

"No, there is no support for my conclusion."

"Speak English and fill in the blanks, doc. What are you talking about?"

Whitehead shrugged. His gaze shifted in the direction of the warehouse. "I have nothing solid on which to base an assumption. There are no legitimate facts supporting my hypothesis." He gave Creed a pained, exasperated expression.

"But your gut tells you those guys are close to completing whatever they're working on." Creed filled in the blanks for Whitehead.

The man nodded. "Yeah, they could be. What are we going to do if we go in there and they are done with what they are working on?"

Creed placed his rifle beside him after ensuring the weapon was on safe. He leaned his elbows on his knees and stared directly at Whitehead. "If they are complete, you are going to determine if they are safe to move."

"And if they are?"

Creed glanced at where McGowen was sleeping. Browning was doing his own recon. They'd have to discuss this possible twist. His eyes shot around the small clearing. Mariella was watching the building after sending one of Rafa's men out to trace the powerline and set up a disruption of power. He returned his gaze to Whitehead. "Then we adapt the mission."

"Do you want me to wake him up?" Whitehead motioned to the shaded area where McGowen slept.

"No, let him sleep. We'll talk about it when he wakes."

"Fuck, why do you still want to do this shit? McGowen told me all of you volunteered to be here, to do this. Why?"

Creed laid another rifle across his lap and considered that question. "For over twenty years I ate, slept, trained and lived the life of a Navy SEAL. Service to my country is grafted into my DNA."

"It isn't an easy life." Whitehead shook his head. "You're out of the military. Why not relax?" He waved a hand around him. "This is insane. I don't understand what made you wake up one morning and say, hey, let's go hang out in the ass-crack of Cuba and hunt down people making dirty bombs."

Creed laughed. "Dude, you're here."

"I am, and I can tell you that while it has been an educational experience, I'll never agree to do this again."

"No?" Creed cocked his head. "Why not?"

"Because of that." He pointed to the M-4 Creed had just finished working on. "I was under the impression this was a 'go in, take a look and get my ass back out' operation. Not this... mess. How do you deal with it?" Whitehead picked up one of the radioactivity meters at his feet. "The complications are exponential."

"Dude, life isn't complicated. People are. I trained with the best the Navy had to offer. Individual men became a team, one body of many parts. We learned to depend on each other. That made life simple because we all had the same goals, the same focus, and the same training." Creed chuckled and grabbed the M-4 on his lap and his roll of black electrical tape. "Besides, the only easy day was yesterday."

Whitehead's eyes snapped to him. "Yesterday wasn't easy. Rafa's man tripped, and the guards came to investigate. They almost found us."

Creed smiled across the clearing at the man. "Were you found?"

"Well, no." The man's brow furrowed.

"Are you alive?"

"Obviously."

"Then yesterday was easy." Creed grabbed the electrical tape and went to work muffling any potential for noise.

CREED HAD JUST FINISHED GOING THROUGH ALL the equipment they'd hauled off the boat when he saw Browning approaching. He waited until the man fished out a bottle of water and drank half of it.

"Did you find a suitable position?" He glanced at his naked wrist for the twenty or thirtieth time since he'd given his watch to Mariella this morning. He needed to remember to get that thing back from her.

"Yes." One-word answers seemed to be easiest for the man.

"We might have a wrinkle in the plan. Whitehead thinks the bombs may be done or are close to being done. If so, when McGowen wakes up, we'll discuss what we are going to do."

Browning opened his mouth to speak, but the low drone of a motor and the blaring of a radio coming from the direction of the warehouse spun both men. The music cut off suddenly. Creed and Browning moved as one through the low sawgrass and up to the dense foliage. It took almost five minutes to work themselves into a position where they could see. A large green military truck had pulled into the compound, and four of the six guards were busy unloading supplies. The men laughed and joked among themselves as they transferred the cargo from the covered bed of the deuce-and-a-half into the warehouse by a back entrance. The two guards who remained positioned themselves at opposite corners, facing the facility.

He nudged Browning and pointed to the two men. Browning scanned the area and nodded. From their positions, the two guards had complete coverage of the facility's perimeter. Getting in tonight wasn't going to be a walk in the park. Browning nudged him and nodded down the access road. A banged up old Fiat bounced toward the ware-house. They watched as the thing parked in front of the building and two men got out. Definitely civilians. They exited the car and stretched, waiting beside the old vehicle until a guard made his way from the truck to the Fiat.

He and Browning weren't close enough to hear any words, but one civilian pulled out several sets of papers and handed them to the guard. The man read them and called over another guard from the truck. They motioned up the road where the old Fiat had traveled and then to the door through which the guards had carried a bulky and obviously heavy equipment container.

The four men parted company. The guards returned to the supply truck and the civilians used keys to unlock the front door to the warehouse. Creed watched it slam shut and bounce open before one of the men inside the facility pulled the door shut.

He and Browning jumped slightly when the supply truck's music started blasting again. The driver put the truck into gear and called out a friendly salutation to the men as he was leaving. Two guards carried some supplies back to the shelter where they slept, and the other two ambled over to the warehouse. One sat on the trunk of the Fiat, and the other strolled around the building. McGowen was right. They weren't consistent or predictable, but one thing was sure, the guards were trained and focused on that structure.

He and Browning backed out and made their way back to the clearing. McGowen was up and sitting on one of the fallen logs. He nodded toward the warehouse. "Noisy fuckers."

"Yeah, well, they think they are alone." Creed acknowledged. "If that changes we need to worry. The civilians came back." Creed grabbed a bottle of water and tossed it to Browning, who caught it in mid-air. He grabbed another one and drank the entire thing in one go.

Whitehead pushed out of the brush and headed straight to them. "The civilians are back."

"Yeah, we saw." Creed motioned between himself and Browning.

"Oh. Okay." Whitehead headed to the cooler and grabbed two bottles of water. "When are Rafa's men changing out?" He opened one bottle and took a drink.

McGowen glanced at his watch. "Mariella told them to relieve her in about a half hour." He motioned to a shady area where two men were starting to stir.

"Good, when Mariella gets back, we need to have a discussion."

"What happened?" McGowen's eyes snapped to him and then to Browning.

"I'll fill you in when she gets back." Creed motioned to the rifles, NVGs, body armor, and ammo. "In the meantime, I've done a field check and secured everything. Get those vests and ammo belts loaded and fit the NVGs."

McGowen grabbed an M-4, ensured it was on safe and pulled back the bolt locking it to the rear with a flick of his finger. "Who's the fourth rifle for?" He raised his head and looked at Whitehead. The man shoved his arms into the air and stepped away.

"Nope, not me. I have my equipment. I refuse to carry a weapon."

"The fourth is for Mariella."

All three men looked at Creed at the same time. He couldn't have scripted a more concise move on the parade field. "She's one of us. She's proven herself, and I'm not leaving her out here in the jungle unarmed."

"Does she know how to work one of those things?" Whitehead pointed to the rifles like they were poisonous snakes. He took another step away from them.

"I'm sure she's fired a rifle before, but if not, I'll give her a quick class." Mariella undoubtedly had firearms experience. That was evident by the automatic she routinely strapped to her thigh. "There is a vest and a helmet for you." Creed toed one of the Kevlar vests. "Adjust a set of those night vision goggles to your head."

McGowen rose and stretched. "I'm going to fill them in on the basics. They've been tight with me."

He motioned to the two men who now stood underneath a shady tree.

"Go ahead." Creed watched McGowen leave.

Browning moved next to him. "P-problems."

Creed nodded. "Yeah." Browning was sharp. He'd seen exactly what Creed had seen. McGowen had been watching at night. Whitehead during the day. While the intel that McGowen had gathered was invaluable, the five minutes he and Browning had observed today was telling, to say the least.

Creed dropped back down and watched as Browning helped Whitehead fit the NVGs and then helped to adjust his flak vest. Once Whitehead gave him a thumbs up, Browning gathered the man's gear and helped him figure out how to carry his equipment. They settled on a small backpack and worked the equipment into the confines while using a couple of t-shirts to pad the sensitive meters and keep them as soundless as possible.

Mariella came back to the camp and grabbed a bottle of water before sitting down next to him. "The supply truck came today."

"It did." Creed acknowledged. "It looked like a government truck. This may be a regime operation after all."

"No. It wasn't government. That is one of our trucks."

Creed blinked at her. "Rafa's people are supplying this warehouse?"

She nodded. "That is probably how Rafa knew about the site so quickly."

McGowen ambled over and sat down. "Okay, Skipper, what's the new wrinkle."

Creed drew a deep breath. "We now have less than three days before the prisoner transport." Everyone nodded. This wasn't new, but he wanted to lay out the situation, step-by-step.

"Whitehead has a hunch the people building the bombs may be finished or very close to it."

Whitehead ducked his head at the glare McGowen sent him. "Would have been good to know that, partner."

"If true, that will change our plans. Additionally, we saw some issues today when the supply truck came"

Browning nodded. "L-locks."

"Right. The civilians had a key to the front door. Looked like a deadbolt to me." He sent a quizzical glance to Browning. "You?"

The man nodded his head in agreement.

"Which wouldn't be a problem if we were breaching the warehouse with a full tactical team, but the noise in this situation would be a liability."

"So, we go in the rear door where they deliver supplies. There is no lock on that door."

Creed nodded at McGowen. "We could do that, or we could move up our timetable to enter the front before the civilians leave."

"Fuck." Browning's word was echoed by McGowen.

"You got the logistics figured out?" McGowen asked.

"I think I do." He turned to Mariella. "I want you to reach out to Rafa again."

"What do you need?" She leaned forward. His watch dangled off her forearm.

"First, I'll have that back." He pointed to his watch. "Second, remember that villa Rafa talked about? The one the government official owned by the beach?"

"Yes... the one for the honeymoon?"

"That's the one. This is what we are going to do..."

# CHAPTER 25

*M*ariella shrugged out of the flak vest. It wasn't horribly heavy, more cumbersome and awkward. The night vision goggles were still a mystery. She'd finally figured out that's what Creed referred to when he mentioned NVGs. Creed said she'd be able to see when it was completely dark. Light made the screen unusable. He'd fitted them to her face and then lifted a rifle. "I'm assuming you've fired a rifle."

Creed made a statement instead of a question, and for that she was grateful. Once again, he didn't assume she was a stupid, useless woman like so many men in her past.

"This is the M-4." He displayed the weapon and held it at hip level. "The rounds are 5.56mm, and it weighs 8.79 pounds with thirty rounds loaded in the magazine. The muzzle velocity is 3100fps, and the chamber pressure is 52,000psi." He looked up and chuckled. "Don't worry, there won't be a test. Suffice to say this bad boy will take down anything you shoot at. Here is the selector level. This is safe, next is semi-automatic. The semi-automatic setting is where you need to stay. If you go to the third setting, burst, you'll use up your ammo and won't be any support to us. Keep it on semi."

He moved to stand beside her. "This is the charging handle. Hold it like this and pull back. When the handle is back, use your thumb, here. Push this portion of the lever down, and it locks the handle back." He demonstrated for her. "Magazine ejection is here." He pushed the button, and the magazine dropped out of the weapon. He caught it, not allowing it to fall to the ground.

"If you have to clear the weapon or if it misfires, remember some basic simple steps. Slap the magazine release. Make sure you carry it down, don't let it fall. Pull the extractor level back like this. That should clear the spent brass or the round. Lock the bolt back. Insert the magazine, like this, and let the charging handle go forward." He pressed the button, and the bolt slid forward.

He handed the weapon to her. "Get the feel of her and work the upper receiver. I want you to know how to do this in the dark."

Mariella took the weapon. The first thing she did was place the selector level to safe and send him a withering glance. She pulled the charging handle back, locked it to the rear, dropped the magazine, reinserted it and sent the bolt forward.

Creed did a quick glance around. "Fuck, that was way hotter than it should have been." He adjusted himself, and she laughed. "This is not your first time with a weapon like this is it?"

"I've fired the AK-47. It is similar but doesn't have an external charging handle. I like this for dislodging misfires." She lifted the weapon and tucked it against her cheek leveling her sight picture. "What is the maximum effective range?"

"550 meters, but it has a maximum range of 3600 meters. If you miss, that bullet will travel until something stops it or it is way the fuck out of here."

"So, the lesson here is not to miss?"

"Gawd, I think I'm in love." Creed laughed as he handed her a full magazine.

Mariella faltered at the exchange of magazines. Creed's words floored her. If only he were in love with her. *If only*. She took a breath and handed him the empty magazine without looking at him.

"Hey." He put his fingers under her chin.

She made sure her weapon was on safe and slung the rifle over her shoulder. She drew a deep breath and looked at him when the pressure of his fingers didn't falter.

"We okay?" He pushed a stray piece of hair away from her face. "I meant what I said last night."

"Was it only last night?" She smiled up at him. "It seems like a lifetime ago."

"A lot has happened today. A lot more will happen before we can breathe easy, but when we do, I want to take you out on a date. I want to get to know you better, Mariella."

She tried to stop the smile that spread across her face, but she couldn't. "I think you know me better than any man on the island."

He ran his thumb across her bottom lip. The feel of his warm skin and the intensity of his stare sent a shiver of desire through her. "I may, but I have a feeling there is so much more to you."

"Maybe." She smiled coyly, stuck her tongue out and flicked his thumb. His eyes darkened, and his breath held for a second. She'd do anything to remain the focus of his attention.

"Skipper, you ready?" McGowen moved up from the deepening shadows.

"Yeah," Creed called, still staring into her eyes. "You be careful tonight. Don't take any chances." He took off his watch and grasped her hand. He held it, so her fingers were pointed in the air before he slipped the heavy watch over her wrist. It fell down her arm almost to her elbow. "Don't be late."

He picked up his weapon and strode to where McGowen, Browning, and Whitehead waited. He walked through the group and melded into the foliage. McGowen gave her a two-finger salute, and

Whitehead brought up his hand in a half-hearted wave before they turned and followed Creed into the underbrush. Browning nodded, turned on his heel, and slipped into the darkness.

Mariella had dispatched her men to the locations where they needed to stand watch. The ones that had been up all day were given a few hours' sleep. If they did not succeed tonight, the men wouldn't need more sleep. If they did succeed, her men could sleep the day away tomorrow.

Mariella picked up her NVGs and the helmet. The helmet she attached to her belt with the chinstrap. No matter how she adjusted the webbing, her head was too small. There was no way she could see and wear that damn thing. If a bullet went through her brain, she wouldn't have any concerns, but she wouldn't leave the helmet in their campsite for just anyone to find. She glanced around one last time and ensured they'd left nothing. Creed's men hadn't left so much as a footprint. Her men had cleared their equipment. She took a deep breath and shifted away from where the Americans had ghosted into the darkness.

The moon crept up. It was almost a quarter moon, so the darkness was a friend tonight. She glanced at the watch which had stayed lodged on her arm near her elbow. Ten thirty. She moved forward and stopped. Watching, listening and waiting. She had plenty of time to reach the small building where the guards slept. Her men should already be there, with the exception of the one man down the road who would bring down the power line. She had no doubt her man could cut the power. They'd perfected the technique in order to make approaches or departures in certain areas easier. The government was slow to respond to outages. It could take months before they came out to this location—unless her government was responsible for the dirty bombs being built. If that were the case, the power crews would respond immediately. For many reasons, she prayed her government wasn't responsible.

She moved along the leaves and between the blades of sawgrass and slightly moving palms until she reached her destination. Checking down the trail and staying quiet for a moment, she listened to the sounds of the night. The bug song and small noises of the night were the only sounds she heard. She made her way to the small building. Soft snores could be heard coming out of the open windows. The door was closed. She slid on her NVGs and turned them on. The sudden light and clarity stunned her. She and her men were in charge of ensuring these men did not make it to the warehouse and for making sure no alarms were set off. She scanned the area around the building and easily picked out her men. Creed warned her not to look at anything that emanated a light, so she resisted the temptation to watch the small glow on the moon when the clouds parted momentarily. Everyone was to move at exactly eleven thirty. Her men would see her moving and back her up.

Eleven twenty-five. She closed her eyes and said a prayer Rafa had managed to keep his end of the arrangement. If he didn't, all of the careful planning tonight would be for nothing.

CREED HELD UP HIS HAND, and all motion ceased... except for Whitehead who bumbled forward. McGowen grabbed his shoulder and pushed him to the ground. Browning's hand slid over Whitehead's mouth, stifling the man's gasp. Browning touched his lips with his finger and Whitehead nodded his head quickly.

Creed listened. He'd heard something other than his men's movement. He surveyed in short bursts working from close in to farther out. There. He focused on the back of the man ahead on the trail about fifty feet from where they crouched. Creed watched and then smiled as the man shook and spun, tucking his cock back into his pants. The guard picked up his rifle that had been propped against a tree and crashed through the underbrush.

Creed waited for several minutes before he lowered his hand and his group followed him forward. When they were within fifteen feet of the clear zone around the building, he maneuvered his small group to one of the largest clumps of sawgrass in the area and positioned behind it. He grabbed Whitehead's arm and glanced at the watch he was wearing. They had eight minutes. McGowen and Browning settled, immediately motionless. Whitehead fidgeted until McGowen put a heavy hand on the man's shoulder. He glanced up at Creed and cringed, settling immediately.

Creed motioned for Browning to take his place. The man would lead the movement. He moved swiftly and almost silently through the underbrush. Creed glanced at McGowen and then motioned to Whitehead. The man's hands were clasped together, and he was visibly shaking. McGowen rolled his eyes. He dropped his lips to Whitehead's ears and whispered something to the man. Whitehead jumped but nodded. He shook his head after a moment, and McGowen tapped him on the shoulder. McGowen winked at Creed.

Creed glanced at Whitehead's watch again and through the leaves, watched the light from the warehouse. He counted the seconds. The lights flickered and then went out.

There were several calls from the guards and, "The fucking power went out," was echoed by at least three different voices. Creed dropped his NVGs and moved forward, trusting McGowen to keep Whitehead in tow. He saw Browning and counted three guards. The guards had congregated about mid-building. The NVGs limited his scope of visibility. It was rather myopic looking through the amplified light, but he could see the guards. He glanced back to Browning, who lifted his hand. That was the signal that the guards on the far side weren't a factor. They were far enough away from the door that Browning felt it was safe for Creed to move.

Creed rose into a crouch and headed out. Whitehead and McGowen were close on his six. The distance to the door was about three hundred feet. He moved as quickly as possible while still remaining silent. His gaze swung between Browning and the guards huddled on the near side of the building.

They moved closer. Creed lost sight of the guards as the building shielded them from the men. They were about ten feet from the door when it slammed open, and someone yelled, "What the hell happened to the power?"

Creed and McGowen ducked, pulling Whitehead down with them, huddling suddenly and silently not more than eight feet behind the man who was yelling.

From his right Creed heard, "It went out, moron."

"Are you going to call it in?" The man at the door yelled back.

"No, of course I'm not calling it in. I love standing in the dark. Moron."

The guards laughed, and the man in front of him

swore before he headed back into the building. The door slammed behind him, and a crash from inside the building was followed with another string of Spanish swear words that would singe a seasoned sailor's ears. Creed rose, grabbing one of Whitehead's shoulders, and McGowen moved almost at the same time he did. They pinned themselves against the corrugated tin wall. Creed swung his myopic view to Browning. The man was looking straight at him and lifted his arm telling him there were no guards active on his side of the building.

Creed crab walked to the door, pushed and turned the handle. It moved and then caught. He pulled the door closed and breathed a sigh of relief. Only the deadbolt held it shut. Easily enough to force. He nodded to McGowen who moved to the door and carefully placed a center punch in the locking mechanism. McGowen grasped the handle and waited.

Creed shifted his left arm and cut through the air. Browning spun and launched a rock toward the shrubs. Creed heard a scurry of boots and watched Browning. The man lifted his arm again, and Creed nodded at McGowen. With one strike, he destroyed the locking mechanism and opened the door. Creed grabbed Whitehead and pushed him through after McGowen. He snagged the handle and pulled the door closed behind, him flipping the deadbolt. The door rattled not more than thirty seconds later—a guard checking it was locked. Creed crouched just inside the door. Whitehead and McGowen were further down the hall.

He signaled McGowen to follow and moved away from the door. There were no windows. He made quick work of walking down the hallway. A sudden clink of metal against metal and two Spanish voices stalled their advance.

"Fuck, I can't see shit. Where are the battery operated lights?"

"The batteries were dead the last time this happened. There are some candles in the bedroom."

"We might as well call it a night. We can't finish without power."

"Yeah." A loud thud followed. "Fuck, here are the stairs. Seriously, working under these conditions is ridiculous."

"The money makes it worth it."

"We will be set for life."

"Do you think they'll want more?"

"I don't know. You heard the lady, right now, just these three."

"At least they let us connect the triggering devices on these."

"You're sick. Do you actually want to see one of these things blow up?"

"What difference does it make as long as I'm nowhere near it?"

The voices softened as their tread on the stairs

KRIS MICHAELS

moved farther away. Creed waited, listening to the men's trek across the floor above.

He nodded and they moved silently down the hallway. There was a door at the end. Creed carefully turned the handle. The door opened, and the hinge squealed in complaint. They froze and waited. All remained quiet. Sweat poured down his face and rolled down his neck. He motioned for McGowen to enter first, holding up Whitehead when the man made to follow. He held up a finger. Whitehead didn't move an inch.

McGowen came back and gave Creed the all clear sign. He guided Whitehead in but left the door open. McGowen led the way to the next door, which was ajar. Whitehead straightened and looked at Creed. Creed lifted a finger to his lips, and Whitehead nodded. He removed his backpack straps from his shoulders, his stare focused on the table just inside the door. The pack slipped out of his hands. Creed lunged for it at the same time as McGowen did. The pack landed in both of their hands. As a team, they rolled their heads toward Whitehead. Even with the myopic view that the NVG's provided Creed could see the horror on the man's face not covered by his own NVGs.

Creed lifted his finger to his mouth again. Whitehead nodded. Fuck his life. The man was an unstable ball of nerves. He should have demanded the geek show him how to work the damn equipment.

Whitehead pulled the pack toward him and quietly unzipped the top. He took out two different meters and laid one down. He worked flipping switches and moving dials for a few moments before he stood and walked toward the table. McGowen's hand shot out and moved the device Whitehead left on the floor.

Creed and McGowen exchanged exasperated looks before they followed the man into the workshop area. Whitehead held out a hand keeping them at the doorway. He circled the table, twice. Finally, he set the equipment on the table and started to look at the boxes that lay on the worktop. Creed stood and grabbed the backpack. McGowen straightened, still holding the equipment that Whitehead had left on the floor.

Whitehead motioned for them to come forward. Creed moved in and glanced at the sturdy equipment boxes. What he saw looked identical to the devices Branson had shown him.

Whitehead pointed to the first one and ran his finger along a wire that was connected to what appeared to be a triggering device. He motioned to the other two boxes. The wire wasn't there.

Whitehead raised one finger and nodded his head up and down. He pointed to the other two devices and shook his head. Okay, one live and two not ready, but those two were too fucking close to being done for Creed's liking. They were a go.

He leaned forward and whispered in Whitehead's ear. The man nodded and started working carefully and quietly, packing up the devices.

Creed pointed to the ceiling and McGowen moved. They made it up the stairs and down the hallway. There was a small glow of candlelight that showed as a brilliant light green in the NVGs. Creed pulled them off at the same time as McGowen. They clamped their eyes shut giving nature time to adjust their vision.

He opened his eyes and waited. McGowen held soundlessly beside him. Creed gave it another minute before he motioned for them to move. Silently they ghosted into the room. It was a small sitting room. The men they'd heard were in the next room. One was reading a book beside a candle and the other lay on the couch, his feet on the armrest and his elbow flopped over his eyes.

Creed directed McGowen to the man on the couch and entered the room with his weapon lifted.

The flash suppressor of his barrel lodged on his target's temple before the man realized Creed was there. McGowen's man startled and jumped. It was the last voluntary move he'd make for a while. The butt of McGowen's rifle knocked him out.

"You can die, or you can talk to me," Creed spoke in Spanish to the man.

"I don't want to die." The man's accent wasn't local. He spoke Spanish, but it wasn't his first language. Creed didn't have time to figure out what type of accent he had, he needed answers. Now.

"Who are you making the bombs for?"

"I don't know. A woman. She set us up out here. She's paying for the guards, the equipment; and she's paying for the food."

"The guards?"

"They are dangerous."

"Most guards are."

"No, these guys are hardened. They take our phones, and we are almost prisoners here. We only get to leave when we are called into Havana. We have to request permission to leave, request all our supplies and explain if something breaks or doesn't work. We are followed. Always."

"How do they know when you are leaving?"

"The guards here call ahead. They have a Sat phone. I've seen it. They kill for money. They brag about it. They've threatened us. The woman is the only reason they don't take what we are making and sell it themselves. She is very powerful."

Creed didn't doubt it. Money and power usually walked hand in hand. "How are you getting paid?"

"She sends the money through a Canadian broker." That would be easy enough to track. Undoubtedly the woman had safeguards, but they could find the broker.

"How much were you paid?" The man glanced at his friend and McGowen, who had ziptied the man's arms behind his back. He was in the process of restraining the unconscious man's legs in the same manner. "Don't worry about him," Creed growled. "You want to live, right?"

The man's gulp was audible in the quiet room. "Ten thousand dollars for each box."

"How many devices have you made?"

"Eight."

"Are they all functional?" Creed nudged the man when he glanced over at his friend and stalled again.

"Three are supposed to be. Two downstairs need the timer installed."

"Are you delivering them?"

The man nodded. "We were told to take them to Havana. I have the address." The man nodded to a small notebook.

Creed grabbed it, "Show me."

The man fumbled with the pages, his hands shook violently. "Here. This is where."

"When?" Creed grabbed the entire notebook, it had drawings and other squibbed notations that Branson's people might find useful.

"Next week, Friday. She wants an update by tomorrow night. I give it to the guard. He calls." The man flinched when McGowen stood and headed across the room.

Creed glanced at McGowen. "You ready?"

McGowen nodded and leveled his rifle on the man Creed was talking to.

"What? No! You said I'd live if I told you the truth."

"But you didn't, did you?" Creed went with his gut on this one. "We know you left out information. Tell me now, or I'll let him finish both of you."

The man's eyes bugged out, and he stammered, "She's American."

"And?"

"She's got a special passport. I saw it. It was black. That's something, right?" He swung his eyes from the end of McGowen's rifle to Creed. "I swear that's all I know."

Creed stood and held his finger to his lips silencing the man. McGowen moved while Creed held his weapon on the guy. "Keep very quiet, or I'll end you." The man opened his mouth for McGowen as he pushed in a rolled-up sock he'd found somewhere. The gag was tied so tight it put indentations in the man's cheeks. McGowen ziptied the guy's hands and pulled him out of the seat, taking him to the small sitting area. After checking to make sure they were not going to give, he used another tie to strap the guy to the exposed metal struts in the wall. He dragged the unconscious man over, zipped him to a lower strut and gagged him.

Creed stood over the conscious man. "I hear anything from you or your buddy, and you're dead. Got it?"

The man nodded his head and pushed into the

wall away from Creed.

Creed nodded to McGowen. They moved as one out the door, down the stairs and to the front door, passing Whitehead. The man knew to stay where he was until they came back. Creed unlocked the deadbolt, cracked the door open, and glanced out. He lowered his NVGs and waited to let his eyes adjust. He searched the area he could see. Nothing. He slipped out the door and waited, slowly scanning his field of vision, which was basically like looking through a tube. He cleared the area and motioned for McGowen to follow. The man slipped out and silently shut the door behind him. Creed used hand signals to indicate he'd go right. McGowen nodded and spun, heading left.

He moved to the corner of the building and peeked around the corner. Two of the three guards he'd need to take out leaned against the Fiat. One lit a cigarette and pulled a lungful off the coffin nail. The action lit the tip up like a ball of light in Creed's NVGs. He ducked back and closed his eyes tightly for a count of ten before he crouched low and soundlessly moved forward parallel to the men. He settled about ten meters behind them. Their low conversation and frequent chuckles played on his ears.

He moved forward. Five feet at a time. Up-move-pause-move. He lifted his NVGs and settled at the rear of the Fiat where he waited. A low audible grunt brought both guards to attention. Creed pushed off his back-right foot and flew at the men. The one on his right turned just in time to meet the business end of his rifle stock. The collision was violent and the impact, lethal. Creed ducked to his right, pushing the dead man to his left. He rolled and came up, grabbing the AK the guard had attempted to bring into position.

Creed grabbed the barrel and pushed the weapon back into the guard. To keep his balance, the guard shifted his right foot off the ground. Creed kicked his standing leg and the guard's left knee snapped backward with a sickening crunch. Creed shoved his forearm under the man's chin, snapping his mouth shut and stifling his scream of pain. He ended the struggle with a violent twist of the man's neck and slowly dropped to the ground with the dead guard.

He regulated his breathing, staying still by the downed guards. A scrape to his left snapped his head in the direction of the guard's sleeping quarters.

Creed strained but didn't hear anything else. He carefully lowered his NVGs again and scanned the side of the building. There was one man down. He saw movement at the side of his vision and swung his head. Browning was moving toward him. He waited until the man was looking his way and held up two fingers. Browning pointed to himself and held up one finger. Three guards taken care of. That left McGowen to deal with the other three.

He pointed to the other side of the building, and

he and Browning sprinted across the cleared zone and stopped at the corner. Creed signaled he'd take high and Browning crouched taking the low position. Creed tapped Browning's shoulder, and they rolled around the corner, their rifles ready to fire should McGowen need assistance.

*Holy fuck.* If he wasn't watching it in shades of very visible green, he wouldn't have believed it. McGowen, sans rifle, was walking up behind the three guards on this side of the building. The animated guards motioned to the right and started to move. McGowen shadowed the movement.

"Fuck." Browning's almost there whisper echoed Creed's thoughts. McGowen snapped the first guard's neck. The man hadn't even dropped before the second man was down and the third was in McGowen's grasp. The entire fight took less than twenty seconds. Creed had never seen such a devastating show of deadly aggression. McGowen dropped into a crouch and scanned the area.

Creed tapped Browning and pointed to his wrist. Browning flashed his watch. Creed gave him the signal and the man flew across the clearing where Mariella and her people were waiting. He turned his attention back to McGowen, who was now pulling the dead men out of sight. He turned on his heel and entered the building.

He made enough noise to alert Whitehead he was coming. "Take off your NVGs," Creed said as he entered the room. Whitehead peeked up from behind the table where he'd been crouched.

"Dammit, you scared the fuck out of me." The man stood and pulled his goggles off.

Creed pulled a glow stick from his vest and popped it as he lifted his own NVGs. "Are we ready?"

"I need to pack the back of the tubes on this one. Give me five more minutes, and then you can give these to the baggage handlers in the biggest city in the world, and there would be no damage." The man shook a can in his hand and aimed the attached straw behind the tubes. He sprayed what looked like expanding insulation foam under the sealed containers. Creed assumed they held the radioactive material. Foam bubbled up and surrounded everything in the device. Smart. "This will harden in seconds, preventing anything from jostling the contents of the containers. By the way, they have quite the little lab built here. There is a clean room, where they probably vacuum sealed the cylinders. Suits, breathing apparatus, ventilation system, all compact and all extremely high tech."

"Understood. Get that stabilized. I'll be back in five minutes. Be ready."

"Roger that, Skipper."

Creed was out the door before the man finished his sentence. He opened the door just as McGowen was striding toward it. They both spun when a single shot echoed through the stillness.

# CHAPTER 26

*M*ariella glanced at her watch and moved forward to the bunkhouse. There was no call for help from the guards when the power went out, although she did hear some conversation and then laughter. The men inside the shelter didn't even stir.

Her mission was to contain the men, alive if possible. She made her way to the door and examined the bunkhouse. It was nothing more than four walls and a roof, and it stunk of sweat and filth. Her nose curled at the stench. How could they sleep? She didn't need the NVGs to see the men in the cots or to hear the rustle of sawgrass against clothing from behind her. She stepped to the side of the door and into the shadows.

Rafa's men appeared and moved toward the building. She stepped back into view and pointed at the front man and then to the door. He nodded and glanced at the man behind him. They both entered the cabin. Mariella swung in and stood in the doorway for a moment. Her men ghosted toward the weapons rack at the back of the shelter.

Mariella pulled down her goggles and searched the small table/kitchen area to the right of the door. There was a notebook, a big clunky looking phone and the radio box that McGowen had told them about. She glanced at her men and bent down to look at the box. It was connected to a cable that ran up to the roof. She carefully reached around and unscrewed the cable. She picked up the box, and it scraped along the table. Her men froze. One of the guards stopped snoring.

Oxygen was sucked from the room, but that was okay because she wouldn't risk breathing. The man turned and sighed. His breathing regulated. She picked the radio straight up and carefully took it to the door, positioning it outside. Her men followed with the weapons from the rack. They carefully laid the guns down in the dirt outside the building.

Mariella re-entered first, gazing at the sleeping forms. She moved out of the way and her men slipped inside to gather the rest of the weapons. The big phone and notebook went into her pockets. Mariella lifted her goggles and let her eyes adjust to the darkness again. They exited as quietly as they'd entered. She took up position outside the building and waited.

She glanced at the watch lodged next to her elbow. There was a stir inside the building. She dropped down as did her men and a guard appeared at the doorway. He scratched his belly as he headed toward the latrine. When he turned the corner, she motioned to one of her men. He nodded and faded into the darkness going after the guard.

The sound of a scuffle reverberated through the small area. Mariella could hear the men in the building stir. *Fuck.* She moved into position and readied her rifle. There were muttered comments, too low and muffled to be heard, but the tone she understood.

She moved up, closer to the door. "The guns are gone!" A guard inside the sleeping quarters shouted the words.

She stepped closer to the door and flicked the weapon to semi as Creed had directed. The metallic click of the weapon's selector level changing positions silenced every man inside the building.

"You have no weapons. Put your hands on top of your heads and walk out. Slowly." Mariella's words were met with more silence. "You have thirty seconds." She counted to ten. "Twenty."

The first man appeared at the door. His eyes bugged out when he finally saw her. "Move forward."

The man did. Slowly. His eyes scanning the darkness for who knew what.

"On your knees."

The man hesitated for a fraction of a second before he dropped to his knees and lunged forward toward her.

Mariella dodged the lunge. Her shitkicker caught the bastard in the head. Rafa's man jumped on him just as two more men flew out of the building. Mariella swung her rifle toward the door and came face to face with a revolver. "Drop your weapon." Spittle flew from the guard's mouth when he spoke. She didn't see it, but she felt it.

"No." She moved the M4 to hip level. Her finger on the trigger.

"I will kill you, bitch," the guard threatened.

"Maybe." Mariella smiled in the dark. "But, I'm ready to die. Are you?"

She saw his eyes narrow. A rush of movement from her right drew both her and the guard's attention. A black figure flew through the air, the guard in front of her swiveled and fired.

She lifted her rifle at the same time as Rafa's men. The men who rushed to the door stopped as one. Their hands in the air, they stared at the fight happening not more than five feet in front of them. Mariella glanced to the ground and the life and death struggle happening beside her. Her eyes flitted to the men at the door. "Hands on your heads now, or

357

you're dead!" Her command broke through to Rafa's men who moved forward with force and dropped the men to their knees as she kept the assault rifle trained on them.

The sounds of fighting stopped. She waited to turn until all the men had been ziptied and pushed onto their faces outside the door. As the last man dropped, she spun and drew a bead on the guard lying lifelessly on the ground.

Browning stood. He was bent at the waist over the dead guard. Creed and McGowen flew into the small clearing.

"Mariella?" Creed called from across the clearing.

"I'm fine. I think Browning needs help."

Creed and McGowen forced the man to sit down and she dashed to him.

Browning glanced up at her. "O-Okay?" he stuttered. His eyes closed in pain when McGowen moved his flak vest.

"I'm fine. Thank you." She dropped in front of him and took his hand.

"Shoulder. Through and through. We need to pack it." Creed pulled off Browning's vest. He cut the shirt away from the wound, and McGowen handed him packs of white gauze. Mariella watched in silence, holding Browning's hand. He squeezed it when Creed pushed the padding against the wound before he taped the injury and grabbed Browning's vest. "You good to go?"

"N-never q-quit."

"Damn straight." McGowen grabbed both his weapon and Browning's before he and Creed helped Browning to his feet. "Where is the truck supposed to be?"

She pointed in the direction of the main road. "Down the road beyond the bend."

Creed snapped, "Your men got these guys?"

Mariella spat out several commands, and the men nodded. "Yes, they will secure them and then get out."

"Can you help him? We need to grab the equipment."

"Yes." It was her fault Browning had gotten hurt. How could she have let that guy get the drop on her? She hadn't seen the pistol. Hell, her men hadn't mentioned any side arms. Browning's injury was all on her. She'd stay with him as long as he needed her.

Browning shook his head. "G-good t-to go." The man grabbed his gun with his good arm. He nodded toward the warehouse.

Creed nodded. "All right, let's go." He glanced at the guards one more time before he spun on his heel and headed back to the warehouse without giving her another glance.

She drew a deep breath. She could hardly blame him for not wanting to look at her. She was a liability. Creed had trusted her with a task, and she hadn't been able to do it without almost killing one of his men.

∽

CREED'S HEART rate still hadn't returned to normal. He'd broken through that clearing and breathed a sigh of relief when he saw her. Until she told him Browning was hurt. Fuck, had he missed something? What happened? How did a sidearm come into play? Had he missed that intel from McGowen or Whitehead? His mind circled the questions as he led his people back into the main compound. He canned his emotions, putting a lid on everything. Mission first.

His head snapped around and he barked, "Mariella and McGowen. Get the men from upstairs, take them and Browning to the truck."

Browning made to object, and he shut that shit down fast. "That's an order. You are down here on the door, and then you will go with them." He glared at Browning who finally nodded, although his jaw clenched and worked like the man was biting back a slew of words.

Creed followed his people into the building. "I'll get Whitehead and the devices. Whitehead?" Creed bellowed as he moved down the hall.

"Here." The man appeared in the doorway. "There was a shot!"

"Yeah. You got those things ready?"

"I do. Who got shot?"

"Browning."

"Is he okay?"

Creed spun on the man. "We need to get the fuck out of here. Grab your shit and a case."

Whitehead moved and strapped his backpack on his shoulders. "Did he die?" He grabbed a case and started trudging to the front of the building.

"No. Shoulder injury, but we don't know who else could have heard that shot. Get going." Creed muscled the other two devices like suitcases, one at the end of each arm, and gritted his teeth at the combined weight. He turned sideways and double-timed it down the hall. They hit the door at the same time that McGowen, Mariella, and the two civilian men made it downstairs. Browning was leaning against the building.

McGowen pushed one civilian in front of him and used the sling of his weapon to level the gun at the man. "Move, fast. If you try anything, you're dead."

He nudged the man in the back with the flash suppressor at the end of the weapon's barrel. The man did exactly as McGowen directed. McGowen held the rifle with one hand and grabbed a device from Creed with the other.

Creed switched hands to take the device in his left and with his right he grabbed Browning, getting under the man's good shoulder. Together they brought up the rear of the rag-tag team.

They moved down the road quickly and semi-quietly. Creed kept surveying the area, expecting trouble. They rounded the bend, and thank God, Rafa had delivered. The green truck with the enclosed back sat at the side of the road.

"F-fuck." Browning breathed out the expletive when his foot went into a deep hole. Creed corrected them before they face planted.

"Everyone in the back except Mariella. You drive." Creed bit out the order as they shoved the boxes into the truck.

The man who'd answered Creed's questions earlier cried out. "Don't! You can't move them like that!"

"Shut the fuck up. I stabilized them, you moron," Whitehead hissed and pushed the civilian into the truck.

"We'll make a fighter out of you, yet." McGowen said to Whitehead before he pushed the other captured man in. "Sit the fuck down." He snapped, and both of the men dropped to their asses next to the devices.

Creed nodded to Whitehead. "Get in and help us." He waited until Whitehead was in the truck before they moved Browning to the tailgate. Whitehead reached down and took Browning's good hand. McGowen and Creed practically hoisted the man into the back of the truck. Whitehead took off his pack and put it under Browning's head as the man reclined. Even in the dark, it was easy to see how pale Browning was. Creed glanced at McGowen and nodded to the side of the truck. They walked several feet away, and Creed whispered, "If you need me to stop the truck, pound on the window. I'm not taking any risks with him."

"He's tough. I'll monitor him. He just needs to stop fucking moving."

"We are traveling straight through to the villa." Creed gave McGowen his rifle and took off his flak vest and helmet with the NVGs attached. They walked back over to the truck. "Keep it buttoned up back here. We can't let anyone see inside."

"Will do, Skipper." They dropped their equipment in the bed of the truck and McGowen hefted himself up into the bed. Creed handed him his weapon. "Hold on." He went up to the cab of the truck. "I need all your gear."

Mariella passed the equipment through the window and then the rifle, stock first. He checked the safety as he walked back to the rear of the truck. "Here." He handed Mariella's PPE and weapon to McGowen.

He helped snap the canvas fabric into place before jumping into the cab of the truck. "Let's move."

CHAPTER 27

*M*ariella drove in silence, but the ugly voice in her mind berated her. She gripped the steering wheel, white-knuckling the urge to beg for any information on Browning or the mission. She'd seen the cases. They had the two men who'd built them. Dirty bombs had been built in her country and she had been the fault point in the mission. Everyone, including Whitehead, had done their job. Rafa's men had performed well, but she'd failed. She glanced out the side view mirror, making sure there was no one behind them. This time of night there was rarely any traffic on the roadways.

If all went well, they could reach the villa by daybreak before the town started to wake. The truck was in good condition and had a full tank of gasoline. She nudged the accelerator further and upped the speed. They'd have one day and night to hide, rest and make a plan of action. She glanced at Creed.

He had his foot on the dash of the truck, his elbow on his thigh. He chewed his thumbnail as he stared sightlessly out the window. His strong jaw flexed and relaxed over and over. He was lost in thought. No doubt worried how to get the agents free without Browning.

Mariella swallowed down the emotion that threatened to consume her. Finally, she gathered the guts to speak. "I'm sorry."

His head snapped toward her. "What?"

She jumped at the harshness of his tone. She whispered, "Nothing," and concentrated on keeping the truck on the road and away from the harshest of the cracks, bumps, and potholes.

"What did you say?" Creed dropped his foot to the floorboard and shifted to face her.

"I said I was sorry." She didn't look at him. Whatever verbal berating he'd lash her with was deserved. She braced herself for it, expecting the tirade she'd earned.

"What are you sorry about?" His attention seemed riveted on her.

She flicked her eyes away from him. Okay, so he wanted her to admit her sins. She cleared her throat. "I didn't handle my portion of the mission. It is my fault Browning was hurt."

Creed dismissed her admission. "Browning made a decision to act." His voice sounded distracted.

"Because I couldn't handle the situation."

"What happened?"

"The guard had a pistol. I didn't know it. He pulled it on me. We were in a standoff. I was going to kill him, or he was going to kill me." She shrugged. What else could she say? That she wanted to cry? She swallowed hard. "I hesitated. I waited and prayed the man wouldn't call my bluff."

"Fuck me." He leaned forward and rubbed his hands over his face. His beard had grown in nearly full now. "You're not to blame. Shit happens in situations like these. Split-second decisions get made on almost no information and nothing but your gut to go on. I trust Browning did what he felt he had to do."

Mariella shook her head. "He did what I forced him to do."

"Stop taking the blame for something that isn't your fault," Creed spoke to the floorboards. "I'm just glad you're safe."

"At Browning's expense?"

"At any expense!" She jumped at the shout. "Fuck, don't you get it? I almost lost you tonight, and I will always thank Browning for stopping that from happening." He leaned back and stared out the windshield.

Mariella whispered, "I didn't want to die. I didn't

want to leave you." She swiped at the tears that built in her eyes.

Creed reached out his hand and laid it on the seat. She reached out with hers and laced her fingers between his. His thumb caressed the back of her hand. "Collins told me something interesting last night."

Mariella blinked at the radical topic change, but okay. She'd go with it. "Oh?"

"Well, he has to do some more research, but he and Browning believe we may actually be married."

Mariella's head whipped toward Creed and so did her arms, sending the truck to the right. It caught the edge of the road, and she broke free of his hand, struggling to pull the old truck back up onto the hardened surface. "Shit." She barely managed to correct the vehicle, and it took her breath for a moment. Her heart beat a rapid dance in her chest.

"Shit." Creed echoed and turned his head and stared out the passenger side window.

"What are you going to do?" she asked, keeping her eyes firmly on the road. She hoped Browning hadn't suffered too much from the lurch to the side of the road.

Creed shrugged. "Not sure."

*Not sure?* Mariella wanted to scream at him. Berate him. Hadn't he said he wanted this thing between them to go further? He just told her he was glad that Browning had stopped what she knew in her heart was her last moment on earth.

*Could it be? Married to this man? Could the fates be so kind?* She wanted to jump up and down and laugh. Could this man actually belong to her, tied to her through law and the eyes of God? She wanted to stop the truck and launch across the seat and kiss him, but doing so would only expose how deeply she'd fallen for him.

She felt his eyes on her and sent a sideways glance his way. "What?"

"What do *you* want to do?"

Was it her imagination or did he sound anxious?

She sent him another long look before she returned her attention to the road and shook her head. "I don't know. I guess that is something we will deal with when we leave here." She shrugged. "Nothing we do will change what is. Besides, you could do worse than me." She sent a smirk his way.

"You could do better than me," he teased in return.

"Yes, where is Brad Pitt when you need him?"

"Brad Pitt? Woman, don't sell me short." His laughter relaxed the tight, heavy places in her heart. The tension in the cab of the truck lightened, and she took a deep breath for the first time since they pulled onto the roadway. His hand found hers again. She gave him a quick smile. Her mind flitted back to the moment that handgun was in her face. She straightened her shoulders and checked her side view mirrors again. Clarity sailed through her mind like a boat across a glass top lake. She'd do whatever it took to maintain this relationship. She'd never wanted anything like she wanted Creed and he'd opened the door. Hope filled her heart. Hope for a life with Creed and for a forever kind of love.

CREED RUBBED his eyes removing the grit that seemed lodged in them. Mariella navigated the narrow streets as if she'd driven them every day. The night sky had just started to lighten in the east when they pulled in front of the villa. Creed jumped out and thumbed the combination to the gate left on a slip of paper in the ashtray. Four numbers that would mean nothing to anyone but them.

He swung the gate open, and Mariella pulled the truck into the small compound while he secured the gate behind her. There was a one car garage. Creed trotted over to the door and yanked it up and waited until Mariella pulled the truck into the stall. She had to pull it in, touching the bumper to the front wall before he could snake the door down and shut out the rest of the world. The villa actually boasted a door into the home from the garage. A perk of wealth and class of the owner, no doubt.

Creed tapped the side of the truck. "Side panel, Tigger." The flap opened. "How is he?"

"Been out of it most the trip. The bleeding seems to have stopped, but we need to get that wound cleaned out, packed, and that arm wrapped so it doesn't move."

"Roger that. Whitehead, help Mariella get the two civilians out." He grabbed a rifle from the four lying in the bed of the truck and tossed one to her as she exited from the passenger side of the vehicle. Fuck, it was a damn tight squeeze.

"Do me a favor? Kill the first one that says a word." He pointed at the two men responsible for building the bombs.

"Gladly." She reached down and slapped the release sending the bolt forward with a terrifying clank. Creed turned away so the men wouldn't see him smile. They didn't know there wasn't a round chambered in the gun. The sound effects alone should keep them in line.

Whitehead scrambled over the side of the truck and was none too kind to the former guards as he pulled them over and down to the concrete. Bound like they were, it was a miracle they didn't fall on Whitehead and splatter him on the concrete.

Creed motioned to McGowen to stay in the truck. "Give me a minute." He grabbed his forty-five from the holster at his back and headed into the house. He held up a hand, and Mariella stopped the procession before they left the garage. Creed cleared the house and made his way back to the garage. "There is an interior room. Down the hall, second door to the right. No windows. Put them inside. We'll rig a fail-safe on the door. If they open it, they die."

She nodded and started the procession inside with Whitehead leading the way.

McGowen looked at him from the bed of the truck. "A fucking failsafe?"

"Hey, they have no idea I was bluffing." Creed chuckled as he took possession of one the devices. He carried it into the house and placed it in the room closest to the garage door. It appeared to be a small bedroom. He trotted back out and repeated the trip two more times.

Finally, they moved to Browning. "Are you ready?"

"Fuck, man, if we didn't need to clean that damn wound, I'd leave him here rather than jostling him."

"And if we don't clean it, he could die from infection." Creed shook his head. "You help him to the side. I'll control the burn as he slides down the side. Just make sure he's facing out, so his bad arm doesn't get pinned against the truck."

"Roger that." McGowen spent a minute or so waking Browning and explaining what they were going to do. The man nodded and sat up with help. Fuck him, Browning looked harsh. He was game, though, and helped as much as he could. When he repositioned his second leg over the side of the truck, Creed grabbed him by the waistband of his camos and wrapped his arm around Browning's uninjured side. His man collapsed, and Creed took Browning's weight.

"Where to?" McGowen grabbed the remaining rifles and turned to the house.

"There is a bedroom on the left next to the bathroom." They'd need plenty of clean water and hopefully some type of antiseptic.

McGowen opened the door and went ahead of him into the bedroom, pulling the bedding back from the top of the bed. They both helped Browning to lie down, and McGowen went back out to empty the truck of the rest of their equipment. Creed stepped out of the bedroom to see what type of antiseptic he could find in the bathroom. Mariella was already there filling a bowl with water while she ransacked the curtained area under the sink. Whitehead sat on a chair outside the room where the men they'd appropriated had been stored. His jaw clenched tightly, he caught Creeds attention while he waited for Mariella to finish and nodded toward Browning's room. "Will he be okay?"

Creed nodded. "He's tough."

He stepped out of the way when Mariella exited the room. She had a sheet, scissors, a bowl with a washcloth and a bottle of rubbing alcohol. Fuck, Browning would need to be tough. Creed grabbed the medic kit from the packs as McGowen trudged by.

He opened the pack and sat it out beside Browning. The man's eyes tracked to him. He was pasty white, but there was a look of determination in his eyes. "You ready for this?" Creed asked.

Browning closed his eyes and nodded. Once.

Creed drew a deep breath and sent Mariella a look. It was going to be a long fucking day.

AN HOUR later he and Mariella walked out of the room and closed the door slightly behind them. Browning was one tough son of a bitch. Thank God for Mariella. She worked diligently, disinfecting the wound. Her tears rolled down her cheeks as she worked and she suppressed a small sob when Browning had gone rigid, seconds before he passed out. Creed kept his hands on task but his heart swelled with acknowledgement that she was crying for his man.

"Hey, I'll say it again. It wasn't your fault." He tipped her chin up and made eye contact. "We work in dangerous environments. Shit like this happens even though we take every precaution." Her lips trembled but she nodded and tried to smile. "Okay?" he said softly.

"Yeah…um…I'm going to wash up." She motioned

to the bathroom. Creed glanced in and noticed a small shower off to the right. High-class digs.

"I'm going to check in with McGowen and White-head. Come find me when you're done?"

She nodded. He could see the exhaustion painted across her expression. Hell, he felt it, too, but there was far too much to do to give in to his body's demands.

He passed the room with their unwilling visitors and chuckled at the rigged lock. The men wouldn't get out of their bonds, but the rope tied to the door handle and then cinched to the bars on the window in another bedroom was interesting. He peeked into the room. Whitehead was stretched out on one of two single beds in the room. He carefully stepped under the rope and headed into the kitchen. McGowen sat at the table with a cup of coffee. He pointed to a battered French coffee press on the stove. Creed groaned at the beautiful sight. "Fuck, I think I'm in love with you, man."

"Sorry, you're not my type. How's Sage?"

"He'll live. He needs to rest."

"Which leads to my next question. How in the fuck are we going to manage two prisoners, three devices, Rafa, who is also injured, and Browning, while still freeing the CIA agents that are possibly injured, definitely guarded, and oh, by the way, about thirty minutes from any support, as in our troops in Gitmo?"

Creed took a sip of his coffee and leaned forward. "Alone, I am lethal..." he began.

"As a team we dominate," McGowen smirked and nodded. "SEAL forever man, but that doesn't answer my question."

"We are going to divide and conquer, my friend." Creed had to make big leaps of faith when making this plan, but he liked their chances. "This is what we're going to do."

MARIELLA USED the comb that she found in the bathroom and worked it through her freshly washed hair. She braided it quickly and redressed. She didn't have any clean clothes, but at least *she* was clean. She slipped out of the bathroom and stopped short, staring at the rope that led from the doorknob into the other bedroom. She tiptoed to the rope and gazed along the length to where it was tied off on the security bars of the window. Whitehead's soft snores made her smile. She turned around and opened Browning's door. The man was sleeping or perhaps still passed out. She had no idea how he kept from screaming when she was cleaning the injury. She'd almost lost it. She did notice the man had more than one scar on his body. His chest had several long, ragged scars and there was a wicked looking one just under his ribs on his side.

Browning had seen more than his fair share of injuries.

She took a damp cloth and wiped his brow. He frowned in his sleep. "Shhh... you're safe." She smoothed the cool cloth against his skin again and watched as he visibly relaxed. "Thank you." She whispered her words before she bent and kissed his forehead. His brow wasn't hot, which was a godsend. She watched him for several more seconds before she silently backed out of the room.

Mariella ducked under the rope-slash-lock and headed into the kitchen. McGowen and Creed looked up and stopped talking when she came in. She halted and blinked at them before she put her hands on her hips, "Well, that won't make a person paranoid."

McGowen chuckled and stood. "I'm going to take the village idiots to the head before I give them a drink of water and lock them back up. I'll take the first watch. Grab some shuteye. I'll wake you if I start to nod off."

Creed reached out, and they bumped fists as McGowen left. When they heard him shuffling the men down the hall, Creed rose and stretched. "Shall we?"

Mariella motioned out the door and headed to the room at the other end of the house. There was a full-size bed. For that she was grateful. She pulled off her t-shirt and dropped it as she walked to the bed. She sat down and bent down to pull off her boots. She hadn't tied the laces when she redressed after her shower. With her boots off she flopped back on the bed, exhausted.

Creed lifted her feet. She unbuttoned her camos, and he tugged them off. She pushed up on the bed to the pillows with her bra and panties on. Creed tugged off his shirt and then sat on the side of the bed just as she had to untie his boots. She watched the muscles of his arms and back move when he unlaced them. She heard one boot drop, then the other. Creed stood and retrieved a small silver packet from his pocket before placing it beside the bed. He dropped his camos, tossing them to the side. He kneed onto the bed and walked on his hands and knees until he was beside her before lying down.

He turned so he faced her. The bright light of the morning sun let her see the tiredness and stress etched in his features. She shifted her hand and ran a fingertip over his brow. "Do you think your plan for tomorrow will work?"

Creed closed his eyes for a moment. They'd discussed the pros and cons of what he wanted to do all the way to the villa. She didn't doubt for a second that all parties involved would agree, but as he'd said before, he didn't really have any choice in the matter.

"I think we've accounted for everything on our end. Rafa is the only unknown, and you believe he'll cooperate?"

"I do." Rafa was a proud man, a man of his word, even if he was a thief and a smuggler. If he said he would do something, it was done.

"Then we do our best." He reached over and traced her collarbone with his finger.

Mariella nodded. "Our best." She smiled and rose. His finger dropped as she sat up and popped the back of her bra and wiggled out of her panties. She pushed him onto his back and pulled his boxers down. His heavy cock thickened, and she couldn't resist the need to taste him. She bent over and licked a stripe up the underside of his shaft, not stopping until she reached the tip. She sucked his crown in her mouth and teased the underside of the cap with her tongue. His hand snaked to her braided hair. He grabbed the long plait and held it firm in his strong hand. She opened her eyes and looked up at him. His striking blue eyes burned as he gazed down at her. The look was fiercely intense, just like the man himself.

He pulled her up against his long body. Stretched out and on top of him, she dropped down, taking a kiss. She was in love with him. Maybe she could show him with her body and actions what her foolish heart had been so slow to admit.

She hovered, suspended over him. The distance that separated their bodies was perfect. Her nipples brushed against the springy hair on his chest. She moaned at the sensation that was compounded a million-fold when his hands caressed her, trailing paths of heat all over her exposed skin. She took each gentle touch and absorbed them, cherishing the moment and the honesty. She ground her hips down and smiled through their kiss when he moaned. She broke their contact long enough to reach behind her and lift his cock.

He gripped her hand. "Condom."

She glanced at the nightstand and the small packet he'd placed there before she reached out and grabbed it. She put the small envelope to her teeth and tore the packet open. It took her no time to roll the sheath down his stiffness. She leaned down. "Where was I?"

He grabbed the back of her neck and brought her down to him with an enthusiastic tug. "You were going to ride me." He gathered her, gently moving her so her mouth could slide against his lips. Their tongues dueled in a sensual battle. She broke the kiss to breathe. "Oh yes, that's what I was doing."

She positioned his cock and placed him at her entrance. His hands lifted, holding her breasts as she leaned into his support. She closed her eyes and grabbed his forearms as she found a rhythm. With the exertion of her movements, her thighs burned, and her body tightened.

"Look at me," Creed commanded from under her. Her eyes popped open. She saw a look of reverence on his face. "You are beautiful and you are mine." His words echoed through her, their volume increasing until they filled her very essence and exploded around her heart in a tactical assault she couldn't avoid.

He ran his hand up her neck, his thumb traced her bottom lip. She took his thumb into her mouth and circled it with her tongue. "Fuck. Mariella." He shifted his right leg, planting his heel on the bed and pulled her to him, flipping them on the small bed. He pulled her leg up to his hip and thrust into her. "Not going to last." His forehead rested on hers. She looked up into his eyes. He sighed over her, "I'm never going to let you go." His thrusts sped up.

She gasped against his lips and whispered, "Don't. Don't ever let go." She arched against him and bit her lip, stifling the cries of rapture that begged to be released.

His orgasm shattered him as he held himself over her. She gazed in wonder at his masculine beauty. The cords of his neck strained in release. She tugged him down on top of her. It didn't matter that she couldn't breathe. She'd die happy with this man consuming all of her air. Creed moved to his side on the bed. Her mind registered the fact but her exhausted body refused to respond nor could she make her eyelids open. She snuggled into him and let herself drop into much-needed oblivion.

# CHAPTER 28

*C*reed's eyes popped open at the light tap on the bedroom door. He extracted himself from the tangle of his and Mariella's limbs. It took him only a minute to get up and get dressed. He opened the door and slipped out, carrying his boots in one hand. Padding down the hall to the kitchen, he gave McGowen a quick nod. "Browning?"

"He's doing okay. Low-grade fever, but he's sleeping."

Creed dropped his boots in a chair and made his way to the coffee pot, glancing out the window to the beach as he crossed the kitchen. "Sit rep." He poured his coffee as he waited for McGowen to run down the watch.

"This is an active community. Nothing unusual that I could see. I've burped and diapered our guests. They are quiet as church mice. Whitehead hasn't moved. There are sandwich makings in the cabinet and a few things in the fridge. Coffee is behind that curtain." He pointed to a shelving unit that had a red and white checked piece of material suspended across the front.

"Got it, sack out. I'll wake you when it's time to take over for me." Creed raised his cup to his mouth but stopped McGowen before he could leave the room. "Do you have your burner on you? I'm going to have to brief Branson. Mine are buried in the packs, and I don't want to rummage around and wake people up."

McGowen patted his camo pants until he found the cell, reached into the pocket and pulled it out. He tossed it to Creed. "Good luck with that." He gave an exhausted wave of his arm before he trudged the few steps down the hall to where Whitehead was sleeping. Creed watched the man slip under the rope and head into the room. The springs of the small bed complained under McGowen's weight.

Creed looked at the sun. It was starting to set. The western sky radiated dark hues of pink and orange. Tomorrow morning the agents would be moved. He turned on the phone McGowen had tossed him. He entered the number and leaned against the counter. "Go." Branson's voice snapped across the connection.

"Change of plans. Two shipments to the secondary export point. First shipment will be with primary mission at 0900 tomorrow, medical required. Second shipment sometime in the afternoon. Keep an eye out. We'll be coming in hot."

"Roger, I copy all," Branson replied. "I'm flying in tonight. I'll be waiting for you."

"Affirm. There are two you'll need to speak with before anyone else does."

There was a pause on the line. "I copy. I'll ensure we have the proper people on hand to make that happen. Good luck."

Creed ended the call, turned off the phone, and pulled the battery. He sat down and shoved his feet into his boots before he laced them up and leaned back. He tapped the Formica table top and considered how to deal with Rafa. Head on and straight up. It was the only way to go. Rafa had a fuck-ton riding on this mission, so making the events successful tomorrow was in his best interest.

Creed straightened from the chair and ensured the perimeter of the house was secure. He moved slowly from window to window, checking the beach and street behind the house for any indication they were being watched. He ended up in Browning's room. The man blinked at him when he entered. Creed held out a hand, stilling the man as he struggled to sit up. He moved to the window and checked outside before he moved to the bed and sat down beside Browning.

"You hanging in there, brother?" Browning nodded and winced as he tried to move again. "What do you need? Water?" Creed grabbed at the bottle of water Mariella had left on the bedside table when Browning nodded.

He lifted Browning up and folded a blanket and the pillow behind the man to keep him at an incline before he lowered the man slowly onto the cushioned support. He unscrewed the cap and handed Browning the bottle. He was shaky, but the man tipped it up and damn near finished all of it in one go.

"S-status?" Browning asked once he caught his breath.

"We are secure now, holing up at the villa as we had planned." Browning nodded and waved at his arm.

"We've come up with a plan. We are splitting up. Again. I'll need you to take Rafa, his aunt, Street, the two fuckers that were building the bombs, the bombs and Whitehead to Gitmo. They will be waiting for you. 0900 tomorrow morning. That's five civilians you'll need to corral along with three dirty bombs. We'll track you until you reach the main gate. Think you can deal with that little boo-boo like a man and help a brother out?"

Creed laughed at the middle finger Browning flashed him before he pointed a forefinger at Creed.

"Me? Well, if the plan goes right, Rafa's men won't know he's going to be on the first transportation leaving the island, and they'll give us heads up in time to get in place. McGowen, Mariella and I will get the agents and haul ass to Gitmo."

"C-collins?"

"Is waiting for us. You'll get medical. If you're released, you'll head home with us."

Browning narrowed his eyes and glared at Creed. He chuckled at the determination he saw there. "Yeah, you'll be with us. I getcha, man." He took the water bottle from Browning and put it back on the nightstand. "Now you need to rest. I'm asking a helluva lot from you."

Browning lay back, still elevated, and made a fist raising his arm with effort. Creed bumped it. "You want to lie flat?"

Browning shook his head and closed his eyes.

"All right, man." He rose and checked out the window one last time before he left the room.

Creed remained vigilant as the sun slowly sank. He didn't turn on any lights in the house, not wanting to silhouette himself. He fixed himself a sandwich and watched out the kitchen window as the moon rose over the ocean. There were occasionally people who strolled along the beach, but they moved past at a leisurely pace, no indication that they paid any attention to the villa. He took another bottle of water in to Browning and some soda crackers he'd found. The man ate a few, took some over the counter pain meds Creed had in his pack, drank the water and fell asleep again.

Creed chuckled to himself every time he glanced into the bedroom where Whitehead was sleeping. How the hell McGowen slept through the man's snores was beyond him. He'd checked on Mariella several times. The woman was snuggled up with his pillow. He pulled the curtain in the living room back a few inches and gazed outside. His life had changed seemingly overnight. He'd been treading water and never realized it. Not until those beautiful doe eyes locked on to his. Creed caught a slight movement down the road and shifted his position to get a better look. He found the spot where he'd seen the movement and kept watch. A cat jumped from the ground and walked along a cement wall that held back an elevated yard. The yard and the wall had seen better days. The cat ambled along while Creed watched.

A shuffling sound behind him drew his attention away from the outside. "Do you need me to watch?" Whitehead scratched his head and yawned as he asked.

"Nah, man. I got this. You can go back to sleep."

Whitehead nodded and ambled back down the hall. Creed heard him in the bathroom before the springs of his bed complained again. The sound wasn't as loud as when McGowen had relaxed, but enough Creed knew he was alone again.

He made his way back into the kitchen and poured another cup of coffee. Rafa was supposed to arrive sometime tonight. The man would bring

Street and Amelia with him. How many men traveled with them was questionable, but the man had survived and thrived in the political web of the Cuban government, so he'd know best how many people to bring.

Creed walked the house for hours. He planned to wake McGowen at four and grab two or three hours of sleep before they started the day. Outside, gravel crunched under tires. At the distinct sound, he flew through the dark house to the front room. He flicked back the curtain and breathed a small sigh. The purple and white 1957 Chevy he'd become very familiar with pulled up in front of the house. The headlights were out. Two trucks silently pulled to a stop by the car. Rafa's form rose from the driver's side. He spoke with the lead truck momentarily before he went around the car and helped Amelia out.

He opened the back passenger door, and Street got out of the car. Creed cracked open the front door. Rafa entered the combination to the bicycle lock that held the front gate shut. He allowed his party to go before him. After he secured the gate, they moved forward. Creed opened the door and stepped back into the house, hiding himself from the street and the trucks waiting there.

When she finally entered the house, Creed took Amelia's hand and escorted her to the kitchen, where he turned on the small lamp over the stove. She sat down and glanced behind her. Street shuffled in and sat down at the table. Creed's eyebrows rose when Rafa came into view. The man looked gaunt and ashen, a mere shadow of the robust figure of authority he'd left days ago. "What happened to you?"

"Adalberto wasn't easy to kill." Rafa waved him off and moved toward the coffee pot.

"Did you find it? The location?" Street asked, capturing Creed's attention. He sat with his head in his hands.

Creed glanced at Rafa, and the man shrugged. "Yeah, man. We found it, and we got the guys building them."

Street turned his head and blinked up at Creed. "My team?"

"We'll get them too."

"Okay." Street closed his eyes and laid his head down on the table.

"Amelia, would you like to lie down?" Creed asked out of courtesy, but of all the people who'd just walked through that door, she seemed the strongest.

"No. I will rest here for a moment, and then I'll find what is in this kitchen and make breakfast." She glanced at Rafa. "You talk out there, out of my way."

Rafa chuckled and pushed off the counter where he leaned, motioning to Creed as he passed. They ended up in the living room.

Creed took the couch, and Rafa sat on the chair next to him. "How bad are you hurt?"

"I'll be fine." Rafa dismissed his question. "My men brought the car back. They told me one of yours was hurt."

"He was." Creed placed his elbows on his knees and leaned forward. "Look, I'm going to lay this out, man-to-man. I need your help, and I don't give a flying fuck if you like what I'm going to ask. I'm looking after the safety of way too many people and I need your help."

Rafa leaned forward and pulled out a pack of cigarettes from his shirt pocket. He shook one out and lit up before he responded. "What is it that you need to say to me, man-to-man?" He drew deeply on his cigarette.

"We are going to do this exit in two stages. I need you to drive the truck we have in the garage taking Amelia, Street, two of my men, the men who built the dirty bombs and the dirty bombs to Gitmo."

Rafa blew out his lungful of smoke and leaned back in the chair. He stared at Creed as he took another deep inhale off the cigarette. "No."

"What do you mean, no?" Creed straightened, "I'm telling you, man, I need you to get these people and the fucking bombs to safety."

"No. I cannot drive. I have people who watch me. If they see me drive to the American base, they will not do as I ask." He looked at the cherry of his cigarette. "Have an American drive. Amelia, Street and I will be in the back of the truck with the two who built the bombs. I will ensure they do not escape." The man took another toke off the cigarette. "I realize I am a liability in my current condition."

"Is everything set for the transfer?"

Rafa nodded. "Although, if the guards from the warehouse are found missing before the transport leaves, there will be trouble."

"Then let's hope nobody checks on them." Creed glanced toward the window willing the hours until they moved to speed by.

MARIELLA WAITED in her uncle's '57 Chevy until the truck backed out of the garage. Whitehead and Browning were in the cab of the truck. Whitehead drove. She pulled out in front of the man and headed to the American base at Guantanamo Bay. Creed sat beside her, McGowen in the rear of the car. They'd stowed their gear in the trunk before daybreak. The men were armed with their automatic pistols, and their assault rifles were in the trunk. The road in front of them was completely empty. It was early, and it was Sunday. A fortuitous advantage.

As they'd discussed at length this morning, once she pulled onto the main road, she slowed, allowing Whitehead to pass her. Neither he or Browning looked over or acknowledged them. The fabric flaps hiding the valuable contents in the rear of the truck were snapped down tight. She allowed the truck move on and put a half mile or so between them. They maneuvered carefully around the chunks missing in the pavement.

"Mark that. Remember that the left-hand lane is clearer." Creed spoke to her and McGowen. They had no idea who would be driving on the run to the base, but they conceded it would be better to actually drive most of the route while escorting their team to Gitmo, or as close as they could go without raising suspicions.

Mariella pointed to their turn off. Creed nodded. She took the turn and immediately worked through the small village to gain a vantage point where they could see the main gate of the American military installation. The truck Whitehead drove was inside the first set of two gates. The second set opened, and the truck was escorted into the installation. Blue lights lit up on the roof racks of the escort vehicles in front and behind the old green truck. She closed her eyes and said a prayer of thanks. Whitehead, Browning, Rafa, her great aunt, the dirty bombs, the scientists, and the CIA agent, Street, were now safe in the hands of the Americans.

"Phase one, complete," Creed said to no one in particular.

"Now we wait to hear the route they are taking to transport the other CIA agents."

Mariella drove back in the direction they'd come

to the town of Guantanamo where they ate and filled the car. She pulled back onto the Carreteras Principales and worked her way to the road that led away from Tortuguilla and toward La Maya. Mariella glanced at the watch lodged on her arm, almost to her elbow. She glanced at Creed, "Rafa's men should have called with the route by now."

"They'll call." McGowen's steady voice from the back of the car was the only indication the man was awake.

"But they should be here by now." Mariella took her eyes off the rearview mirror, glanced at the road and then at Creed.

"They'll call," both men said at the same time. Mariella wrinkled her nose at them and drove on. Fifteen minutes later, after several similar, one-sided conversations that ratcheted up her anxiety level, the phone rang. She fumbled it in her hurry to pick it up. Creed held up a hand, reached to the floorboard and picked it up before he connected the call and handed the phone to her.

"Yes?" She answered a little breathlessly.

"Where is Rafa?"

"He's busy. Why are you asking stupid questions? Where are they?" Mariella found it easy to slip back into the need to demand respect.

"They have turned off the highway onto the secondary road that runs south of La Maya."

"South?"

"Yes. They just turned. We did not follow. You have about thirty minutes before they could turn north again. There is only one truck. Blue with black tarps. There are at least three guards. Two in the front and one in the back. The back flaps are not secured tightly. When we passed, we saw an armed man in the back of the truck."

"Anything else?"

"Tell Rafa the guards are not regular Cuban Army, and they are well armed."

"I'll make sure he knows. You can return to the compound." Mariella waited for the man to acknowledge her and tossed the phone down.

"Blue truck, black tarps, two guards in the front and at least one in the rear." She slowed enough to make a U-turn in the middle of the highway and sped back to the cut off. It should intersect with the road the truck was traveling.

"Why would they turn off the main road?" She asked the question out loud, but in reality, she was talking to herself.

"They probably suspected they were being tailed. They turned off to make sure they didn't have someone following them." Creed answered her. He shot her a questioning look. "Did Rafa's men follow them after they turned off?"

"No." She turned right and sent them on a collision course with the armed guards holding the three American spies they needed to get out of the country.

"Okay. See that hill?" Creed pointed to a hill in the distance. Mariella nodded. "When we get there, I want you to position the car in the middle of the road. They will either stop or slow down enough that we can make our play.

She nodded and slowed as she topped the hill. She could see for miles, and there were no cars on the road either coming or going. Mariella positioned the car as Creed asked and they went to work. McGowen popped the hood and lifted it. They kept the passenger door open and with the car angled away from the direction of the approaching truck. They wouldn't see her rifle nicely fitted between the bumper and the chrome of the radiator cover of the Chevy.

Mariella grabbed the clothes she'd brought with her and dropped her camos after shedding her boots. She wiggled into indecent jean shorts—the half moon of her ass cheeks peeked out the bottom of each leg. Creed had made her sacrifice a perfectly good pair of jeans because she'd never wear these again, and grabbed the front of her black t-shirt. She reached into the collar of her shirt and pulled the bottom of the hem up through the collar. Doing so bared her midriff and accentuated her breasts. She wrapped the material around once and tucked the tail. She snarled at the backpack but pulled out the heels Creed had found in the villa. They were too small, but she could wear them. She put them on and pulled the string from the end of her braid. After loosening her hair, she flipped her head forward and mussed it. She looked down at herself and sighed before she moved from behind the car to where the men stood looking down the highway.

Creed glanced back at her and immediately did a double take. His eyes ran up and down her before a wide smile spread across his face. "We are not going to have any problems stopping the truck."

McGowen turned his head, and he, too, did an immediate double take. "Fuck."

"Mine, eyes on the road." Creed cuffed the man on the back of the head and walked back to her.

"You look amazing. Are you ready?"

"I am. I think." She drew a deep breath. "I fucked up last time."

"You didn't." Creed cupped her cheek, and she grabbed his forearm.

"Skipper." McGowen's voice interrupted the moment.

Mariella glanced at the black dot on the horizon.

"Go time." He leaned down and left a searing kiss on her lips. "Don't take any chances."

"You either." She watched as he ran to the side of the road opposite of McGowen. The men were hidden by a slight rise they lay behind. Clumps of weeds and scattered bushes spotted the roadside. Mariella watched as the truck drew closer. She closed her eyes and turned her back to the truck, bending over the engine compartment of the car, her long legs spread enough to show off her ass. She could hear the truck downshift as it slowed.

Mariella straightened and wiped her cheek, smudging a small amount of grease on her skin. She flipped her hair back and gazed over her shoulder at the slowing truck. The men didn't look happy, but their gaze was fixed on her. She dropped the wrench in her hand and stood, turning to give them a perfect view of her breasts.

The passenger motioned for her to move her car. She looked at him then to her car and then back at him. Throwing her hands up in the air she reacted. "How? Would you like me to push it?" The man motioned again, and Mariella put her hands on her hips. The truck came to a complete stop.

The driver's side window came down. "Move out of the way."

"Don't you think I would have done that if I could have?" She motioned to the car.

"Try again." The man yelled at her, and she threw her hands up in the air.

"Fine, I'll try again." She strutted back to the car, moved past where she'd been displayed over the engine compartment and stopped in front of the car. "The least you could do is help." Mariella made a show of not being able to get the hood to shut.

The man on the passenger side turned and spoke to the driver. The driver shook his head and motioned at Mariella. The passenger threw up his hands, and they held a brief, animated conversation before the guard on the passenger side of the truck opened his door.

*Yes...just a bit further.* Mariella lifted her hand shading her eyes. She pouted and stuck her hip out. "Please?"

The driver shook his head, but the passenger smiled and jumped from the cab. He trotted over to her. She smiled and leaned down, pulling her rifle out of the confined space. As he passed the passenger side door, she grabbed it.

CREED WAS up over the embankment the second the guard cleared the cab of the truck. He flew across the terrain and launched into the open door of the cab. The driver's hand never left the steering wheel.

Creed held the muzzle of his rifle against the man's cheek. "You move, you die." He hissed the words. The man stared at him and didn't move an inch.

"McGowen?" Creed yelled the man's name.

"Clear!"

"Mariella?" He'd lost sight of her.

"We are right here."

His eyes flitted from the man behind the wheel to where she stood, her eyes trained on the other guard.

"Get on your knees!" Mariella spat.

Creed returned his attention to the driver. "You, out." The man started to move, and Creed dug the flash suppressor of the M-4's barrel into the man's cheek. "Slowly."

The guard sneered at him and opened the door. Creed kept in close proximity to the driver, crawling over the seats to do so. On his way past, he reached for the handbrake and engaged it.

"On your knees," Creed demanded and jabbed the man in the back with his weapon to prompt the motherfucker to comply with a little more expediency. He put his boot in the middle of the man's back as soon as he hit his knees, sending him face-first on the hot asphalt. "Hands on your head." The man complied and Creed motioned to Mariella.

She nodded and shoved the other man to his hands and knees. "On your stomach."

Creed backed away, watching to ensure she had control of the two guards before he spun and made it to McGowen. The guard from the back of the truck was splattered unconscious on the concrete. He wasn't going to get up anytime soon. McGowen shrugged when Creed sent him a questioning look.

He turned his attention to the men remaining in the back of the vehicle. "Homeland sends their regards." A smile spread across his face at the expressions of relief on their faces.

"Fuck, thank God." Each one of the men deflated.

They'd been beaten, the visible bruising a testimony to the treatment they'd received. "Can you get us to the interior of the island?"

"No need. We got that taken care of."

"You found it? There was a workshop?" the third man asked.

"Yes, we found the workshop and three bombs." Creed glanced at Mariella to make sure she was solid. He didn't have any need to worry. She watched the men like a hawk.

"They were waiting for us." That comment redirected his attention quickly. The first man leaned his head back against the tarp. "Someone had to have sold us out."

"Your man, Street, is alive." All three sets of eyes snapped to him at his words.

"Skipper." McGowen's voice jerked his head around. "Car... no, truck. They're coming fast. Too fast."

"Fuck." He grabbed two zipties from his vest and made quick work of cuffing the men on the ground. "Mariella, you're driving!

She'd kicked off the heels and flew up into the cab of the truck. "Weapon!" Creed called, and she tossed it back down to him. McGowen was throwing their packs into the back of the truck as Mariella put the damn thing into gear and revved the engine. Creed grabbed the back tailgate at the same time as McGowen. "Go!" He yelled the word, and Mariella floored the damn thing.

He and McGowen half climbed, half fell into the back of the truck. Creed threw his pack behind him. "Ammo's in there. Get it for me." The agents were banged up, but they could help.

He cringed at the crash and even over the grinding of gears he could hear Mariella cursing. She'd pushed the purple and white Chevy out of their way and was gaining speed.

Creed planted his ass on the bed of the truck opposite McGowen and both men braced their feet against the tailgate. "Coming fast."

Yeah, he could see that. The truck... no, it was a small SUV, was hauling ass. "Get down. Lie down flat." Creed barked the order at the CIA men, wanting them out of the way of any stray bullets. They flopped to the bed of the truck even though their hands were still tied. Creed pulled his knife from his belt. "Here." He tossed the damn thing back and gauged the distance to the SUV. Less than a half mile now.

"Help me get rid of this damn tarp! I need a clear field of fire." He and McGowen yanked the tarps down. The black fabric sailed behind them. The SUV swerved dramatically and hit the soft shoulder trying to avoid the fabric as it flew back from the truck. They overcorrected and headed to the other side of the road. The SUV launched from the concrete and tore up the area next to the road, but they didn't stop.

"Definitely not friends," McGowen shouted at him.

"You think?" Creed shouted back.

"Here!" Two ammo belts immediately followed the voice behind him. Creed nodded to McGowen, who lowered his weapon long enough to strap on the additional ammo. Once the man was armed again, Creed took a couple seconds and strapped on his own tan web belt and ammo pouch.

"Where are we going?" One of the men yelled over to him.

"Gitmo!"

"Do they know we are coming?"

"They know!" Creed shouted back. "Get down!"

Mariella downshifted, and the truck skittered as she turned to put them back on the main road. She floored it again and weaved around the biggest potholes.

The SUV flew onto the highway and skated almost to the far side of the concrete road before it started after them. "Here they come!" Creed announced.

"You think?" McGowen replied.

Creed smiled despite the situation. "Tires, engine, then the driver."

"Roger that." McGowen acknowledged. They both settled and waited. They were flying. Mariella had the truck red-lined, but the SUV was lighter and catching up. He and McGowen waited, holding off until guns appeared out the side window of the chase vehicle. Creed wasn't sure who fired first but two, three-round bursts spat out of each of their weapons and the SUV careened wildly. It hit a pothole and flipped, rolling sideways over and over. Both he and McGowen sat staring behind them.

They saw the Cuban National Police car as they flew past. It was going the other direction until it wasn't. McGowen glanced at Creed. "We are going to have a fucking international incident."

"Yeah."

A small passenger truck passed them going the other way. It cut sharply and smashed into the police car. Both vehicles careened off onto the shoulder of the road.

"Score one for Rafa's men!" McGowen pumped his fist in the air, before he changed positions, jamming his feet on both sides of the tailgate. "I'll take the rear."

Creed moved up to the cab of the truck and stood on the lip of the truck bed to see over the top of the roof. He could see the coast. The main gate to Gitmo was at the top of the fucking hill. The road leading down to the beach wound down to the main canton-ment area and then pushed back into the detainment area.

"Skipper!"

Creed's head snapped back. Three sets of blue lights flashed behind them. He grabbed the side of the cab and leaned down to the driver's side window. "Don't slow down. Don't stop. If the gates are closed, ram those sons of bitches!"

He didn't wait for an answer. "Fucking grab something and hold on tight!" Creed grabbed the side of the truck. McGowen braced against the tailgate and the three men lying on the truck bed bracketed themselves across the bed of the truck.

The truck fucking flew toward the gate, but the cars were gaining. Creed ducked down when a shot smacked next to his head. He swore.

"Skipper?" McGowen had his rifle raised and ready to fire.

"No! Do not return fire!" Creed yelled back. They had less than a quarter of a mile left to freedom. He saw a scurry of activity at the main gate. Fuck, they didn't have the main gates open. "Hold on!" This shit could hurt.

"The police cars are stopping!" McGowen let out a whoop of excitement.

"We aren't! Brace!" Creed gripped the side of the truck as Mariella unexpectedly slammed on the brakes. Creed flattened against the cab. The vehicle's momentum changed, slamming them sideways. Four men careened into him.

Creed gasped at the sharp pain in his back. He rolled a pack off his face and moved, trying to lift enough to move the damn ammo pouch currently puncturing his spine. *Fuck! How the hell?* He pushed a foreign foot from where it was lodged under his chin. How did he get on the fucking bed of the truck?

"Shit."

"Fuck."

"Holy hell, what the... uh... Skipper?" McGowen's voice rang stronger than the other muttered voices.

Creed pushed up and hissed, pulling his hand out from under the boot matching the one that was all up in his shit. The man rolled away and groaned an apology.

"Commander Lachlan?" A strident voice bounced around the bed of the truck.

Creed responded, "What the fuck? Where the hell is Branson?" He lifted his head and blinked at the three-hundred-sixty-degree curtain of very pissed off military police who surrounded them. Each and every one had a weapon trained on the truck.

"I'm Commander Lachlan." Creed stumbled up and winced. Somehow, he'd rolled his fucking ankle. He glanced around for McGowen. The man was behind him. How the fuck?

"Sir, I've been instructed to escort everyone to Camp Four."

He glanced at the petty officer who spoke. "Chief, I've been to Camp Four. I'm not going there as a prisoner."

The man smiled. "It's empty now, sir. Mr. Branson has set up operations there."

Creed reached down and picked up his rifle... or McGowen's, he wasn't sure. Every damn last member of the security cordon moved at once, lifting weapons to the ready. Creed froze. He held his hand out and laughed. "Chill." He used his thumb and index finger to hand the weapon to the closest military member. "There are two of these in this mess somewhere." He glanced down at the slowly untangling mass of humanity. His head snapped around. "Mariella?"

"I'm here. Not moving. Not moving at all!" she yelled. Obviously, the armed curtain had weapons drawn on her, too.

He released a sigh. "I guess this is where I say take me to our leader?"

"That would be the only thing that is going to happen at this point, sir." The petty officer confirmed. "One at a time, exit the back of the truck. Sir, you can get down." The man motioned to Creed. He limped to the end of the truck and jumped down, landing on his good foot and tweaking his fucking knee in the process. He hissed and grabbed the truck. It had been a really fucking long day.

# CHAPTER 29

*M*ariella struggled under Creed's weight. He moved slowly. She gripped his waist as they hobble stepped into a long white building. The extensive pathway to the building and the length of ten-foot-high chain link fence and the rolls of barbed wire on top were intimidating as fuck.

The Americans had three guards leading them and three following them. Although these didn't have their weapons drawn. The CIA agents had declined medical care and followed them. McGowen brought up the rear. Mariella glanced past the CIA agents and smiled at him. He winked at her and stuck his hands in his pockets, whistling.

The guards stopped and pulled open the double doors to the long white building. The CIA agents were directed into a room on the right. Creed was asked to proceed to the end of the hall. Mariella's heart leaped when she saw her uncle sitting at one of the tables. He stood when they entered and walked over to Creed. "You did it?"

"We did it." Creed acknowledged.

"Excellent. This man Branson. Is he one you trust?" Rafa crossed his arms and spread his feet.

Mariella knew that pose. "What is going on?"

Rafa glanced at her. She braced herself for the usual brush off. "He and the other man have offered me a deal I don't know if I can refuse." Okay, well that was more information than he usually offered her.

"What deal?" Mariella looked from her uncle to Creed.

"That is between the men and me. They want me to work for this Guardian." *Ah, there was the attitude she knew and did not love.* Rafa turned his attention to Creed. "Do you trust this man? He said Guardian is solid. This solid means they are good people?"

"I do trust him, and Guardian has an excellent reputation," He acknowledged.

Rafa nodded. "Good enough for me." He snapped his fingers at one of the guards. "I need a cigarette." He glanced at Mariella and frowned deeply. "They do not allow smoking in their buildings. Pfft. Americans." Rafa headed toward the door, and the guard followed directly behind him.

"Commander Lachlan."

Mariella's attention snapped to the other side of the room. Two men crossed to them. Creed extended his hand when they offered theirs.

One of the men said, "I told you this mission was custom made for your skills."

"It is damn good to see you, but do you mind if next time my skills aren't tumble-dried in the ass end of a pick-up?"

Both men laughed. "We have that entrance on video in case you'd like to watch it."

Creed groaned. "No thanks, I lived it. Mariella, this is my boss, Silas Branson."

"That was some fancy driving. I believe you were the reason for the dramatic entrance?"

"No! The people shooting at us were the reason for that." Mariella stood her ground. *She* hadn't done anything wrong this time.

The man standing next to Creed's boss chuckled but tried to hide it behind his smile. He was bigger than McGowen and had black hair and intense green eyes. "Ms. Diaz, I'm Jared King." He extended his hand and they shook. He turned his attention to Creed. "Commander Lachlan."

"Sir." Creed acknowledged him and shook his hand. He turned and nodded to McGowen. "This is Tigger McGowen. I'm assuming you met Browning and Whitehead, the rest of my team?"

"Met and debriefed. My people are here to take control of the individuals you brought in. We are in a conversation with POTUS as to where they will be held, but we believe our history working this issue will sway the decision in our favor."

"And who is this 'we'?" Mariella asked as she looked between the four men. *And what the hell was a potus?*

Creed nodded at the man who'd introduced himself as Jared King. "He runs Guardian Security."

"What's that?" She gazed intently Creed.

"They own the boat."

"Oh, the rich people."

Jared chuckled. "We have also been appointed by POTUS to work all leads on certain incidents we believe are tied to a case already in-house."

*Ah, so potus was someone important.*

"You believe what is happening here is linked?" Creed put weight on his knee and stood on his own. His arm dropped from her shoulder.

"We do." Jared King nodded and indicated a door at the end of the large room. "If you and your team will follow me, we'll do our debrief and get you off this island."

"My uncle?" Mariella glanced back at the open door. She could see him standing at the fence looking out toward the hills that blocked the base from the rest of the island.

"He is an interesting man," Mr. King acknowledged. "I'm sure you'll speak before long. As you know, we will talk to each of you separately." He extended his hand, and they all moved forward.

Fear clenched her gut. Surely, they wouldn't make her leave without Creed. Mariella sent a worried look his way. Creed smiled at her. "I promised. I keep my promises."

Mr. King turned his head in their direction and raised an eyebrow but didn't say a word. She gave Creed a thankful smile. Yes, he had promised he wouldn't leave her. She drew a deep breath and pulled that truth into her heart.

CREED RETURNED the bag of semi-melted ice that had slipped to his ankle. It was the third ice pack he'd used since they'd started the debrief. He'd answered all of Branson's questions first and now was answering the same questions, phrased differently by Jared King.

Creed shook his head. "No, not really." He leaned back in the chair and grabbed the bottle of water and took a drink. "I don't know why I thought it was important enough to call Branson. My gut told me that if the intelligence had been tainted or was off, that perhaps the reason and rationale for the dirty bombs wasn't limited to destruction and terror. Thinking out of the box is a habit. The displacement of people could be a secondary, but it could also be the primary reason. I guess I called Branson just to ensure the powers that be would step back and look at everything again."

King nodded his head. "That would fit a couple of scenarios we've come up with. They were watching what the individual country's response entailed."

"Who is they?" When Jared King simply shrugged, Creed stopped with the water bottle halfway to his mouth. "So you think I was on to something?"

"We do. Branson brought it to my attention. He also got one of his experts into the evidence locker at the CIA. Those bombs that were found weren't active, and the radioactive material was negligible." King leaned back and threw the pen he had been using onto the table. "Bottom line, what you, Branson, and your team did... fuck, it was impressive."

"Any repercussions from the events at the warehouse?" Creed hadn't heard anything about that portion of the mission.

"None, and from the information we've gathered from the people you sent in with Browning and Whitehead this morning, the operation wasn't sanctioned by the Cuban government. We feel sure they knew what was happening, and I'm sure many, many palms were well greased, but they can't say a word." King chuckled. "You'd be surprised how many times that happens."

Creed shook his head slowly side to side. "Nope.

Don't think I would be." He twirled the water bottle in his hands. "Do we know who sold out the team?"

"Street did."

"What the fuck? Do we know who he was working with?"

"We have a money trail and will find out where the money originated." King leaned forward. "Branson is working with the few people he trusts in the CIA to try and determine if the leak of information goes deeper than Street. If the man hadn't been picked up by Rafa, he'd be free to take the money and disappear."

"But he's fucked up, with the concussion and all." Creed made a movement around his head.

"According to our doctors, there is nothing wrong with him. He didn't escape because Rafa didn't leave him alone for a second. He was injured, but he wasn't injured how he said he was. His team figured out he was the person who sold them out, and they jumped the man prior to them being surrounded and taken."

Creed spun the empty water bottle again, thinking. "Why would he give us the general location of the lab?"

King shrugged. "One of the many questions yet to be answered."

"So he sold out the team? For what?" Creed couldn't comprehend an instance where he'd do that.

"Greed. The people who paid him made him an offer he didn't choose to refuse or report." King sighed and steepled his fingers together. "Tell me, Mariella Diaz, is it true you married her?"

"Ah... yeah." Creed rubbed the back of his neck. "Rafa tell you that?"

King made a sound Creed took for agreement before he said, "You do know that *technically* you are legally married to her, right?"

Creed chuckled humorlessly. "I didn't know it was legal when it happened."

King sighed and leaned back in his chair. "I can get it annulled by the time you get back to the States."

"No!" Creed may have yelled that and by King's reaction, he had. "We're good," Creed assured the man.

King grinned and dipped his chin so he wasn't looking at Creed when he spoke, "Okay, then perhaps I should offer to amend the marriage certificate to reflect your actual name?" King glanced up at him, waiting for an answer.

"Yeah, that would be good. Can you get me a copy of that certificate? The legal one, with my name on it?" Creed smiled across the table, and hoped asking nicely would get him his way.

"Dude, after the shit you pulled off, it would be an honor." King stood. "If you ever get tired of playing part-time gigs with Branson, you give me a call. We have room for your entire team."

"Yeah, but you'd scatter us to the wind." Creed chuckled as he stood to shake the man's hand.

"See, that's where you're wrong. We need strong teams who trust each other." King picked up his tablet and pen.

"Can Branson keep Collins?" Creed asked, tongue in cheek.

"Ah, no... he's a part-timer. Comes and goes as his schedule allows." King winked at him and turned to walk away.

"Hey, did anyone ever tell you he looks a lot like–"

King interrupted him with a shout of laughter, "Yeah, yeah... he hears that all the time!"

King opened the door and held it open for Mariella. She edged past him and scurried into the room. "Are you okay?" he asked as she folded into his arms.

"I'm fine. How is your ankle?"

"Just twisted it. Are you ready?" He limped toward the open door.

"For what?" Those beautiful brown doe eyes turned up to him.

"To go home."

Her beautiful smile fell from her face. "You mean I have to stay?"

Creed stopped and pulled her into him. "No. I meant we are going to our home, in Key West."

She tucked her chin down. Her body shook, and she whispered, "Our home?"

Creed tipped her chin up so he could see the tears filling her eyes. "Our home. Seems we *are* legally married. You okay with that? Think you could live with this beat up old SEAL? Forever?"

She laughed as tears bridged her lashes and trickled down the sides of her face. "I know I can. You are my SEAL. Forever."

 wo years later

CREED TWISTED HIS WRIST, pushing his Harley over the speed limit. Not much, but enough. He pushed the legal limit every night because home was now his favorite place on earth. There was a corny old saying about "Home is where the heart is." Yeah, his heart was there all right. He was so fucking lucky. Lucky Jared King had worked his magic on the license. Lucky Mariella was on board with what he'd asked King to do. Hell, when he told her what he wanted, the smile planted on her face had been as big as his. Thank God. Lucky that Branson had worked his magic and Mariella was a legal citizen of the United States. She'd been working for his family's company in accounts receivable. She was happy and her education in accounting had come in handy. Lucky they'd had an opening and lucky she loved the work. Fuck, he should just change his name to Lucky Lachlan. It had a ring to it.

He pulled into the small driveway and recognized the vehicle blocking his way. With a snort, he pulled to the side, cut the engine, and punched the kickstand down before he leaned the bike on the metal stand.

Mariella appeared at the top of the steps. The soft wind tossed her long hair around her face. Fuck, he didn't have words to describe how damn good it felt to have her waiting for him every night. Perfect came close.

He long-legged the stairs two at a time to reach her quicker. Of their own accord his arms wrapped around her, lifted her up, and pulled her into his body. Her tan legs wrapped his waist, her arms his neck, and she giggled like a carefree girl. They made up one piece that had been cut in two and cast into the universe. Only the joke was on the universe. They'd found each other and filled the voids that had consumed both of their lives. Not many were that lucky. He smiled as he reached the top of the stairs. He was definitely considering a legal name change.

"Mrs. Lachlan, you couldn't wait until I got inside?" He nuzzled his lips against her neck. She shivered and sighed into him.

"I can never wait for you to be inside me." Her words and low laugh punched heat through him. Damn, she still did it to him, even after two years.

He arched away from her and gazed down into those beautiful brown eyes. "Remind me to thank Rafa the next time he calls."

"For what?"

"For making us get married. Best thing that ever happened to me."

"Best idea Rafa ever had."

"I agree." His hand traveled up her waist to cup her breast.

"Ah, no." She grabbed his hand, and he stilled immediately. "We have a guest. He's waiting for you in the living room." She grimaced slightly. "Hope you don't mind, but I felt sorry for him. When I got home from the grocery store, the poor man was sitting on the front porch in that wool suit. It's got to be ninety in the shade."

Creed straightened and let her slip down his body until her feet touched the ground. He held her hand as he opened the front door, walked into his living room, and stopped.

"Branson. It's been a while. What can we do for you?"

The End

# SILVER SEALS SERIES TITLES AND LINKS

SEAL Strong - Cat Johnson

SEALs Love Legacy - Sharon Hamilton

SEAL Together - Maryanne Jordan

SEAL In Charge - Donna Michaels

SEAL In A Storm - KaLyn Cooper

SEAL Forever - Kris Michaels

SEAL Out Of Water - Abbie Zanders

Sign, SEAL and Deliver - Geri Foster

SEAL Hard - J.m. Madden

SEAL Undercover - Desiree Holt

SEAL For Hire - Trish Loye

SEAL at Sunrise - Caitlyn O'Leary

SEAL of Fortune - Becky McGraw

ALSO BY KRIS MICHAELS

Jacob, The Kings of Guardian - Book One

Joseph, The Kings of Guardian - Book Two

Adam, The Kings of Guardian - Book Three

Jason, The Kings of Guardian - Book Four

Jared, The Kings of Guardian - Book Five

Jasmine, The Kings of Guardian - Book Six

Chief, The Kings of Guardian - Book Seven

Jewell, The Kings of Guardian - Book Eight

Jade, The Kings of Guardian - Book Nine

Justin, The Kings of Guardian - Book Ten

Drake, The Kings of Guardian - Book Eleven

A Christmas with the Kings - Novella (Book. 11.5)

Guardian Shadow World

Anubis

Asp, Guardian Shadow World Book 2

Guardian Novellas

Montana Guardian - A Guardian Security Novella

Backwater Blessing - A Guardian Crossover Novella

The Everlight Series:

Made in the USA
Middletown, DE
19 July 2020